THE PLAYBOY SAVORED SEDUCTION

THE PLAYBOY SAVORED SEDUCTION

SHIRLEY JUMP

This is a work of fiction. All of the characters, organizations, and events portrayed in this novel are either products of the author's imagination or are used fictitiously.

eISBN: 978-1-937776-66-4
ISBN-13: 978-1-937776-85-5

Other Books by Shirley Jump

THE SWEET AND SAVORY NOVEL SERIES:

The Groom Wanted Seconds:
A Novella (Prequel)

The Bride Wore Chocolate (Book One)
The Devil Served Desire (Book Two)
The Angel Tasted Temptation (Book Three)
The Playboy Savored Seduction (Book Four)
The Boss Courted Trouble (Book Five)

The Beauty Charmed Santa: A Christmas Novella
The Millionaire Tempted Fate: A Novella

MORE FROM SHIRLEY:

The Sweetheart Bargain
Really Something
Around the Bend
Return of the Last McKenna
Simply the Best

CHAPTER ONE

"**S**old!"

The auctioneer's gavel came down with a final slam, and Boston's 28th most eligible bachelor walked off the stage of the Worth Hotel ballroom—and straight into the open arms of his new female owner.

Her prize was one Jerold Klein, a forty-year-old rare bird dealer with a hooked nose and graying head to match his prize cockatiels. Geraldine Hawkins let out a squeal of joy at her successful purchase, as if she'd just nabbed a four-thousand dollar ermine bargain on the fur rack at Macy's.

Daniel Worth IV scowled. Why the hell he'd signed up for this, he didn't know. Actually, he did know. He'd agreed after the third or fourth round of a damned good Scotch, too mellowed by the liquor to refuse when Kyle Montague had asked him to participate in the early February "charity" event.

Yeah, it was a charity all right. One where men who knew better gave away their dignity and called it a tax deduction.

All night, the women had been straining forward in their seats, waving their checkbooks like dollar bills while the auctioneer listed the assets of the each bachelor with the drama of Bob Barker giving away a Caddie.

This was as much charity as a Chippendales performance was a garden party.

"For our next eligible bachelor, we have Percival Howard the Third," the auctioneer began. Percival, who'd always been on the pink side of shy, lingered beside Daniel in the shadows, his white-knuckled hands glued to the wrought iron railing.

Daniel shook his head. What the man in front of him needed was a good shot of testosterone, or at least a fourteen-ounce rib eye. Babied by his mother, because of his "weak constitution" and his inability to digest anything containing protein, Percival's diet was filled mostly with carrots, his vegetable of choice. The result—a perpetual orange tint in his skin.

It gave "you are what you eat" a whole new meaning.

Percival's dietary choices had had the dual effect of greatly improving his eyesight but leaving him with the unfortunate nickname of "Persimmon." Being known as a fruit hadn't exactly helped Persimmon develop his social graces. The poor orange man shook and sweated his way up the two steps to the stage.

Regardless of his menu restrictions, the audience wanted its next bachelor. Particularly one who had a second house in Tuscany and a reputation for treating women like crystal. Still, Persimmon lingered outside the glare of the spotlights, the color in his cheeks deepening from under-ripe carrot to crimson.

"Where is he? Give him to us!" shouted someone in the back.

"Yeah, get him on stage!"

"Are these the same women who organize the annual Support an Orphan party?" asked Jake Lincoln, sidling up beside Daniel. "That fancy shindig where we pay a grand a head to eat Marcy Higgins's cousin's crappy version of standing rib roast and listen to her father drone on about the tragedy of growing up alone?"

"Wasn't he raised in a family of twelve?" Daniel said.

Jake chuckled. "The rich empathize with everyone, don't you know that?"

Daniel knew that spiel. Particularly around tax time, when Grandfather Worth was looking for an extra deduction.

"Give us your poor, tired and hungry," Daniel said. "Just don't make us walk in their knock-off high heels or eat their store-brand canned food."

The auctioneer went over to coax Percival onto the stage. A cheer went up from the crowd, checkbooks raised in tribute. Moments later, a price was put on Percival's persimmon-colored head.

"Ain't that the truth." Jake shook his head. "You want to mosey on over to the bar or continue watching our peer group being sold off like prize livestock?"

"Sold!" The auctioneer declared again, giving Boston's 29th best a nod and a slam of his gavel. "And now, our final bachelor of the night, our *piece de resistance*," the auctioneer said, waving his hand to add a touch of drama to his words, "and the man you ladies have been waiting to see. The one *Boston* magazine called 'the most eligible bachelor in the city.'"

"Can't," Daniel said to Jake. "I'm up."

"*You're* the *piece de resistance?*" Jake laughed. "The icing on the cake? The cherry on the sundae? The—"

Daniel raised a finger in warning. "Don't forget, I know about that slightly illegal thing you did trading small caps last year. So if I were you, I'd stop right there."

Jake clapped him on the back. "Go get 'em, tiger. Remember, this is for…" He paused. "What the hell charity is this for, anyway?"

"I don't know." Daniel let out a long breath that said he'd been to too many of these things in recent weeks. It seemed *this* had become his job. It wasn't a job Daniel liked, but it was one Grandfather Worth insisted Daniel do, exerting his iron grip on everything in Daniel's life, as he had for twenty-eight years.

Daniel could think of several things he'd much rather be doing, but Grandfather would have his head—and his inheritance—if he stepped off the carefully planned family path.

The prep school Daniel had attended, the college he'd graduated from, even the courses he'd taken, had all been decided by Grandfather. All Daniel had to do in exchange was abide by the elder Worth's rules and the money would continue to flow into Daniel's bank account, as regular as Old Faithful.

But one misstep—such as the time Daniel had dated a woman whose pedigree Grandfather had deemed "inadequate", like she was a substandard poodle at Westminster—and the money vanished. A simple break-up, and the floodgates were opened once again.

When Daniel had been young and more concerned with his social life than his future, Grandfather's rules had been a tolerable annoyance. Slug back a whiskey with friends and he'd forget the future waiting for him at the helm of Worth. Forget how much he'd hated business school. Forget that every element of his adult life was set in a pattern as unchangeable as a DNA strand.

But today, as he waited for the auctioneer to finish listing his assets like he was a 2006 Escalade, the whole thing grated. And made Daniel wish for...

Something. *Anything* but this.

"Why are you selling yourself anyway?" Jake asked, as they waited for the auctioneer to finish his spirited recap of Daniel's personal résumé.

"My grandfather makes me do this crap. Says it makes the family look good."

Jake's raised eyebrow as Daniel walked away told him what he thought of that.

The women whooped and catcalled Daniel as he made his way across the ballroom stage. He'd known many of these women all his life and they'd never acted like this. What the hell had the waiters been passing around in the drinks anyway?

Was it just the thought of turning the tables, of being in control? Of having a man at their beck and call?

Twin canister lights were directed at the spot where he was to stand—conveniently marked with a duct-taped X. White beams shone like a police interrogation in his face, making it hard for him to see the audience. Just as well. He didn't want to know if it had been Mary Jo Williamson or Lauren Templeton who'd let out that wolf whistle.

After all, he had to face them in mixed doubles tennis on Tuesday.

"As you ladies know, Daniel Worth the Fourth is single," the auctioneer paused long enough to allow a few appreciative hollers from the crowd. "He's twenty-eight years old, and, as a member of the Worth family, valued at ninety-three million dollars."

Technically, that wasn't correct. He only had that net worth *if* his grandfather kept him on the family dime. As long as Daniel towed the family line, there wasn't any reason to think that would change, considering Daniel had been born into wealth, as had his father, and his grandfather, and all the Worths before them, ever since the first Worth had started a chain of hotels in Boston and made a mint, practically from the day the colonists were looking for housing.

The Worth family excelled at one thing: finding what people wanted in a bed. And charging them a damned good rate for a pillowtop, room service and a maid who would pop in and turn down the covers just before you were ready to retire. A dreamy experience, Grandfather Worth called it, chuckling all the way to the bank.

Now there were Worth hotels in seventeen countries, each pouring a steady stream of money into the family coffers.

Which meant that yes, Daniel Worth was, pun intended, worth a hell of a lot of dough, and he didn't have to do a whole lot to get the money—besides show up at things like this and eventually take the reins of the family business, carrying on the Worth mantle of ownership.

Daniel had already done all the hard work by being born into the right family. His father had died of a heart attack at forty-eight, leaving a gap between Daniel Worth the Second and Daniel the Fourth—and placing an extra generation of expectations on Daniel's shoulders.

Expectations he hadn't been very good at fulfilling. Hell, he wasn't much good at anything beyond playing the bachelor, as his grandfather reminded him on a weekly basis. That was probably why *Boston* magazine had done that stupid article on him last month. His reputation, it seemed, had seeped into the collective media.

"Now, who'd like to start the bidding?" The auctioneer looked out over the crowd. "Remember, ladies, this is all going to a good cause: the Juvenile Diabetes Foundation."

Oh yeah, that's what they were raising money for. Explained the lack of cake, too.

"Two thousand dollars!" said a woman in the back who sounded a lot like Lauren Templeton.

"Two thousand, five hundred!"

"Three thousand!"

"Four!"

"Four thousand, five hundred!"

Daniel's stomach twisted. When he'd arrived at the hotel tonight, he'd thought this might be fun. Some woman, maybe one he'd dated before, would buy him, they'd go out, have a few laughs and a few drinks, and he'd have done his charitable work for the year. Might even be able to write off the bar tab.

But with the women yelling out price tags on him—

"Six thousand!"

"Six thousand, three hundred!"

—like he was a twelve-carat yellow diamond they all wanted, he felt—

Cheap.

Hell, this wasn't fun. It was freaky.

"Eight thousand!"

"Nine."

"Nine thousand, five hundred!" Whoever raised that price gave out a little whoop-whoop at the end.

When this was over, he was going to strangle Kyle. Surely Grandfather had enough money and influence to get Daniel off on self-defense. Or at least temporary insanity.

"Twelve thousand, three hundred and twenty-two dollars!" called a woman's voice Daniel didn't recognize. He scanned the crowd but couldn't see past the blazing lights. A heavy hush descended over the elaborate ballroom.

Everyone was probably wondering the same thing he was—who had put that large, precise dollar tag on Daniel Worth...and why?

More importantly, what did she intend to do with him once she had her bachelor? Each woman was paying for the right to twenty-four hours with the man of her choice.

Twelve grand... What was she expecting to get for her five hundred dollars an hour?

"Do I hear twelve thousand, five hundred?" The auctioneer looked around the room. Apparently, most of the bank accounts in the room had been drained by the first twenty-nine offerings. None of the women leapt to the next level in bidding. Granted, not a man tonight had gone for more than eight grand. Why should he think *he'd* go for the equivalent of two dozen pairs of Jimmy Choos?

Hell, he'd already dated half the women in the room. Sort of took the air of mystery out of the equation. He stepped forward, out of the glare in his eyes, and scanned the group again, all seated in a room as familiar as the back of his hand. Okay, half might be an exaggeration.

Of sorts.

"Twelve thousand, three hundred and twenty-two going once, going twice," the announcer paused, his gavel hovering over the wooden stand, "and sold! To the woman in the back row."

Just like that, it was over. The lights dimmed a bit, Kyle Montague was back on the stage, thanking everyone for their donations, and Daniel was being shepherded off to sign some papers, probably saying he wouldn't sue for abuse of a donated object or something.

Outside the ballroom, he saw the twenty-nine other paired "couples" for the evening. Persimmon had been bought by moon-faced Sadie Yearwood, whose *nouveau-not-so-riche* mother had thrown her a debutante ball eight years ago—at a Holiday Inn. Sadie had one arm tucked into Persimmon's, and was smiling up at him with the adoration of a kitten who had latched onto a fishmonger.

Jock Crandall, whose father had made a bundle in inflatable toys—and not the kind used in pools— had hungry eyes for every other woman in the room except the one who had just torn a check out of her monogrammed checkbook and handed it to the cashier.

Typical Jock behavior. The man had all the staying power of wet tape.

Then there was Marvin Hall, who'd never actually dated a woman. His father, a lingerie millionaire, was convinced his son just needed to toughen up. He'd enrolled poor scrawny Marvin in every sport offered at Brighton Academy, until the boy had broken enough bones to be given an engraved seat on the football team's bench.

Marvin was with a slender blonde in a red evening gown who apparently found him fascinating—and clearly didn't believe any of the rumors about Marvin's preference for men over women, despite growing up in a sea of garter belts and thigh highs.

"Hefty price tag on you," Jake said, handing Daniel a new scotch on the rocks. "Think you're worth it?"

"Want to poll the ladies?"

Jake scoffed. "Half of them would say you're a terrible boyfriend."

True enough. Daniel had never had much interest in settling down, because that meant growing up and being a "Worth man"—working in a field he hated, going to a job he'd dread. Daniel had had enough of a taste of business in his hands-on practicum at Harvard.

If things had been different, if he'd had a last name like Jones or Smith, then maybe—

Stupid thoughts. His last name wasn't changing and neither was his future. Daniel returned his attention to Jake. "I doubt she bought me to be her *boyfriend.*"

"Now you'll see what it feels like to be a kept man." Jake put a finger to his lips. "Oh wait, you already know about that. You've been kept all your life."

"Ha, ha, very funny. So have you and most of the men in this room."

Jake shrugged and tipped more drink into his mouth. "Yeah, it sucks being rich."

"Did you see who she was?"

"Who?"

"The woman who bought me." Daniel took a swig of scotch, the alcohol a smooth hot burn on his throat. "Damn, that sounds so—"

"Cheap? Tawdry?" Jake grinned. "Welcome to my world. I live there every day, remember. I work in *Hollywood*."

Jake's family owned a studio with a hit cop show on NBC that often shot on location in Boston. He'd been an extra in seventeen episodes and had dated more starlets than Warren Beatty had in his heyday. It kept him in *People* magazine, which he said was good for his career, such as it was.

Daniel knew Jake. Had known him all his life. His best friend had no designs on a career any more complicated than calling for room service the morning after. What he did do, he did for fun. Anything more was work, something Jake avoided like most people avoided public toilets.

Work was the one word that made most of the people in Daniel's peer circle shudder with fear.

And yet, as the crowd milled around him, paying for their "purchases" and talking about the same things with the same people, Daniel wondered—not for the first time—what it would be like if he wasn't living this life. If he hadn't grown up in a world that told him he needed a Swarovski crystal chandelier over his head and an Oriental carpet beneath his feet to be happy.

Daniel tipped the glass into his mouth again. Yeah. And maybe he just needed more scotch.

"Excuse me."

He pivoted at the voice. It was softer and sweeter than when it had been shouting out dollar amounts, but still, he recognized it. The voice was paired with wide, deep green eyes and a heart-shaped face framed by long brunette curls. Lithe and petite, she lacked the designer labels, nine-hundred dollar high heels and ten-pound diamond earrings the other women wore. Instead, she was clad in simple black satin slacks and a soft teal sweater that skimmed over her curves and had a small, teasing scoop in the front. Interesting. And different. *Very* different.

He didn't know her...but he knew he would, soon. "It's you."

She cocked her head. "If you mean, am I the one who bought you, yes, I am. Or I will be, if I could get over to pay the cashier." She waved her checkbook at him, one of those free ones banks gave out with new checking accounts. None of that fancy mono-grammed stuff for her. Just a plain old blue vinyl cover.

Did she even *have* twelve thousand dollars? She wouldn't be crazy enough to bounce a check to a charity, would she?

Daniel decided he didn't care. Suddenly, he wanted to be out of the stuffy, cloying environment, away from the hotel where he'd spent half his formative years, following his grandfather around, "learning the business." A business he wanted nothing to do with, then or now.

"Right this way," Daniel said. With one arm, he cleared a path, murmuring "excuse me's" as he eased the crowd out of the way. She gave him a nod of thanks, then moved past him and up to the register.

"*That's* your date?" Jake said.

"Seems so."

"She's hot. But she's not from our side of the block." Jake peered over Susan Whiteman's blond up-do to get another glimpse of Daniel's buyer. "I take that back. She's *very* hot."

"She's mine."

"Ooh, getting all territorial already?" Jake grinned. "Down, boy. She's only yours for twenty-four hours, or until she's done with you, whichever comes first. This time, you're not in control."

Daniel swirled the ice cubes around in his drink. "We'll see about that."

"Worth arrogance. Plenty to go around." Jake shook his head. "A thousand dollars says you don't even get to first base with her tonight."

"A thousand?" Daniel gave his friend a smile. "Your mommy lets you bet that much of your allowance?"

"Hey, it's my money."

Daniel arched a brow.

"Are we on, or are you too chicken to take the bet?"

Daniel put his nearly empty drink on the tray of a passing waiter. "I hate to take money from a friend. But, if you insist…"

Jake chuckled and thrust out a hand. "Just promise that you won't be grumpy tomorrow when you're emptying your wallet into my palm."

"Oh, I won't be grumpy," Daniel said, watching his buyer weave her way back through the crowd, a receipt for her purchase in her hands. She had a perfect figure and a strong, confident stride. Exactly the kind of woman he liked going toe-to-toe with. "Because I know *I'll* be the one with a smile on my face tomorrow."

"Worth arrogance," Jake repeated, shaking his head. "One of these days, it's going to be your downfall."

"Hey, I can't sink any lower than this," Daniel said, waving a hand at the stage. "I went for less than a used Toyota."

Jake grinned. "Too bad you don't come with a warranty, my friend."

Daniel's Spent-a-Mint Chocolate Brownies

Brownie Batter:

3/4 cup cocoa, unsweetened

1/2 teaspoon baking soda

1/3 cup butter, melted

1/2 cup boiling water

2 cups granulated sugar

2 large eggs, slightly beaten

1 teaspoon vanilla extract

1 1/3 cups all-purpose flour

1/4 teaspoon salt

Mint Layer:

1/4 cup butter, softened

2 cups confectioners' sugar

4 tablespoons crème de menthe

Frosting:

1/2 cup butter

12 ounces chocolate chips

I know, it looks as intimidating as a family dinner. But really, this is pretty easy—even a non-cooking, spoiled bachelor playboy can do it. No need to call in the maids for help. Well, maybe just for a minute so they can show you how to turn on the stove and preheat it to 350 degrees.

Find a mixing bowl (I know you've got one in your kitchen somewhere). In it, combine the cocoa and baking soda, then stir in the butter. When that's mixed, add in the boiling water and mix until well blended.

See how easy that is so far? Now add the sugar, eggs, vanilla. All in one bowl so far—can't get much better than that for clean-up. Of course, doing the dishes with a sexy woman in an apron is even more fun, so we'll break in some more bowls later.

For now, add the flour and salt, then pour the whole thing into a greased 13 x 9 ½ inch baking pan (if you need to get out a tape measure to check those dimensions, it's a sure sign you aren't spending enough time in your own kitchen. The lazy option, of course, is to ask the cook which one is the right pan). Bake at 350 degrees for 35 to 40 minutes, or until a toothpick inserted in the center comes out clean. Cool and get ready for the layers that add that taste of extravagance to the dessert.

In a separate bowl, mix the mint ingredients. Spread on top of the brownies, then chill them for an hour. I'm sure you can find something to do with that hour—and someone to do it with.

Finally, melt the butter and chocolate chips in the microwave in 30-second bursts, stirring each time until smooth. Spread the chocolate frosting over the mint layer—carefully, so the whole thing doesn't look like a man did it. Then put the brownies back in the fridge, letting everything get firm and hard again. I meant the brownies.

Slice and serve to a woman who has just spent her very last dime making sure you're the one she's going home with tonight.

Chapter Two

Olivia Regan had either made the biggest financial mistake of her life, or the smartest marketing move in the history of bakeries.

After emptying her business checking account in one swoop of a pen, she was sure it was the former. This had seemed like a damned good idea when she'd seen Daniel Worth IV's picture in *Boston* magazine last month as "the most eligible bachelor in the city of Boston" but now...

Well now it just seemed crazy.

She was all out of options. Short of turning herself into a human popover and standing in the middle of Herald Square, offering passersby a taste, she saw no other way to drum up business. Ads hadn't worked. Free tastings hadn't worked. Going door-to-door with flyers, samples and shameless begging hadn't made much more than a dent in business.

Daniel Worth had better damned well live up to his name. Especially since she'd just sunk her very last nickel into him.

Her cell phone rang and she dug it out of the purse dangling on her wrist. Hopefully, it was her sister, telling her business was brisk at Pastries with Panache. The name displayed on her Caller ID screen, though, was "Pauline Regan."

Her mother.

She considered not answering at all, but knew her mother would keep calling. Thank God her parents lived in Maryland, a place they'd moved to ten years ago when her father had accepted the job of dean of a women's college, because otherwise her mother would be here, poking and prying until she found out exactly what Olivia was up to. Not out of nosiness, but out of concern that her headstrong entrepreneurial daughter would end up destitute and selling pencils on street corners.

Given the last few weeks of shaky profit-and-loss statements, it was a career choice Olivia had considered.

Olivia cupped her hand over the phone, hoping to drown out the background noise of the auction. In front of her, elderly Wendall Montague was taking his sweet time writing out her charitable deduction receipt. "Hi, Mom."

"Olivia Jean, why is your sister at the shop this morning instead of you?"

"Uh…" Olivia scrambled for an answer that was close-ish to the truth. "She's helping me while I'm out buying something."

"She should be studying for her permanents exam. Those chemical equations can be quite difficult, you know. Josie needs to complete beauty school. To complete anything, for Pete's sake. Lord knows I can't have anyone else in the family ending up like your father."

The implied words—ending up like Olivia. Mom believed anyone who went into business for themselves was either crazy or suicidal, or both. Over the years, Harold Regan's dozen different get-rich-quick schemes had given her mother what she called "a nervous condition."

Meaning she couldn't open the bank statement without first taking a Valium.

Dad's investments had always been a fifty-fifty thing. Half of them actually made money while the rest drained his bank account like a Hoover on high. As her mother went on about Josie's hairdressing future, Olivia thought of her dad's ventures.

There'd been the dog massage parlor—a pooch disaster.

The apartment complex for singles only—a huge success, until all the residents paired up, got married and moved into ranches on cul de sacs.

The reptile weighing scales—they'd been a success until Dad realized his partner was using SuperGlue to keep the snakes in place for the TV ads.

The Flower-Power Miniature Golf park— sounded great on paper, but flopped with kiddos who didn't find golfing with tulips fun. Not to mention that little incident with the bees.

Dad's investments had made Mom adamant that all three of her children find a nine-to-five job. Ben had one, Josie was working toward one...but

Olivia was the lone black sheep who'd been a disappointment ever since she dropped out of Boston University to go to culinary school. And then ended up dropping out of that, to take private lessons instead. Apparently the instructors of the culinary school she'd attended didn't find two-alarm kitchen fires amusing.

"Your sister is a smart girl but she needs to settle down," Mom went on. "Get a job she can stay with for more than a month. Today it's photography, tomorrow it's dog walking. What's it going to be next? Zookeeping? You have to encourage her. She's got a talent for this beauty thing. Did you know she got the highest score on her hair dyes quiz?"

"That's great," Olivia replied. Wendell leaned forward, the completed receipt quivering in his grip. Olivia took it, smiled a thanks that tested her patience, then moved away from the table. "Listen, Mom, I need to go—"

"And you, dear, I wish you'd chosen a more stable career," Mom continued, not hearing Olivia. "I thought you'd have learned from your father's mistakes. And then, look at his brother, Uncle Morty. That toilet factory of his was your dad's latest 'investment'. Flushed half our savings down with his "every home needs a bidet" ship."

Olivia cupped her hand over the phone as she wound her way through the crowd at the cashier's desk. She stood on her tiptoes, looking for Daniel Worth.

There he was, a man who seemed to tower over the others, his dark hair standing out in a sea of blondes. "Mom, not every small business fails," Olivia said into the phone.

"Four out of five do." Her mother paused, drew in a breath. "I worry about you, honey. About your future."

The soft tones in Mom's voice made something in Olivia's eyes sting. She blinked the feeling away, redoubling her resolve to make the shop work. "I worry, too. But I'm going to be okay."

"It's just…." Her mother hesitated before going on. "Are you sure this pastry thing is right for you?"

A guy in a tuxedo brushed past Olivia, nearly spilling his champagne on her slacks. She weaved past another giggling couple, bringing her within six feet of Daniel. "Mom, I researched it, studied the trends, evaluated the competition—"

"I mean in your heart, are you sure this is the field for you?"

"Of course." But even as Olivia said the words, she wondered if they were true. She had trend reports and business plans, but something seemed to have gotten lost along the way, like a light dimming ever so slightly each day.

Back when she first started laying the groundwork, she'd felt that light burning hot and bright, but somewhere between the endless hours spent pleasing the Board of Health, wading through the red tape of a business start-up, the continual worry about profits…the excitement she'd started with had dissipated.

She was tired, that was all. Tired of running an uphill race. Tired of trying to think of new ways to turn Pastries with Panache around. Tired of being the one with all the responsibility on her shoulders.

"Honey, I don't want to be the wet blanket at your beach party," her mother said. "All I want is for you to be happy."

"I am happy," Olivia insisted. *Or I will be, once the general ledger has more in the receivables column than the payables.*

"Just promise me one thing," Mom said. "You won't keep pouring good money after bad. And you'll jump off that ship before it sinks."

Olivia looked up and caught Daniel Worth watching her, his blue eyes as vibrant as a butane flame. Heat pooled in her veins. If he had that much effect on her in a crowded room, imagine what that look could do in her shop? "It's not going to sink."

Her mother sighed. "That's what they said about the Titanic, dear."

Jake's Fast-and-Easy Chocolate Trifle

1 chocolate cake
8 ounces chocolate pudding
1 8-ounce container whipped topping
3 candy bars, your choice

You want the woman, right? Then don't waste any time in the kitchen. Send the butler out to the bakery, have him get the cake, pudding, whipped topping and candy bars. What kind of candy bars? Her favorite, of course. You're not making this for her nutritional benefit, if you know what I mean.

Have the cook break up the cake into chunks. Then, while you're busy putting on the Barry White and pouring champagne, the cook can be busying layering in one third of the cake pieces in a bowl, then topping with one-third of the pudding and whipped topping respectively. Crumble a candy bar in, then repeat all layers.

If the cook isn't handy, pay the butler extra to do it. No need for you to dirty up a spoon, not when there's an inheritance to spend. And a lady waiting for you to show her your best assets.

CHAPTER THREE

Olivia finally managed to get her mother off the phone by telling her she was getting in her car. To Pauline Regan, celling and driving was the danger equivalent of using the third rail of the T as a balance beam.

She tucked her phone away, then took a good, long, close-up look at the merchandise she'd just purchased. And had to admit she was pleased.

Daniel Worth IV was the quintessential playboy: tall, dark, handsome. He had a charming grin, teasing blue eyes and broad, defined shoulders. He was leaning against one of the ballroom pillars with the ease of a man who owned a corner of the world. Which he did, at least many prime real estate corners.

He'd do. He'd do just fine, in fact.

She reminded herself that no matter how sexy, he was a purchase, like the mixer she'd bought last month. Despite his charm, she had no intentions of getting involved with him. Dating men because she had a "good feeling" about them had led her down Disaster Avenue more than once. Olivia was older, wiser and had vowed from here on out to trust her head, not any other part of her body, when it came to dating.

A man standing near Daniel walked away, tossing a grin Daniel's way, leaving Olivia more or less alone with her purchase. "Mr. Worth," Olivia said, putting out her hand. "I'm Olivia Regan. Your new owner."

He quirked a grin and clasped her palm with his own. A warm, large palm that seemed to embody security, comfort. Result of a good manicure, nothing more.

"That has to be the best pick-up line I've ever heard," he said.

"Oh, I'm not picking you up. I'm—" Just then, she was jostled from behind. Olivia lost her footing, teetered on the high heels, and stumbled against Daniel's chest.

When they touched, lightning coursed through her, fast and hard, like a flamethrower toasting her hormones. For a brief second, she wanted to kiss him, to taste what was right there, right above her. She'd studied the man for weeks, his face becoming so familiar that it had started starring in a lot of her late-night dreams.

Very sexy late-night dreams. Ones that would have been called soft porn if they'd been on cable.

Some reflex made her tip her chin up at the same time he lowered his. Between them, she could feel the steady beat of his heart, the rhythmic movement of his chest. *Oh boy.*

"If this isn't picking me up, I don't what is." Daniel's voice was low, husky. Tempting.

Too tempting. Like touring the Hershey factory after giving up chocolate for Lent.

Olivia inhaled, then drew herself up and pulled away. "Sorry. I, ah, stumbled."

His lips curved into a grin. "You weren't about to kiss me?"

Been there, did that, last night around three in the morning.

"For one, I didn't think about anything more than whether someone had spilled a drink on my pants." *Lord, Olivia, come up with a better lie than that.* "For another, this room is terribly stuffy so I'm sure it's affecting everyone's thinking. Especially yours."

"So you aren't interested in me?"

"I am, but not for kissing." *Liar, liar, lips on fire.*

"Really?" He raised a brow. "I assumed you wanted a date with me, bad enough to pay for it."

Ugh. The man had an ego to match his bank account. What had she expected? That the hottest playboy in Boston would be humble, well-mannered? That he would assume a woman would pay twelve thousand dollars to use his name and likeness, instead of his body?

Then again, taking another glance at Daniel Worth's lean, V-shaped frame, maybe *she* was the crazy one. Using his body suddenly didn't seem like such a bad idea.

Whoa, business only. Remember? Sleeping with him isn't part of the equation.

Not unless you can think of a way to make it turn a profit.

"I have other uses in mind for you," Olivia said.

"Other uses?" He smirked. "Not ones involving whips and chains, I hope. I'm not a fan of pain. I much prefer pleasure."

The way he said the word, it sounded as decadent as her chocolate ganache. Something hot melted in Olivia's gut. She should have chosen someone else, someone easier to manage. A beagle instead of a Great Dane.

But when a girl needed a big job done, she called in the big dog. And Daniel Worth was the biggest dog in town.

"Let's go. We need to be alone for what I want."

"Already?" His smirk widened.

After she was done with him, there would be time enough to knock his swagger down a notch or two—and baking implements aplenty to do the job.

Olivia shifted a bit on her high heels. She never wore shoes this tall and her arches groaned beneath the strain. She'd gotten all dressed up for the event, telling herself when she'd slipped on the shoes— left over from being a bridesmaid—that she wasn't doing it to impress the bachelor, but to fit in. But as his gaze skimmed over her with clear appreciation, the shoes suddenly stopped feeling uncomfortable.

"I have plans for you, as I said, and I'd like to get started."

Business only, she reminded herself again, tearing her gaze away from his lips and focusing instead on the least sexy part of his face she could see—the tip of his nose.

"How about we go to my townhouse in Beacon Hill? It's not that far from here."

"I was thinking maybe...my place." Olivia reached into her bag, pulled out her keys and dangled them with an invitation in her eyes.

Like a puppy spying a new toy, Daniel nodded. "You lead, I'll follow. I am, after all, bought and paid for."

"And since I paid damned good money for you, I expect to get every last dime's worth."

"Oh you will, Miss Regan," he said, bringing up the rear as they exited the room, "you most certainly will."

Olivia pushed the call button for the elevator, hoping like hell that her investment was going to leave her flush at the end—unlike Uncle Morty's bidets.

Olívia's Drive-Him-Bananas Muffins

2 cups flour
1 teaspoon baking powder
1 teaspoon baking soda
1/4 teaspoon salt
1/2 teaspoon ground cinnamon
1/4 teaspoon grated nutmeg
3 large ripe bananas
1 egg
1/2 cup dark brown sugar, firmly packed
1/4 cup vegetable oil
1/4 cup walnuts, chopped fine

If the man keeps trying to steal your attention, focus him on one of these instead. Guaranteed, he'll opt for nabbing a muffin, thereby distracting him from your heart. Start by preheating the oven to 375 degrees and lining your muffin cups with paper liners—to make later stripping much easier, of course.

Sift together the dry ingredients and put aside. Mash the bananas, then beat in the egg, sugar and oil. Without spilling, forgetting yourself, or getting distracted by the sexy bachelor in your kitchen, slowly add the dry ingredients to the wet, mixing on low speed until blended. Fold in the walnuts, then fill the muffin cups two-thirds full.

Bake them for 20-25 minutes. Just long enough to share a cup of coffee with a man who isn't all he seems. Or maybe…more than he seems.

Chapter Four

Daniel quickly learned two things about Olivia Regan: she didn't need a man to take care of her and she liked to be in control. She waved away the offer of his personal limo, opting to drive him to their destination in her six-year-old Volvo instead. When he came around the car to open her door, she beat him to it, seating herself before he could do the chivalrous thing.

Clearly, this was one woman who didn't need a knight in shining armor. He suspected, in a pinch, she'd knock the knight off his horse and take the reins herself.

She rolled down the window and looked at him. "Are you going to get in? Or jog behind the car?"

"I..." She'd also done something few women had ever accomplished—left him at a loss for words. He stood in the middle of the Worth Hotel parking garage like an idiot—knowing some security guard was yukking it up behind the video cameras—and came around the other side. He barely had his seatbelt buckled before Olivia had the car in gear and was whipping it around the curves of the garage like Jeff Johnson on crack.

"Hey, slow down," he said. "You could kill someone."

She tossed him a grin and depressed the accelerator more. "Why do you think my insurance rates are so high?"

His jaw must have dropped because she banged a hard left out of the garage and onto School Street. "I'm kidding, Worth. Don't look so shocked. Don't your society princesses make jokes?"

"Not about killing pedestrians."

"I've never run over anyone in my life. I'm merely driving Boston-style." She increased her speed again, then swerved into the left lane of traffic, in a space only six inches bigger than her car. The Honda behind her laid on his horn in aggravation with her commando driving.

Or maybe at the horror of seeing his life flash across his windshield.

"Why are you in such a big hurry?"

She flicked on her blinker, then took a left before the directional had a chance to flash twice. "I only have you for twenty-four hours. I don't intend to waste twenty-three of them stuck in traffic."

"Eager, are you?"

Olivia gave him a non-committal smile and went back to concentrating on weaving in and out of the cars on Tremont, as if playing traffic dodgeball would save her several of those twenty-four hours.

Daniel had no idea who this woman was or why was so damned determined to have him. It had to have been that spread in *Boston* magazine. He'd told his grandfather it was a stupid idea, one that would only perpetuate the paparazzi's endless fascination with his dating life, but Grandfather had insisted, saying the publicity would give the family hotel chain a much-needed infusion of "sex appeal."

Hell, he didn't even know his seventy-five-year-old grandfather—whom Daniel had rarely seen in anything less formal than a three-piece suit—thought about anything more passionate than his weekly bridge games. Especially since Grandmother Worth had passed away three years ago.

Nevertheless, if there was one thing Grandfather was good at, it was keeping Daniel on his toes.

"So, what kind of stamina do you have?" Olivia asked.

"Stamina?" He blinked. "You get right to the point, don't you?"

"Oh, for God's sake. What makes you think I meant sex?" She hung another left onto Kneeland and let out a gust. "I know you're rich and gorgeous and every cliché that's supposed to make a grown woman weak in the knees," she let out a dramatic, sarcastic sigh that told him what she thought of women who did that, "but not every woman you meet wants to take you to bed."

"Not every woman I meet pays five hundred dollars an hour to spend time with me, either." He clutched the dash as she made a perilous right turn down a narrow side street. A burly construction worker setting up a detour sign leapt out of her way, releasing a string of obscenities at Olivia's retreating taillights. "Why did you buy me, anyway?"

She smiled at him. "You'll see."

Daniel checked to be sure his seatbelt was snug. He could see the headlines now: Worth Heir Dies In Old Volvo With Crazy—

Then he realized he knew virtually nothing about the woman who held his life in her lead foot. Did they even have a picture of her back at the hotel? Some kind of evidence, should he end up hanging off the Tobin Bridge at the end of her smashed-up auto? Or worse, spirited off to some Mexican dungeon until his family coughed up a Lotto drawing's worth of ransom? "Who are you, anyway?"

"I told you my name." She short-braked at a light, sending both of them careening toward the dashboard, saved from hitting it by the seatbelts.

I'm in a Volvo. Safest car on the market.

Yeah, safest on the market with your average driver. Olivia Regan is anything but average.

"That's not a lot to go on," he said. The light turned green and Olivia jetted into the next lane, spurting ahead of the cars slow to accelerate, then zipped down Essex Street. "I know more than that about the people who stay in my hotels."

At that, she laughed. The car slowed a bit, as if the act of releasing humor made her relent a little on the traffic, too. "I won't give you my credit card number, but I will tell you that I'm twenty-six, single and I prefer a king over two doubles."

That particular tidbit of information sent an image rocketing through Daniel's brain that had nothing to do with business. Olivia, spread out on one of the famous Worth mile-high mattresses, in something sheer and white and silky, smiling up at him and no longer wanting to speed past the good parts.

"I'm a king man myself," Daniel said.

"I expected you would be," she replied.

"Is that a smear on my wealth?"

"Hey, if the dollar signs fit." She gave him another impish grin, then sped past a little old lady driving a bright yellow Volkswagen.

"I take it you aren't from a wealthy background."

"Gee, what gave it away? The JC Penney labels on my back or the car that I'm making payments on?"

He heard the sarcasm in her voice and knew it wasn't directed at him. She'd only known him for twenty minutes. The tone was for his kind—wealthy people who'd never had to worry about money. He'd run into that attitude from time to time, whenever he'd stepped out of his own circle of friends. It made him uncomfortable. Perhaps that's why his kind stuck together, huddled in a bunch like emperor penguins on an iceberg. Because they knew if they stepped into the frigid waters of the general populace, the middle class polar bears would gladly eat them alive.

How could he explain being handed something he hadn't asked for, hadn't earned? But something he sure as hell wasn't turning down.

He was rich, not insane.

"You know," he said to Olivia, "I never put down the way you dressed or the car you drove."

She let out a gust and the car slowed again. "You're right. I've simply had to work my butt off for every dime I've ever made and you...well, people like you—"

"Haven't."

Olivia shrugged, displacing the long brown waves of her hair. They resettled around her shoulders with an easy messiness that said she wasn't one of those women who hairsprayed like they were girding up for a hair gladiator battle.

"Anyway," she said, changing the subject. "I didn't mean to get off on a have's and have-not's discussion. I have no intention of trying to instigate social change in the next twenty-four hours."

"Pity. That's what I was hoping we'd do. It'd be a hell of a lot more fun than drinks and dinner."

She laughed again, this time a deeper, throatier sound that came from some well far inside her. It told Daniel that Olivia Regan was the kind of woman who did things with passion.

Passion. The stab of envy that went through him surprised Daniel. Where did she find that hungry drive? And most of all, what would it do to him if he let her into his complacent, predicted-from-birth life?

"Bullshit," she said. "You were hoping I'd take you straight to my apartment and we'd have wild, kinky sex. Over and over again."

He grinned. "Well, *after* we changed the world, I figured we might need to blow off some steam."

"Uh-huh. You're a bad liar, Worth."

She slowed the car and parallel parked on a small side street between Atlantic Avenue and Surface Street, a few blocks from Boston's busy financial district. He looked out his window and saw a bright teal-and-white awning hanging over a small storefront. The letters Pastries with Panache decorated the plate glass windows in a gold hand-lettered script. Beside it was another small shop named Gift Baskets to Die For, gaily decorated for the upcoming Valentine's Day holiday.

Though it was nighttime, Daniel could see through the windows and into the shop, which was softly lit by a pair of wall sconces. He spied café-style tables ringed by chairs. A Closed sign hung in the window, with the operating hours of 7 a.m. to 2 p.m. displayed in black script below. "This isn't your apartment."

"No, but I do live here. Or it feels like it most days." She turned off the Volvo and got out. Once again, not waiting for his help.

Hell of a woman. One he didn't think he'd want to arm wrestle. Or race at Daytona.

Beneath the puddle of the streetlight, stood one thing that didn't go with the bakery's décor—a man. Tall, he wore faded jeans and a worn brown leather jacket. When Olivia stepped onto the sidewalk, the other guy jerked forward. "Where have you been?" he said.

"I was buying a man."

"You did *what?*"

"I told you, I bought a man." Olivia thumbed the remote and with a double beep, locked her car, then waved for Daniel to follow. He cast an amused glance at Mr. Bewildered and did as Olivia asked.

She flipped through her keys, found the one she wanted and slipped it into the steel security gate that had been rolled down to protect the front of the shop. She unlocked and lifted that, then inserted a different key into the handle of the door. The scent of chocolate drifted through the air around them, coming from the gift shop next door, Daniel presumed.

The sweet aroma did nothing to temper the annoyed look on the other guy's face. As soon as Olivia withdrew her key, he stepped forward and blocked her from entering. "Olivia, you can't *buy* a man."

"I can and I did." She turned to Daniel. "Didn't I?"

"She did. I'm like an indentured servant. But more fun, I hope." Daniel shot Olivia a grin, just to torture the poor sap.

Judging by his possessive annoyance, Mr. Bewildered was either a boyfriend or an ex. If Olivia had been Daniel's girlfriend, she'd never have been going out to bachelor auctions, much less purchasing eligible males. Either way, if she had to go out and *buy* her dates, then this guy had to be really horrible.

"Who are you anyway?" The other man took two steps toward Daniel, in a gesture that would have been construed as menacing in a rooster colony.

Daniel gave him a polite smile. "Daniel Worth."

The other guy's jaw worked up. Down. Opened. Closed. "You bought a *millionaire?*" he whispered to Olivia.

"Multi-millionaire," she corrected. "As in more than one million."

Mr. Bewildered backed up a step. Nothing like a little money to get another rooster out of the chicken coop, leaving the best hen behind.

"I told you, Ben, what I do with my life is my business. So don't think you can tell me what to do anymore. That stopped after I turned ten." Olivia brushed past him, pushed on the door and entered her shop, not bothering to look behind her to see if the men followed.

Ten? How young had Olivia started dating? The glass door shut, signaling that she was clearly done. With both of them.

Ben looked at Daniel. Daniel looked at Ben. They each shrugged, then took the argument inside. Where the pretty woman was, after all.

They might be men—but they weren't complete idiots.

Daniel stepped inside Pastries with Panache and was immediately wrapped in the homey scents of

Olivia's shop. For a second, his mind rocketed back twenty, maybe twenty-one years, to when he'd been a little boy.

Lewiston, the Worth family butler, had brought Daniel home to spend the weekend at his family's house, on the first of many such weekends. Daniel didn't remember why now but it was probably because his mother was off in Europe again, his grandparents were likely vacationing in Florida and the nanny had the weekend off. He'd been forgotten in the shuffle, as he often had in the busy-ness of the Worth world.

But Lewiston had been there, as always, to pick up the pieces.

He'd been eight or so, but he remembered the weekend like it was yesterday. Especially the kitchen. There'd been cakes. Pies. A turkey the size of a Hyundai. All homemade, not five-star chef creations from some restaurant with a fancy name. And a warm, large woman who smothered Lewiston in a hug, then drew young Daniel in with her free arm, smushing him into the family. The two days had passed in a blur of simple food and laughter, something so foreign that Daniel almost felt like he'd stepped into an alternate reality.

When he returned home to the stilted elegance of the Worth family home, he realized he had.

Olivia's shop was like that weekend. Filled with the scents of what a home should be. Sugar, cinnamon, custard, apples. Sweet, warm. Homemade. It was almost enough to make Daniel sentimental.

Almost. If he could afford to be a sentimental man.

Ben shrugged off his leather jacket and draped it over one of the scrolled wrought-iron chairs. "I worry about you, Olivia."

She didn't reply, instead moving to flick on the lights, bathing the room in a warm yellow glow that increased the intimate feel, as did every element of the décor. Though he barely knew her, he could see Olivia in each detail, feel the vibrancy of her personality in the yellow walls and crimson flooring. In the center of the tables sat squat bowls with thick vanilla pillar candles surrounded by tiny kiwis, tangerines and lemons. A long lighted glass case stacked with scones, bagels, muffins, cakes and other baked goods ran the length of the back wall, flanked on one side by a short bar and four bar stools. Ready and waiting for someone to sidle on up, slather on some butter and indulge. If everything Olivia baked tasted as good as it smelled, and as good as she looked, he'd be happy to try a bite. Or two.

Daniel took a glance at his new "owner" and hoped indulgence went along with her plans for him. Then he remembered Ben standing over there, perfecting his glare. There wouldn't be much decadence happening here, not unless Daniel dipped a finger into the coconut cake in the case.

Ben let out a gust. "Olivia, if you won't listen to me, will you at least call home and let them know you're alive?"

She paused mid-step, halfway to the commercial coffeepot on the back counter. She let out a sigh and her head dipped a bit. "Yeah, I will."

"Good. Then Mom will get off my back. My work here is done." Ben swung his coat off the chair and sent Daniel a glance. "Though why you bought a man—"

"Hey, you don't care what I buy at Macy's, so don't worry about this. Just think of it as a bigger purchase." Olivia grinned. "Besides, I don't butt into your life."

"I don't screw up mine."

She arched a brow. "You're divorced, living with a cat and working a job you hate."

Daniel draped a confidential arm over Ben's shoulder. "I'd get out while the getting is good. I think she's going in for the kill."

Ben chuckled. "You know her well already."

"I've seen her drive."

Ben shook his head, his laughter coming stronger now, a bit of détente between the two men because they belonged to a rare club—those who had survived a life-threatening experience in the passenger's seat of Olivia's Volvo. "She gives the Boston P.D. a run for its money," Ben said.

"I do not," Olivia said, dumping water in the coffeepot, then flicking the switch.

Ben snorted. "I'm your brother. You can't lie to me."

Her *brother*. Not her boyfriend. That information suffused Daniel with a relief he hadn't expected.

He looked again at Olivia, studying her petite frame with renewed interest. Hell, if he were honest with himself, interest that hadn't died one bit since the moment he saw her.

"After she talked to you," Ben continued, "Mom called me, concerned because she heard noises in the background. She thought you were at a wild party and sent me out to make sure you didn't end up on the wrong end of a police raid."

Olivia chuckled. "Okay, I'll call home, I'll even make plans to drive down to Maryland for a weekend." She put up a hand to head off Ben's next question. "Soon. I promise. Now, go back to Tabby."

"Rex. My cat's name is Rex. Like the dinosaur."

"She's a calico. You can't call her that forever."

"Long as I have a can of tuna in my hands, she'll come. Even if I call her Snuffleupagus."

Olivia laughed, a sound as rich and sweet as the treats that filled the back case. For a second, Daniel felt a weird pang of longing. For a little of this... repartee, this teasing. Only children like him didn't trade barbs—and jabs—with a sibling.

Except for Lewiston and Daniel's frequent-visitor cousin Madison, the Worth house had always been a silent museum filled with antiques and rules for behavior. After his father died, Daniel's mother had retreated to her late husband's house in France, saying she couldn't stand living there anymore. She'd left Daniel behind, at Grandfather's request, to grow up "properly." Meaning a young boy would cramp her efforts to find another wealthy husband in Paris.

Over the years, he'd barely seen or heard from her. And thus, the main duties of mothering Daniel had been left in the hands of the butler.

He shook his head. He was probably experiencing food poisoning or after-burn from the auction's crappy champagne. It wasn't like he saw Olivia with her shop and wished he had a little of that purpose for himself.

Well, maybe he did. Up till now, his sole purpose in life, according to Grandfather, had been seeing how many times he could star in the weekly Gloria's Gossip column in the *Herald*. Daniel snorted. Now *there* was a mission in life.

Years ago, he'd had a dream for a different mission—until it became clear his plans weren't his own. Grandfather's big talent—besides his acting hobby—was to squash dreams that weren't in keeping with his vision for a Worth.

Daniel shook himself mentally, watching Olivia and Ben continue the friendly argument as she walked him to the door. The food *had* to have been spoiled. Otherwise, why was Daniel standing in a bakery, for God's sake, questioning a life anyone in their right mind would kill to have? And some had, if the rumors about Larson Cullers were to be believed.

Yet despite the money, the limos, the vacation homes, Daniel still wasn't satisfied.

Insane. That was like going to the all-you-can-eat buffet and leaving with a craving for dog food.

"Nice to meet you," Ben said, extending his hand to Daniel. The two men shook, though Daniel could see Olivia's brother didn't trust him as far as he could throw a donut.

"Despite my reputation, I'm a decent guy," Daniel said.

Ben gave him the uh-huh nod. "Don't try to kid me. I speak guy, too, you know." Then he turned and pressed on the brass handle to open the door. He paused a second. "Hey, sis?"

"Yeah?"

"Remember even wolves sometimes wear gentleman's clothing." He cast a glance toward Daniel. Then he was gone, leaving that little tidbit behind and but ruining the hell out of Daniel's plan to press Olivia against that glass case. To taste the lips that alternately drove him crazy when they were moving and teased at him when they weren't.

Olivia returned to her spot behind the counter, readying two cups of coffee and then putting out sugar, creamer and spoons. She glided through the space, clearly at home.

"This is your shop." The words were a statement, not a question.

"Yes," she said, handing him a cup. "My sister works here with me, but that's it. We've been open about a year."

"Can I ask what you have planned for me?" Daniel said, leaning against the counter and accepting the cup she handed him.

"Pictures."

He took a step back, the java sloshing in the floral-print mug. That kind of thing *definitely* wouldn't go over well with the Worth Corporation board of directors. Not to mention how Grandfather would react at the next family dinner. He could just see the seventy-five-year-old patriarch flinging the bouillabaisse at the wall. *After* he'd whipped Daniel's butt with a French baguette.

When it came to protecting the family dignity, Grandfather took no prisoners and left no visible markings.

"Pictures?" Daniel asked, putting his coffee on the counter. "Of me doing what? Exactly?"

Olivia sipped from her mug, her emerald gaze connecting with his over the rim. "Eating."

"And you propose to do that by getting me into a compromising position, taking a photograph that *People* will pay a boatload for and then blackmailing me for money?"

She laughed, that same genuine sound he had heard before, only ten times deeper this time, as if the release of humor gave her something she didn't find elsewhere. Even under the gas pedal.

"Oh, God, no." Olivia tipped a finger to her chin, a bemused smile on her face. "I hadn't thought of blackmail. Maybe I'll reserve that idea, in case you don't cooperate. Sort of a plan B."

"Okay then, it must be something more nefarious." Daniel said, lifting the glass dome off the cake plate on the counter and withdrawing a muffin. He waggled it in her direction. "You have a baked goods fetish and I'm your sex toy?"

Olivia's face flushed deep pink, a color Daniel decided he liked very much, even if her plan was setting off alarm bells in his head. "I do *not* get kinky with my food." She yanked the muffin out of his hands. "What I have is a bakery that needs help."

"So you spent twelve thousand dollars on me instead of…what, rent? Advertising? Utilities?"

"I've done all that. Did a nice half-pager in the *Herald.* A slew of thirty-second spots on three different radio stations. I even hired a marketing consultant." She let out a very unladylike sound and moved to add more cream to her coffee. "Fat lot of good that one did me. The 'consultant' didn't tell me anything I didn't already know. He was a waste of time and money."

Daniel took advantage of her distraction and snagged another muffin, biting into it before she could turn around. It was good. Damned good. A hell of a lot better than the too-dry chateaubriand they'd served at the auction. If Olivia could do this with bananas, walnuts and flour, he could only imagine what other talents she had.

Daniel took a second bite, then hid the remains behind his back before Olivia caught him. "What did the consultant say?"

"I need more business." She pivoted and waved her free hand at the empty shop. "Well, duh."

"So why not take the easy route?" he asked, intrigued. "Get a partner, a loan from the bank?"

She shrugged, as if the answer was inconsequential. "I prefer to earn my way to the top. I accepted help once, and I don't want to do it again."

Daniel forgot the muffin behind his back, his gaze centered on Olivia's, on the intelligence and spark residing in her dark green eyes. "You're not like anyone I know, Olivia Regan."

"Because I'm not wearing Prada?"

"A woman can look good in any label," he said, his gaze skimming over her form and deciding that Olivia would, indeed, look good in a potato sack. Or in couture. Or in his bed, wearing nothing. "No, I meant because you're …well, a hard worker. I mean, you run this place pretty much by yourself, you clearly took a huge financial risk with the auction. Most of the people in my peer circle don't believe in big financial risks or in working."

"Ever?"

"Not if they can help it. I mean, if you're born with money, work is a hobby, not a necessity."

Olivia ran a hand through her hair, and the brown waves resettled into haphazard curls around her face. "I'd love that luxury for, oh, about six months. Then I'd go stir-crazy."

"Sometimes, I do." Maybe that's what he'd been feeling lately. Crazy. For something different. Something like…

Her?

As he'd said, she was a woman unlike any of the ones he'd ever met. It was like finding out there was an exotic island he'd never visited. And Daniel definitely wanted a vacation at Olivia beach.

"That's good to hear," she said, circling around him and plucking the second muffin from his hands with a devilish grin. She teased the bitten part under his nose. He gave her the who-me shrug he'd perfected when the maids had caught him raiding the dessert trays at his parents' cocktail parties.

"Oh, all right, Worth, you win. I can't sell it when it has your teeth marks in it." Olivia gave him back the muffin.

"Hey, you never know. Britney Spears's chewed gum went for a few hundred on eBay."

"Well, I'm not auctioning off anything of yours yet. As I said, I have plans for you. And we better get to work before you eat all my profits." She reached under the counter, withdrew an apron and tossed it to him. The white fabric unfurled as it sailed the few feet into his grasp, displaying the name of the bakery in teal letters swirling across the front. "Put that on and start earning your keep."

For the bargain price of twelve thousand dollars and a bite of muffin, Daniel had been purchased—but for a lot more than just a little baking in the back room, he suspected. Olivia Regan had plans for him. Big plans. Ones his family would undoubtedly disapprove of. Which could only lead to one thing—

Trouble.

Something quickened in Daniel's veins and for the second time that day, he had the feeling that letting Olivia drive—anything—was a bad idea.

Olivia's Something's-Cooking Fudge Brownies

1 cup butter
6 ounces unsweeted chocolate
2 cups sugar
4 eggs
1 teaspoon vanilla
1 cup flour
1/2 teaspoon salt
2 cups walnuts, chopped

There's one thing you didn't count on when you bought yourself a bachelor—that you'd find him sexy as hell. And distracting. And a lot more stubborn than you expected. There's only one thing to do—bake some brownies and let the chocolate soothe your frazzled nerves.

Preheat the oven to 350 degrees and grease an 8- or 9-inch square pan. In a small saucepan, melt the butter and chocolate. Mix the sugar, eggs and vanilla, then add the flour and salt. Fold in the chocolate, then do the same with the walnuts. Heaven in a bowl—heaven deluxe after you bake it for 45 to 55 minutes.

Whenever your imagination starts to travel down Bachelor Lane, stuff one of these in your mouth. Before you say something you might just regret.

CHAPTER FIVE

Within ten minutes, Olivia had everything ready to make good use of Daniel Worth. With only twenty-three hours left with her rented bachelor—since one hour had been lost to travel time and a pointless argument with Ben—she needed to take advantage of every second.

And at fourteen cents a second, he was pricier than calling long distance to Canada.

Her baby sister Josie had returned to the closed shop to help execute phase two of their plan. Everything was in place to hopefully take Pastries with Panache to the next level. Heck, to any level, considering customers hadn't exactly been streaming through the door since she'd opened nearly twelve months ago.

Her neighbors next door, Candace, Maria, Rebecca and Meredith, the four women who worked at Gift Baskets to Die For, had been supportive, often sending business her way, and working out co-arrangements on weddings and bar mitzvahs. She'd taken over a lot of their baking needs, leaving the trio to concentrate on basket design and sales. But it hadn't been enough. Olivia needed to triple, hopefully quadruple, her sales in order to make this crazy venture repay what she'd put into it.

Essentially, everything. All her free time, her nonexistent love life, her savings. Every bit of Olivia Regan had been poured into this shop. To feed a dream, a career, that wasn't hers alone.

She *had* to make it work. Before she did what half her family expected her to do—

Fail.

"Are we ready?" Josie asked, coming up beside Olivia, her digital camera in hand. Josie had held down almost every job known to man—a fact that drove their parents crazy—but made her a valuable asset to Olivia. She'd once been an assistant to a guy who was composing a coffee table book of weed photos. Though his artistic renditions of dandelions and crabgrass never made it into print, Josie learned the workings of a camera. "The time is right for doing this, Liv. I checked your astrological chart this morning, and it says your moons are in the right alignment."

"My moons are what?"

"Don't you read your chart before you go to work? Geez. It can dictate your whole day."

Olivia loved Josie but found her a tad...unusual. Besides her fondness for the astrological, Josie believed in fairy tales, UFOs and humanzees. A clear consequence of watching too much Discovery Channel.

"Daniel, what sign are you?" Josie asked, stepping up to one of the wealthiest men in the city as if he were sitting at the end of a bar, chugging back a Coors. "It's very important for me to know so I can capture your aura in the right light."

"Uh, I have no idea," he said, shooting a glance Olivia's way, as if she could supply the answer.

"Capricorn," Olivia said. "His birthday is January third."

Daniel stared at her. "How'd you know that?"

"*Please.* You're as much a part of the public record as Ted Kennedy's senate votes."

Josie held the camera in her hands, staring off into space for a second. "Ooh, this is so perfect! It's, like, destiny! You're January third and Olivia is April twentieth—"

"Whoa!" Olivia said, knowing exactly where Josie's thought bus was heading. "I'm not here for a dating connection. This is *business*. Only."

Josie shook her head. "Everyone is a potential date for you, Liv. Your soul mate could be standing right there," she said, pointing at Daniel, "and you'd never know it if you didn't explore your goat-bull connection."

"I'm not exploring any connections, Jo." Olivia gestured toward the camera. "Can we get started?"

"You need to explore *something*, sis. I mean, how long has it been?"

Olivia felt her face heat up when she saw Daniel turn and look at her, an eyebrow raised in question and a grin on his face. "This isn't about me. It's about the business."

"Yeah, yeah. Like I haven't heard that one a million times. You need to loosen up. Live a little."

"I am loose." She shook her hands to prove the point.

"Not the right kind," Josie said, grinning. "Did you know you are more likely to be abducted by aliens if you're a single loner than if you're happily married?"

"I'll keep an eye out for the blinking lights," Olivia replied. "But for now, let's get this photo shoot started."

Daniel's cell phone rang and he excused himself to answer it. Thank goodness he wasn't listening to Josie's planetary connection spiel anymore.

"You should stand near him," Josie said. "Let his aura rub off a bit. He's—"

"He's not my boyfriend, he's a marketing ploy," Olivia reminded her sister. "That means no thinking of him in a sexual way."

Yeah, like she'd stuck to that rule. Every five seconds, a sexual image involving Daniel Worth popped into her head. Sometimes more often than that.

No one could say Olivia Regan didn't have a damned good imagination.

Josie sighed and turned the camera on. "Fine. But if you prefer to go through life without understanding why your Sun isn't always in alignment with his Venus, then fine."

"All I care about is getting his Venus on film," Olivia said, her voice low and hinting.

Josie leaned in close. "I have a good feeling about him. Last night, I had this dream—"

"Jo, I love you, but I don't want to hear—"

"And he was on your bed, in a pile of rose petals, bringing your every wish to life like Cinderella's prince." She put a hand to her chin. "Except without the horse and the mice. Oh, and the evil stepsisters. Or the glass slipper, come to think of it. But, you get the idea."

"He's not going to be on, in or even under my bed. Ever." Olivia directed the words to herself as much as her sister, bringing up visual reminders of the gossip column accounts of Daniel Worth's dating history to cement her resolve.

Josie wagged a finger at her. "Don't be so sure. Today is the seventh and seven is your lucky number." Her sister grinned. "Maybe you'll get lucky yourself."

Olivia groaned, threw up her hands and sent a muttered, "can we just do this" at Josie.

Her sister shrugged, then circled the small café table, envisioning her picture. Josie's waist-length straight brown hair shimmered like a curtain against her tight dark jeans and pencil-thin body. "Think you could get him to strip?"

"Sorry. That's not part of the deal."

Josie sighed. "Pity. He has very good bone structure and nudity is *so* hot today. Why, there's even have a nudists' convention for Trekkies. Do you think they do a different Vulcan wave with all those body parts flopping around?"

Olivia decided not to ask what kind of bone structure Josie meant or what Daniel Worth might look like among the Spock imitators. Instead, she headed over to the counter, out of the way of the photos and Josie's astrological matchmaking.

On the table where Daniel was to sit she had set up a New York style cheesecake on a delicate china plate. Strawberry glaze dripped over the sides, puddling on the plate in a bright crimson circle. The cheesecake looked delicious, and so did the man, she had to admit, taking a look at the man standing a few feet away. Beneath the store apron she had finally convinced him to put on, Daniel's tailored black tux fit him with ease, the fabric skimming over broad shoulders and a V-shape that would give most men waist envy.

Tall, dark, handsome and a little dangerous. He was the exact kind of man she'd be attracted to—assuming she had time for a man in her life. Desire brewed inside her, whispering to get closer, to flirt a little.

But Olivia had already learned a painful lesson about trusting her gut when it came to men. Daniel Worth was a marketing tool, nothing more.

Really.

When he was done making the cheesecake look good, her only intention was to have him do the same with the white cake and the tortes waiting on a nearby table. This was all about the pastry, not him.

Daniel finished his call and tucked his phone back inside his pocket. "Sorry about that. Family business."

When he said the words, she got the feeling it wasn't a business he enjoyed.

"Are you ready?" Olivia asked.

He swept a hand over the apron. "I'm not so sure about this."

"Why? It's just some ads."

"Ads that feature me endorsing a product. With my name, I might add."

"A product you believe in," she said, crossing to him. She leaned forward to pluck a crumb of muffin off his collar and show the incriminating evidence to him. "Evidently."

"But why me? There were twenty-nine other men there tonight."

"Not all of them were Capricorns," Josie said. "A Gemini would have been a disaster."

"They also weren't ranked as the top catch for a single girl," Olivia said. "When I run my ads with your image and the message "Looking for what tempts Boston's most eligible man?" women will hopefully stream into my shop."

"*That's* your concept?" His features turned stony. "*Playgirl* with pastries?"

Olivia nodded. "Hey, sex sells."

"Not using me it doesn't." Daniel undid the strings of the apron blaring her logo across his chest and slid it off his body. "I didn't ask to be voted "most eligible" and I have no desire to exploit that stupid title."

"Ooh! He's stripping. Yes!" Josie's camera flash went off again and again. "Can we go for the pants next? I bet we can capture the nudist market!"

"What are you doing?" Olivia said. "We had a deal. I paid for you."

"You paid for a *date* with a bachelor. Ads weren't part of the deal. Sorry, but I've changed my mind about this whole thing." He stood and faced her, their gazes connecting, only a few inches separating them.

Well, that and a bit of tension.

"That's perfect!" Josie shouted. "Emotion, desire, heat. Heck, it's a soap opera on a stick!"

"You have to do this." Olivia pressed the apron to his chest. "I invested everything I had in you."

"Why? What's in it for me? I already gave at the charity. In fact, I gave fifty thousand to the diabetic kids fund."

"Give me a smile, guys," Josie said. "Your auras are glowing like freakin' Christmas trees."

"Of your personal money?"

"Well...no, of my family money."

She snorted. "Then you have no idea what this is costing me. You throw your family's money around like it's yours, but you have no clue what it's like to empty your pockets and invest every dime you have in your business. To jump off the bridge and hope like hell the water is deep enough so you don't break your neck."

"Speaking of water, maybe we could do this in a pool," Josie said. "Or maybe we should do this on some red velvet. He's a Cardinal sign, you know. Makes for great passion."

"Maybe I don't," he said, taking a step closer to her, throwing the apron into a nearby chair and with it, her equilibrium, "but that doesn't mean that you can use me like some baking pan you got a bargain on."

"I wasn't—" She didn't finish the sentence. She was, indeed, doing exactly that. Though she might quibble—

He was more the Calphalon variety than Pyrex.

Josie was behind them, the lens whirring as it zoomed closer. "Oh! I just had a vision. His face everywhere: T-shirts, subways, bus backs, Happy Meal bags—"

"Like I said," Daniel went on, ignoring Josie's continual shooting, "what do I get out of this?"

Olivia put her hands on her hips. She hadn't expected him to be this...difficult. Obviously, she hadn't thought through all the potential cogs in her plan. One, that Daniel Worth would be more than just a pretty face, as all the reports about him said. And two, that he would be such a complete pain in the butt. "What do you want?"

"He's ruled by Saturn," Josie put in. "What do you think he wants?"

Daniel leaned forward, his deep blue gaze connecting with hers. "You."

Olivia snorted. "Are you that stereotypical? You want sex in exchange for working with me?"

"No, I want more than that. Much more."

Olivia inhaled and the warm air rushed down her throat, filling her lungs. "What do you mean...more?"

Click went the camera. Click, click, click. Josie scooted around them and bent to one knee, now shooting somewhere to the side. Daniel closed the space by taking a step forward. Everything within Olivia went as hot as a torch firing on crème brulee.

"I want what you have," he said.

"Me? I have nothing. I gave at the office, remember?"

"If I could just get some rose petals in here," Josie muttered.

"You have these," he said, taking her hands in his and holding them up like two works of art, then releasing them to pick up one of the muffins from a nearby table loaded with additional treats, "and these. I want all of that."

"You want my muffins?"

Josie zoomed and clicked. "Think we could move a bed into the shop? This is faboo stuff. Real sexy."

"No. I want your business." He tick-tocked the muffin before her. "You're an amazing baker. I'll invest in this little shop, solve your problems and give the Worth Hotel chain something to talk about at breakfast."

Steam rose within Olivia, boiling and furious. How dare he think he could just march in here, throw some money at her and she'd succumb like a puppy at the sight of a bone? How dare he try to suck her and Josie's dreams up into some corporate vacuum?

How dare he...bother her and distract her and annoy her to the ends of her admittedly thin rope of patience?

"You can't have it. Or me," Olivia said, jerking her hands out of his grasp, the anger rising within her like Mount Vesuvius. Before she could think twice, she turned, snatched the frosted white cake off the table beside her—

And slammed it into the handsome, presumptuous face of Boston's most eligible bachelor.

"Perfect!" Josie exclaimed, her fingers working the camera in a frantic frenzy of clicks. "Talk about using your body for art!"

Daniel's Not-Going-Back-There Buttercream Frosting

4 egg whites
1 cup sugar
Pinch of salt
3 sticks unsalted butter, softened

A woman with a cake in her hands is a dangerous thing. All that stuff about the way to a man's heart doesn't apply when she throws the cake in your face (very undeserved, I might add). Just stay away from an armed, angry chef who knows how to put her frosting to work.

Or, you can learn how to make your own frosting and have a damned good food fight with her. Start by putting the egg whites, sugar and salt in a double boiler. Whisk continuously until the sugar is dissolved and the egg whites have reached 140 degrees.

Then put it in the big mixer and let the thing go to work for about five minutes, creating a thick, fluffy concoction. Add the butter a little at a time, beating until it looks like frosting—and looks like a weapon you can use in a battle of the wills.

Or, if she ever forgives you, you can put this frosting to work in other, very interesting and much more fun ways. It never hurts to keep a little on hand in your refrigerator—just in case she returns.

CHAPTER SIX

Daniel still had buttercream dripping off his tux when he hailed a cab and headed back to his townhouse in Beacon Hill. He'd stormed out of the bakery, swiping off the remains of what had been, he had to admit, a tasty facial. Though unwelcome and damned unwarranted.

He'd only been trying to help that she-devil. That was the last time he offered to buy a business without cladding himself in full-body armor.

His cell rang and he dug it out of his inside pocket, flipping the Nokia open as the cabbie pulled onto Atlantic Avenue and away from Olivia Regan. Far, far away. "Hello?"

"How's it going with that feisty brunette?" Jake asked.

"It's not. I just left her—five seconds too late, I might add." A glob of white frosting clung to the back of his hand. He was tempted to eat it. No. That would be aiding the enemy. Instead he withdrew a handkerchief from his pocket and wiped off the dollop. The front of his tux was streaked with the sweet confection, like a zebra with watery stripes.

From the front seat, the cabbie glanced at him in the rearview mirror, raised a questioning brow, but didn't say anything. He'd surely seen far worse in the back of his Taurus than a cake-smeared guy in a tux.

Jake chuckled. "A lover's tiff already?"

"Very funny. She threw a cake at me."

Now Jake roared with laughter. Behind him, Daniel could hear the sounds of Barry White crooning through a stereo and the clink of ice in a glass. The unmistakable sounds of Jake preparing for female company.

"I bet you deserved it," Jake said.

"I did not. All I did was offer her some help."

"Let me guess. In the guise of money?"

"Well, yeah."

"Danny boy, when are you going to learn? A woman like her doesn't want a handout. She's the kind that's filled with the fire of independence. I could see it, in the way she bid for you and the way she handled you."

"Handled me? I don't need handling."

Jake laughed again. "You, my friend, need as much handling as the rest of us. Hell, we can barely function in the real world. God forbid your grandfather ever cuts you off from the family fortune. You'd need a guide dog just to cross the street."

Daniel scowled. "I am not that helpless."

"Okay, maybe not. But tell me, when's the last time you had to make yourself a meal? Set up your own social calendar? Make your own bed?"

"I could do those things." Probably. Besides, for every chore there was a book of some kind. A resource for making hospital corners and prioritizing RSVPs.

Jake snorted. "Uh-huh. And Cher does her own hair, too."

"Superstars don't count. They're in a whole other category from us."

"And what about looking for a job? How would you do that?"

Daniel swayed with the cab as it rounded a corner so fast, he was sure two of the wheels lifted off the pavement. "Why would I have to?"

"Come on. Didn't you tell me your grandfather threatened to cut you off again the other day?"

"He says that all the time." Every time the paper ran another picture of Daniel on the town with a woman Grandfather deemed "unsuitable" or the *Herald* caught him carousing at a bar, singing karaoke off-key after a few too many scotches. Charitable event attendance was good—but unseemly public behavior was not.

Grandfather tossed out the money card whenever he thought Daniel wasn't living up to the Worth name—something that had been happening practically since the day Daniel learned to tie his shoes with bunny ears instead of the way two generations before him had done it.

If Grandfather didn't approve, you either learned to do it right. Or learned to do without. *Really* learned to do without.

For Daniel, that meant skating by just enough to not have to worry about being kicked to the poverty curb.

"Yeah, but one of these days, he's going to mean it," Jake said, the ice in his glass clinking as he took a drink on the other end.

If the whimsy hit him one of these days, Grandfather would indeed sever the financial strings. Just as he'd cut off Daniel's cousin Louis and his mother, Aunt Helen, for buying stock in the Adams Mark hotel chain. Both were living in Alabama now, working at a dress factory and making ends meet by a thread.

"By the way, I believe you owe me a thousand dollars," Jake said, laughing.

"I'll have my butler send you a check, hopeless monkey that I am."

Jake laughed again. "Hey, the day's not over yet. You still have time to go back and grovel. Double or nothing?"

"I don't think so. I'm done with that woman." Daniel brushed at another clump of dried frosting. It crumbled under his touch, scattering across the seat. In the narrow rearview mirror, the cabbie sent him a glare. "Hey, buddy, clean that up."

"Uh, yeah." Cradling the phone between his shoulder and his ear, he scooped the white crumbs into his hand and tossed them out the open window. The last thing he needed to do was tick off his ride and end up walking through Boston in a tux that had been through a food fight. The press bloodhounds would be on him in seconds.

"She leave you?" The cabbie asked, jerking his head at Daniel in the mirror. "Dump you for the best man?"

"Uh...no." Daniel glanced down again at himself and realized he did, indeed, look like a jilted groom. The tux was as close to marriage as he was *ever* going to get, so the chances of his being jilted at the altar—or ending up with bridal cake smeared on him by his new wife—were slim to negative ten.

"My girlfriend, she do that. Leave me for another man," the cabbie continued. On the other end of the phone, Daniel could hear Jake greeting someone. "I take care of that. Nip it in the buds." He punched one fist into the other, releasing the wheel to do so. The yellow cab swerved to one side.

"Hey, listen, Daniel," Jake cut in, "my date's here. I gotta let you go so I can hold on to Evelyn, if you know what I mean."

"Evelyn Wood?"

"The one and only...I think."

Daniel chuckled. Evelyn Wood was one of the Wood triplets who were well known for playing games with their dates. "Are you sure it's Evelyn? I hear those women are famous for trading places."

"I'll just have to play the guessing game. Evelyn loves to play that, don't you, baby?" Jake's laughter was low and filled with hints of what was to come.

Daniel suspected Evelyn had already started laying the ground rules for the evening. Most likely with an interesting part of her anatomy. He said goodbye and hung up, knowing Jake wouldn't miss him.

At all.

The cabbie squealed to a stop in front of Daniel's townhouse and pointed at the red numbers on his dash, indicating the price. Then he put out his hand and waited for the money to come through the window. No longer talking to him or even bothering to be friendly. Probably because Daniel hadn't taken his offer to nip those problems in the "buds."

Ah, Boston hospitality. He could always count on service with a smile. Daniel paid, gave the guy a nice tip to make up for the crumbs, and hopped out, then headed up the wide granite steps and into the bow-front mansion masquerading as a townhouse. The 7,000-square foot property, a gift from his grandfather upon his twenty-first birthday, overlooked Boston Common and was larger than most starter homes.

It was, and always had been, too big for Daniel. Two stories, four bedrooms, five bathrooms, a four-car garage. But it was situated in exactly the right zip code, which made it perfect for a Worth grandson.

"Mr. Worth! What happened to you? And to your suit?" His butler, Lewiston, greeted him at the door, gloved hands immediately at the soiled tux, removing the jacket before Daniel was five feet inside the ornate marble floored entryway. Daniel didn't even have to lift a shoulder.

Damn Jake for being right.

"It's nothing, Lewiston. I'm fine." Or he would be once he got the damnable image of Olivia Regan out of his mind.

"I don't know if I can get this out, sir," Lewiston said, brushing at the stain, his nose crinkling. "Is this…cream?"

"Frosting." Daniel put up a palm. "Don't ask. It's a long story."

Lewiston sighed. "Food fight *again*? I thought you gave those up in third grade, sir."

Daniel shook his head. "A woman, Lewiston."

"Oh. Those you *started* in fifth grade. A little harder to give up, too." He looked again at the coat, gave it a glance that called it a hopeless case and draped it over one arm. "Was she one of those Thompson girls? They're like elephants when they eat. No manners at all. I once saw Emily Thompson fling a lobster claw across the room and into Louisa Thibodaux's nose." Lewiston shuddered at the memory.

"No. She's no one you know. She's not part of the regular crowd." Daniel chuckled. "Not at all."

He paused at the Chippendale console table in the hall, avoiding his reflection in the matching mirror and flipped through his mail, not really seeing any of the letters. A half dozen inscribed invitations were mixed in the stack amongst the letters and financial reports his grandfather sent as regular as fiber laxatives, "to keep him in the loop" and undoubtedly prepare him for his future at the helm of Worth. Daniel tossed them to the side, unopened. They landed atop a small stack from last week, also unopened.

He was pretty damned far out of the Worth Hotel loop. Which was exactly how he liked it. He didn't care who Grandfather hired as a chef, what kind of sheets the guests slept on or whether more people used Visa or MasterCard.

"Expanding outside your usual circle, sir?" Lewiston asked.

"Hmm?" Daniel laid the rest of the mail back on the silver dish and turned toward the impassible face of the butler who'd been with him his entire life.

"Nothing. Just I've never heard you mention a woman who wasn't one of "us," so to speak." Lewiston glanced down at the jacket again. "Or one who had such a great right arm."

Daniel smiled. "She's different, that's for sure."

"Good."

"Good?"

"I think a woman who tests you is a good thing, if you don't mind my saying so, sir. 'A woman simply is, but a man must become.' Lewiston nodded. "Camille Paglia, the author, said that."

"And what does that mean?"

Lewiston was famous for quoting literary wisdom. A well-read man, he had also inspired that love of the written word in Daniel. But sometimes, despite years of education and volumes of books, Daniel had no idea what the hell the butler was talking about.

"That a man who meets a good woman is encouraged to become more of the man he should be by her influence."

Daniel chuckled. "Well, I'm already the man I'm going to be, or will be with Grandfather's help, not Olivia's."

Lewiston didn't say anything. He merely brushed again at the frosting on Daniel's jacket.

Daniel gestured to the smears. "In case you're worried about my wardrobe, I won't be seeing her again."

"Such a shame, given the influence a woman like that could have over your evolution." Lewiston tsk-tsked. "But I *am* glad to hear the laundry will be safe."

Daniel ignored the bit of advice about Olivia. Lewiston always thought he knew best when it came to Daniel's life... but he didn't know how outraged the Worth patriarch would be if his grandson dared step outside their social circle.

"Think of it this way. You won't have to hear my grandfather berate you for the overuse of Tide." Daniel wagged a finger at his butler and affected the stern, upper-crust attitude of his grandfather. "Such a waste, Lewiston. You really must be more careful with your detergent dispensing."

Lewiston smiled, then he paused, the smile disappearing. His eyes widened and his jaw dropped. "Sir, you might want to—"

"And watch those softener sheets, too," Daniel went on, striding forward, his shoulders back, his finger raised in imitation of his grandfather. "Too much Downy and before you know it, the Worth family value has dropped one-one-hundredth of a percent—"

"Uh, sir—" Lewiston pointed at a spot past Daniel's right shoulder.

And then, like a rush of cold air, Daniel knew. "He's right behind me, isn't he?"

Lewiston nodded. "I meant to tell you earlier but got distracted by the frosting. He's been waiting for you."

"I suppose there's no good way to get out of this, is there?"

"No, there isn't." Grandfather's deep-timbered voice covered for the whirr of his electric wheelchair, now in motion and coming up the length of the hallway, fast and furious. Daniel was sure Grandfather had had a nitroglycerine booster installed in the thing, just so he could increase his sneakability.

Daniel pivoted. "Hello, Grandfather. How nice to see you."

"Bullshit. You hate it when I surprise you. You know it, I know it. Hell, even Lewiston knows it." He raised a still-powerful hand at the butler.

"Dusting to do," Lewiston said, producing a feather duster from behind his back and disappearing fast.

Daniel leaned against the wall, nearly displacing a half-million dollar Revolutionary War painting with his shoulder. "To what do I owe this visit?"

"You need to settle down," Grandfather said, as always getting right to the point and skipping pleasantries. He stopped the wheelchair a foot away from his grandson. Despite his seated position,

Grandfather Worth seemed somehow taller, more imposing. And always in control.

In the Worth family, the one with the checkbook made the rules. And everyone else followed along, hoping they could sneak past Go a few extra times.

"I *am* settled. I'm living here."

Grandfather snorted. "You need a woman. For God's sake, Daniel, you've sown enough oats to feed all of Africa."

Arguing that he saw his bachelor activities in terms of a much smaller country wasn't going to work in Daniel's favor, so he kept his mouth shut.

"Get married. Come to work for me. Make something of yourself."

"I was just at a charity auction." Daniel swept a hand over his frame, indicating the remains of his tux. "That's something."

"Those things are a bunch of crap and you know it. Get a real job. In the hotel. I'll make you a president of something or other. And marry someone. Lauren Templeton is on the market, and she's got good stock. But for God's sake stay away from the maids. Your cousin did that and we were untangling *that* disaster for a year."

"I thought Godfrey was happily married."

"The maid he married wasn't interested in him. Just citizenship." Grandfather cursed. "You'd think he could have figured that out on the wedding night. He told me the woman lit her green card on fire as "mood lighting," for God's sake."

Daniel headed into the parlor, straight for the mini bar. Behind him, he heard the soft whir of the wheelchair speeding across the wood floor then up and onto the Oriental carpet. "Scotch?"

"Do you have the Dewars?"

"Of course." Daniel gave his grandfather a grin. "You're funding my life of decadence, after all."

Grandfather harrumphed. "In that case, make it a double. On the rocks."

Daniel poured two drinks, then handed one to his grandfather. "To net worth."

Grandfather clinked with him. "No, to *increasing* net worth."

Daniel sipped, then took a seat on the ridiculously small and uncomfortable love seat. He hated the formal living room. Hated the red cushions of the furniture, the gold drapes, the deep bronze walls. He hadn't decorated any of it; in fact, he hadn't chosen a thing in his townhouse.

Not even the brand of scotch. He was a kept, bossed around marionette, strung along by his grandfather. Daniel might as well cut off everything below the waist and leave his masculinity at the door.

Damn Jake to hell for being right, he thought again.

The doorbell rang. Both of them ignored it, as they had all their lives. In the Worth homes, some-one else answered the door, the phones. While the Worths did whatever important thing they were doing at the time.

Like sipping scotch and trying to avoid the subject.

"So, Daniel, are you going to do as I asked?" When it came to holding onto a conversational topic, Grandfather would have given any terrier a run for his money. "I'm done supporting you. Either you say yes now or I'll cut you off. It's high time you grew up."

"I—" A commotion sounded in the front hall. Lewiston shouted, then there was the clatter of two pairs of shoes rushing along the wood floor.

A second later Olivia Regan stood in the doorway, her dark brown hair in disarray around her face, her fists on her hips and a determined set to her jaw. "I want what I paid for, Worth. Now."

Olivia's When-Among-Tigers Striped Pound Cake

4 ounces semi-sweet chocolate
3 cups all-purpose flour
1 teaspoon baking powder
2 cups butter, softened
3 1/3 cups sugar
10 eggs
1 tablespoon vanilla extract

Before you step into the tiger's den, you have to gird yourself for battle. What better way to do that than by using a cake that will hopefully calm the vicious beast (and keep him from eating you alive). Start by preheating the oven to 350 degrees. Line a bundt pan with parchment paper, then grease and flour the paper, just to be sure your cake won't stick. You might need to get it out of there in a hurry, after all.

Melt the chocolate, either in a microwave or a double boiler. In one bowl, mix the flour and baking powder. In a separate bowl, cream the butter and sugar until as light and fluffy as an innocent little kitten. Add the eggs, a couple at a time, then the vanilla. When it's all mixed, add the dry ingredients—careful not to get dust all over the place.

Keeping your eye on the tiger who wants only to eat you alive, put half the batter in the bundt pan, then add the chocolate to the other half and mix well. Pour the chocolate batter on top of the plain. Using a knife, swirl the two colors together, in a tiger stripe pattern if you want. Bake for 1 ¾ hours, while you're arguing with the tiger about who's really in control here. Let it sit in the pan till cool, then unmold and serve. If the tiger isn't appeased by your pound cake, then be sure you're wearing your running shoes.

CHAPTER SEVEN

Olivia knew she was in trouble the minute the man in the wheelchair gave her the evil eye. Actually, it wasn't an evil eye, more a look of disdain mixed with a whole lot of other D words—displeasure, disgust and distance-yourself-from-my-family-this-instant.

She had no intention of doing that. Not until she got what she'd paid for because if she didn't, her business would tank. Too many people were depending on her to make it work. And right now, it wasn't working at all.

A shiver of nerves ran through her as she paused long enough to take in her surroundings. Ten-foot ceilings, triple crown molding, mahogany paneling and, outside the doorway, even an elevator with a brass entry. All this wealth, so much it seemed to close in on her like being suffocated by ermine, and then, these people, who clearly saw her as the cockroach climbing up the silk drapes. Olivia squared her shoulders and took in a deep breath, determined not to let them scare her off, or worse, win this battle of the wills.

Heck, the Red Sox had won the World Series. Miracles *could* happen.

Even in Daniel Worth's parlor.

She'd once seen some pop psychologist on TV who'd suggested visualizing something you could conquer. Fine. She'd imagine Daniel Worth and his grandfather—because she knew from having seen his picture in the papers that the man in the wheelchair could only be the senior Worth—were a couple of kittens.

Yeah, *tiger* kittens with one-foot fangs and razor-sharp claws embedded with Hope Diamond chips in their pinkies—

Okay, that wasn't helping.

"How did you find out where I live?" Daniel crossed his arms over his chest.

"Oh, *please*," she said, laying her purse on a buffet table and entering the room, making herself at home in the tiger's den. "You were voted the most eligible bachelor in Boston. Any female under the age of sixty knows where you live." Behind her, she heard the distinct sound of the butler snickering.

"My address is not a matter of public record."

"It's on the Quacker tour," she said. The amphibious vehicle—a knock-off on the famous Duck tourist rides—ran on sea and land, providing tourists with a unique perspective of the city's most gossiped-about sites. "All the women give you two quacks up when they pass."

"They do?" He looked horrified and she bit back the urge to laugh. For Pete's sake, didn't the man have any idea what the combination of wealth, good looks and the words "single and available" could do to some women? He might as well hang out a sign advertising a stud service.

"I do my research, Worth," Olivia said.

"With a *quacker?*" his grandfather said, scooting his electric wheelchair forward a few inches. Sarcasm dripped from every syllable. "How…innovative."

"I also used a computer, the library and stock reports. I know all there is to know about Daniel Worth, the Worth Hotel chain and you, Mr. Worth." She eyed the second Daniel Worth, who she knew headed everything in the family, with "an iron fist and a steel jaw," as *Hotelier* magazine had said in their November 2005 issue.

"All that proves is that you can manage a library card," the older man said, his silver hair not moving an inch as he leaned forward to study her, brown eyes narrowing nearly to slits. "Just what do you want with my grandson, Miss—?"

"Regan. Olivia Regan." She refused to flinch beneath his probing stare. "And that's between me and him."

"Grandfather," Daniel said. "I can handle my own life."

"Right," the elder man replied drolly. "That's why you're running around Boston with cake on your trousers." Then he turned to Olivia again, flicking a button on the chair so that it jerked even closer. "I'll ask you again, what do you want with my grandson?"

She met his stare, drawing in a breath as she did. Kitty, kitty, she repeated to herself. He's nothing but a big, harmless, *rich*, vicious kitten who can squash me like a—

Not helping, Olivia.

"Simply to get my money's worth," she said.

"No pun intended, of course," the elder Worth said. He perched an elbow on the arm on the silver-and-black chair and pondered her for a second. Despite being paralyzed from the waist down from a polo accident fifteen years ago (another fact she'd garnered from her library research), he was wearing a well-fitted gray pinstriped suit and cranberry tie with a white shirt. His immobile feet were clad in dress shoes, an expensive Italian label, Olivia was sure.

"This is ridiculous, Grandfather. Leave her alone," Daniel said. "I told you, I can handle this."

Lips pursed, Daniel Worth II studied Olivia for a second longer, then looked to his descendent. "Fine. But remember what I told you earlier."

Olivia saw Daniel bite back the first thing he thought to say. Instead, he ground out a "Yes."

"Good. And, Daniel? I expect to see you in my office Monday morning. Nine o'clock sharp." Then his grandfather flicked the button on his wheelchair and sailed down the hall between the two of them as easily as Mario Andretti navigating the track in Indianapolis. A moment later, he had left the townhouse with the help of his driver, leaving Olivia and Daniel alone.

"Gee, with family like that, who needs enemies?" she muttered. The tiger had left the building but she still felt like a chewed-up piece of meat.

"He's not all bad. At least most of the time." Daniel ran a hand through his hair, displacing the dark brown waves. In the unbuttoned tuxedo shirt and disarrayed hair, she had to admit he looked even better than he had dressed up on that stage. Even handsomer than in the *Boston* magazine spread.

No wonder women quacked at the sight of him.

"Listen, I'm sorry about the cake," she said. "Sometimes my temper gets the best of me."

"Sometimes?"

She laughed. "Okay, often. I just don't appreciate anyone telling me how to run my business."

Daniel cast a glance toward the hall where his grandfather had gone. "That makes two of us."

"Anyway, I hope you'll forgive me. I was wrong and impetuous and—"

"Grumpy?"

"I was going to say stressed. Stress makes people do stupid things, especially if there's a cake handy."

"No harm done, except to my jacket," Daniel said. "Besides, sometimes I deserve a cake in my face."

"Sometimes?" she teased back.

"Okay, often," he parroted, a smile curving across his face as easily as sunshine on a lake.

She would not melt at his smile. Would not let that charming grin wiggle its way into her heart.

She'd done that once before with someone else—
and realized too late she'd let a porcupine near her
heart.

"Now, about us—" Olivia began.

"There is no us," Daniel cut in, putting up his
palms. "You don't seem to understand me or my
position in this family. I'm glad to help you, within
reason, but I'm not wearing an apron again. No
matter what you paid for me at the auction." He
crossed the room in three fast strides, stopping at a
cherry secretary. He withdrew a set of keys from his
pocket, unlocked the middle drawer, then opened
it and took out a leather checkbook. He selected
a Waterford pen from the globe-shaped holder
before him and twisted the ink down. "Why don't I
just reimburse you for your donation and we'll call
it even?"

"No." Yet, as soon as the word left her mouth,
Olivia thought of the dozen grand, just waiting for
her across the room. Was she insane? She could
undo this, put some money back in her bank
account instead of living on the edge of a very dangerous cliff.

Daniel's hand hovered over the page, the pen
at the ready. In a few seconds, her bank account
could be filled again and this crazy idea could be
forgotten.

"No?" he repeated.

As easy as it would be to let him wipe everything away with a few swipes of his pen, the last
thing Olivia wanted was to go back to the status

quo. The status quo, after all, wasn't working. She needed something drastic to take Pastries with Panache over the top and prove the shop could be a success.

Besides, it wasn't like she had a choice in the matter. It wasn't only her future at stake here. And that meant she had to stay focused on her goal—to turn her business into one heck of a lucrative slice of pie.

To do that, she needed to jump off the cliff, and take her chances that there'd be some sales next week to cushion her fall. The demographics reports she'd run all told her there was a market for her pastries—all she had to do was reach it.

Olivia was prepared to do whatever it took to make that happen. Even if it meant coercing a millionaire.

To be honest, she liked that cliff. Liked the excitement of not knowing what was coming around the bend. It was the same fuel that had ignited her father's ventures into business and now, that energy flowed through her blood, too. It was either that or typhoid fever.

"I want what I bought, Worth. You." She eyed the remaining tiger and took three steps forward to lean upon the desk and come within inches of the sexy magnetism that a thousand women in Boston would have killed to be near. "Now, what do you want from me so that we can make this happen?"

Daniel lowered the pen to the cherry surface. He planted his hands on either side of the secretary and brought his face to hers. A whisper, a breeze, that's all it would take and his lips would be on hers, and Olivia Regan, who'd lived a life that had never had enough money, would be kissing one of the richest men in the city.

"What can I have?" he asked.

She swallowed. *Anything.* "I can...work for you."

"I don't need any employees." His lips curved into a grin. "Unless you want to be my personal valet."

Something hot churned within her stomach. Oh, this had been a bad idea. No wonder that female reporter at *Boston* magazine had gushed so much in her story about Daniel Worth. Had he gotten this close to her? Had his eyes held that same power over her, making her pen still over the slim reporter notepad, until all she was writing was gibberish?

"I'd rather have a less, ah, intimate job." *Yeah, right,* her brain said. About now, she'd get as intimate as he wanted. On this desk, on the Oriental carpet, on the fireplace hearth. Heck, even on the loveseat that looked about as comfortable as a pincushion.

"Really?" he said, raising a strong, warm hand to cup her jaw. All images of kittens disappeared from her mind. Definitely nothing cute and cuddly resided there now. Not unless she counted the image of a bearskin rug.

And her. And Boston's most eligible man. Naked. Sweaty. And working off the calories from that cheesecake.

Whoa. This was *so* going down the wrong path. Olivia jerked back, out of his grasp. "*Really*. Worth, this is a business arrangement, not some twisted gigolo/hooker arrangement."

"Funny, that's what I thought your marketing plan was all about." He came around the corner of the desk to face her. "Didn't you buy me, over all the other men, for sex appeal?"

"Well…yes."

"Then what's wrong with a little *quid pro quo?*"

She drew herself up as haughtily as possible. "I'm hardly using you for real sex. Just your image."

"A little beefcake to help sell your cheesecake, huh?"

"Yes."

He moved forward, invading her space again, his body inches from hers. He'd loosened his bow tie and undone the top button of his tuxedo shirt, giving her an all-too-brief peek at his chest. Tiny, perfect pleats flattened against the torso of his shirt, pearl buttons trailed a visual downward path, begging to be followed, while starched white material curved over his broad, firm shoulders. Her heart betrayed her words by thudding faster in her chest, sending a rush of heat through her veins.

Oh yeah, he was a beefcake. And a half.

"So if I kissed you, you wouldn't respond at all?" he asked, his voice low and seductive, the words teasing at the air between them.

"Oh no, not one bit."

I'm a strong woman.

Yeah, and Eve had no trouble resisting that apple.

"What if I told you," at this, he moved even closer, his fingers reaching up and dancing at the back of her neck, mamboing with her hair, "that I wanted a little cheesecake for myself?"

"I'd, ah, tell you the bakery is closed." There. She'd managed to get those words out. More or less.

"Closed, hmm?" And he lowered his mouth within kissing distance to hers.

Damn, he had a fine mouth. Lips that weren't too thin or too generous, perfect, straight, teeth, and a tongue that hinted at pleasures to come. How long had it been since she'd been kissed? Months at least.

"Closed and locked tight," she added. Olivia had already learned that mixing business with pleasure was stupid with a capital S. She'd journeyed down Stupid & Heartbroken Lane with Sam Reynolds, the marketing consultant she'd hired to help her promote Pastries with Panache.

Sam had been more interested in promoting his case with Olivia than her business. By the time she realized he was only after one thing—and that thing wasn't her muffins—her business was out a few thousand dollars and her heart needed some SuperGlue.

"Too bad," Daniel said, "because those are my terms." He withdrew, taking all the heat with him and leaving her feeling like a Schnauzer left out in the cold by an owner too busy to open the door.

"Your *terms?*"

"It's simple. I'm interested in you and you want me, for 'business reasons'," he added little air quote marks around the last two words, clearly not believing her motives. "If you date me, I'll lend you my image for a *tasteful* ad campaign." He pointed at her. "As long as I don't have to wear an apron or humiliate myself, I'm yours."

"What do you think I am, a hooker?"

A grin tipped up one corner of his mouth. "Are you? It would explain all that money."

She felt heat of another kind rise to a boil within her veins. "I am not some desperate girl from the wrong side of the tracks that you can pick up on a whimsy and date for kicks. So that when you're done with me, you can go back to the country club and tell them you were slumming with the chick from the auction."

His blue eyes glinted like steel. "Is that what you think I wanted?"

"Well, isn't it? I'm not exactly your type." Olivia waved a hand over her frame, sweeping over her department store clothes and three-year-old high heels, the edges scuffed despite a determined polishing job earlier today.

"How do you even know what my type is?"

"I did my research, Worth, remember?" She turned away and yanked her purse off the buffet table behind them. "And in it, you were always on the arm of one debutante after another. Never, in any of those articles, were you with a woman like me."

"Maybe because I've never met a woman like you before."

She thrust a fist onto her hips. "Maybe that's because you've never ventured across your side of the tracks."

"Touché," he said with a grin. "The lady has a temper and a way with words."

"And a way out of here." She swung her purse over her shoulder. "Listen, buster. I'm not some hard-up middle-class version of an escort service that you can use for chuckles. I bought you fair and square. If you're not going to comply, then I'm going to the auction people and demand I either get my money back or a more cooperative bachelor." Olivia spun on her heel and headed for the door.

"Olivia, wait!"

She didn't. She kept going, striding across the Oriental carpet, hitting the wood floor of the hall, ignoring the priceless Revolutionary War art on the walls and the crystal chandelier that hung over her head. Behind her, Daniel's dress shoes clattered against the oak as he came around to the front of her, nearly toppling a Ming vase off its marble pedestal.

"What?" She bit off the word.

"Don't go. I'm really not the jerk I appear to be."

"You could have fooled me." She shook her head. "And to think I wasted a quacker on you."

A grin took over his face. "You quacked at me? Twice?"

"Oh, get over yourself. I was in a crowd. It was peer pressure."

"Uh-huh." He swallowed the grin, and sobered his face. "I swear, I do not want you for nefarious sexual purposes."

"Then what *do* you want me for?"

He let out a breath and draped an arm over the curved oak banister, seeming taller and yet more vulnerable with the gesture. "I meant what I said. You aren't like the other women I've met."

She snorted.

"You stood up to my grandfather, for one. And you're independent, for another."

"I have to be. I wasn't born with a trust fund in my diaper."

He laughed. "And you're a hell of a conversationalist. So let me take you out, once or twice, and I'll pose for your ad campaign. Then we'll call it even—"

"And go on our way," she finished for him.

His gaze met hers. "If that's what you want, yes."

"That's what your grandfather would want."

"He doesn't make the decisions in my life."

She arched a brow, but kept silent, though she suspected he was telling her one of those-save-the-manhood lies. Olivia thought about his offer for a long second, her gaze on the oval of beveled antique glass in the door. A rainbow of light caught on each of the prisms in the glass, spiraling off it and onto the floor, like a flower of color.

She had no other options, really. Get her money back and start over again—

And be left in the same predicament as she had been last month and the month before.

She knew, from all her research, that her idea for a pastry shop that brought a homey touch to the shadows of the cold brick-and-mortar Financial District would work. There were tons of businesses there, just waiting for high quality, decadent goods to show up in their breakrooms, at their company parties, at client events. She wasn't worried about having a customer base.

What she was worried about was the six-foot-two bachelor standing before her.

He was the one contingency she hadn't counted on. She'd handled an unruly Kitchen Aid mixer before. How hard could one randy bachelor be?

"Worth, you have a deal," she said, putting out her hand.

But when Daniel Worth IV grasped her palm with in his own firm grip, she had to wonder whether she'd just committed herself to the most insane deal of her life. Or a temptation no sane woman would resist.

Well, if worst came to worst, she could probably auction him off on eBay before the twenty-four hours were up. Undoubtedly, a man like him, with a pedigree better than an AKC-registered hound, would fetch quadruple the price of that one lady's moldy grilled cheese sandwich.

Sometimes, there was no accounting for taste.

Josie's The-Stars-Are-Right Cheesecake

For the love match:
1 stubborn sister
1 eligible bachelor
2 compatible astrological signs

For the cheesecake:
3 tablespoons unsalted butter, softened
3 tablespoons sugar
1 cup graham cracker crumbs
2 pounds cream cheese, softened
1 1/4 cups sugar
Rind of one lemon, grated
3 tablespoons fresh lemon juice
1 teaspoon vanilla extract
4 eggs, at room temperature

Everything is perfectly aligned for love, so get to baking quick before the bachelor leaves. Preheat the oven to 350 degrees while your sister and the sexy single guy are preheating a little on their own. Mix the butter, sugar and cracker crumbs, then press into the bottom a 9-inch springform pan. Bake the crust for five minutes.

Beat the cream cheese until smooth, about 30 seconds, just enough time for Venus to intersect with Mars. Scrape the bowl, then add the sugar and mix again for another 30 seconds. Add the remaining ingredients, mixing only until everything is incorporated. No need to take this too far or you'll end up with frosting instead of cheesecake.

Wrap aluminum foil around the bottom of the springform pan, making it come up one inch over the sides (reserve extra foil for a hat, should the aliens ever invade Boston). Pour in the filling (quick now, because that goat-bull connection between the other two can be quite volatile), then put the pan on a jelly-roll pan and pour ½ inch of water around the outside of the springform pan.

Bake for one hour. I know, that's a long time and a lot can happen in an hour (trust me, I know. I watch The Discovery Channel). But it might be just enough time for the stars to sprinkle on a budding romance.

Or, if your sister is being stubborn, for the guy to see stars as she's booting him out the door. Hmm…now that I think about it, you might want to hand the two of them some Oreos and lock them in a closet till they get their hearts aligned with the future the stars have in mind.

CHAPTER EIGHT

The second photo shoot went much better than the first, Daniel had to admit as he sat in Olivia's shop the next afternoon. Because it was Sunday, the shop was closed, giving them plenty of privacy. And keeping Daniel's foray into pastry modeling out of the eyes of the public.

Josie started by reading their fortunes, because she said it would create good karma for the photos. Her tarot had revealed the exact hour and place for a successful ad campaign—something Daniel didn't think those cards were able to do, but with modern inventions, one never knew.

She then insisted on taking a headshot of each of them against the plain, cream-colored walls—to verify that their auras were in a happy place. By the time they started the actual photography, Daniel's moons had been declared fit and his sun found to be in the right quadrant.

Gee, and here all he thought he had to do was throw on a suit and smile.

Olivia ran back and forth between her kitchen and the front of her shop, arranging different settings and then planting Daniel into the scenes like her own personal Ken doll.

She'd done a good job of ignoring him, and pretending their earlier near-kiss in his townhouse hadn't happened. Every time Daniel tried to open up a door with Olivia, she shut it firmly, treating him like a widget instead of a man.

He must have misread the pulse of tension between them yesterday. Because right now, Olivia Regan was about as interested in him as she was in re-reading the Massachusetts BMV's rules of the road book.

Three hours and two memory cards later, Olivia finally decided she had what she wanted and Josie pronounced it all planetarily perfect. She slipped her digital camera into a khaki bag and slung it over her shoulder. "Gotta get back to my apartment. Time to practice my perm rod rolling." Josie put a finger to her chin. "Not sure who I'm going to practice on. My roommates threatened to kick me out after my dye job homework assignment. And the school's kind of, ah, banned me from practicing on anything breathing." Josie put her hands up in a who-me gesture. "That whole thing with the Barbasol was so not my fault."

"Don't you have another option? Some perm-needy person?" Olivia asked, drawing her hair back behind her ears, as if marking it off-limits.

Josie nodded, resolute. "Barbie."

"Who's Barbie?"

"The doll, silly. Actually just her stylin' head. Her hair's not really cut out for perming. It's been colored too much and you really shouldn't mix that many chemicals." Josie sighed, taking a breather from her ramble about the hair options of a doll. "But I guess she's more concerned about her style than the quality of her shaft. So many people are like that."

Olivia didn't even risk a glance in Daniel's direction after the shaft comment. She could practically feel him grinning.

"Anyway, I gotta roll." Josie laughed, then toodled a wave and headed for the door. "Remember, be true to your selves."

When Josie was gone, Olivia sank into the chair opposite Daniel, who was sitting at a table laden with a slice of cheesecake and spring table setting. Five minutes earlier, Josie had been shooting him about to take a bite of a cheesecake he never got to taste. Now he picked up the two forks on the table, handed one to Olivia and took the other for himself.

"Oh, no, I never eat my own food," Olivia said, waving away the offer.

"What? Don't you taste as you bake? I thought all chefs ate their creations."

"Are you kidding me? Have you seen what I make here? I'd weigh ten thousand pounds if I ate a bite of everything." She laid the fork back on the table and started to rise. "I should clean up."

"Sit. The mess isn't going anywhere."

"If I let it sit, it only gets worse," she said, exhaustion weighing down her words. "It's bad enough I forgot to soak the cake pans before I left for the auction. And then, with the photo shoot, I didn't get a chance to get to the dishes. Now they'll be—"

Daniel withdrew his cell phone from his inside jacket pocket and hit one number. As if admitting defeat, Olivia stopped talking and sank into the opposite chair. The other end rang once before being answered.

"Lewiston, would you send Mary and Louisa over here? Let me give you the address." He covered the mouthpiece and waited until Olivia supplied the street number for her shop, then repeated it into the phone. "We could use some help cleaning up. Tell them I'll make it up to them in their next pay-check." He thanked the person on the other end, then flipped the cell shut.

She stared at him, jaw agape. "You-you-you can't do that!"

Daniel tucked his phone back into his pocket. "I believe I just did."

"But this is *my* shop. You can't just call in your maids to clean up my mess."

"And why is that? Because you want to run your-self into an early grave doing everything yourself? Face it, Cinderella, you're exhausted." He picked up her fork, stabbed up a bite of cheesecake and held it toward her mouth. "And undoubtedly hungry."

"You can't..." but her voice trailed off. She eyed the baked delight and sank back into her chair. "I can't...."

"Yes you can. Open up." He inched the fork closer.

"I shouldn't…"

"Yes, you should." He moved the bite so that it whispered against her lips, begging her to taste it.

"I never…" And then, the scent of the bite overwhelmed her. She opened her mouth and took in the cheesecake. Immediately, her eyes shut and she arched backward in enjoyment as she swallowed the rich, creamy delight. It sailed across her palate, smooth and easy. "Mmmm… Oh, that is so good."

"Have more." He readied a second bite.

She shook her head. Without much emphasis. "I shouldn't."

"It's just cheesecake, Olivia, not crystal meth. And besides, it's *your* cheesecake. I say that makes it twice as okay." He picked up his own fork and speared another bite. "See? I'll indulge with you. We can do it together."

It wouldn't take much to push her over the edge and face-first into the entire cheesecake. "Sounds decadent."

"No, this is," Daniel said, taking his second bite. He hadn't lied. It had to be the best cheesecake he'd ever tasted, full and flavorful, with a hint of lemon and vanilla. The morsel went down in an instant, leaving his mouth begging for more. More of the cheesecake. More of Olivia. More of that defiant smile that seemed to challenge and tempt him at every turn. "What's in this anyway? It tastes like heaven."

Olivia flushed. "Uh…company secret." She took her fork out of his grip, then dipped into the dessert again with a sigh of defeat. "And you, Worth, are a bad influence."

"I'm a bad influence on everybody. It's a necessary quality for a playboy." He gave her a grin, then toasted her with his fork and moved the plate closer to the middle of the table. They sat like that for a couple of minutes, sharing the hefty slice and their appreciation for the amazing power an oven could have over some cream cheese and eggs.

Finally, only a few graham cracker crumbs remained. "It's all gone," Olivia said, her voice tinged with sadness.

"There's a whole bakery of goodies left to conquer." He waved his fork toward the case, stocked full with more delicacies. He wondered if everything Olivia created tasted as amazing as that cheesecake.

"I can't. I need those for tomorrow. They're my regular Monday morning orders. Nothing like a little sugar to lift the 'weekend's-over' grumpiness."

"What's one more cake going to hurt? Come on, you know you want to." He reached out, his hand brushing against hers. As it had before, the simple act of touching her soft, delicate palm set off a three-alarm fire—complete with bells—in his head.

He wanted her, definitely more than he'd ever wanted any woman before. He wanted to kiss her, to taste her, to savor every inch of her with the same attention he'd just given to her baked goods.

Olivia flushed, shaking her head. Desire flickered in her eyes but she got to her feet, backing away from the table.

Apparently he wasn't the only one who needed to call in Boston's finest to put out a little person-to-person flame.

Olivia grabbed his fork and laid it on the empty plate with her own, her movements now resolute. "No. That's the kind of thing that gets me into trouble. Thank you for your help today, Worth. I hope the ad campaign works."

He rose and circled the table to stand before her. "That's it? It's over?"

"You did what I asked, and I'm thanking you."

He was losing her, losing the ground they'd gained in the last few minutes, now that the effects of the cheesecake and their earlier repartee had evaporated. All of a sudden, they were about as cozy as two strangers waiting in line at the 7-Eleven for a Big Gulp.

Daniel realized he didn't want to let go of her. Not that easily.

She had something—this woman who drove like some people tangoed. A spark, a passion, that he had yet to find for himself.

And besides, she'd promised him a date. Something he fully intended to collect.

"I envy you, Olivia Regan," he said.

"Me?" The surprise was clear in her eyes. "But you can have anything you want."

"They say the grass is greener on the other side. But this time, I think you have the better lawn."

"Why?"

"Because you got to plant it yourself." He thought of the expectations waiting for him in his grandfather's office tomorrow, the responsibility of the Worth name. Come Monday morning, he was expected to shoulder the load of his pedigree. It was a task Daniel dreaded because if there was one environment he hated, it was the stuffy, boxed-in, straight lines corporate world.

Olivia chuckled, her green eyes dancing with amusement. "Trust me, the gardening isn't all it's cracked up to be. I still have a lot of weeds to pull."

"You made a hell of a gutsy move, spending all your money on me." Stepping out on that limb, without even knowing for sure he'd cooperate. How many women did he know who'd do that? Hell, how many people in general?

The list was so short, he could fit it on a Post-It.

"Not as gutsy as paying in advance for the ad space," she said. "The ones we shot today will run next week."

He grinned. "Pretty confident you were going to win me, weren't you?"

"I always get what I want, Worth." She spun on her heel and headed into the kitchen, pushing through the stainless steel door. It swung slowly shut behind her.

Well, damn. So did he. But right now, Daniel was left wanting something he didn't have. And, as Olivia had made it clear, he wasn't about to get.

Or so she thought.

He gathered up the other rose-patterned dishes that had been placed on the table for the photo shoot and followed after her, determined as a groupie looking for Madonna's autograph.

"You're forgetting one thing, *Miss* Regan," he said when he entered the kitchen.

She pivoted away from the sink, that damnable mask of business still on her heart-shaped face. If he hadn't known better, he'd swear she was a complete stranger, looking for her thirty-two ounces of Diet Pepsi and nothing more.

But he did know better and he knew exactly how to push her buttons.

"What am I forgetting?" she asked.

"You owe me." He grinned and leaned against her counter, not going anywhere. Not now, not later. Not until he had what he was waiting for. "And I always get what I want, too."

Olivia's Senses-in-Turmoil Irish Coffee

1 shot Irish whiskey (1.5 ounces)
3 sugar cubes
8 ounces coffee
1/8 cup heavy cream

When you're around a man as hot as this one, you can do one of two things: leap into his arms and demand he end your gotta-have-him misery, or have a good, stiff drink. The drink is far less dangerous for your heart, believe me.

Pour the whiskey into a tall mug. Add the sugar, then top with the coffee. Pour the cream carefully on top, so that it sits there prettily. Drink heavily and repeat as necessary until the temptation to kiss him has passed.

CHAPTER NINE

Olivia held her breath. She hadn't counted on him wanting anything from her. Sure, she'd made the promise, but that had been words—she hadn't thought he'd actually expect her to *go through* with it. In Olivia's plan, she forked over the cash, got her bachelor photos, and Daniel Worth would just disappear, bored with his walk on the middle-class side of the grass.

Clearly, her business plan needed a little tweaking.

A *little* tweaking? Heck, it needed an extreme makeover.

"It's my turn now," Daniel said, moving closer, making it seem as if the kitchen was a two-foot square.

Olivia could have stepped to the right. She could have shoved him away. She could have given him some haughty response, in the tradition of Scarlett O'Hara. But she didn't want to. It had to be the cheesecake in her system because all of a sudden, every sense within her was pinging like sonar in the middle of a minefield. "Your turn?"

"*Quid pro quo,* remember? I did what you wanted, now you do what I want." His grin turned up at one corner and a tease lit his blue eyes. Olivia wanted to bottle that color, paint it on her walls.

She shook her head with all the vehemence of a balloon on a string. "I thought you said you only wanted a date. For you, I'm assuming that means dinner at some fancy restaurant."

"We can do that…later." His grin widened and he stepped forward, capturing her jaw in his palm as gently as he'd hold a butterfly. "We already ate dessert before dinner, so why don't we start with the goodnight kiss?"

"A little more dessert before the substance?"

"A hell of a good idea, don't you think?"

Oh, she thought so, all right. But what her gut was telling her and what was right for her mind and her business were two different things. Desire for Daniel wasn't a problem—it was the results of that feeling.

Desire got her into trouble. Desire got her caught up in making decisions as bad for her heart as pneumonia was for her lungs. Desire made her think with entirely the wrong body part.

Before she could start heeding the messages pounding inside her, Olivia spun away from him, turning toward the faucet to run hot water over the dirty dishes. "I know what I promised you, Worth, but it was just empty words so you'd fulfill your end of the bargain. For your information, I don't want to date you or marry you or bear your children like all those other women who are—"

"Quacking their quackers at me?"

Damn, she'd done that herself. And with a lot of enthusiasm, too. "Yes."

He came up behind her, his warm breath whispering across her neck. "And what if I wanted to date you? Or marry you? Or...well, bearing your children might be a little hard."

She pivoted back, ready to tell him off, to put him in his place—a place far from her because whenever he was near all her best intentions slipped away like flour sifting through her fingers.

He was close, so close. A rush of attraction ran headlong through her betraying body, undermining her intentions like the Vegas strip blinking its neon at a recovering gambler.

Daniel Worth needed his own twelve-step group. Count on Olivia to bring the quackers.

She wouldn't inhale one whiff of the spicy undertones of his cologne. She refused to see the gold flecks in his eyes, or notice the broad expanse of his shoulders.

He was just a guy, like any other guy.

Yeah, and Man O' War was just another horse.

"Oh, please," she said, slipping on her heart armor of sarcasm. "You are the last man on the planet to get married, bear children or even commit to anything or anyone more needy than a goldfish."

Daniel took a step back, the tease gone from his eyes. Her words had hit their mark. "Ouch."

"Am I wrong?"

"A little."

"I told you, I did my homework." But there was little satisfaction in being right.

"What they print in the gossip columns isn't always the truth," he said. "And I bet Gloria's Gossip section didn't mention that I'm interested in you. Incredibly interested."

"It has to go both ways, unfortunately," she said, lying through her teeth. She was interested in him, in the odd juxtaposition of the man the media depicted and what she had seen in the last few hours.

But a relationship with him... Now that was a bad idea, a very bad idea. The one thing Olivia hadn't budgeted for was a man like Daniel Worth coming into her life. "I've already gotten what I wanted. So thank you." She thrust out a palm.

"That's it? A handshake?"

"Uh-huh. If you want any more than that, I suggest you bid on me when *I'm* up for auction." She gave him a smile that told him the chances of that were about slim to none.

Olivia doubted she'd see Daniel again after this, anyway. She wasn't part of his world and no matter how successful Pastries with Panache became, they'd never run in the same circles. Best to end it now before she filled her head with silly ideas about a future.

Daniel grasped her hand with his but didn't shake or let go. "No."

She blinked. "No?"

"That's not it." He leaned forward and before she could move away or protest, he lowered his mouth to hers.

Daniel Worth didn't just kiss Olivia. He *cherished* her. His lips drifted over hers slow and easy, nipping and teasing at first, then tasting each one with the tip of his tongue before opening to her and encompassing her mouth. His hands cradled her jaw, his fingers dancing a thousand sensations along the sensitive edge of her hair.

Adjectives tumbled through her mind—fantastic, incredible, amazing—but none seemed to fit the thunder of feeling pounding in her body. Her skin flashed hot, then hotter still, and she gave up her mental battle.

Resistance was futile. Her body had betrayed her the instant his lips met hers, as sure as if he'd kissed her a thousand times before. Olivia groaned and opened to him, darting her tongue into his mouth. He tasted of sugar and coffee, richer than the dessert they'd shared, more tempting than the best chocolate in the world. A shudder of need— for this, for him, for more—ran through Olivia. She grasped at his back, urging him forward, closer.

His kiss had awakened a part of Olivia that she had tamped down for months, silencing her self to pour every ounce into the business. Her heart pounded in her chest, the blood pumping faster and faster, like a drum beating a call she hadn't heard in a long, long time.

But…oh, this was wrong. *He* was wrong. He'd be gone tomorrow, back to his world, and she'd be left wanting. Needing. And disappointed as hell.

Olivia pulled back, inhaling some common sense. "We shouldn't have done that."

"Are you saying you didn't enjoy that? Because I didn't hear you say no. Or in any way resist."

She thrust her chin upwards. "I was simply overcome."

"By what? The scent of my cologne? The aroma of vanilla?" He grinned at her. "And besides, I thought that overcome stuff only happened in romance novels."

Olivia moved away, out of his reach, then grabbed a dishtowel and took inordinate interest in wiping fingerprints off the stainless steel surface of the revolving tray oven. "It's simply been…a long time for me."

He came up beside her, gently taking the towel from her hands and turning her back to face him. "I find that hard to believe. Especially with a woman as beautiful as you."

"Oh come on, Worth. You don't have to butter me up." Her body may have become as resistant as a rubber band, but she still had her mouth.

"I'm not. I'm being nice." He trailed a finger under her chin. Every nonsensical part of her body begged for more, for her to stop this stupid resistance and just let the man kiss her again. And again. And again, until her brain became as mushy as a half-baked cake. "The proper response is to be nice back."

Being nice would mean kissing him again and if she kissed him one more time, Olivia would be as powerful as a rag doll in his arms. Olivia Regan never succumbed to anyone, even herself.

Not anymore.

Losing her heart, soul or even something as small as her concentration wasn't part of the deal with this millionaire man. "I am nice," she said. "Most of the time."

He grinned. "About as nice as a porcupine with a stick up his—"

She slugged him in the right shoulder. This was better, this repartee that allowed her to distance herself.

"I take that back. About as nice as a grizzly bear with a pine tree in his—"

This time, she hit his left shoulder. "You've run out of arms, Worth. Say anything more and I'll have to aim lower." She directed her gaze below his belt. "Much lower."

He made a motion of zipping his lips. "I bet you were hell on the playground."

"I never met a dodgeball that could hit me."

"Or a boy who could tag you."

She shrugged. "Most never took me by surprise."

He tipped her chin with a finger. "Until me."

Olivia refused to admit he was right. Doing so was tantamount to hanging out a white flag and offering her surrender. "With you there were exten-uating circumstances."

He smirked. "Oh there were, were there?"

"Yes. I was…overcome by the sugar in the cheese-cake." Sugar in the cheesecake? She couldn't come up with something better than that? Like an allergic reaction to dust motes or an incurable disease?

"Uh-huh. Do you lie as well as you hit?"

"Let me hit you again and we'll see." *Let me do anything but step back into your arms and forget I have a floundering business to run and a lot of people counting on me to make it successful.*

He chuckled. "Have dinner with me, Olivia Regan. You name the place, the time. Make all the rules, and I'll play by them." Daniel traced her lips with his finger, outlining the type of play he had in mind. "Just don't say no."

She opened her mouth to do just that or maybe, say yes—she hadn't quite thought that far—when the kitchen door opened and three people walked in, dressed in black and white and bearing Pine Sol.

"Good timing," Daniel said, clearly meaning the opposite by the tone of disappointment in his voice. He turned to Olivia. "This is Lewiston," he said, indicating the tall man with white hair and impeccable suit who had answered Daniel's door the day before. "Lewiston, this is Olivia."

"Pleasure to meet you," Lewiston said, taking her extended hand in his white glove.

"Same here," Olivia responded. She was introduced to the maids, Mary and Louisa, then quickly got to work assigning them tasks in the kitchen. Within a half hour, they had her kitchen cleaner than she'd seen it since she'd unpacked the boxes and set it up the first day. Which didn't say much about Olivia's abilities as a housekeeper, she supposed.

But people hired her shop for its pastries and baked goods, not whether her stainless steel gleamed after the last pan was dried. Pastries with Panache could out-cheesecake anyone in the Tri-State area, whether or not her Kohler faucet had a few spots on it when she was done.

Daniel's cell phone rang somewhere in the middle of the detergent and drying frenzy. He slipped outside to take the call.

"His grandfather," Lewiston explained. "It's a lot like Pavlov's dogs."

Olivia grinned. "I have a mother. I understand."

Lewiston's face, which had been as unexpressive as a loaf of French bread, broke into a slight smile. "Ah, families are the same, aren't they?"

Olivia shrugged. She doubted the middleclass, sometimes-teetering-on-the-count-the-pennies edge of broke Regans were anything like the Worths. "Perhaps. Though mine has only ridden in a limo for funerals."

"Trust me, miss, it's not all it's cracked up to be." He shook his head. "Altogether too much leg room."

"And that's a bad thing...why?"

"More space for more family members. Sometimes, too many in one place can be a disaster. Plus, there's more room for dirt to settle." He gave her another grin.

Olivia decided she liked Lewiston. Very much. When he'd arrived, she noticed the way he talked to Daniel—professional, yet with an undertone of obvious love. Daniel had said Lewiston had been with him since birth, a loyalty nearly unheard of in today's rush-to-the-next-big-promotion place.

"Lewiston?" Olivia asked, crossing to him as he started polishing the proofing box.

She shouldn't ask. Daniel was a distraction she couldn't afford. Yet, curiosity burned inside her, some masochistic urge to know if those blue eyes were looking at anyone else with the same level of interest.

"Is, ah, Daniel…seeing anyone?"

The butler turned, surprise evident in his features. "Seeing anyone?"

Olivia toyed with a dishrag. "Like ah,… Oh, I don't know, a steady girlfriend?"

Lewiston chuckled. "Mr. Worth isn't exactly a going steady kind of man." He tipped his head and studied her, light blue eyes wise with age and concern. "It would take a very strong woman to keep someone like him interested."

A strong woman. Did he mean her? Well, she was strong, but busy right now. Too busy for a man. Besides, she had no thoughts of keeping Daniel Worth interested in her. None at all.

"Well," Olivia said, reaching for a rag of her own, if only to keep her hands and mind occupied with work. "I'm sure he'll meet someone. Someday."

"Has he already?" Lewiston asked. The question hung in Olivia's kitchen, laden with meaning. The maids paused in their chatter, as if they too wanted to know the answer.

Olivia didn't want to be the Worth heir's girl-friend. She had a business to run—a business that was supposed to be taking care of her and Josie financially—and her love life could wait. Asking Lewiston about Daniel had been a temporary moment of insanity, one she'd experienced once before, with disastrous results. A millionaire wouldn't be any better for her heart than an average Joe—the rich guy just came with better toys and perks. "No, of course not. At least not that I know of."

Lewiston didn't say a word, just returned to his work, his face once again a mask of professionalism.

With her kitchen firmly under control, Olivia headed out front. Through the glass, she saw Daniel outside, standing in the cold and chatting—actually, from her perspective it looked more like arguing— on his cell phone. She thought about what Lewiston had said about Daniel's grandfather. Perhaps the life of a millionaire wasn't as stress-free as she'd imagined. Empathy fluttered through her. Grabbing both their coats, she headed outside. In the interests of being nice, not any lingering curiosity from her conversation with Lewiston.

He was hanging up just as she reached him. She handed him the cashmere overcoat. "Hey, thanks," he said.

"Can't have my investment ending up with the sniffles." She grinned and slid her arms into her own coat.

"Speaking of that... Tonight, your twenty-four hours with me are up, you know." Daniel said, study-ing her face, looking for—

What? Interest? She was kidding herself if she thought a man like him, with millions of dollars and dozens of people at his disposal, was interested in her for anything more than a fling.

"That's okay," she said. Let him off the hook now and eliminate any possibility that she might fool herself into thinking she saw, and felt, a spark of interest from him. "We finished everything I wanted to accomplish today."

"*Everything?*" The word hung in the air between them.

Snow began drifting to the ground, surrounding them in a silent delicate swirl of white. The emerald of Olivia's eyes deepened to the color of a deep, dark forest, telling Daniel there was a lot left unsaid.

"You never answered me before," he said. "Would you like to go out to dinner? You did promise me, after all."

She was shaking her head before he even finished the question. "I don't mix business with pleasure."

"Our business," he said, sweeping a hand toward the shop, "is concluded, isn't it? That means you aren't mixing anything with your pleasure."

"Still, we shouldn't—"

"Are you making excuses, Miss Regan?"

"No." But she averted her face as she said it and he got the distinct feeling that sometimes, Olivia Regan wasn't the best liar. "Well," she said as briskly as the winter wind, "Thank you again, Mr. Worth. It was a pleasure working with you. And I'm sorry about reneging on our dinner deal, but I am quite busy here. Perhaps a raincheck?"

She was dismissing him like he was a door-to-door salesman with a load of outdated encyclopedias under his arm. He should be glad he was being released so easily, that this woman who expected a lot out of herself and everyone around her was so intent on slipping out of his life.

He knew he hadn't misread the kiss between them, or the simmering tension that burned below the surface of her every word. Olivia Regan wasn't immune to him—

Even if she sometimes treated him like an outbreak of bubonic plague.

"Technically, you still own me for six more hours. You should make the most of your investment," he teased.

But the professional demeanor remained. For all the warmth in her gaze now, he could have been a proctologist. If he didn't have a crystal clear memory of it, he'd never know they'd been kissing just a half hour earlier. What had happened between then and now?

And why couldn't he recapture the mood?

"If I think of something else I need, I'll call." Olivia thanked him again.

"What if we—"

"No, don't go there. Don't say we. I know all about you and the string of women as long as the Earth's equator who have been to dinner with you.

I don't want to be at the end of a very long conga line."

Ouch. He didn't bother to quantify his romantic past, because he knew Olivia would never believe him. The media machine had done its work, very well, painting him as Rudolph Valentino with a Viagra drip.

The relationships Daniel had had with women—if one would even call them relationships—had been as meaningful as Twinkies. He'd dated a lot, yes, but only because he'd been searching for some unidentifiable quality he had yet to find.

Until he met Olivia. From the second she'd put up her hand to place an outrageous pricetag on his head, he'd known. There was something different about her. Something dangerous for him to pursue.

Grandfather Worth wanted him to stay within the pack, as if the entire Boston elite were a bunch of AKC wolfhounds. The trouble was, Daniel had learned, that all the inbreeding among his "kind" had created a bunch of Ivana Trump clones who were about as interesting as stale bread.

He didn't want a carbon copy. He wanted the original recipe—Olivia Regan. Yet, even as desire for her surged inside his chest, he wondered whether *she* deserved a man like him.

"I have to get back to work," she said, turning on her heel.

He reached for her hand, trying to delay the inevitable. "Olivia—"

But she cut him off again. "Good day, Mr. Worth." Olivia tugged her palm out of his, her small delicate hand slipping out of his larger grip with ease.

The woman moisturized, dammit.

Then she was gone, out of his life and out of his line of sight before he could think twice. Probably just as well, Daniel thought as Olivia disappeared back inside her store, leaving him out in the cold. The last thing he needed was a woman who drove him crazy, made him work for what he wanted and made "hard to get" into a contact sport.

Because if there was one thing Daniel sucked at, it was fulfilling other people's expectations.

Josie's Their-Auras-Are-Glowing Chocolate-Raspberry Tarts

Pastry:

2 cups all-purpose flour, plus more for dusting

3 tablespoons sugar

1/4 teaspoon salt

3/4 cup unsalted butter, cold and cut into small chunks

1 large egg, separated

2 tablespoons ice water, plus more if needed

Filling:

1 cup heavy cream

10 ounces semisweet chocolate

2 tablespoons raspberry liqueur

1 1/2 pints fresh raspberries

2 tablespoons confectioners' sugar

Read your horoscope before you start baking to make sure all the planets are aligned just right. Check the skies, too, just in case some alien life form is waiting to take your raspberries away. Mix the dry ingredients for the crust, then cut in the butter with a pastry blender. In a separate bowl, whisk the egg

SHIRLEY JUMP

yolk (reserve the white) with the ice water, then work it into the dough.

Preheat your oven to 350 degrees while you roll out the dough and press it into a tart pan with a removable bottom. Make sure the dough is as even and smooth as the outer shell of the space shuttle. Bake it for 20-25 minutes, until it's golden like a pleased aura.

Meanwhile, bring the cream to a boil, then remove from the heat and add the chocolate. Whisk until entirely melted, then add the liqueur. Chill for 20 minutes (gee, isn't it cool how that all works out time-wise? It's like it was meant to be).

Spread the chocolate over the baked and cooled tart shell, then top with the raspberries. Dust with the sugar, and serve. It's best to serve this right away, while the possibility of two lost hearts finding each other is still warm.

CHAPTER TEN

"You have to watch this," Josie said, breezing into the shop that afternoon. She dropped a DVD onto Olivia's lap. "I told you those crop circles were real."

Olivia picked up the plastic holder. "Josie, this is *Signs*. It's a movie with Mel Gibson and that Phoenix guy whose name I can never pronounce."

"A movie? Are you sure?" Josie grabbed the tape, glanced it over, then handed it back. "How do you know it's not a documentary masquerading as a movie?"

Olivia shook her head, refusing to have this argument. Again. "Aren't you supposed to be at school?"

"I got out early. You're looking at the woman who mastered Barbasol usage faster than anyone else in the history of Bella Me Beauty School."

Olivia laughed. "You know your chemicals. You should have become a scientist."

"And spend my whole life cozied up with a Bunsen burner and microscope?" Josie put up her palms, warding off the idea. "I think not. I'd rather be the one *under* the microscope than the one *behind* it."

"Why's that?"

"Because," she said, grabbing the tape again, "when you start looking through those lenses, you see the *real* scary stuff in life. Like diseases and germs that would make the folks at the Raid factory scream. I'd rather live my life in ignorant, what-if bliss."

"Somedays, I wish I could," Olivia mumbled. She was dealing with the scary stuff, the real-life business stuff all alone. How she wished she could pass that microscope on to another viewer. For a second, she looked over at her sister.

Could she share this burden? Relieve a little of the weight on her own shoulders? For a second, she wondered if Josie would understand.

No. She couldn't do that to her sister. Josie had finally found something she loved to do and a job she could stick with longer past the expiration date on a gallon of milk. The last thing Josie needed was for Olivia to throw some scary financial facts into the mix.

Their plan was simple—Josie would work here but keep going to beauty school as a safety cushion. Olivia could risk her own financial future but there was no way she was going to let Josie do the same. A salon in Newton had already expressed interest in hiring Josie once she got her beautician's license. Josie was secure and Olivia wasn't going to do anything to change that.

"Hey, what happened in here?" Josie asked, ducking her head into the sparkling clean kitchen.

Olivia followed her into the room. "Did you get tel-etransported into Martha Stewart's body or what?"

"Daniel sent over a "cleaning crew" so I could relax."

"Sweet. That guy is a keeper. I tell you, he's got the Venus for you."

Olivia let out a sigh and knew for sure that telling Josie about the financial worries would be a mistake. Her sister was too naïve to handle what was happening with the financial end. Bless Josie's right-brained heart, but she wasn't the one to lean on for this.

Or for relationship advice. Not when Josie thought proper planetary alignment insured a happy future.

Olivia reached for some Tylenol and a glass of water. Cutting Daniel Worth out of her life hadn't been nearly as satisfying as she'd expected. She'd gotten rid of one bachelor—but left herself with a hell of a regret hangover.

Josie leaned on the counter, dabbing up the remains of some chocolate frosting from a bowl. "I don't know why you're so resistant to him. He's rich, he's gorgeous and he believes in miracles."

"How do you know that?"

"He asked you out, didn't he? I knew he would. I had a *feeling*." Josie gave her sister a good-natured smile. "Seriously, you need to make time for a guy."

"I don't have time for a man, not now, not for a long time. To me, that's like making room in your closet for the size two clothes when you don't have the bone structure to be that skinny."

It was an argument they'd had many times. Josie thought everything was possible—Pluto landings and happily-ever-afters.

"You paid for him, Liv, and that's one expensive hook-up." Josie grinned. "Take advantage of him."

"I'm not interested in him that way."

Josie waved her hands at her sister. "Hello? Are you dead? On life support? Has some alien pod snatched the real Olivia? That man is better looking than Brad Pitt and George Clooney put together. What's not to like?"

Olivia shrugged. "I don't want to date a millionaire."

Josie rubbed at her ears. "Did I hear you right? I thought you just said you don't want to date a millionaire. You *are* a pod twin. It's like *Invasion of the Body Snatchers* all over again. Quick, tell me something only I would know."

"Josie…"

"See! You can't do it. This is bad, very bad."

"Jo, it's me. *Really*. I'm just not that interested in Daniel Worth."

The two of them left the kitchen and headed to the front of the shop, donning aprons as they went. Olivia renewed her determination to handle this on her own. Josie worked hard in the shop; she deserved to maintain her what-if bliss. Olivia had protected her sister from bad news and the real world for most of their lives. She could do it now, too.

Olivia drew in a breath. Her moment of neediness was over.

"Well, he's sure interested in you," Josie said. "I saw how he looked at you earlier today. He looked like Darwin discovering a humanzee. I say you date him and accept the fringe benefits of a few diamonds." Josie grinned. "Make some new best friends, sis."

"I can't. I'm too busy working."

"Bull. You're using that as an excuse," Josie said. "If you wanted him, you'd make room for him."

Olivia chuckled. "You make it sound like getting a puppy."

"Well, he does have those big, blue, *adoring* eyes. And I bet he'd love it if you stroked his tail."

"Josie!"

Her sister laughed, a devilish grin on her face. "The guy is cheesecake on a stick, Liv. If you pass up the opportunity to date him, you're either nuts or you *have* been body snatched." Josie leaned closer, peering into her sister's eyes. "That *is* you in there, isn't it?"

"Quit it. I can be uninterested in a millionaire and still be a human."

Josie arched a brow at that possibility. "Whatever you want to tell yourself, alien clone sister. But I think the proof is in the Daniel pudding." She grinned. "Help yourself to a bowl. Or two."

As Olivia turned away to straighten a tray of chocolate raspberry tarts, she told herself Josie was all wrong. Buying Daniel Worth had been a mistake. Did the auction have a return policy?

Because buying him had caused her to second-guess herself more than a psychic with a migraine.

Daniel's Tasting-the-Simple-Life Easy Fruit Dip

1 8-ounce tub of whipped topping
1 cup milk
1 1.4-ounce package instant vanilla pudding

Just because you've never had to do anything more complicated than order lunch, doesn't mean you can't learn to feed yourself. This is a simple one, so easy a monkey—or a wealthy bachelor who's never lifted a finger—can do it.

Mix all ingredients. Refrigerate for one hour. Serve with fruit.

There. How hard was that? Maybe there's hope for you yet.

CHAPTER ELEVEN

Grandfather Worth was about as pleased as a cat in a Jacuzzi. And when Grandfather Worth wasn't happy, he was going to make damned sure no one else was either.

After being summoned, Daniel had headed directly to Grandfather's palatial house in Brookline. Now he stood in the entryway on Sunday night and waited. Any minute now, the family flogging would begin.

"I have heard, Daniel, that you are appearing in ads for this..." Grandfather Worth waved his hand vaguely, one corner of his mouth lifted up in a sneer, "this pastry shop. The one *that* woman owns."

"How did you find out? We just finished the photo shoot."

Then he knew. The second Grandfather had met Olivia, he'd undoubtedly called on the private investigator he kept on retainer, just for occasions like this. Within hours, every scrap of information available about the pastry chef who'd dared to invade the Worth cocoon would have been on Grandfather's desk.

His grandfather pursed his lips, revealing no sources. "What we have here, Daniel, is *failure* to communicate." His grandfather paused for dramatic effect, adjusting the cravat at his neck, raising his chin three degrees. "Your destiny is to work at the Worth company, taking my place at the helm. Tomorrow morning, I expect you to step up to your responsibilities and have something to keep your hands occupied. Besides women."

Daniel ignored the jab. "I don't want to work at Worth. I never have. You know that."

"Why not? You can combine the best of both worlds in one place," Grandfather said drolly. "Beds and business."

Familiar frustration rose in Daniel's gut. The man who'd raised him had never understood the grandson he professed to love. There'd always been this wall between them, as strong as steel and as immovable as a sleeping elephant. "Is that what you think of me? That all I do is sleep around?"

His grandfather put on his poker face.

"I won't work for you," Daniel repeated.

Vocalizing the words made them a final decision. The thought of being behind a desk every day caused a knot of tension in Daniel's gut. Despite what he had promised Grandfather earlier, he knew now that he couldn't do it. No matter what threats Grandfather tossed on the table.

Besides, he could only imagine the kind of power Grandfather would exert if Daniel was in the same office building as his namesake. He had heard, from other family members, what working for the family drama king was like.

There weren't enough synonyms for "difficult" in Roget's to describe the experience.

"You need to grow up, Daniel. I've allowed you to dally with your life long enough. It's time for you to show me the money, so to speak." He chuckled at his rip-off from *Jerry Maguire*. "Start earning your keep. Be a man, for God's sake."

Daniel bristled. "I am a man. Just not the one you wanted."

Daniel thought of the times he'd tried to pursue another path. He'd signed up for a creative writing class in college and before he knew it, his grandfather had called the dean. From there on out, every class Daniel signed up for that deviated from his business management track was full. Or canceled. Or otherwise unavailable to him.

To Grandfather Worth, anyone who dared to go outside the predestined family business track ran a close second to Benedict Arnold.

"Don't tell me you've considered that scribbling you do as a career," Grandfather said, scooting his chair closer. "It's a hobby, for God's sake, not a job."

Daniel gritted his teeth and kept the words he wanted to say firmly in check. He and Grandfather had never agreed on Daniel's career ambitions. To Grandfather, Daniel was a Worth and that meant one mission in life—to continue to increase the family value.

Daniel's dream of writing for a living had been tucked away in a drawer in his room, relegated to the position of hobby, pages hidden, never to see the light of day. A Worth businessman didn't pen novels or write sardonic essays about his life. A Worth businessman put on his suit and kept the family image as pristine as its hotel lobbies.

"I told you yesterday, if you won't work for me, then you won't have my money." Grandfather leveled his Scrooge gaze on Daniel, leaning one arm on his wheelchair and furrowing his brows together. When he'd performed in *A Christmas Carol* three winters ago, the critics had said his Ebenezer had had the Ghost of Christmas Future shaking under his cloak.

"I don't want it."

As soon as the words left Daniel's mouth, he knew they were true. He was through with the money, the butler, the maids. All of it. He was through living in a world about as real as the plays and movies his grandfather loved. One where the rules of the game were set by someone else.

Daniel wanted what Olivia had—playing by his own rules. Calling his own shots. Making his own damned decisions, good or bad.

Grandfather sat there, silent. The Broadway masks were gone, replaced by a stunned slackness in his jaw. "You don't want *what?*"

"The money. This." Daniel waved a hand at the Worth mansion, passed down for umpteen generations, gaining in priceless art and antiquities with each succeeding inheritance as if it were a woman putting on more and more jewelry until she began to look gaudy, not beautiful.

Grandfather snorted. "You're insane."

"Probably."

His grandfather pushed on the arms of his wheelchair. For a moment, Daniel thought he was about to stand, but then Grandfather remembered the restraints of his handicap and with a gust of frustration, dropped himself back into his metal prison. "I can't let you do this, Daniel. You're a Worth. You're *the* Worth. The *heir.*"

"I don't want to be. I want to be my own person. Someone other than Daniel Worth the Fourth."

Grandfather scowled. "Don't tell me this is about getting some stupid sex change. I swear to God, you go and get your testicles cut off and change your name to Vivian and I'll kill you myself before the press does."

"It's not about anything like that. I only want the chance to do what *your* father did."

"What?"

"Prove myself. On my own terms. Without the family money behind me."

His grandfather let out a laugh. "One day of poverty, and you'll be crawling back to me. Just like your Aunt Helen and her worthless son. Begging to take your place in the family again."

"I won't." Though Daniel did have a twinge at the thought. How would he make a living? He had a degree, but no job experience. A name he couldn't really use, because the first question out of everyone's mouths would be why he wasn't working for his grandfather. Where was he going to live? How was he going to buy food? Get around?

Panic shuddered in his chest.

He punched it down with an invisible fist. If he was going to make the break, now was the time. Before he ended up like his cousin Reginald, kowtowing to Grandfather at every turn like a pigeon salivating beside a Beemer at the carwash.

"You want to be on your own?" his grandfather said, shouting now. "You want a taste of that life? You can't *handle* that life, believe me."

"I can and I will."

His grandfather waved a hand. "Fine then. You've got your wish."

"Good." A feeling of satisfaction filled Daniel's chest. No more catering to Grandfather's wishes. No more being someone else's vision of himself. No more—

"Now get the hell out of my house. With the clothes on your back and nothing else." Daniel Worth II raised a thin, bony finger and pointed toward the door. "And see how it feels to be a worthless Worth."

Madison's Richer-Is-Better Crème Caramel

1 1/4 cups sugar, divided
4 tablespoons water
2 teaspoons vanilla extract
1 2/3 cups milk
1 cup whipping cream
5 large eggs
2 egg yolks

If you happen to be born into a rich family, don't be stupid enough to throw it all away. Especially not for love—a man isn't nearly as good as a full set of credit cards and a generous spending limit. Whenever you get the urge to be poor, take a taste of these and you'll change your mind as fast as a woman at a Jimmy Choo bargain sale.

Put one cup of the sugar and the water in a saucepan. Stir to dissolve the sugar until it comes to a boil. Then leave it alone until it caramelizes. Can you taste the calories already? Just inhaling requires a half hour on the treadmill to keep your thighs in shape.

Pour the caramel into either a 4-cup soufflé dish or six 4-ounce ramekins. Place the dish(es) in a small roasting pan and start preheating the oven to 325 degrees. In a separate saucepan (don't worry about all the dishes; just smile at a handsome guy and he'll be in the mood to suds for you), mix the vanilla, milk and cream. Stir often and bring to a boil. Set it aside and let it cool, giving yourself enough time to flip through the newest Spiegel catalog.

Whisk the eggs and egg yolks with the remaining sugar in a bowl, until it's as smooth and creamy as a good facial mask. Add the milk, then pour it into the caramel-laced dish(es). Cover them with foil, then put them in a roasting pan and pour in boiling water to fill the pan halfway up the sides of the dish(es). Bake for 40-45 minutes, until its set and firm as liposuctioned thighs.

Cool for a half hour or so (enough time to surf Nordstrom's online site and see what's new in shoes for spring), then run a knife along the edge of the custard to loosen it. Put a plate on the dish and invert both at once to turn it out gently. All that gooey, hip-spreading caramel on the bottom will drizzle over the top and sides, creating the ultimate in dessert.

Share with friends who understand the frustrations of men and pencil skirts.

CHAPTER TWELVE

"I wouldn't go in there if I were you," Daniel said. His cousin Madison paused on the bottom granite step leading to Grandfather Worth's massive brick home. Her silver SL500 Benz sat in the circular drive, the engine clicking a few times as it cooled. Despite the mid-teens temperature and the fact that she'd probably just jetted back from Paris or Milan or someplace equally couture, she looked perfectly put together. Her ermine coat hid a pencil-thin body and offset her sleek blond hair. She was a perfect match for the twelve thousand-square foot mansion, its rolling lawns, stone walkways.

"Why not?" she asked.

"He's in a mood." Daniel tipped his thumb in the direction of the front door. "A really, really bad mood."

The daughter of Grandfather's youngest child, Vivian, Madison had lived inside these walls more often than her own because her thrice-divorced mother spent her days traveling from one poverty-laden country to another, fulfilling her humitarian missions. A young child didn't mix well with building huts in Haiti or treating AIDS in Africa, so Aunt Vivian had left young Madison at Grandfather's house. To live much the same life as Daniel had— one devoid of parents and warmth.

Over the years, Madison had become a close cousin to Daniel—as well as the only one who could understand the frustrations of growing up in a prison made of money and ironclad rules.

Madison lowered her suitcase to the brick walk-way and put her fists on her slim hips. "What'd you do now?"

"Me? Nothing." Daniel paused. "Well…except disown the family fortune."

Madison threw back her head and laughed. "Is that all? Gee, and I thought it was something serious."

"It is. I'm officially penniless." Beyond them, the sun began its slow descent into the horizon, casting the vast snow-dusted acreage in rich orange hues.

"Come on, Daniel. You and I both know you'll be back here before the stars come out tonight," Madison said, gesturing toward the sky. "We may not like Grandfather's rules, but you have to admit, they come with some very nice perks."

"We pay for those perks," Daniel muttered.

Madison waved a manicured hand at him. "So you have to make an appearance in the company offices once in a while. What's the big deal?"

Daniel shook his head. "It's not what I want to do with my life."

"This isn't kindergarten, Daniel. It's real life. You do things you don't want to do because people are paying you to."

"This coming from a woman who makes a living off her pouty smile?"

"Hey, those pouty smiles end up in *Vogue*, I'll have you know. And modeling is hard work."

"Uh-huh."

"Hey, don't make fun of me, penniless no-job boy."

"You're my cousin. You're supposed to support me."

Madison laughed. "Daniel, supporting you walking out on the family fortune is like giving an alcoholic a ride to the bar. I support you when you make *smart* decisions."

"Like what?"

"Like carrying on the Worth Hotel chain so it can support us all in the manner to which we have grown quite accustomed." Madison drew her ermine tighter around her neck for emphasis. "I'll only have these looks for so long, so I'm keeping my bread buttered on the right side."

"Sorry. No can do. I need to make my own way."

She narrowed her gaze and studied him. "You're serious, aren't you?"

"As a stock report."

"Wow." She took a half step back. "You really did it?"

He nodded. The feeling of freedom swelled in his chest. He'd done it. And it felt damned good.

"You're insane." She considered him for a second. "What are you going to do now?"

Daniel shrugged. "I'll figure it out. It's actually kind of exciting to think about what lies ahead. Homelessness," he put out a palm, "or success." He put out the other hand, weighing his two options.

Madison grimaced. "Where are you going to live? I'd put you up in my place in New York, but it's being fumigated this week, which is why I'm here at the happy family home."

"A motel, I guess. At least until I get a job."

"Oh, come on, there are a thousand women in Boston who would *pay* you to live with them. They'd happily make a little room in their beds for boy toy like you." She chuckled. "Though as your cousin, who suffered from your frog and worm 'surprises', I don't quite understand why."

Daniel shifted from foot to foot. "I have a girlfriend…more or less."

"More or less?" Madison crossed her arms over her chest. "What kind of answer is that?"

The Thurgood's Siamese zipped along the boxwoods, undoubtedly pursuing a small rodent. The persnickety feline must have escaped from its own yard, to once again indulge in making deposits in Grandfather's mulch. "It means I'm interested in someone but I'm not close enough yet to show up on her doorstep."

"You? Interested in someone? A single someone?" Madison eyed him. "Since when? You're like a monkey in a field of bananas when it comes to women."

"Hey, I'm not that bad."

Madison smirked. "You, cousin, are a Worth and a Worth doesn't settled down unless he's forced to."

"Grandfather is married."

Grandfather's butler, Charles, came out of the house then, asking Madison if she was going to come inside. He didn't even spare a glance toward Daniel. Already, the family freeze had begun. "Not yet, Charles," Madison said. "But could you take my bag in and tell Grandfather I'll be in shortly?"

Charles turned his cold shoulder on Daniel, then did as Madison requested. As soon as the heavy oak door shut, Madison took Daniel's arm and pulled him down the walkway and out of view of the front windows. They strolled along the driveway, past the six-car garage and onto the manicured grounds.

"Don't you know the story about that?" Madison asked as they stepped onto the stone path that wound its way through the prize roses, merely stalks in the winter. "He met Grandmother at a party and dated her for ten years before finally getting married. And that was only because Helen was on the way."

Daniel had forgotten. "You know Grandfather. He's so picky, he makes Morris the Cat look like a pushover."

Madison laughed, her high heels clicking against the smooth pathway stones as she walked. "You can say that again."

Daniel thought back to the other men in his family and realized Madison might have a point. His father hadn't married until late in life, after dating most of his social circle before being forced to settle down. Grandfather, he'd heard, had laid down the law and told Daniel the III to either get married or get out.

Daniel didn't like facing that generational reflection. Like grandfather, like father...like him. Was Daniel just a carbon copy of his paternal relatives? Had he become the one thing he'd vowed *not* to be? A man who'd someday end up married to Lauren Templeton or Mary Jo Williamson, because he'd been told to get a proper wife?

"Don't worry," Madison said, patting his shoulder. "There's still hope for you."

He laughed. Being with Madison had always been good for him. She was the only person in his life besides Lewiston who understood the craziness of being a Worth. "Oh, you think so?"

Muted landscape lights peeked out from the mounds of snow covering the shrubs. Silence coated the estate, as if nothing dared disturb Grandfather's peaceful setting.

"You already turned down a fortune and an easy excuse to get into a woman's bed," Madison said. "I'd say that means the no-commitment buck stops with this generation of Worth men."

Daniel wasn't ready for any kind of commitment—except one to Bellevue for throwing away ninety-three million dollars on a whim.

Though, whenever he thought of Olivia, the insane urge to become a responsible, two-point-five kids kind of guy roared to life. Yet, how could he do that? He had nothing to offer her right now—literally. He wasn't even going to consider commitment, not until he'd proved himself in the real world—the one without a trust fund for a cushion.

"What about you?" he asked. "You're twenty-six, unmarried and not committed to anything."

"I am too." Madison grinned. "My frequent flyer miles."

Daniel put his arm around Madison and steered her toward her Benz. "Well then, do you care to grab a cheap burger with a disinherited millionaire whose got all the job prospects of lame duck?"

Craving-a-Worth
Chocolate-Peanut Butter Candies

6 ounces semisweet chocolate chips
10 ounces peanut butter chips
12 ounces peanuts, shelled

When you're wanting a millionaire, waiting isn't an option. Go after what you want, girls, and while you're at it, end that boxers or briefs debate once and for all. To tempt him to come closer, make these little candies, quick and easy.

Start by melting the chips in a microwave for two minutes on medium (50%). Stir. Cook for one more minute, then stir in the peanuts. Drop by tablespoon onto waxed paper, then let stand till they're as firm as a certain bachelor's awesome anatomy. Then they're ready for enticing a Worth.

CHAPTER THIRTEEN

Olivia was busted.

The ads hadn't worked. She'd opened Pastries with Panache early on Wednesday, the day after the ads featuring Daniel had run, hoping there'd be a line of people outside her door, dying to taste the same treats as the most eligible bachelor in Boston.

People *were* lined up. Unfortunately, across the street. At Sweets without Sin, which was celebrating its grand opening.

Today.

Olivia had seen the empty storefront across from her, craft paper taped over the windows to maintain the suspense about what was going in there. And now, a little over a week before Valentine's Day, a day she'd expected to be busy, they'd unveiled their "Holiday Health" series of soy flour products, throwing a sugar-free wrench into her plans.

"What's with all the people?" Josie swung her purse off her shoulder and stowed it under the counter. "It's like the Trekkies have invaded again."

"Blame it on Atkins," Olivia grumbled, abandoning her masochistic window watching. "Everything over there is six net carbs or less. While we—"

"We take carbs to a new level." Josie finished with a grin of pride. "Come on, sis, it'll work out. It always does, doesn't it? Besides, when I read your tarot last week, it said great things were on the horizon. Trust the tarot, sis. It's never wrong." Josie paused, a finger to her lips. "Well, except when there's an operator error."

"I'd rather trust the bottom line," Olivia said. She pushed a button on the cash register. When the drawer popped open, she held up the few dollars inside. "And this says a storm is brewing if we don't increase sales."

Not just a storm, but a mini typhoon.

Josie slipped on an apron and tied it behind her back. "We'll blow over the scent of our fresh Danishes and before you know it, those former sugar addicts will cross back over to the dark side."

Olivia shook her head and plopped into one of the bar stools. "I don't think so, Josie. I'm out of customers, out of ideas and worse, out of money."

Josie pulled Olivia into a one-armed hug. "You still have me. And that millionaire."

Olivia sighed. She'd never had Daniel Worth to begin with. Not really. "My twenty-four hour millionaire expired."

"Come on, let's cook something. We'll all feel better then." Josie straightened, pushed on the stainless steel door and headed into the kitchen.

Olivia trailed after her and headed for the tall, wide cabinet of dry goods. Like a surgeon prepping for a complicated transplant, she loaded the counter with flour, sugar, baking powder and everything else they'd need for the first recipe of the day.

"Well, you do have one more option," Josie said. She pulled a recipe out of the plastic bin beside the counter and ran a finger down the list of ingredients, double checking as she always did.

In the year since Pastries with Panache had opened, Olivia and Josie had developed a predictable pattern of working together, becoming a human assembly line. They made the same basic pastries every day, then offered special recipes on certain weekdays. After all this time, each of them had memorized the pattern.

Olivia pulled a white cake they'd baked the day before out of the freezer and put it on a revolving cake stand. "What's that?"

"The Frosting on the Cake contest for professional bakers."

"Oh no. No, no, *no.*" Olivia put up her palms at the thought of the annual competition hosted by the Restaurateurs Association. The head chef of a local establishment was supposed to prepare three dishes in one day in front of an audience of spectators and judges. And since she was the one listed on the menu as the head chef, that would mean Olivia would be doing the cooking. That was akin to putting a blind man in charge of aesthetic lighting. "You know I can't do that. *Especially* in public."

"Sure you can." Josie loaded flour into the stainless steel scale, adding until the contents reached the exact weight she needed. "And if you win, it's a fifty thousand dollar prize."

"Fifty thousand?" Olivia had missed that little tidbit when she'd received the entry flyer. The minute she'd seen the words "baking in front of an audience," she'd tossed the thing aside like it was an invitation from *Fear Factor*.

She withdrew a bowl of chocolate buttercream frosting from the refrigerator, then pulled out a long, thin knife to apply it. In seconds, she had a crumb coat on and was starting the final coat.

"It's not just the money. You also claim the title of the best pastry chef in the city of Boston." Josie grinned. "That's the kind of PR they'd hear about on Mars." She laughed. "We could have Martians landing, just to try our tarts."

"I doubt word would spread that far." Olivia mixed green food coloring into a fourth of the remaining frosting, then put it into a piping bag and began laying leaves around the perimeter of the frosted cake. She trailed some of the leaves over the edge, making it look like ivy climbing the sides. "And that's assuming I could even win that thing. You know about those disasters in culinary school, Jo." She mixed some pink into another clump of frosting, then used a second piping bag to top the leaves with flowers. "Still...I could do a lot with fifty thousand dollars."

"*Big* things," Josie said. She measured the sugar, turned the mixer on, then dropped in eggs one at a time, watching the machine swirl them into the dry ingredients.

Josie paused and looked over at Olivia's nearly completed cake. "That's like art, sis. You're amazing with that thing." She waved a hand at the piping bag.

Olivia stepped back, judging her work with a critical eye. She shrugged. "I like to decorate."

"And you're good at it. Your apartment looks like something out of a women's magazine. And this place, well, it's just perfect. Cozy and sweet, all at once." Josie turned the mixer off and skimmed her recipe again. "You really should consider entering the Frosting on the Cake. Because you sure as heck have the frosting part down pat."

"I don't know." Olivia weighed the pros and cons for the hundredth time since Josie had first mentioned the competition months ago, and as they had before, the cons won. As wonderful as the money would be, the chances of her actually winning were slim to zero. "There has to be another option."

"Well, there might be," Josie admitted. "But this is as close to get-rich-quick as you can get. Besides marrying that millionaire, of course."

"I'm not even dating him, much less thinking about marrying him," Olivia said. "Besides, he's not even my—"

The bell over the door jingled. Olivia hurried out to the front of the shop, hoping like hell half the line from across the street had gotten tired of fake sugar and soy flour. Olivia halted mid-step, her breath caught in her throat.

It wasn't a gaggle of customers—it was someone far more dangerous for her arteries.

"Hi." Daniel Worth stood in the doorway, dressed in a navy blue suit, looking a little more rumpled and sleep-deprived than usual.

Usual? How did she know what his usual was? All she knew was what she saw in the gossip pages and in those few hours they'd been together. But still…something lingered in his gaze that told her this wasn't the same Daniel Webster standing before her. He didn't look like the same bachelor she'd read about, nor the same one who'd been on the other end of Josie's lens three short days ago. He seemed weary…almost like he needed a shoulder to lean on.

Or…a woman to take care of him.

Insane thoughts. This was one of the richest and most desired men in the city. He didn't need anything, especially not anything Olivia could give him. Heck, she could barely keep her own head above water, never mind tread for two people's problems.

Yet, some crazy part of her wanted to jump in the deep end with him and take her chances. No doubt about it—Daniel Worth should come with a swim advisory.

"I didn't think—" She cut herself off. "Well, I didn't expect you to come back." Especially not after the way she'd ended things. With a handshake, for Pete's sake, like he was some new acquaintance she'd met at a Chamber of Commerce meeting. And yet, that kiss—that hot, steamy, turn your toes up kiss—hadn't been far from her mind either.

"I had a craving," he said, stepping closer to her. Damn, he had nice eyes. Really deep blue eyes, as vibrant as the ocean after a storm. And teeming with just as much hidden danger.

"I, ah, don't have any cheesecake in the case right now," Olivia said, "but if you come back, I can have one ready later today."

"I don't want cheesecake." Now he was inches away, close enough for her to catch the spicy notes in his cologne. To feel the heat emanating from his body. To reach out and touch him, if she raised her hand just a little bit.

The urge to do that rose within her, strong as a tidal wave.

"How about a Danish?" Her voice squeaked on the last word. Nerves. Nothing more. This man—the wrong man—shouldn't have an effect on her.

But damn it all, he did nonetheless.

"No." A slow, sexy smile curved across his face.

She swallowed. "Uh…muffins?"

"No." Daniel reached out and cradled her hands. His touch sent soothing warmth through her, followed immediately by a heat that flooded her veins so fast, she felt a rush akin to leaping off a building. If he'd been any hotter, she'd need to slip into something more comfortable—like a pair of oven mitts.

"I never said I was craving anything to eat," he said.

"Oh." Olivia opened her mouth, then closed it. "Oh," she repeated. And then she knew. What was more, she knew he wasn't the only one craving something. She may have told herself she didn't want him, wasn't interested in him, but she'd be a liar.

Olivia held her breath, wanting to hear the words. Knowing she shouldn't want them—or him.

"Olivia, I've missed—"

"Oh my God, that's him!" a female voice squealed outside the window. "It's Daniel Worth!"

Before Daniel would get a word out or even better, run like hell, three women rushed into the shop. One hauled a toddler behind her, the towheaded boy struggling to keep up with his mother's frantic race toward the Worth heir. The women shrieked and grabbed one another, as if the trio felt faint at the mere sight of an eligible, wealthy bachelor.

"Get his autograph!" the mom shrieked, still trying to get her reluctant son to come along faster.

"Get his phone number!"

"No, get his *boxers!*" the third one yelled, charging forward, fingers ready to snatch at him.

Daniel's eyes widened. "Hide me," he said to Olivia, only half kidding.

"Sorry." Olivia grinned. "I think the quackers finally caught up to the duck."

Josie's Nuts-for-Him Pecan Pie

1 stick butter
1 cup sugar
1 cup light corn syrup
3 eggs, beaten
1 cup chopped pecans
1 unbaked 9-inch pie shell
1/4 cup pecan halves

I just knew he'd be perfect. He loves pie, he's interested in you—what more do you need for a sign? A UFO to drop from the sky and conk you on the head? Geez. Some people couldn't see a soul mate if they were in an alternate dimension.

Start by preheating your oven to 350 degrees. Melt the butter in a small saucepan, then stir in the sugar and corn syrup (double sweetness, definitely a sign of sweet things to come!). When the sugar has dissolved, add the eggs and then the pecans. Easy-peasy done! Pour it into the pie shell, decorate with the pecan halves, then put it in the oven for one hour, or until it's as firm as your belief in the afterlife.

CHAPTER FOURTEEN

The women rushed him with all the force of the Patriots' first line of offense, but Daniel pivoted quickly, keeping his trousers—and his dignity—intact. "Ladies, ladies," he said. "I appreciate your interest, but—"

"He's a briefs boy!" the first woman shouted, triumphantly jerking up Daniel's suit jacket. "I'm calling the *Enquirer!*"

"Ladies," Daniel tried again, reaching behind himself to loosen the woman's bulldog grip. "*Please.*"

The fan club shoved Olivia to the side. She'd thought of ducking for cover behind the glass counter, but then, watching Daniel nearly get mauled by a pack of wild bachelorettes, she surged forward, straight into the fray.

Not in her store. And not with her millionaire.

"Ladies, Mr. Worth would *love* to chat with you," she said. That got their attention. Three heads swiveled in her direction.

"Go Mickey D's," said a fourth voice—the lone sound of dissent—waving two grubby hands in the direction of the door. "Want fresh fries."

"However," Olivia went on, "he was just getting ready to try one of our menu items. I'm sure, though, that he wouldn't mind chatting with you if you all wanted to sit down and share some goodies with him."

Daniel's gaze connected with Olivia's. He smirked, clearly understanding her diversionary tactics. He crossed to a table and pulled out two of the wrought iron chairs. "Right this way, ladies. May I recommend the Danishes? I hear they're just as delectable as the cheesecake."

He sent another glance Olivia's way, sending with it the heat of a shared memory.

The women shrieked with joy at the offer of a meal with Boston's Most Eligible Bachelor. They scrambled over each other, vying for the seats closest to Daniel at the little round table. The toddler lagged behind, unimpressed by all the hoopla surrounding a stranger, until his mother scooped him up into her lap and snagged the last seat across from Daniel.

For twenty minutes, the Daniel Worth Fan Club ordered nearly every item on the menu, eating and giggling like a bunch of seventh graders who'd snagged backstage passes at a Ricky Martin concert. They went through plates of Danishes, tarts, muffins, coffee and finally, juice and mini chocolate chip cookies for the little one.

Throughout it all, Daniel was a gracious host. He took time to speak to each of the women, nearly causing a mass swooning. He didn't flirt, exactly, but

Olivia noticed he had a way of directing his attention fully on a woman, causing her to flush and stammer.

All her life, Olivia had thought of herself as pretty much immune to anything with testosterone. She'd dated men, and made a lot of bad choices—Keith Manning and his obsession with combing every hair on his body topped that list—but she'd thought she'd become smarter since that and the Sam disaster. Making decisions with her head, not her hormones.

Yet Daniel had an appeal she couldn't deny and knew went way beyond the way he made her insides quiver whenever he directed those deep blue eyes at hers.

Clearly, she had plenty of company in that opinion.

The toddler, who had had enough of the fawning, started banging his hands on the table, causing coffee to slosh and crumbs to bounce onto the floor. "Home!" he shouted. "Home! Home! Home!"

His mother flushed. "I'm sorry. He's impatient."

"No problem," Daniel said with a patient smile. "He probably figured it worked for Dorothy in Oz, why not try it here?" He withdrew a quarter from his pocket, then bent toward the child "Hey, Jonah, do you like magic?"

The little boy paused and gave Daniel a wary look.

"Watch this." Daniel showed him the quarter, then wiped one palm across the other, making the coin disappear.

"Money!" Jonah shouted. "Money! Money!"

"A boy after my own heart," Daniel joked, sending the women into fits of laughter. "Here it is, Jonah." Daniel curled his right hand behind the towheaded boy's ear, then pulled it forward, revealing the silver coin in his palm again.

Jonah blinked, then shoved a crumb-coated fist at his ear. "Money?"

"Want me to do that again?" Daniel asked him. When Jonah nodded, Daniel repeated the trick, entertaining the young boy until he burst into gales of laughter—and the heart of every woman in the room melted.

Finally, when the treats were gone, the woman left as they'd come in, chattering excitedly and flirting shamelessly with Daniel until the door shut.

"Thanks," he said to Olivia. "I owe you for keeping my BVDs safe."

Olivia swallowed. Secretly, she'd been rooting for that woman to get his trousers off. "A smart businesswoman would rather have her customers grabbing for the Danishes than your underwear."

Daniel chuckled, his gaze on hers. He opened his mouth to say something, but Olivia turned away, stacked the empty plates in a pile, then headed toward the kitchen.

Confusion warred inside her—between her brain in the North and everything else in the South. He was sexy, undeniably so, but he was also so much more. He had something she'd never seen in any of the men she'd dated, and definitely not in Keith and his hair fetish. Or Sam and his ongoing admiration for himself.

Yet, even as he followed her into the kitchen, she vowed not to tell him how sweet it had been to see him with the child, how touching it had been when he'd taught the three-year-old the trick, then pretended to be surprised when Jonah pulled a fumbled, obvious version. Because saying any of that would expose a weakness in Olivia—and if there was one thing she refused to be, it was vulnerable.

To anyone.

"Well," she said, "if the Danishes didn't work, I was going to get out the fire hose."

He chuckled. "A little jealous, were you?"

"Not at all." Olivia raised her chin. "I was just protecting my investment."

"Do you mean me? Or the store?"

Olivia gave him a non-commital smile. Damn, he was still amazing and hot and a hundred other things she tried to ignore. Not just in the traditional way, with his broad shoulders and lean waist, but in another way that went straight to the core of her as a woman.

His attention on her was undivided. A heady feeling filled her, like being the lone float in the Macy's Thanksgiving Day parade. "That all depends. Which one is going to give me the better payback?"

He laughed, the sound as rich and hearty as the fresh pot of coffee brewing behind her—and as tempting as that first energizing cup of the day. Unable to resist, Olivia joined in, the laughter coming from some deep part of her that hadn't been used in a long, long time.

A part she'd missed.

This wasn't what she'd bargained for when she'd emptied her checking account on this man. For once, Olivia didn't know what to do. How to act. Whether to push him away or demand he do more of that…that *something* he did so well.

Josie came in through the back door of the shop, fresh flowers in one arm and a bag of perm rods in the other. "How was business today? Wait. Don't tell me." She closed her eyes and pressed a finger to her temples. "You had a crowd in here that couldn't get enough." She opened her eyes. "Am I right?"

"In a way." Olivia grinned at Daniel. "We were practically a male Hooters. With him as our star." She told Josie about the women, glad to be saved by the human bell instead of dealing with the way Daniel had made her feel. She'd revisit that later. Much later.

"Cool," Josie said, eyeing Daniel. "So now you're our new male stud muffin?"

"Uh, I don't think so," Daniel muttered, clearly embarrassed by the title.

Josie put the flowers in a vase she filled with water, then straightened, leaning against the counter. "Well, you should be. It's like this shop is the Bermuda triangle and you're the mysterious force bringing everyone in."

"To drown and never return?" Daniel asked.

Josie laughed. "No, silly. To have that big of an effect, you'd need to be able to disrupt the space-time continuum. I don't think this shop is big enough for that." She tapped her lips. "But it is just the right size for a Millionaire Dating Club. I can see it now—make a love match and get a discount on your wedding cake." Josie turned to Daniel. "Care to bring over a few rich, sexy and single pals?"

Daniel gave Olivia a wry, almost sad smile. The weariness invaded his shoulders again. For a second, she wanted to reach out and take away the weight of worry. She knew that heaviness all too well herself.

"Sorry," Daniel said quietly, "but I'm not a millionaire anymore." He ran a hand along the curved back of one of the chairs, tracing the floral pattern in the wrought iron. "My grandfather and I had a 'disagreement' about my future. Basically I didn't want to go into the family business and so we decided I'd see what poverty felt like."

"You-you did?" Olivia gaped. Beside her, she heard Josie's sharp intake of breath. "Every dime?"

"With my grandfather, it's an all or nothing deal. You either go along with his grand scheme, or you get nothing."

Olivia shuddered to think of someone else calling all the shots in her life. Though she hadn't been a success—yet—she'd rather know the failure was her own instead of another's plan. When she'd gone into business, she'd done it because she had a need to be on her own, to control the reins herself.

Ownership, Olivia realized, was a powerful thing. Now, maybe for the first time in his life, Daniel was taking ownership of his path—and paying a steep price for that choice.

She looked at him, at the pride, peppered with a bit of fear, in his eyes, and felt a surprising respect for this not-so-rich millionaire. "What are you going to do now?"

"Act like your average bum." Daniel grinned. "Nah. Pound the streets, look for a job and live out of a Motel 6. Glamorous, huh?"

"That's quite the step down, isn't it?" The words were out before she could stop them, some inbred reflex passed down by her struggling parents to hate the rich, the corporate America types, who had wiped out most of Mom and Pop land. "I'm sorry. That sounded snotty and mean."

He shrugged, letting the words roll off his shoulders. "Hey, I'd say the same thing."

"You have to excuse us," Josie said, handing each of them a cup of coffee. "We've never been around anyone who gave up that much money *on purpose.* Our dad says his last penny will be pried out of his cold, rigid fingers at the wake."

Daniel laughed. "I think your father and my grandfather would get along very well."

Olivia sipped her coffee and eyed the tall, dark-haired man beside her. When she'd plunked down the sum total of her checking account on his handsome head, she'd never imagined they'd have anything in common. And now they had plenty—financial ruin and the knowledge that they didn't live up to other people's expectations.

When Olivia had first decided to bid on Daniel, she'd expected him to be the person she'd read about in the gossip columns—a bratty, self-absorbed playboy with as much regard for the middle class as your average slug. Clearly there were two sides to Daniel Worth: a public persona and then a private man few people had glimpsed. Olivia's reservations about him began to melt.

She took a step forward, drawn to him in a way she hadn't been before. "That was really brave."

He laughed. "Or really stupid. But, it does leave me free for the first time."

"Freedom? When you're broke, that's an oxymoron," Josie said. "Well, unless you have a lot of Visa cards. Then you're free for thirty days. Forty-five if you get the good grace period."

"To me, being able to succeed or fail on my own is worth the price," Daniel said.

"That I can relate to," Olivia said quietly, thinking of how much it was costing her to succeed… or fail. How much she'd kept secret from the people who loved her, how much she'd shouldered herself instead of sharing the information with Josie. Protecting, as an older sister should. "And admire."

A long second passed between them, punctuated only by the ding of the oven timer. "I better get that," Josie said, putting a set of cooling racks onto the counter. "And you two should, ah, go mind the store." She grinned. "And see what happens when your sun intersects with his Venus."

Which was code, Olivia knew, for "go be alone and deal with all the stuff you're doing a damned good job of avoiding, sis."

"Uh, how about we go grab a snack?" she asked Daniel. Keep his mouth full and then he wouldn't talk to her. Or kiss her. Or push her off that very teeny cliff again.

His interest piqued. "What kind of snack?"

"Pie?"

"I'll follow you anywhere for pie," Daniel said, grinning.

It was just pie, Olivia told herself, as they went out to the front part of the shop where she sliced him a hearty portion of pecan. "Here you go."

"I never pie alone," Daniel said, gesturing toward his dish, that familiar teasing twinkle in his eyes. "Join me."

How tempting that thought was. The pecans crusted on top of the sugary base would be sweet and crunchy. The crust flaky and tender. Every bite one to savor.

Her stomach groaned, putting in its two cents. She looked into Daniel's eyes, and another part of her groaned, too.

He didn't know what he was asking of her. Besides the dessert, there'd be sitting with, looking at him, allowing her thoughts to travel down a one-way street with no room to turn around, back up and forget she'd ever met him.

She'd already put that car in gear, though. Doing anything more would be like adding high octane fuel to an already racing carburetor. "No, not the pecan pie. *Anything* but the pecan pie."

"Don't you like it?"

"Too much. One bite and before you know it, I've inhaled the entire thing. I'm a pecan pie nut." She chuckled. "Pardon the pun."

The smile that crossed his lips had nothing about friendship in it. It went further, much further.

Oh damn. She'd already passed her self-imposed relationship speed limit. Where the heck was a good cop when she needed one?

"I'll have to remember that," Daniel said. "For later."

Oh my. Olivia inhaled, willing herself to stop responding to his every facial gesture like a fish spying a juicy worm. Before she knew it, she'd be hooked—and this playboy would fillet her heart.

Daniel sliced another piece of pie, loaded it onto one of the shop's plates, then handed it to her with a fork. One serving of temptation, with a side of bachelor. "Join me, Olivia. And I promise, if you go after the rest, I'll hold you back. I'm a sucker for pecan, too."

Admitting defeat, Olivia took her pie and the seat across from Daniel. "You are a hard man to resist."

He forked a piece of pie into his mouth and grinned. "Does that mean you're starting to find me irresistible?"

"Nope. Just the pie, Romeo." The lie slid easily off her tongue. To stop herself from saying anything more, Olivia popped a bite into her mouth and nearly cried with pleasure at the sweet delight.

Outside the shop, a group of people had congregated on the opposite sidewalk. For the first time since she'd opened Pastries with Panache, Olivia hoped the customers would go away and leave her to her pie.

Yeah, like that was the only thing that had mouth watering as regularly as a sprinkler system.

Daniel made quick work of his slice, and pushed the empty plate to the side. "You know, you're the first one to say anything nice about me walking out on the money."

"Really?"

He nodded. "Even my own cousin told me I was nuts."

"I know what that's like," she said quietly, fiddling with her fork and avoiding his gaze. "Not having people who believe you can do it."

"Even yourself?"

Olivia circled the plate with her fork, pushing the crumbs to one side. Should she be honest? He was, for all intents, still a stranger. She'd never told anyone, much less someone she didn't know, her fears about the business.

And yet...could a man who'd renounced millions for the chance to make it on his own understand why she'd made the choices she had?

Olivia nearly laughed at thought of the millionaire understanding what the poor girl in the apron was enduring. That was like Prince Charming empathizing with Cinderella's kitchen drudgery.

Maybe that had been the attraction on that ballroom floor. Both of them were suckers for the fairy tale.

"There are days when I think of calling it quits," Olivia said finally. "Sometimes more than once a day."

"Well I'm glad you didn't. You give the rest of us hope that where there's a will, there's a way, as they say." He smiled. "I guess there's a reason that's a cliché."

She shrugged. "At least you can go crawling back to the family millions. My only option is bankruptcy court and the unemployment office for me and my sister. You haven't lived until you've been there."

He chuckled. "I'm trying to avoid both my grandfather and the unemployment line at all costs."

She finished her last bite of pie, then rose, grabbing both empty plates. "More?"

The light in his eyes sent a shiver down her spine. "Oh yeah. And some coffee, too, if you don't mind."

Olivia hustled over to the pie and the coffeepot. She didn't want him to disappoint a customer—even one she had no intention of charging.

Yeah, right. She wanted to see him grin at her again, with that smile that reached all the way to his vibrant blue eyes. In seconds, she had pie and mugs on the table and was already diving in—to the dessert. "Any luck in the job department?"

"I have an interview at four. Considering my resume consists solely of RSVPing to parties, the fact that anyone is talking to me about employment at all is a step up." He sipped his coffee, then leaned back in his chair, a man still powerful in looks and presence, despite what was in his bank account. There was just something about Daniel Worth that told people he was somebody.

Somebody interesting. Somebody powerful. Somebody that Olivia desired as much—no, a hell of a lot more—than a five-speed on the floor.

Josie brushed through the kitchen door, the new flowers trimmed and ready to be replaced in the table vases. Olivia rose to help her, taking half the blooms.

"I heard you mention that you were looking for a job," Josie said. "If you want a career enticing young, single female customers inside our doors, you're welcome here. We pay in crumbs, though." She laughed. "Literally."

"As much as I'd love to be here with Olivia every day—" and something hot pooled in her gut at the words *love, Olivia,* and *every day* "—I think I'm going to try to make it on my own. See what I can do, without a credit card in my pocket."

"I think that's cool," Josie said. "Dangerous, even."

If only Josie knew the truth, she wouldn't be thinking poverty was cool. If she knew…

Where the start-up money had come from. And how quickly the business was hemorrhaging.

No. She could never tell Josie any of that. For the first time in her younger sister's life, Josie had a bit of stability. A job she was excited about. Words like "in the future" and "next year" had started to slip into her vocabulary. And with beauty school in place as a worst-case scenario back-up plan, Olivia could sleep at night, knowing her sister's future was secure.

As for herself, the business was a worry—yes—but there was something exciting about the challenges ahead of her. *That* was what kept her here everyday, kept her from throwing in the towel. The thought that her answer to success could be just around the corner, waiting to be discovered.

"One thing I've learned in the last few days is that I like living on the edge." Daniel draped an arm over the back of the chair and smiled. "Except when Olivia's driving."

She reached over and slugged him. For old times' sake.

"Hey! Here I was, innocently stopping in to ask you to lunch and I get hit."

"Make fun of me behind the wheel, Worth, and you're asking for it." Secretly, she smiled. He'd had three women nearly prostrating themselves at his feet, and yet, Daniel Worth had stayed behind—to ask her to lunch.

It was only her competitive nature. She shouldn't care. Shouldn't feel the thrill of excitement at the thought of being alone with him again. Shouldn't remember exactly what his lips had felt like on hers, and then anticipate more. Much more.

He wasn't the only one who was excited by living on the edge. Heck, right now, she was dangling on a precipice with nothing to break her fall—not a bungee cord, a parachute or even a cheap foam pillow.

And that feeling, Olivia realized, added a sharpness to her days that she'd never found in a "real" job.

"My offer still stands," Daniel said. "Will you go to lunch with me?" He leaned forward, his gaze dancing with a tease. "We'll walk, of course."

"Go," Josie whispered, giving Olivia a nudge. "I can stay. I've got plenty of time before my buzzcut class."

Why not, Olivia thought. She felt the excitement of possibilities revving within her. Who knew what potential waited for her around the Daniel Worth corner.

Or how sweet it might taste.

Two minutes later, Olivia found herself and Daniel bundled up in winter coats and gloves, heading toward a small deli two doors down from the pastry shop. The scent of roast beef and chicken wafted toward them as people went in and out of the small restaurant, their breath hitting the outdoor air like smoke pouring out of a bingo parlor.

When Daniel reached out and took her hand in his, warmth and security flooded her palm, despite the gloves. The deli, Olivia realized, wasn't the only steamy place in Beantown.

Flour-Is-Your-Foe Flourless Chocolate Cake

4 ounces unsalted butter, cut into small pieces
8 ounces bittersweet chocolate, cut into small pieces
5 eggs, separated
Pinch of salt
2/3 cup sugar substitute, divided
Unsweetened whipped cream, for garnish

If you're looking for a culprit to blame all your problems on, take a look at that addictive white stuff. Yes, we're talking about flour, a substance so dangerous, a smart consumer will avoid the baking goods aisle altogether. One whiff and before you know it, you've crossed back over to the sugar side.

Preheat the oven to 325 degrees. Line the bottom of a 10-inch round cake pan with parchment paper, then grease the inside with butter (butter can be your friend, but not flour). In a double boiler, melt the butter and chocolate (hey, it's bittersweet chocolate, the carbs are in control), then whisk in the egg yolks, salt and all but four tablespoons of the sugar substitute. In a separate bowl, whip the egg whites with the remaining sugar, getting them as frothy as a cloud. Fold the egg whites into the chocolate mixture.

Pour into the pan, then bake for one hour and fifteen minutes. Just enough time to make up some pork rind nachos for supper. When the cake is done, immediately remove it from the pan and top with whipped cream. Then invite all your friends over to join the lower net carbs revolution!

CHAPTER FIFTEEN

They never made it to lunch. The mob got them first.

Not the crazed Daniel Worth female fan club, but a group of people chanting "Sugar is Evil" with all the fervor of a cult.

And here Olivia had thought they were a nice, innocent group of potential customers. They weren't customers, they were clearly sharks in sheep's clothing.

"Cut the carbs!" a woman, dressed in head to toe yellow spandex, shouted at Olivia. She hoisted her sign high with pride. On it, a bag of sugar had been vilified, a skull and crossbones marking the innocent white powder as toxic. "Sugar-free is the easy way!"

A man with a waistline spilling over his size-42 jeans rhythmically slapped the side of his own sign, like a drum call to war. "Join the low-carb revolution! Overthrow the sugar kings!"

A conga line formed behind him, echoing his words and marching along in a circle, pumping their signs in one hand and making victory symbols with the other.

"I didn't know I'd need battle armor to take you to lunch," Daniel said.

"What is their problem?" Olivia asked. Daniel put out an arm, offering her shelter, but she ducked her head and blazed her own path through the crowd. "All I want to do is sell my muffins."

"Publicity. Don't you see that animal at work here?" He pointed toward a camera crew from Channel 7 setting up on the corner. A few reporters were already trying to grab comments from the carb-conscious crowd.

"Publicity? But—"

"They're evil, I tell you! Evil!" A scrawny man who looked more like Gollum than a human shook a bony fist in her face. "Throw the Twinkies out!"

Before she could back up from Gollum's continued advance, Daniel had pulled Olivia into the narrow alley between two buildings. She stumbled against his chest, plowing into the warm, hard planes of his torso. A zing went through her and for one crazy second, the world dropped away. The urge to grab him and haul his mouth down to hers roared in her head. Or better yet, haul *all* of him down to the ground.

Maybe there was something to that sugar rush mumbo-jumbo. Because she sure as hell had a craving for a high she couldn't find in a plate of bacon and eggs.

"Your neighbors opened a new store today," Daniel explained, pointing to the Sweets without Sin window, as if their soft collision hadn't happened.

"What better time to have some "protestors" drawing attention to the wonders of going sugar-free, than today?"

"They *planted* this?" Olivia shook her head. "What kind of lunatics do that?"

"Ones who haven't eaten cake in a long, long time."

Olivia laughed.

"Anyway, the media comes down," Daniel continued, "talks to the protestors and the owners of the shop, and whammo, an ad they didn't even have to pay for. On all three networks and in every major newspaper."

"That's just…slimy." Olivia peeked around the brick building and watched the pandemonium for a moment. "But damn, I should have thought of it myself."

Daniel chuckled. "There's still time to get in on the "revolution," he said. "Why not go in front of the media and defend your creations?"

"You mean, counter-attack?" Hmm. Almost as good an idea as starting her own revolution. The rush of a challenge roared through her veins, quickening her pulse. Olivia nodded. "Sounds like a damned good idea."

He grinned, clearly impressed by her risk-taking. "Be sure to give out some of those Danishes while you do it." He winked. "Ready?"

As much as one could be ready for battling people who considered one of her main ingredients poison. She drew herself up. "Let's do it."

She and Daniel made their way back down the sidewalk, hurrying past the white-foods denying mob. But they weren't fast enough. They'd almost reached the shop when they were spotted by an eagle-eyed "Flour is Fattening" sign toter.

"Get them, before they go into that den of sugar!" screamed the woman in spandex, wagging her finger and rushing toward them. "They know not what they do to their waistlines!"

Several people turned and started running, signs thrust forward like javelins. "I think we should—" Olivia began.

"*Run,*" Daniel finished, grabbing her hand before she could protest and hauling her into the shop just before a "Eat Meats, not Sweets!" screamer thrust his steak-scented words inside.

"What the heck is going on out there?" Josie asked. "Are those women back for their millionaire?"

"They're here to protest the evils of our wares," Olivia said. "Apparently, chocolate cake is contributing to the decline of the nation."

"Or the expansion," Daniel quipped.

Josie laughed. "That's what the big hullabaloo is about? I figured it was either an alien abduction or a dog-eat-dog race for the position of Worth arm candy."

"Arm candy?" Daniel asked. "Well, last I checked, there was a vacancy." He turned a teasing smile toward Olivia. "Interested in the job?"

"Not one bit." Olivia told herself she didn't care if that particular position was open. She needed to keep her eye on the business, not the firmness of Daniel Worth's rear end. Especially when she was at war.

A war she intended to win. The business meant too much to her to let it go down in a flurry of soy flour and wheat bran.

"Give me your apron," Olivia said, gesturing to Josie. "And a plate of the Danishes."

Josie undid the white strings and tossed her apron over to Olivia. "Why? Are you going to start a food fight? That's probably not the best thing to do on a day when your moon is out of alignment. You could end up with a muffin in the wrong place."

"Nope, not a food fight. I'm taking on the revolution. And maybe creating one of my own." She slid the apron on, then accepted the plate of pastries Josie handed her. A deep breath, then Olivia headed toward the door, ready to take on the flourless world.

"You want some company?" Daniel asked.

For a brief second, she wanted to say yes. She wanted to rely on him, to accept the shelter of his arms. But no—that was what she'd done with Sam. And in the end, his "help" had been nothing more than a gimmicky ad campaign to get him into her pants, leaving her heart high and dry.

Relying on others only threw her off a well-planned track. The last thing Olivia needed right now was to be derailed.

She didn't need Daniel Worth. Or anyone else.

"I'm a big girl," Olivia said. "I can do this on my own."

Then she stepped out into the fray, armed only with twelve-hundred calories of strawberry-filled weapons.

Olivia's Not-Really-Lethal Danishes

1 envelope dry yeast
3/4 cup milk, warm (about 110 degrees)
1 egg, lightly beaten
1/4 cup sugar
1 teaspoon salt
1 teaspoon vanilla extract
2 1/2 cups all purpose flour
1/2 pound unsalted butter, cold
raspberry jam
egg wash (one egg beaten with two teaspoons milk)
sugar

Things outside are starting to boil into a frenzy, so you better arm yourself with something that will calm the mob. Start by sprinkling the yeast in the milk and letting it sit for five minutes, until the yeast is bubbly and ready to go to work. Whisk in the milk, egg and sugar.

Using a pastry cutter, cut the butter into the flour until you end up with large crumbs (almost as crumb-y as your business is going right now). Fold the dry ingredients into the wet, mixing until the flour is moist.

Cover with plastic wrap and refrigerate overnight. Everything looks better in the morning, including dough. Now you're going to put in the layers, creating a dough that's light and fluffy (hopefully the problems outside are getting lighter, too). On a lightly floured surface, roll out the dough into a rectangle that measures about one foot by two feet. Fold the dough in thirds, then turn it and fold it in half. Roll out again to the same size as before and repeat the rolling process. There—nice, flaky layers ready to be refrigerated again for another 20 minutes.

Preheat the oven to 350 degrees. Roll the dough into a rectangle again, cut into six even pieces and spread filling across the top. Form the pastries by bringing the opposite corners to meet in the center. Allow to rise for a half hour.

Brush with egg wash, sprinkle with sugar, then bake on a parchment-paper lined tray for 20 minutes. When you're done, you've got the perfect ammunition for a little bakery battle.

Chapter Sixteen

"That had to be the sexiest thing I've ever seen," Daniel said when Olivia returned twenty minutes later, bearing an empty plate and a triumphant smile.

"Sexy?" She laughed and headed into the kitchen, with Daniel close behind. Josie remained out front, tending to a window display, which left the two of them alone.

Very alone.

The swinging door slowly came to a stop. Warm silence surrounded them, scented with citrus and chocolate.

Olivia put the plate in the sink, then filled it with warm water. *Stay busy with work, so you don't get busy with him.*

"I don't consider dispensing breakfast treats sexy," she said. The small victory *had* felt good, though. The thrill of taking the crowd on, then turning the reporters' heads with some baked delights, still pumped in her blood.

Daniel took a step forward and caught a tendril of her hair between his fingers. He was behind her, his breath a whisper on her neck, warmer than the heated water coursing over her hands. Heat of a whole other kind raced in her. "You out there, taking on the media. No prisoners, no thought of defeat. That kind of confidence should be bottled."

"Confidence?" She pivoted and snorted in disbelief. "I was shaking in my boots, terrified the reporters were going to ask—" She cut off her sentence, shaking her head. She wouldn't admit that to Daniel—or anyone. "Anyway, it wasn't confidence. More stubbornness."

"Well, you did a damned good job either way." Daniel moved closer. The sink was behind her, leaving no room to back up, to distance herself from his approach. She should have run, but she stayed, as rooted to the spot as a hundred-year-old maple.

There'd been a reason she'd quacked her quacker when she passed by Daniel's house on that tour bus.

Because the man she'd studied with the intensity of college Calculus was fascinating. Gorgeous. Cut with more facets than a crystal vase.

Despite all her business intentions and non-involvement resolutions, she wanted him. Damn. When it came to the war between her brain and her hormones, her cerebellum was clearly outnumbered.

Only a few inches of heated air, filled with the intoxicating scents of chocolate, lemon and cinnamon, separated them. He circled her waist with his arms, reaching behind her back to grasp the strings holding the apron. Daniel's gaze locked with hers.

Deep and blue, brimming with the same dark heat running through her veins.

Resistance was futile.

She nodded, just once, a slight whisper of movement. A knowing smile curved across his lips. He tugged one side, then the other, releasing the white cotton until it hung loose about her neck.

Olivia inhaled, her mind a jumble. The scene outside, the problems inside, everything disappeared from her mind. Everything except the deep blue of Daniel's eyes and the tender heat in his touch.

"I…" She tried to get a word out, but nothing came. Never had she met a man who could take such complete control of her faculties, like a testosterone-filled tranquilizer.

"Me too," he whispered. Then he grabbed the edges of the apron in two tight fists and tugged it gently over her head. His hands skimmed down her sweater, brushing the edge of her breasts, sending a zing of pleasure through her.

Oh, God. More of that. Please.

"You are…amazing."

"I'm not—"

He pressed a finger to her lips. "Don't. Let me admire you."

"But—"

He ticktocked the finger, gliding against her lips in a long, slow movement that nearly made her cry with desire. *Kiss me,* she wanted to scream, but still, she resisted, her brain reluctant to give up the fight…yet.

"You've had a hard day and I think you need a break," Daniel said. "Let me give it to you."

It was clear he wasn't talking about boosting her benefits package with an extra vacation day. Her mind raced with images of all kinds of benefits— most of them based in a bedroom, not a boardroom. "A break?" Her voice squeaked.

Without a word, Daniel hoisted her onto the countertop and slid himself into the space between her legs. He cupped her chin, then brought his lips to hers. He didn't kiss her, just teased along the edges, sure and easy. "Open sesame," he whispered.

She did. He had asked nicely, after all.

Daniel slipped his tongue inside, urging her to respond. His fingers glided through her hair, kneading the sensitive places along the base of her skull. Desire ignited inside Olivia and she surged forward, wrapping her arms around his neck, pressing her pelvis to his. Roaring fire blazed inside her, demanding to be quenched.

Now. On the counter, on the floor. Anywhere that he was willing, ready—and able. Olivia wasn't about to be picky at a moment like this.

She stopped caring if he was all wrong for her. Stopped caring if the business needed her or she was crazy to get involved with a man who didn't just come from the other side of the tracks—he owned the whole damned railroad.

His kiss deepened, fueling her need even more. With a jerk, she tugged his shirt out of his pants, ranging her hands up his back. Firm, hard muscles flexed beneath her palms as he reached to tug her even closer. She nibbled at his lower lip, then groaned when he did the same back to her. *Good. So good.*

Now, now, now, her body screamed. *Find a bed and get him in it. Before I self-combust.*

"My car is, ah, out back," Olivia managed. "Let's go to my place. It's closer."

Daniel filled the centimeter of space between their mouths with a sexy grin. "I'm not sure you're in any condition to drive."

She laughed, the sound deep and throaty, resonating in her chest. "I'll manage. Just keep your hands off my stick shift."

He quirked a brow at her. "Is there something I should know?"

Olivia gave him a jab. Albeit, a nicer, softer jab than before, but a jab all the same. "Let's leave a few surprises for my bedroom," she teased.

"Mmm…I like surprises. Especially ones in the bedroom." He scooped her off the counter and into his arms. She barely had time to shout out to Josie that she was taking a *long* lunch break before Daniel had opened the back door with his foot and carried her to her car, parked in the alley space behind Pastries with Panache.

It took less than eight minutes to zoom down Atlantic Avenue, onto Route 3, then Storrow Drive, until they reached The Fenway building on Westland Drive. She nabbed a parking space on the street, parallel parked her Volvo like it was a loaf pan she was shoving into the oven, then hopped out and grabbed Daniel's hand, leading him through the lobby and up to the fourth floor.

"Nice building," Daniel said. "Though it's going by in a blur."

"You can enjoy the view later. Much later." Olivia slid her key into her door and unlocked it before he had time to draw another breath.

Still holding his hand, she rambled off the rooms as they barreled through the small apartment. "Entry, kitchen, bath is down there to the left, living room, then…" she opened a door on her right, "the bedroom."

"My favorite," Daniel said.

She gestured toward the double mattress. "Not enough room for a king in here, unfortunately."

"Still plenty of room for what I have in mind." Then Daniel lowered his mouth to hers, capturing her once again in a dizzying kaleidoscope of sensation. She tipped her head back, allowing him full access to her throat, the V opening of her shirt, heck, anything he wanted.

It had been so long. Too long, Olivia realized, since she'd been with a man. Especially with one who was so *good*. Too many months of working hard, of worrying about bottom lines and mark-up percentages. She needed this.

Needed *him*.

Olivia slid her hands under the shoulders of his suit jacket, pushing it back and off his arms. It fell into a puddle on the floor behind him. She reached for his tie, tugging at the knot to loosen it, then slipping one maroon end out of the other. With a final yank, she slid the Brooks Brothers silk off his neck and tossed it aside. Where it landed, she didn't look and didn't care.

Daniel's hands went under her shirt, cupping at the soft lace of her bra, his palms covering the fullness with warmth. His thumbs rubbed across her nipples, igniting an instant explosion. She groaned and arched backward, thrusting her hips against his. He was hard. Ready.

And so was she.

Olivia took a step backward, pulling Daniel with her. They tumbled onto the bed, landing on the dark blue comforter in a tangle of body parts and kisses. Two pairs of shoes dropped to the floor. She wrenched at his shirt, pulling the rest of it out of the waistband so hard, the bottom button popped off, went flying and pinged against the window.

"I see you have sex like you drive," Daniel said.

"Uh-huh. Fast, hard. And good." She grinned, then reached for his pants.

"Fast isn't always better," he murmured, pushing her gently onto her back. He straddled her, then raised her shirt, exposing skin and lace to the warm air. "Patience, Olivia, is a virtue."

"I'm not worried about my virtues right now." She tried again to grasp his trousers, but he blocked her, taking her wrists in one hand and holding them above her head. The feeling of losing control, of being the one in submission, roared through her veins. It was scary—as scary as having someone else behind her Volvo's wheel—and at the same time, exhilarating—like a downward spiral in a toboggan.

She wanted Daniel in her now. And Olivia was a woman used to getting what she wanted, when she wanted it.

His teasing nibbles made her feel like a dieter who was forced to sniff the chocolate cake instead of inhaling it.

Then, an instant later, the cake was there for the taking. Daniel reached forward with his free hand and flicked open the front clasp on her bra. He drew in a deep, appreciative breath. "Beautiful."

The air whispered against her skin. Olivia flexed beneath him, pressing her pelvis to his. "Stop admiring them, Picasso, and do something." But there was no anger in her voice.

"As you wish, milady," he murmured, lowering his head to kiss her. He trailed his mouth along her neck, above the fine bones leading to her shoulders, then down, down, down, slow and easy, to one of the two areas screaming for his attention. Her nipples were stiff and sensitive, and she nearly cried when he brushed against them with his chin. The rough stubble of his five o'clock shadow tingled along the nerve endings, making her moan with want.

Beneath him, she raised her hips, seeking what wasn't there. Yet. She twisted in his grip, wanting him to hold tighter and at the same time, let go, so she could torture him the same way.

Then her nipple was in his mouth, and he was sucking at it, stoking the fire of sensation with a butane, flame-throwing tongue. She cried out, all but shouting his name, her body bucking and thrashing as the orgasm rolled through her, spreading fireworks into her veins, her muscles. Everything, everywhere, rushing in a rippling blur over her skin.

Daniel lifted his head to look at her, blue eyes teasing and dark. "And that was just one breast," he said in a low, husky voice. "Imagine what I can do with the rest."

"I don't want to imagine." Olivia squirmed out of his grasp, then yanked her jeans off and tossed them to the floor along with her shirt and bra. She kneeled on the bed, wearing nothing more than a pair of white lace panties, and smiled. "Now it's your turn."

"Just drive the speed limit," he said. "I don't like to rush this part."

"Hush up. And give me the wheel." She grabbed his belt buckle, undoing it in a split second and then moving on to the clasp of his trousers. In seconds, she had his zipper open, his pants off and a view of some very nice BVDs. "Hmm…what does this say about you?" she asked, running a finger beneath the elastic, teasing against the flat expanse of his waist. "That you wear briefs instead of boxers?"

"It says if you don't take these off in the next five seconds, the whole debate will be a waste of time."

She laughed, then reached for his waistband with both hands, ready to tear his underwear in half if necessary.

"Wait," Daniel said, putting a hand over hers.

"*Wait?* For what?" She looked into his eyes and saw he was serious. The fire of desire still burned in the blue depths, but it had been pushed aside by something far deeper.

Daniel raised himself up on his elbows. "Olivia, this is going to sound nuts."

"It already does. You have a mostly naked—and willing—woman in a bed with you and you want to take a *break?*"

"You've read about me; you know my reputation," he began.

"Yeah, but I don't care about that right now. Besides, it's the gossip column. How accurate is it?" She reached for his briefs but once again he stopped her.

"Things do get exaggerated there, but..."

When he didn't finish, she rolled off him and onto her side of the bed. "But what?"

"But..." Daniel reached out and traced a finger along her thigh. The touch sent a shiver tingling through her, reminding her that only two teeny scraps of fabric separated her from Nirvana. "But then I met you."

His words—serious words—hit her with the force of a taser gun. They were the kind of words she tried to stay away from. The kind that implied bigger things than a night in her bed. Olivia Regan might be a risk taker with her bank account, but when it came to her heart, she was as leery as an agoraphobic in a mall. "You met me? And?"

"And I wanted something different." He circled her knee. "Something more than I've had before."

Olivia's heart thudded in her chest. Things were moving rapidly past a sexy romp and into territory she'd vowed not to visit. "Meaning?"

Daniel sat up, grabbed the knitted afghan off the wingback chair and draped it over her, drawing the brightly colored fabric closed. "Meaning I don't want a one-night stand."

She grinned, trying to tease him to return to where they'd been five minutes ago. "Who said we'd only do this once?"

Though she joked about it, Olivia was touched. The tender way he'd covered her up, the way he said he wanted more, with that slight hint of vulnerability in his voice…

This wasn't the Daniel Worth she'd thought she knew. And it wasn't the Daniel Worth they wrote about in the papers.

He was a man who wanted more out of her than she was willing to give. And if there was one thing that Olivia couldn't afford right now, it was more of herself.

"I want you, Olivia, more than I want to breathe," Daniel continued. "But you're not the kind of woman a guy like me should just sleep with." He pulled on his pants, tucking in his shirt as he did.

She had to ask, had to make sure he hadn't pulled away for another reason. "Because I'm not rich? Not one of your 'kind?'"

He laughed and took a step forward, drawing her up and into the circle of his arms. Beneath her bare feet, the wood laminate floor was cold, but everything else that touched Daniel was warm. Very warm. Desire still pulsed in her veins. But it was quickly being cooled by the confusing jumble of emotions running through her.

"You definitely aren't one of my kind. But I mean that in a good way."

"How is that good?"

He cupped her chin, drawing her gaze to his. "You expect more out of me. And what's worse, you make me want to give more to you." He shook his head and let out a sigh. "The problem is, I don't have a lot to offer right now."

"I'm not asking—"

He grabbed his tie, then his suit jacket, draping them over his arm. "You don't have to. Simply by being who you are, you make a man want to deserve you." Then he placed a quick, chaste kiss on her lips, picked up his shoes and walked out her door.

Leaving Olivia confused, cold and wishing he hadn't just touched some place deep in her heart. Because, right now, she would have much rather had him in her bed, touching another much more needy—and far less vulnerable—place.

Daniel's The-Deal-Is-Sealed Phyllo Pockets

3/4 cup apples, chopped
3 tablespoons apple jelly
3 amaretto cookies, crushed
3 sheets phyllo pastry
4 teaspoons margarine, melted

You've sealed the deal you wanted, now it's time to celebrate with a quick treat—especially one you can share with someone sweet (or maybe a little tart). Preheat the oven to 350 degrees. Mix the first three ingredients together.

Cut the pastry into 24 squares, covering the pile of squares with a damp dish towel to prevent the phyllo from drying out like your bank account. Lay one square of pastry down, brush with margarine, then place another on top, on the diagonal. Brush top pastry with the melted margarine, then fill with a teaspoon of apple mixture. Pinch the edges together (in a shape that ironically resembles a money bag).

Arrange your twelve phyllo money bags on a greased baking sheet. Bake for 5-8 minutes, until they're as golden as your intentions. Okay, you're a guy and your intentions aren't golden at all, but there's always hope that even a bachelor can change his errant ways.

CHAPTER SEVENTEEN

He'd done the impossible.

Daniel had found a job and he'd done it without relying on anyone in his family or his circle of friends. He didn't know why he felt such a giant measure of pride at the accomplishment. Hell, sixteen-year-old kids did it every day and here he was at twenty-eight, filling out his first W-4 form and feeling like he'd just climbed to the top of Mount Everest.

"I'll see you tomorrow," Henry Matthews, the managing editor of *Boston* magazine said as he rose to shake his new writer's hand. "And you better make that column a good one. I'm giving you a big shot here, Worth."

"I understand, sir. I appreciate the chance."

Henry returned to his chair, leaning back in it and eliciting a sharp squeak of leather protest. "I have to say, those writing samples you showed me were some of the best I've ever seen. You say you've never been published?"

"It, ah, wasn't in my career plans at the time." He didn't mention how deviating from the Worth image, even with a short story in *Ellery Queen*

196

magazine, would have sent Grandfather running for his nitroglycerin pills.

Henry nodded. "That, I understand. I was going to be a jazz musician when I grew up. But my lips couldn't take the pressure." He chuckled. "Now my sax is in the closet and the closest I get to music is reviewing the latest Nelly CD." He made a face, showing what he thought of modern music. "Well, either way, I think your degree and your exposure to the restaurants in town will give this piece a unique slant. Not gossipy, but more an educated insider's view."

"That's what I'm planning."

"Plus, there's a bonus in having your name in our magazine, especially after we named you 'most eligible'."

Daniel chafed under the label. It felt tawdry, cheap. If he was going to prove he could make it on his own, he needed to do it without dragging his pedigree behind him. "I'd rather use a pen name, if that's okay."

"A pen name? Are you nuts? Just saying *Worth* can get you a table at the best restaurant in this city. Not to mention what it could do for our newsstand sales."

Daniel leaned forward in his seat, steepling his fingers beneath his chin. "This may sound crazy, but I want to see if I can do it on my own. As a regular Joe Schmoe."

Henry snorted. "Yeah, it is nuts. But it's your funeral." He shook his head, thinking for a second.

"All right. We'll try it your way. If it doesn't work, you go back to being a Worth."

That was not in Daniel's plans at all, but he didn't tell that to Henry Matthews. Instead, he shook hands with the man, said goodbye, then headed down the hall to Human Resources.

After leaving Olivia's apartment yesterday, Daniel had pounded the pavement for the rest of the day, looking for a job and facing rejection at every turn. He was too overqualified to salt fries at McDonald's, too underqualified to be an office temp and too manly to work in the ladies' coats department at Macy's.

By the end of the day, Daniel had known exactly how Goldilocks had felt in the three bears' home.

He'd spent another, even more restless night at the Motel 6, then finally admitted he wasn't going to get any sleep, not while the image of Olivia, naked and wanting him, stayed in his mind. He'd done the right thing, he knew that.

It was just a stupid thing to do. Something no warm-blooded man in his right mind would do. As Henry Matthews had said, Daniel was nuts.

Instead of doing what he really wanted to do— taking the first train back to Olivia's apartment— Daniel got to work. He refused to return to her until he became more than an unemployed former playboy.

However, nothing in the classifieds fit with the skills of a wayward bachelor who'd just walked away from a fortune. In the margins of the paper, he'd listed his talents and areas of expertise, but ended up with a pitifully short list: eating, drinking and carousing. It had taken three more hours of brainstorming before he'd found a way to change his playboy lifestyle into a job possibility.

A *single* job possibility.

Which is what had brought him here on a cold February morning a little more than a week before Valentine's Day, to the offices of *Boston* magazine. To a last ditch effort at finding employment that didn't involve registration desks, ledgers or double beds.

At the thought of the last, the image of Olivia Regan sprang to his mind like a daisy in a field of dandelions. Suddenly, he wanted out of the magazine's offices. To see Olivia and share this victory with her.

He walked into the small Human Resources office at the end of the hall and handed his completed W-4 form to the receptionist. She read it over, made sure he'd signed it, then glanced up. "Are you going to be working here now?"

"Yeah, but on a freelance basis," Daniel told her.

She glanced down at the W-4 again, and then back up at him, the interest decidedly stronger in her gaze. "Daniel Worth? Are you *that* Worth?"

"No," Daniel said. A partial lie because he certainly wasn't the same Daniel Worth from a week ago. "Sorry."

"Oh." She tossed his form into her inbox, then turned back to her computer, shunning him as a lesser Worth.

Clearly, shedding millions had made him less attractive. Daniel didn't care; in fact, he didn't give a damn what anyone thought about him. The only reaction he cared about was a certain pastry chef's.

As soon as he hit the cold, bright street, Massachusetts Avenue's crowded presence slammed into him. The blare of car horns, the sick-sweet smell of exhaust, the ambling shuffle of college students heading in and out of the neighborhood delis. A courier on a bike dodged traffic with the courage of a gladiator, zipping down the street and taking his chances among the cell-phone distracted Beemers and SUVs.

Daniel barely paid attention to any of them. He strode down the sidewalk toward the T station, weaving his way among the commuters and down the concrete stairs like a human ping pong ball. In the past few days, he'd learned how public transportation worked, and realized he liked it more than being chauffered around in a limo.

This was freedom, albeit freedom with a decided odor.

"Mr. Worth! Wait!"

Daniel pivoted and saw Lewiston, huffing and puffing his way through the Mass Ave. train station. "Lewiston? What are you doing here?"

"Trying to find you, sir." He stopped, then bent over at the knees, drawing in several deep breaths. Despite the run, Lewiston's black suit, white shirt and gray-striped tie were as impeccable as ever. Daniel bit back a chuckle. He'd always suspected his butler carried a dry cleaner in his pocket.

"How did you track me down here?" Daniel asked. "In the subway, of all places?"

Lewiston straightened, his lean frame easily topping Daniel's height by a few inches. "It wasn't easy. I've been looking for days and just happened to see you when I was driving."

For a second, panic twinged in his gut. Was Grandfather sick? Had something else happened? "Why are you looking for me?"

"Because I wanted to make sure you were all right, sir." Lewiston looked surprised that Daniel had even asked the question. He reached into his inside breast pocket, pulled out a crisp white handkerchief and dabbed at his forehead.

"I'm fine," Daniel said. "In fact, I just got a job."

"A job? Doing what?"

"Writing for *Boston* magazine. As a freelancer to start, but that's okay with me."

"You're...writing?"

"Yep. For pay."

Lewiston's face lit up and a grin spread from ear to ear. He shook his head in amazement, then drew in a breath before connecting with Daniel's gaze, a shimmer in his eyes. "I'm proud of you."

A crowd of business commuters passed by them, chatting on cell phones as they rushed to catch the next Orange Line train, which barreled into the station just then with a whoosh and a high-pitched screech of brakes. For Daniel, the subway could have been a tomb for all he noticed. He stared at

Lewiston, surprised and touched by the personal admission.

"It's all your doing, you know," Daniel said quietly. "You fed me all that Shakespeare when I was a kid and now all I can think about is writing my own stories."

Lewiston grinned. "*Et tu, Brute?*"

Daniel chuckled. "Well, let's wait and see if *Boston* magazine likes it. I could end up being a flop."

"I don't think so, sir. You're going to do just fine."

For some strange reason, Lewiston's endorsement hit Daniel square in the chest. This was his butler, for Pete's sake, the man who had hung up his coat and shined his shoes for the last twenty-eight years.

Yet, despite the employer/employee relationship, Daniel had always thought of Lewiston as someone more—maybe because he had spent more time with Lewiston than with his own blood relatives.

Lewiston had been the one to teach him the Golden Rule. Lewiston had been the one who sat with him after school in the kitchen, the two of them dunking Oreos in milk and twisting the tops to eat the soggy middles. Lewiston had been the one who taught him how to fight a bully and how to protect an underdog.

Over the years, he'd used Lewiston as a barometer for his behavior. If Lewiston approved, Daniel figured it was the right thing to do. "Thanks, Lewiston. That means a lot to me."

The other man nodded, then adjusted his tie as if the words made him uncomfortable. "Are you doing all right? Do you have enough money?"

"I'm fine," Daniel repeated. "I refuse to use any of my credit cards, assuming they aren't canceled already, and be beholding to my grandfather. I don't have a lot of cash left but I have a job; it'll work out." He grinned. "Remind me next time I abandon my inheritance to stop at the ATM first."

Lewiston didn't laugh. "You can still come back, you know. If you come home with me now, I'm sure your grandfather will forget the whole thing. Just say you're sorry—"

"No."

Lewiston considered him for a long moment. "You're determined to do this, aren't you?"

"I don't want my grandfather laying out my future like an expert at Mapquest. Not anymore."

"Sir, if you'll pardon me a question..."

"Anything, Lewiston, you know that."

"Why?"

Daniel looked around, at the ordinary people going to ordinary jobs. None of them had an inheritance waiting for them, or expectations of being handed millions. They were working for their own money. Working hard, if their technology juggling and hurried rush for the next train were any indication.

What had Daniel accomplished in his life thus far? Not a hell of a lot. Until he'd met Olivia, he hadn't thought about it—because he hadn't stepped out of that insular, sycophant world of the rich. Now that he'd had a taste of Olivia's world, he hated what he'd been—a spoiled, lazy man who hadn't committed to anything more complicated than a cologne. Maybe now, out here, among the "ordinary" people, he could find a way to be someone else. A better someone.

Lewiston stood beside him, waiting for an answer.

"Because for the first time, I'm ashamed of who I am. Of the excess in my life." Daniel stepped to the right as an incoming rush of passengers made their way past the two men. "And...I met someone who made me want more."

"Olivia?" Lewiston's blue-gray eyes told him he'd figured it all out. "I'd hoped as much."

"She's as far from my "crowd" as Texas is from China. Grandfather would join a nudist colony before he'd support me being with an "outsider."

Stick with your own kind, Grandfather had always said, *because if they're already rich we can be sure they won't try to suck the family fortune dry. And if they do, there's something there to take when we sue them.*

"I loved a woman like that once," Lewiston said quietly. "A long time ago."

The thought of Lewiston having a romantic life outside of his employment in the Worth household surprised Daniel. It shouldn't have—Lewiston was a good-looking man in his early fifties who was well read and damned hard to beat at Scrabble. Yet, in all the years Daniel had known him, Lewiston had never mentioned a woman. "What happened?"

A harried young mother pushing a stroller with a shrieking toddler rushed past them to catch the next train. As she did, the overfilled diaper bag on her shoulder swung into Daniel's side, hitting hard and low. She just kept going, oblivious to the damage a full can of formula could do to a man's kidneys.

"Let's get out of here," Daniel said. "It's like a war zone."

Lewiston chuckled. "Good idea, sir. I'm double-parked on Mass Ave. anyway."

The two of them headed up the stairs, squeezing past commuters and dodging swinging brief-cases. Just as Parking Control was coming down the sidewalk, Lewiston hopped behind the wheel of his Taurus and popped it into gear. Daniel shut his door and settled in against the gray cloth seats.

"Where to, sir?" Lewiston raised a brow in question. "To Olivia?"

"You read my mind."

Lewiston nodded and slipped into butler mode again, driving efficiently but silently, waiting for his employer to speak.

"What happened? With the woman?" Daniel asked when they'd left the congestion of Mass Ave.

"She..." Lewiston paused as he came to a red light. "She left."

"Why?"

Lewiston glanced over at Daniel and said nothing for a long moment. Daniel got the distinct feeling that his butler was weighing how much he was going to share. The light turned green, prompting the driver behind them to beep a reminder. Lewiston jerked back into professional mode and stepped on the gas. "She had other things she wanted to do," he said.

Daniel wanted to press him, but knew from experience that Lewiston wasn't one to share details about his life, no matter how many times Daniel asked. When Daniel had been nine, he'd asked Lewiston a hundred times to tell him about the day Lewiston had come to work for the family and why he'd picked the Worth family above all others. But Lewiston had deferred the question with a vague, "because it was a good family to work for."

The only peek Daniel had ever had into Lewiston was the weekends he'd spent at the butler's family home. There, Lewiston became someone else—someone who felt relaxed enough to toss a ball with Daniel in the front yard, to shout at the Pats while the two of them sat on the threadbare plaid sofa and stuffed themselves to the gills with potato chips and pizza.

When Daniel entered his teen years, though, those visits had stopped. Lewiston wouldn't confirm it, but Daniel knew Grandfather had intervened. Undoubtedly, Grandfather wasn't pleased that his pride and joy was chomping on Domino's and filling his head with NFL stats.

In one day, Lewiston went back to being simply an employee. A business-like wall had sprung up between them, marked by the butler refraining from calling Daniel by his given name and switching instead to the impersonal "sir."

Daniel had told himself it didn't matter, but it had. That was one of the first of Grandfather's machinations into his life—and far from the last.

"Do you need anything, sir? Clothing? Money?" Lewiston asked as he turned onto Atlantic Avenue.

"I'm fine," Daniel told him for the third time. Though he could use more than the clothes on his back and the few cheap items he'd picked up at Filene's Basement, he didn't want to jeopardize Lewiston's job by having him sneak out a suitcase.

"I really wish you'd reconsider," Lewiston said as he slowed for another light. "You're throwing away an awful lot."

"But I'm gaining just as much."

""To gain that which is worth having, it may be necessary to lose everything else." "Lewiston turned toward Daniel. "Bernadette Devlin Mcaliskey in *The Price of My Soul.*"

Daniel chuckled. As always, Lewiston had a literary lesson for him. Somedays, Daniel felt like his whole childhood had revolved around the best in literature: Austin, Faulkner, Twain. It had given him a love for the written word that he'd never given up, despite Grandfather's attempt to mold him into the perfect left-brained businessman. Daniel would rather read *War and Peace* for the twentieth time than analyze a profit and loss statement.

Grandfather called that attitude laziness. Lewiston just smiled and handed Daniel a copy of Dickens.

They reached Olivia's store and Lewiston parked along the curb. He got out, locking the vehicle with the button on the door because the car was so old, it had rolled off the assembly line before the dawning of remote controls. Guilt twinged in Daniel's chest. One of the things he'd wanted to do this year was gift Lewiston with a new car for his birthday. Which he would have undoubtedly refused, but which Daniel would have insisted he keep.

He owed Lewiston, not for the work he'd done, but for what Lewiston had given him beyond a love for literature. Something Daniel had never been able to name, quantify or even vocalize with his butler. Whatever that something was, Daniel kept trying to repay with bigger and bigger gifts every holiday.

Then again, the gifts weren't really Daniel's to give. And the money wasn't his either. He wasn't giving Lewiston anything *he'd* actually bought. It was all coming out of the Worth allowance.

Which came with strings that Daniel had severed. This February twenty-first, Lewiston wasn't getting a new car—or hell, even a pine tree air freshener—until Daniel actually had a paycheck. Then he'd go really wild and maybe get him two green felt trees.

Whoo-hoo.

"This Olivia," Lewiston said as they stepped onto the sidewalk. "I like her. She's good for you, sir, if I may say."

Daniel grinned. "You may. I agree completely. Though I'm not sure she would, at least right now." He thought of how he'd last left Olivia—in her apartment, confused and as mad as a bee that had been dumped in the desert.

But as soon as he opened the door to Pastries with Panache, a little honey greeted him.

"Daniel!" Olivia's voice rose in surprise when they entered the shop. "You're back."

She stood to the right of her counter, looking as delicious as a petit four in a pale pink sweater and dark jeans. Her hair was pulled back into a simple ponytail. The fire in his gut roared with renewed desire, every sense in his body on high alert.

He'd missed her. More than he wanted to admit, even to himself.

"Beauty and honor in her are so mingled/ That they have caught the king," Lewiston whispered in Daniel's ear. "Henry—"

"The Eighth. I know my Shakespeare," Daniel returned. "I think even the Bard would have been hard pressed to capture Olivia on paper."

From across the room, Daniel caught the feisty glint in Olivia's emerald eyes. How could anyone describe this woman who was such a mix of beauty, brains and sass?

As he headed toward her, a realization slammed into him. He was starting to care about Olivia. A lot.

Caring about people meant committing to them. Meant being dependable. Honest, true.

And most of all, it meant trusting that the other person would care back for him, for the person he really was. The problem—

Since walking out of his grandfather's house, Daniel Worth had yet to figure out who he really was—or if he was the kind of man who could be trusted with another's heart.

I'd like to see Shakespeare try to put that in a sonnet.

Pauline's The-Sky-Is-Falling Mud Cake

2 cups flour
1/8 teaspoon salt
1 teaspoon baking powder
1 1/4 cups strong brewed coffee
1/4 cup brandy
5 ounces unsweetened chocolate
1 cup butter
2 cups sugar
2 eggs
1 1/2 teaspoons vanilla extract

Frosting:
1 pound confectioners' sugar
1/3 cup cocoa
1 cup melted butter
1 teaspoon vanilla

Oh, dear, it's all a big muddled mess now. If that man had one smart bone in his body, he could have avoided all of this. But no, he had to go and lose the one thing you held dear in your living room. Deep breaths. Again.

Let's make a cake. We'll all feel better then. Preheat the oven to 350 degrees and grease a 3-quart bundt pan, then dust it with cocoa powder. Sift the flour, salt and baking powder together. A lumpy cake will only make everyone more miserable.

Combine the coffee, brandy and butter in a double boiler, whisking occasionally. Then put it all into a bigger bowl (don't worry about the dishes; if your man loves you, he will have installed a dishwasher, thus saving you the toil of doing them yourself) and beat in the sugar, then add the dry ingredients.

Pour the mix into the pan and bake for 40-45 minutes. While you're waiting, have a seat at the table and make a list of all the ways he's wronged you in nearly 30 years of marriage. Get an extra sheet of paper if you must.

When the cake is cool, unmold it and then start the frosting. Beat all ingredients together until smooth, then spread it on the cake. Don't bother serving this to anyone. After the day you've had, you're going to need to eat the whole darn thing.

CHAPTER EIGHTEEN

"I've left him," Pauline Regan announced, breezing into Olivia's two-bedroom apartment as soon as her daughter opened the door on Monday morning. "And here I am, in the arms of my oldest child. Whom I know will support me as I go through a traumatic experience."

Olivia let out a sigh and turned off the stove, abandoning the scrambled eggs she had ruined. The bottoms were burned, the tops runny and the entire mess had a scary pale cast to it. She'd been daydreaming again at the stove—clearly her mind and any kind of kitchen appliance was a dangerous combination. She'd been thinking about Daniel, about the way his face had lit up like a little kid's when he'd told her about the job at *Boston* magazine. How ironic, she thought, that the gossiped-about bachelor would get a job in the very industry that had made him their bread and butter.

Quid pro quo, indeed.

"Olivia, didn't you hear me? I've left your father."

"Again?" Olivia said. "What for this time?"

Her mother took a seat at the round black-and-chrome kitchen table, helping herself to the stack of green seedless grapes on Olivia's plate. "Honestly, Olivia, you could be more supportive."

Olivia removed the pan from the stove and scraped the remains of the eggs into the garbage disposal. When she did, the flimsy potholder in her hand slipped, leaving her thumb exposed to the heat. Olivia let out a very unladylike curse, then tossed the whole thing—pan and all—into the trash. "Mother, you've separated from Dad seventeen times in the last twenty years. Last time, it was because he lost the *TV Guide*."

"Do you know how much I pay for that subscription? The least the man could do is keep the thing on the coffee table. It's not like Kelly Ripa's face is hard to miss."

Olivia rinsed her hands, dried them on a towel, then glanced at the clock. Great. "I'm late for work. I really don't have time for this conversation."

Mom popped a grape into her mouth. "I'm filing for divorce and you don't have time to listen?"

Olivia crossed her arms and leaned against the counter. Around her, the yellow kitchen walls and red accents were as cheerful as ever, modernizing the retro look of the black appliances and furniture. Despite the zippy decor, another Regan family disaster was looming. "You're actually filing?"

"Well...I will. If Harold doesn't shape up."

Olivia had heard those words a thousand times over the course of her life. Her father had heard them probably ten thousand. Which was why none of her mother's threats worked anymore. Dad simply continued about his daily life the same as always, doing the things that annoyed Pauline to no end and figuring either his wife would come around or he'd die waiting.

Either way, his best solution to Pauline's marital dissolution litany was to take the battery out of his hearing aid.

Her mother tossed another grape into her mouth. "I'm telling you, Olivia, he's really done it this time."

This was why Olivia wasn't married. Because she didn't see the point in locking her life with someone else if one of them was going to call it quits over something as trivial as losing track of Lifetime's movie of the week.

Then the image of Daniel Worth popped into her mind. Daniel on her sofa. Daniel at her kitchen table. Daniel cooking her breakfast because he knew she was egg-challenged.

Daydreaming about Daniel was a ridiculous exercise. They were worlds apart and always would be, whether he'd given up his fortune or not.

Besides, he made her think about things other than work, made her daydream of a future that was impossible to have. And what was worse, thinking about him made her burn her breakfast.

The nether parts of her body might consider him a perfect fit, but Olivia knew better than to trust any organ that didn't function on statistical input.

"Olivia, are you listening to me?"

Olivia sighed and wondered if she'd have time to finish her make-up before she had to run out the door. "What could Dad have possibly done that was worse than running over the petunias with the lawnmower?"

"He…" Mom paused, drawing in a breath that was half sob, "he bought me a food processor."

"You're leaving him after thirty-seven years of marriage because he bought you a kitchen appliance?"

"On my *birthday*, Olivia." She shook her head. "For God's sake, don't you understand the ramifications of that?"

"Uh…no." Olivia glanced over at her Cuisinart on the counter, a little battered after a mishap with a butternut squash last month, and figured a man who bought her a food processor definitely wouldn't be all bad in her book, especially if he hung around long enough to operate it.

"He should know me better than that. A *food processor?* He might as well have given me joint compound and a paintbrush." Mom grabbed more grapes, dispensing them one-two into her mouth. "Not that it would kill him to stop with his big ideas and actually *do* something around the house."

The microwave clock changed to ten of seven. Considering it was an eight-minute ride to the shop—if she broke all the rules of the road—Olivia decided she could get by with mascara and lip gloss.

If she ignored her mother now, Mom would just end up following her to work. And that was the last place she needed her mother to be.

Then she'd find out about Josie working at the shop. If there was one thing Olivia couldn't deal with right now, it was a lecture on ruining Josie's future and the stupidity of luring her younger sister into Olivia's "big idea."

"What's so wrong with the food processor?" Olivia asked. "Didn't you need one?"

"Well, yes, but that's beside the point." Pauline was done with the grapes and reached for a banana in the bright red Sedona bowl. "It was my sixtieth birthday, Olivia. I expected something nice. Like your father usually buys."

A warning bell sounded in Olivia's head. She shouldn't ask the next question; she should just let it alone. If she heard the answer she was dreading, it would only add to the mountain of troubles on her shoulders.

"He told me he had to cut back for my birthday this year," Mom said, continuing on as if she'd read Olivia's mind. "Because our retirement account is fluctuating or struggling or something or other and money is tight." She sighed. "Again."

Olivia glanced at her computer on the small secretary in her dining room. QuickBooks hadn't sported wings or multiplied the digits in her business account in the last few minutes. If her father was having money problems, that meant only one thing—

She needed to turn Pastries with Panache around. Now.

Her father was depending on her; Josie was depending on her. They believed in Olivia's entre-preneurial dream and had laid their own financial futures on the railroad tracks. Olivia had better get her business train rolling along a lot faster.

"So," Mom said, rising to walk into the living room and returning a second later, "I've decided to stay with you." She deposited an oversized hard-as-cement navy Samsonite suitcase on the laminate floor.

Olivia looked at the luggage behemoth. Clearly, this wasn't an overnight visit. "Stay...with me? But why?"

"I told you, Olivia, I have *left* your father. For good this time. I'm tired of his get-rich-quick schemes and his lies and his—" She let out a breath and sank into the chair again. "—inability to understand a woman he's been married to for thirty-five years."

"Mom—"

"No." She put up a hand. "Don't try to talk me out of this. It's too late." Then she crossed her legs and her arms and took up residence in the suede recliner.

This would be impossible. How could she keep up the charade that she was the only one working at Pastries with Panache with her mother underfoot? If Mom showed up at the bakery...

Well, she wouldn't. Undoubtedly, Olivia's parents would be back together before the week was out. They'd never been separated for more than a day; things weren't going to change now.

But as Olivia went to unfold the sleeper sofa and find some pillows, she wondered if she'd just welcomed one more disaster into her life.

Daniel's Your-Appeal-Has-Paled Meringues

4 egg whites
1/8 teaspoon salt
1 1/4 cups sugar
1/2 teaspoon vanilla extract

You might as well be a ghost for all your "former" friends care about your dilemma. Lose a fortune and you disappear off the face of the earth—or at least off society's guest lists.

With these meringues, you'll have a dessert that looks like your new reality. And, you can take it to a certain pastry chef as a way to make amends...and maybe convince her you're not so bad after all.

Start by preheating the oven to 225 degrees. Beats the egg whites and salt in a metal bowl until they form soft peaks. Add half the sugar and continue beating until you create nice, stiff peaks—sort of like the mountain you're about to climb to get your penniless life on track. Fold in the remaining sugar and vanilla.

Pipe the meringue onto parchment paper covered cookie sheets, making little rosettes that are sure to earn brownie points with that fiery woman who expects more out of you than anyone else you know. Bake for two hours, then turn off the oven. Loosen the meringue from the sheet, then let them finish cooling in the oven, while you cool your heels, waiting to see if society will take your penniless self back.

And if it doesn't, don't worry. A little change in attitude and lifestyle might be just the thing to convince the chef that something should be cooking between her and you.

CHAPTER NINETEEN

On Tuesday morning, Daniel stood outside the Suffolk Country Club, caught in the beginnings of a good old-fashioned New England blizzard. Still, he lingered at the door and considered his options.

Okay, there weren't any to consider. He was flat out of possibilities. His first column had been accepted by *Boston* magazine—which was great—with payment thirty days after acceptance—which sucked. When he'd accepted the job, he hadn't considered that little snag.

He was the stereotype of the clueless wealthy. He'd overlooked the little detail of when the check would arrive, because he'd assumed the money would be handed over when the column went in. Like *Boston* magazine was a gumball machine, dispensing a colorful choke hazard for his quarter.

Well, now he was all out of quarters. Daniel shivered in the chill of the February air and drew his topcoat closed. To the right of the door, he spied an ATM. He hated himself even as he slipped the card into the skinny machine slot, but without a place to stay or a job, he was pretty much out of choices.

The card went in, he punched in his password, and hit Withdraw.

In an instant, he saw that Lewiston had been right. Grandfather hadn't wasted any time. The account was closed, the money gone. The machine spit back his card like a baby gagging on spinach.

Daniel lingered on the sidewalk, the snow piling up around his dress shoes. His wallet was empty, and the Motel 6 wasn't taking in charity cases. There was nowhere else to go, at least not until he had a job and a paycheck. Before he could change his mind, Daniel withdrew a second card out of his wallet, crossed to the entrance of the country club and stepped inside, swiping his ID under the bar code reader as he entered.

"Hello, Mr. Worth," said the doorman, who clearly hadn't heard about Daniel's suicidal dive into poverty. "Been a while since you've been here, sir."

Daniel nodded, opting not to say anything rather than lie. He headed past the pro shop, kept going beyond the entrance to the locker rooms and strode past the racquetball court, not even looking inside the glass to see who was getting pummeled by the little ball.

Daniel headed straight for the bar. To beg for mercy.

Though it was barely past ten in the morning, he found Jake exactly where he'd expected him to be—leaning against the smooth oak surface, a half-drunk rum and Coke in his right hand. Persimmon and Kyle Montague were on either side of him, each with a drink of their own. A little green umbrella was sitting in Persimmon's orange drink, cocked at a jaunty angle.

"Hey, Daniel." Jake said. "Join me in a drink?"

If there was one thing he could use right now, it was a drink. But there was no way he was going to put it on Grandfather's tab. Or anyone else's. "No."

"As I was saying," Persimmon cut in, "the antioxidant value in carrots is underappreciated."

"Hey, I heard a rumor," Kyle said, pivoting to face Daniel. "That you were kicked to the curb by your grandfather."

"It was a mutual decision," Daniel said.

"If you maintain your vegetable intake, you can reduce your heart attack risk by..." Persimmon paused, counting with his fingers. "A lot."

Kyle snorted and shook his head in disbelief. "Well, old boy, go home and apologize. Right the hell now. What are you waiting for? Your allowance is going to dry up pretty fast."

Daniel shrugged. "It already did."

"You're...broke?" Jake said. When Daniel nodded, the three men around him fell as silent as mourners at a wake.

"No money?" Kyle said. "None?"

"But...how can that be?" Persimmon said, looking a little worried for his own future. "You're a *blood* relative. I mean, you're part of the family garden, so to speak. And they just yanked you out? Like a weed?"

"Apparently you've never met his grandfather." Jake propped an Italian leather shoe on the brass ring of the stool's base, then leaned back, with the confidence of someone used to owning everything around him. "He'd cut off his own arm if it didn't stay in line with the family plan."

True or not, Daniel didn't feel like listening to Jake's interpretation of his family. "Listen," he said. "I didn't come here to bash my family. I just wanted some help."

"Help? Like a handout? Hey, I can do that. Support you in the manner to which you were accustomed, at least for an afternoon." Kyle chuckled and reached for his wallet. When he opened it, a thick wad of hundreds peeked out, like they were waving hello, long time no see.

Had he been that cavalier before? Peeling off dollars as easily as stamps on a roll?

"I can give you some of my carrot stash," Persimmon said. "Help you keep up your strength and your antioxidant levels."

"I don't want any money," Daniel said. He *needed* it. He just didn't want to take it from his friends. The whole thing was humiliating enough. "Or vegetables. All I need is a place to stay for a couple of days. Till I get paid or find a second job."

"Two jobs? You've *really* gone off the deep end," Kyle said.

"You could go into farming," Persimmon put in. "Organic farming is growing like crazy. And hey, if you do start a farm, I'll buy your products."

Jake was already shaking his head. "Man, I wish I could help you, but if I bring home a disowned heir, my mother's going to have a heart attack. She thinks that kind of thing is as contagious as chicken pox."

The refusal stunned Daniel. His best friend—or so he'd thought. Apparently his friendships were also based on his societal status. For the first time in his life, Daniel realized he had nothing in common with his peers—and didn't want to.

"This isn't a venereal disease, Jake." Daniel let out a gust. "I had an argument with my grandfather. That's all."

"Sorry, dude, but I just can't get in the middle of that. I have to worry about my own ass." Jake finished his drink, then gestured toward the bartender for another.

"Hey, I'd love to have you over. But we're, ah, disinfecting," Kyle said.

"Disinfecting?"

Kyle's laugh was a nervous sound. "Did I say disinfecting? I meant decontaminating. No, ah, exterminating. Yeah, that's it."

"Yeah, I'm sure it is." Daniel looked at Persimmon, who dipped his head and stirred at his drink with the umbrella. "You guys are real friends." He didn't bother to hide his sarcasm.

"Hey, Daniel, we'd love to help you. It's just…" Jake's voice trailed off. He looked to Kyle for help.

"You're not one of us anymore," Kyle said. "I mean, we can't bring you to the yacht club or out for doubles on the tennis court. How would we ever explain it to everyone else?"

"That I'm your friend and it doesn't matter if I have money or not." And yet, he knew that wasn't true. Almost the minute Aunt Helen and Louis had been turned out by Grandfather Worth, they had lost the friends they'd had. She'd been shunned as surely as an Amish woman who'd traded in her long black skirts for a fuchsia thong bikini.

Kyle laughed. "Now I know you've gone crazy. Geez, just go home, will you? We all have to suck up at some point. But look at the benefits." Kyle gave him a good-natured jab in the arm.

"Benefits? You call doing what someone else wants all your life a *benefit?*"

"No, I'm talking about the money. And the girls." Kyle winked.

Daniel turned toward Jake, silent, giving his former best friend one more chance to come through.

But Jake, as always, disappointed. He shifted in his seat. "You understand, don't you, Daniel?"

"No," Daniel said. "I don't understand at all."

Then he turned on his heel and walked out of the country club. He no longer belonged in this world.

Trouble was, he didn't know what world he belonged in. Or if he'd ever be able to afford the rent.

Ben's It's-All-Downhill-From-Here Lemon Curd Tartlets

Filling:
3/4 cup strained lemon juice
8 tablespoons unsalted butter
3/4 cup sugar
6 egg yolks

Tartlets:
3 sheets phyllo
1/2 cup butter, clarified
3/4 cup sugar

If you're looking for a recipe for disaster, mix your parents' pending divorce with bad media press and a playboy who's hanging around your sister like a killer bee with a rose. Since you want to avoid the whole damned thing, head on into the kitchen and work on these. Your mother will think you're cultivating culinary skills to make yourself a more marketable man.

Start with the lemon curd and get the hard part out of the way early. Combine the lemon juice, butter and sugar in a heavy saucepan and simmer over low heat. Whisk the eggs in a separate bowl then temper them by adding a ½ cup of the lemon juice mixture (and I bet you thought I didn't know what temper meant). Add the eggs to the pan, whisking for three or four minutes. Don't let it curdle or it'll be as ruined as your sister's life.

Put the lemon curd into a glass bowl, cover with plastic wrap and refrigerate for three hours. Leave the bickering behind and escape to a bar or some other equally quiet place (compared to anywhere your parents are).

In the meantime, preheat the oven to 375 degrees, then lay the phyllo dough out and cut into 36 squares. Lay out 18 tartlet molds on a baking sheet, then lay one square of phyllo dough on top, brush with the butter, sprinkle with the sugar, and top with another square. Keep the phyllos from poufing by laying another cookie sheet on top to weight them down. Bake for about ten minutes, enough time to grab a cold beer and a set of earplugs.

When cool, add the filling. If you want to get all fancy, pipe it in. Me, I prefer a spoon. In fact, I usually just skip the damned spoon all together and just use the phyllo shells like scoops. A single man is nothing if not inventive with his food.

CHAPTER TWENTY

"Heard you have a roommate," Ben said as he came into Pastries with Panache early Tuesday afternoon. His entrance whisked in a cold breeze and a tiny snowdrift from the storm that had started up that morning, dropping five inches so far on the city. Ben stomped the snow off his boots on the mat at the door, then shrugged out of his coat and hat.

"It's only temporary," Olivia said. She stashed the catalog of kitchen utensils under the counter and crossed to her brother. In the back, Josie was putting the finishing touches on a cake order for a baby shower at a nearby insurance company.

"Uh-huh." Ben gave her a knowing look. "Then why did Mom ask me to go with her to the court-house this morning?"

Olivia let out a sigh. "She really did it?"

"Yep. Says she's sick of their finances being as steady as the San Andreas Fault and sick of Dad's big plans that turn out to be nothing more than costly puffs of smoke."

Olivia dropped into one of the chairs and buried her face in her hands. "This is all my fault."

Ben laid a palm on her shoulder. "Don't take all the credit. This has been going on for years."

"Yeah, but this time—" Olivia cut off the sentence. She couldn't tell Ben. She couldn't tell anyone. This time, the burden was all hers. She'd dragged her sister into this, sure that this time, the family entrepreneurship would turn into something lucrative because she'd done her homework. But thus far, despite her best efforts, Olivia had seen more red than black on her profit-and-loss statement. The excitement of not knowing what each day was going to bring was quickly becoming a continual knot of anxiety.

"Does Dad know she filed?" Olivia asked.

"No, not yet. I'm going to go down there and try to talk some sense into him before this gets out of hand."

"Now? All the way to Maryland?"

Ben shrugged. "Hey, I have no life, remember? The cat knows how to use a litter box and I'll fill her bowl with food before I head out. Then I'll bring Dad back with me and make sure he gets this straightened out."

Olivia lifted her head. "Really?"

"Yeah. I figure I owe you for the free food," at this, he crossed the room to grab a muffin out of the serving dish and take a bite before returning to her side, "and I know eventually Mom is going to drive you crazy—"

"Eventually? She already has."

"Eventually, you'll drive her crazy, too, and then Mom's going to come looking for another place to live. Since I'm the only other one not living with roommates, I figure I'm next on the list."

Olivia laughed. "So you're doing this out of purely selfish reasons?"

"Nah. I'm worried about my cat." Ben gave his sister a lopsided grin. "Every time she sees Mom coming, she runs away. Apparently living on the streets is better than being dressed up by Mom as a ballerina."

Olivia chuckled. Last year, her mother had stopped by Ben's on Halloween and decked out his cat as one of the dancers in the Nutcracker for the trick-or-treaters. From what Ben said, the male feline hadn't been the same since.

Ben shook his head at the memory. "She needs another dog. Ever since Petunia the insane pug died, Mom's been looking for another victim to inherit those cutesy clothes. I don't mind Mom visiting, but I gotta draw the line at my cat."

"All right. I'll keep Mom at my house, purely for animal protection reasons."

"I appreciate that," Ben said, following Olivia into the kitchen. He tossed a hello toward his other sister, swiped a dollop of frosting from the bowl, earning a smack on the hand from Josie.

Olivia slipped on an apron, then took a bowl of prepared lemon curd and a package of phyllo dough out of the refrigerator. She laid both on the marble counter and began unwrapping the dough.

"So, how's business?" Ben said, swinging his lanky frame into a stool and scooting it closer to the counter where Olivia worked.

"Lousy."

Josie grunted agreement from her place in front of the devil's food cake.

"Too many net carbs, huh?" Ben asked.

Olivia put a bit of butter in a pan and turned on the gas so it would melt, then returned to her phyllo. "Don't tell me those card-carrying carb loonies are out there again."

"No," Ben said, toying with a spoon on the counter. "It's something worse."

"Worse?" That's all she needed right now. More bad news. Olivia took her frustrations out on the tartlet pans, laying them out on a cookie sheet with firm pushes that nearly dented the metal. "What could be worse than protestors?"

"They installed a carb counter on their front window. Apparently, your shop is losing the waistline wars." Ben got to his feet and rooted around in the refrigerator. He came back out with two macaroons from the day before. He popped one into his mouth, then retook his seat.

"Are you serious?" Olivia abandoned the dough and crossed to the front door, grabbing the binoculars she'd brought in that morning—for just such a spying purpose. True to Ben's word, a new poster hung in the shop window across the street. "Their cheesecake: 35 carbs. Our cheesecake, 6 net carbs. Who cares about your waistline more?"

Olivia shut the door. "Shit."

"When you couple it with this," From his hip pocket, Ben pulled out a page from that day's *Globe* and unfolded it for Olivia to see. "You've got a bit of a mess on your hands."

Olivia looked at the newspaper, then closed her eyes. When she opened them again, the headline still blared back at her from the Food section: Poor Worth Heir Can't Save Rich Sweets Shop.

Olivia scanned the story. Most of it was about Daniel, and his parting of the ways with his grandfather and the family company. But at the end, it chronicled her bidding on him at the bachelor auction, the ads he'd appeared in and the dearth of traffic to her store now that Sweets without Sin had opened. The reporter ended with a suggestion that maybe Olivia should try to get a refund on her bachelor for failure to live up to his pedigree.

All those damned danishes and this is what she ended up with for coverage? Whatever happened to the media taking a good old-fashioned bribe?

She shook her head and tossed the page onto one of the tables. "They didn't even interview me. They only talked to the people across the street and some anonymous maid who works for Daniel's grandfather. What kind of journalism is that?"

Ben shrugged. "The usual kind."

Olivia ran a hand through her hair and for the first time, truly regretted her decision to go into business for herself. She'd tried so hard, done everything the books told her to do and yet it still hadn't been enough. Sales were down sixty percent from her grand opening. If anything, all her efforts to drum up business had made things worse, as if she lacked the right touch to motivate customer buying.

When it came to business, clearly she was a failure.

"I can't afford this anymore," Olivia said, sinking into a chair. Angry at herself for letting this get to her, but tired of pretending everything was under control. "Putting money into this place has become like using a water pistol to put out a three-alarm fire."

Ben laid a hand over hers. "Why not call it quits? Go back to working nine to five like the rest of us schmucks?"

"That's what everyone wants me to do. It's what they expect out of a Regan."

Quitting. That's what her mother had predicted she'd do before the first year was up. It was what her Aunt Eloisa, Mom's sister, had said would be the smart thing to do.

And it was the one thing she *couldn't* do. Not with people depending on her.

She sighed. "I can't do that to Josie. She's finally found her niche. She's depending on me."

"Liv, you don't have to be the oak tree of the family. It's okay to fail," Ben said quietly. "Josie will be okay."

Olivia shook her head, redoubling her resolve. "No. I refuse to become another of the family failures."

Ben shrugged, his eyes sad, knowing a debate of the Regan history was pointless. He'd heard it all before, at the Christmas parties and the birthday dinners. It was why he'd opted for a regular job instead of pursuing anything remotely entrepreneurial. "Maybe this just isn't the right business."

Olivia wouldn't hear that. Not from her brother, one of her biggest supporters when she'd first opened. If Ben thought she wasn't cut out for self-employment...

Then maybe it was true.

No. That was one thought Olivia refused to entertain. It was too dangerous to even consider. "This *has* to be the right business. I did all the research, pulled all the demographics—"

"There's more to business success than statistics," he said gently.

She turned away from him and got busy rearranging the flowers in the little vase on one of the tables. The pink tulips drooped, as if they had given up on her, too.

A niggling feeling told her that Ben was right. Olivia shook it off. She had everything she needed for success: the research, the facts, and most of all, a willingness to take a risk. She just needed to trust that what was around the corner was better.

And not a Mack truck bearing down on her.

"Well, I better hit the road if I want to get to Maryland before dark." Ben came up behind her and laid a hand on her shoulder. "Don't listen to me, Liv. I'm just your older brother. It's my job to be annoying."

Olivia swiped at her face and turned to face him. "You do it well."

He grinned. "Hey, I may not have any talents, but there's always that." Then he ruffled her hair, just like he had when she was ten, and left the shop, detouring to snag another muffin on his way out the door.

Leaving Olivia in her sinking rowboat of business troubles. Clearly, her donuts weren't going to be any good as life preservers.

Daniel's A-Man's-Gotta-Eat
Cranberry Orange Bread

2 cups flour
2 teaspoons baking powder
1/2 teaspoon salt
3/4 cup sugar
orange rind
2 eggs
2/3 cup fresh orange juice
6 tablespoons unsalted butter, melted
1 1/4 cups fresh cranberries
1/2 cup walnuts, chopped

If there's anything that can give a man a sense of his worth, it's a job. The problem is, it's pretty damned hard to keep your mind on your work when there's a pretty woman waiting for you just on the other side of the door.

All that work—and all that thinking about that hot woman—means you've worked up a hell of an appetite. Try this quick bread to answer at least one urge. Preheat the oven to 375 degrees, then mix the dry ingredients in a big bowl. Add the orange rind, then mix in the eggs, juice and melted butter. Don't get too ambitious in your mixing or you'll end up with a clump instead of a loaf. Fold in the cranberries and walnuts, then pour into a greased and floured loaf pan.

In the 45-55 minutes it takes to bake, start feeding your other cravings with a spunky woman who's damned determined not to fall in love.

CHAPTER TWENTY-ONE

Sweat poured off his brow and his arms ached like the muscles had been put through a shredder. Despite all of that, Daniel felt good.

Damned good. In fact, better than he'd ever felt in his entire life. It was a good feeling, this working for a living. Since he'd left the country club, he'd already logged six hours out in the cold, stopping only for lunch. His adrenaline had yet to ebb, as if hard work only fueled his energy level.

What a hell of a speech that would make at the next society garden party. Want to feel worthy? Want to find that elusive sense of self? Then pick up a shovel and put it to work.

He started in on another pile of snow, hefting it up and to the side. The wet, thick snow clumped together, in a sidewalk mountain. Daniel stood back and looked at the mound, feeling more personal satisfaction in that pile than in all the varsity letters hanging in his childhood bedroom. This was real, tangible, measurable. Not to mention heavy as hell.

There was definitely something to that working for a living thing.

"What are you doing?" Olivia came outside her shop, her arms wrapped around herself, shivering in the cold. He paused, the shovel in his hands forgotten. She was gorgeous, in a soft blue cowl-neck sweater that set off her eyes, tingeing the green in them with a slight hue of sky. Black pants tapered down her legs. She looked simple, elegant. Like she could go toe-to-toe with the abrasive Lizzy Montague during one of her martini-infused harangues.

Daniel smiled. He'd known a very different side of Olivia just a few days ago. A hot, sexy, elegance be damned side. He hoped to know it again. Soon.

Hard work had also made him hungry—for a hell of a lot more than a cheeseburger and fries.

"What are you doing?" she repeated.

"Shoveling your walk."

"Why?"

He hoisted the shovel. "Because that's my new job." He was actually glad he hadn't taken charity from Jake and Kyle. It was hard to feel manly when a friend paid your room and board. But with a shovel in his hands and a few bucks in his pocket, he'd transformed into Rambo.

"Your *job?*"

"Yep. No one would hire me, so I hired myself. I've been clearing paths all day for little old ladies. They don't think my Harvard degree makes me overqualified."

"You have? In this sticky stuff?"

He reached in his pocket and pulled out a can of non-stick spray. "I came prepared."

Olivia laughed and shifted her arms tighter over her body. When she did, her breasts rose. His libido reminded him how long it had been since they'd been together. Too damned long.

"How did you think of that?" she asked.

"You're not the only one who can use the library for research." He grinned. "The spray keeps the snow from sticking to my shovel. It was one of those ask Helen or someone hints. I also know the best way to clean a microwave and I can bake a hell of a mac-and-cheese."

She laughed again, then stepped forward and took the shovel out of his hands. "Come on inside and have some coffee before you get frostbite."

"Let me finish first." Half her walk was still covered with snow, making the path from her store to the next one hard to traverse without boots or a mush team.

Olivia grabbed his arm. Through the layers of his clothing, he could feel the heat of her touch, the strength in this woman who seemed so fragile, yet packed a powerful punch. "It can wait. Right now, I want to thank you."

The seductive smile she added to her words had him inside and stripping off his winter outerwear in five seconds. When he was finally down to normal clothes, Olivia reached up to brush the snow out of his hair, a tender gesture that touched Daniel in some deep, nameless place in his gut.

"Thank you," she said softly.

He felt a huge, goofy grin take over his face. "It was nothing."

"No, it was huge. No one has ever done anything like that for me. It's like you read my mind." She wrapped her arms around his neck and raised on her toes, her gaze meeting his. "I've had a really bad day and then, here you are, like an answer to a prayer."

He chuckled, then tipped her chin up. "You were praying for a sidewalk shovel?"

"No." She stepped back and shrugged her shoulders. "For someone to bring me something good today. At this point, I'd take anything. A visit from the IRS. A near-death experience...I'm easy."

"Aw, come here." He opened his arms. She hesitated. "Olivia, you don't have to carry your troubles all by yourself, you know."

She paused a moment longer, then she stepped into his hug and laid her head against his sweater.

Women had cleaved themselves to him before, as if he were the other half of a piece of Velcro. But never had he felt this sense of vulnerability in a woman. A surge of protectiveness rose in Daniel. He wanted to take away her worries. Solve them all with a swipe of a pen and a check.

But he didn't have a check register anymore. All he had to his name right now was a hundred and ten dollars. It was partly his fault. He could have made a lot more for his drive shoveling efforts. But he hadn't bothered to charge half his customers because it was clear they needed the money more than he did.

And now, in his arms, he held someone else who was in need—for a solution money couldn't buy.

"Tell me what I can do," Daniel said into the soft glossy brown of her hair.

She shook her head. "Nothing. Just hold me."

"*That* I can afford."

She laughed softly and burrowed herself tighter into his embrace. They stood there for a long, quiet moment. Outside, the snow fell in silent, skating flakes down the window. Somewhere in the back of the shop, a machine whurp-whurped as it mixed dough, releasing the smell of cinnamon into the air.

This was good. Very good.

For a second he allowed himself to imagine the two of them together in the future, holding hands in front of a roaring fire. Enjoying the Caribbean breezes from the deck of a cruise ship. And most of all, lying in bed. *After.*

He indulged in thoughts of a life with her, of more moments like this in paradise. Then he spied the open newspaper on the table beside them. His visions of paradise came to a screeching halt, invaded by a flock of vicious journalist seagulls.

Poor Worth Heir Can't Save Rich Sweets Shop.

"I'll sue them," he said, the anger boiling up inside him.

"Don't look at that," Olivia said, turning and seeing where his gaze had gone. "It's just some stupid article my brother brought over."

Daniel released Olivia to scan the story. It was one of those tabloid-ish pieces, filled with half-truths and exaggerations. "Daniel Worth, renowned as one of the hottest playboys in Boston, walked out on his fortune…an apparent rift with his grandfather… Rumors abound that the elder Worth didn't approve of the tart pastry chef…whose shop is embroiled in a bitter fight-to-the-death carbohydrate battle… despite the attentions of the bachelor, the shop is floundering. Perhaps, speculated a Worth household insider, the public has tired of sweet confections and spoiled brats."

"Insider." Daniel snorted. He knew the media. Their version of an insider was a part-time gardener who'd been plied with a couple of beers to fill in exactly the right blanks.

Still, as he looked around the empty shop, he realized he'd done this. His personal life had leaked over into Olivia's business, backfiring on her plan to use his celebrity to boost sales. His choice to walk away from Grandfather's demands clearly hadn't impacted just his life with money problems.

"Olivia, I didn't want you to get dragged into the mess I've made of my life."

"Trust me, Daniel. I don't get dragged anywhere." She grinned, then put a finger to her lips, a tease in her eyes. "Actually, wasn't I the one doing the dragging to my bedroom the other day?"

He smiled. "We'll definitely revisit that. Soon. But this…" He glanced again at the article, which was as much about journalism as a McDonald's jingle was about poetry. "This is wrong."

She shrugged, as if it didn't matter, but he could tell it did. "I'll be fine. The shop will be fine." But the words lacked the ring of truth.

"The ads didn't work?" He asked, even as he knew it was a rhetorical question. He could see the answer in the line at Sweets without Sin, and the empty pastry shop he stood in now.

"I had a few calls the first morning after they ran, until the Splenda addicts set up shop." She ran a hand through her hair. "It's like having the headquarters for PETA renting space on your mink farm."

"Well, the way I see it, you have two choices. Either move the farm. Or launch a counterattack."

Olivia paced, circling the room, the stress clear in the set of her shoulders. "I tried that, remember? Clearly, the way to a reporter's heart isn't through his heart." She shook her head. "Short of winning the Frosting on the Cake competition on Valentine's Day, I don't see another way to boost my sales and visibility."

"Frosting on the Cake? Isn't that being held at one of my grandfather's hotels?"

She nodded. "But I can't enter. It'd be suicide."

Daniel began to ask why when the door opened and Josie breezed in, her arms loaded with sacks of groceries.

"I'm back. I—" Josie stopped short when she noticed him. "Oh! Hi! The goat has returned to the bull, I see." She gave them an I-told-you-so grin.

"We were just talking." Olivia brushed her hands together, as if the subject of herself and Daniel was over.

Daniel sensed something beneath the surface of Olivia, some burden she refused to share. That there was more weighing her down than just a slump in business and a snide reporter.

He had enough to worry about in his own life right now—like affording a place to live and eating three squares—but still, the urge to help her nagged at him. Hell, whenever he was around her, he had a lot of urges.

And they had nothing to do with getting a balanced meal.

"Here, let me get those for you." Olivia walked away, crossing to her sister and taking the bags out of Josie's arms. She left to carry them into the kitchen.

Josie hung her coat on the rack by the door and looked at Daniel. "Someone was in here looking for you earlier this morning."

"Let me guess. A reporter from the *Herald?*"

"Nope. A man named...Louis?" Josie's brows knitted together. "Louis's son? He looked like a Pisces. Does that help?"

"Do you mean Lewiston?"

"Yeah, that's it. He said to call him right away." She shrugged. "He wouldn't say why, just that you had to call." Josie tapped her forehead. "I have a feeling that it's important. And my feelings are always right. Well, most of the time. When there's no interference from satellite signals."

"Uh, thanks." Was this just some ploy by his grandfather to get him back? A trick to reel him back into the family fold and a corner office at Worth?

Then he realized Lewiston would never do that, never be Grandfather's pawn. If Lewiston needed him to call, then it had to be important.

As Daniel headed for the phone behind the counter of the shop, he had the distinct feeling that this was a call he didn't want to make.

Lewiston's Get-Back-to-Tradition Boston Creme Pie

Cake:

2 cups cake flour

1 tablespoon baking powder

1/2 teaspoon salt

1/2 cup butter, softened

1 cup sugar

2 eggs

1 teaspoon vanilla extract

Filling:

1 cup milk

3 egg yolks

1/2 cup sugar

1/4 cup flour

1 tablespoon butter

1 tablespoon brandy

Chocolate Glaze:

1 ounce unsweetened chocolate

2 tablespoons butter

1/2 cup confectioners' sugar

1/2 teaspoon vanilla extract

1 tablespoon hot water

This is a dessert rich in history, much like the family that gave you your name. Originally served and created at the Parker House Hotel, it was a favorite for Longfellow, Thoreau, Emerson and Hawthorne at their "Saturday Club" meetings. In my opinion, any dessert with that much literary support should be on your table on a regular basis. If nothing else, it'll at least make you feel more writerly.

Start by preheating the oven to 375 degrees. Grease two 8-inch round cake pans, then line them with greased wax paper. Sift the dry ingredients for the cake, to improve texture.

In a separate bowl, beat the butter and sugar until it's as light and fluffy as a sitcom (which does nothing for your literary education). Add the eggs one at a time, then add the vanilla. Now alternate adding milk and the dry ingredients, blending well. Don't over-beat this, however, or you'll find yourself with one tough cake.

Divide it between the pans, giving them a tap on the counter to settle the cake mix evenly. Bake for 25 minutes, then cool.

That leaves you plenty of time to make the middle. After all, what's a Boston Cream Pie without the cream? Using a heatproof bowl, beat the egg yolks, then add the sugar and keep beating until it's as pale as a yellow diamond. Add the flour, then stream in the milk, beating constantly. Put the bowl over a pan of boiling water, cooking for about two minutes. Remove from the heat, then add the butter and brandy. Let it cool while you make the glaze.

Put the filling between the two layers, sandwiching them like a family that's gotten a little too close. Melt the chocolate with the butter in a double boiler, then remove from the heat and beat in the sugar, creating a nice, thick paste, then add the vanilla. If it's too thick still, beat in some hot water.

Now it's time to create the *piece de resistance*. Spread the glaze over the cake, then serve immediately to people you love a great deal. While you're at it, give them a great book to read, too.

CHAPTER TWENTY-TWO

Lewiston got right to the point. "Sir, you have to come home. Now."

"Lewiston, you know I can't—"

"Your grandfather has had a heart attack."

Silence hummed across the phone line. Daniel stood in Olivia's pastry shop, the words processing through him in sharp tiny slivers that seemed so incongruous among the muffins and scones. In the kitchen, an oven timer buzzed. His reflection glimmered on the glass display case. Beneath his shoes, the tile floor was hard, solid.

But inside, shock reverberated through him. To Daniel, Grandfather had always seemed immortal, indestructible. Except for his accident fifteen years ago, Grandfather never got sick. Never got the flu. The sniffles. Daniel suspected that the germs, like everyone else in the family, were too afraid of Grandfather's cantankerousness to come anywhere near him.

Daniel put a hand over his face and his mind rocketed back two dozen years. He'd awoken in the middle of the night and found Grandfather slumped in the chair in the corner of his room. "I have something to tell you," Grandfather had said, rising and crossing to sit on the edge of Daniel's twin bed.

Daniel, still bleary and half-asleep, protested and tried to roll back over into the comfort of his pillow, but Grandfather had turned on the light, shocking him first with the harsh glare, then with the harsh words. "Your father has died."

It was the only time Daniel ever saw his stoic grandfather betray any emotion. There'd been a catch in Grandfather's voice and a glimmer that had to be tears on his cheeks. He swallowed hard and averted his face.

But when Grandfather had reached out a hand to grip his grandson's, it had been shaky, unsure. Grasping his tightly, almost hurting him.

Father dead. The words had taken a moment to sink in, but when they did, Daniel began to cry. He was only six, but he knew that somehow, his world had changed, had lost something irreplaceable. His tears turned into a sob that shook his small frame and soaked his pillow.

"Stop that. You need to be a man now," his grandfather had said, his voice gruff. "You're the only one I have left," Grandfather added quietly.

Daniel choked back his tears and tried to be stoic. Grandfather rose, standing there for a long, silent time. Then he gave Daniel's shoulder an awkward pat and left the room.

That was the sole extent of Grandfather's words of wisdom for a little boy who'd just lost his father.

Grandfather never again spoke of his son's heart attack, and expected the same out of everyone around him.

Lewiston had been the one to comfort Daniel that night. He'd been the one to come into the room, turn off the light and then sit on Daniel's bed, with his young charge's head cradled in one arm, uttering soothing words as the grief poured out.

"Sir, are you still there?" Lewiston asked, pulling Daniel out of his memories.

Daniel swallowed. "How...how bad is it?"

"He'll be okay," Lewiston said. "But he needs you right now."

There was no hesitation in Daniel's answer. "I'll be right there." Daniel wrote down the number of Grandfather's room at Brigham & Women's, then started to hang up the phone.

"Daniel?" Lewiston said.

"Yeah."

"Are *you* okay?" There was no mistaking the quiet concern in his butler's voice.

"I'm tough," Daniel said, trying to turn the worry into a joke, because he could deal with that, "I'm a Worth, remember?"

As he hung up the phone and turned to leave for the hospital, Daniel realized that for the first time in many, many years, Lewiston had called him by his first name.

Once again, Lewiston was there for him when it was dark and scary.

Olivia's Lies-and-Promises Apple Tart

1 ready-made piecrust
4 apples, sliced
1/4 cup sugar
1/2 teaspoon nutmeg
2 tablespoons butter, cut in cubes
confectioners' sugar for dusting

When you're busy covering one lie with another and making promises you hope like heck you can keep, you don't have time to make a real piecrust. Preheat your oven to 425 degrees, then form the crust into a circle.

Mix the apples with the sugar and nutmeg, then spread them over the crust, leaving two inches from the edge. Dot with butter, then fold the edges of the pastry in toward the center, creating a free-form apple tart that's as unique and inventive as the stories you've been telling.

Bake at 425 for 15 minutes, then lower the temperature to 375 and cook for another 35 minutes. As soon as it's cool, start shoveling it into your mouth quick—before you say something you might regret.

CHAPTER TWENTY-THREE

Olivia heard the voices before she even got to the third floor. Her mother and father—together again, but not happily. She'd come home after a long, confusing day at work—long because she'd kept the shop open an extra couple of hours hoping to make a few more sales—confusing because Daniel Worth had thrown another monkey wrench into her carefully assembled life.

Heck, every time she was around him, he disrupted her. Emotionally, mentally and *yowza,* physically. Now she worried about him, knowing he was at the hospital with his grandfather. It had been clear when Daniel dashed out of the shop that despite everything, he loved his grandfather. She should have insisted on going with him because if anyone looked like they needed moral support, it was Daniel. She said a quick prayer for the two of them, then started ascending the last flight.

Ben was just coming down the stairs as she headed up. "I thought bringing in Dad would help," he said. "But it's only made it worse."

"Wasn't Mom glad to see Dad?"

Ben waved a hand toward the muffled commotion coming from her door a few feet away. "Does she *sound* glad?"

And indeed, her mother wasn't. When Olivia entered the apartment, her parents paused only long enough to nod a hello before getting back to marital strife.

"I am not coming back just to cook for you, Harold," Mom said. "You have a can opener. Use it."

Dad scowled and plopped his large frame into the black La-Z-Boy. He ran a hand over his bald spot and shook his head. "That damned stove doesn't like me."

Mom crossed her arms over her chest. "That makes two of us."

"Mom, Dad, please." Olivia moved to stand between them, hoping they'd throw up their hands and call a truce, like they had so many times before. "All this over a food processor?"

"It's not about the food processor," Mom said, pouting now. Olivia noticed that her mother's light brown hair seemed grayer, her eyes a little sadder than usual. Had she really given up on her marriage? "It's about him not showing that he loves me."

"Throw a wad of cash at her and she calls it love," Dad said, gesturing at his wife. "Me, I just want my dinner."

"You've never had a wad of cash to throw at anyone. You spend it all on your crazy ideas." Her mother waved her hands around her head.

"One of these days, Pauline, we'll be rich." Dad wagged a finger at her. "You mark my words."

"One of these days, Harold, we'll be dead and all our kids will inherit is a hell of a lot of debt and that damned food processor."

"My investments are going to pay off." He cast a glance Olivia's way, then back at his wife. Olivia wished aliens would zap her out of the room right now. Or at the very least, offer to pay her for their experiments.

Mom rolled her eyes. "Right. And Elvis is going to come back from the dead, too."

"It'll happen," Dad said. "Trust me."

Olivia swallowed back a load of guilt. Her dad was clearly looking at her to save the day. Unless some doctor came out on national television saying danishes were the new diet food, Olivia didn't see that happening in the near future.

She was going to buy a shovel tomorrow. Right now, snow removal had to pay better than pastries.

Olivia rubbed at her temples. "Mom, can't you and Dad just *talk* about this?"

"There is no talking to that man. All he wants is his mashed potatoes. He could care less who cooks them or if the cook is happy."

"The cook would be happy if she went home to her own kitchen," Dad muttered.

Mom shot him a glare, crossed her arms over her chest and pursed her lips. Clearly, the cook wasn't going anywhere.

Ever since she could remember, Olivia's parents had been like this, pecking at each other like two crows intent on getting the last roadside French fry. Yet, beneath it all, there was a love there. She'd seen it in the way they never went to bed without a kiss, never left the house without exchanging a hug, and the way her mother's hand always rested on her father's shoulder when he drove.

But this time, there was a different tone to their fight, as if years of issues had suddenly blown off the teakettle lid.

Her parents needed to make up—quick—before things got any more out of hand, or worse, her father left—without taking Mom home. In a day or two, her mother would get bored with seeing how much drama TNT could pack into an afternoon and journey on down to the pastry shop. There, undoubtedly, she'd have questions. About Josie. About the financing.

Olivia couldn't answer those questions. She'd made a promise. One that couldn't be broken, not until the shop was a success.

Olivia took her mother's elbow and gave it a gentle tug. "Mom, why don't you and Dad sit at my kitchen table and talk? I'm sure you can work this out."

"I don't know." She paused, as if she might relent, then raised her chin. "Did your father find the *TV Guide* yet?"

"For God's sake, Pauline, we don't need that one anymore. The new issue is on the coffee table at home. It's got that George Clooney you like on the front," Dad said, extending an olive branch. Of sorts.

"I don't like George Clooney. I like *Rosemary* Clooney." Her mother let out a sigh that seemed to say, *see, I told you he doesn't love me.*

Was her father that clueless that he didn't know which TV actors her mother preferred? After all these years of marriage? Maybe there was something to Mom's dissatisfaction.

"Rosemary Clooney is *dead,* for Pete's sake. Why would *TV Guide* put her on the cover?" Harold threw up his hands and glanced at his daughter. "See what I have to deal with?"

"You two can solve this, I'm sure." The entire argument made no sense to her, but maybe that was because it was all masking some deeper issues than where the *Better Homes & Gardens* spring garden guide had gone.

"Only if he returns that...that appliance and gets me a real gift." Mom swiped at her eyes, as if wiping away a tear. "Then I'll know he loves me."

"Oh, for Christ's sake, Pauline." Dad pushed the recliner button and popped out the footrest. Then he grabbed the remote off the end table and flipped on the TV, switching stations until he found a basketball game. "You know I love you. If I didn't, would I have ridden all the way up here in that cramped thing Ben calls a car? I swear, you've taken ten years off my life with all this crap about the damned *TV Guide.* You don't even read it."

"The print's too small for my eyes."

"Then why the hell do you subscribe to it?" Dad threw up his hands again and looked to the ceiling, as if hoping for divine intervention.

If she let them go on, Olivia's parents could argue from here to heaven's gates about the merits of one magazine over the other. Olivia didn't see any hope of resolution today, short of staging an intervention with Dr. Phil and Oprah serving as referees.

"I give up," she said. "You two can battle it out. I'm going to make a snack." She headed for the small galley kitchen. Since the apartment was tiny and one room opened into the other, it didn't make for separation as much as a statement.

Mom stomped off to the bedroom, tucking the box of Kleenexes on the coffee table under her arm as she left. Clearly, there'd be no truce, not without some jewelry involved.

Olivia filled a small saucepan with water, then put it on the stove and turned the gas on high to start preparing her specialty—ramen soup.

Her dad ambled in and poked his head into the refrigerator, looking for something to eat since his regular cook was now on strike. "So, Liv, how's the business doing?"

"Uh...fine."

Dad pulled out a Tupperware container, peeked under the lid, made a face and put it back. Probably a good thing, considering Olivia didn't remember what was in there. "You earning a profit?"

As much as she wanted to, she couldn't lie to him. She'd never been able to lie to him. When she'd been a little girl and got caught painting his car red because she thought it needed a new look, it had been her father's patient waiting for an answer that had made Olivia cave and admit her automotive decorating spree. There was just something about the look in her father's eyes, as if he knew he could count on her to eventually tell him, that always made Olivia spill the truth. "I will, Dad."

He clapped a hand on her shoulder. The touch was warm, full of confidence. "I know you will, honey. And you'll do it soon. You're smart and good at everything you put your mind to." He popped the top on a can of soda and tipped some into his mouth. "And when you do, I'll show your mother that investing my retirement in your business was a smart idea. I'm glad one of my kids caught my entrepreneurial bug."

Olivia froze. A lead weight sunk in her gut. "You gave me your retirement money? But I thought you told me it was a savings account. That you'd never touch your retirement." Her voice raised several pitches as the realization hit her. "If I'd known, Dad, I never would have accepted the money."

Her father took a seat at the small kitchen table and spun the Coke can between his hands. "Well, I put a lot of the savings on another horse."

"You *bet* your retirement?"

"Nah. I just backed another business venture that...well, isn't going as well I'd hoped."

Those were words she'd heard a hundred times growing up. It was part of the ongoing argument between her parents—Dad was a risk-taker while Mom liked the security of a Roth IRA and a CD that her husband couldn't touch. The few times when

Dad's investments had worked out, he'd gone and poured all the profit into another idea.

Throughout it all, though, as a promise to his wife, he'd always maintained his retirement account. His job as a Dean of Admissions at Maryland University provided a steady paycheck, good benefits—and the job security to blow his savings every so often.

But now, that was all gone. No wonder he'd skimped on Mom's birthday. No wonder he was looking at her to be the winning horse in his race to make the money back before sixty-five.

"What venture was that?" Olivia asked, stirring the noodles as they softened, pretending she wasn't worried and feeling about as strong as the long, skinny ramen.

Her father's eyes grew bright with the excitement of a new idea, another potential for wealth. Olivia loved him when he was like this, raring to move forward with an idea, excited about the possibilities in the future. When she'd been young, seeing him like this had filled her with the same anticipation she got at Christmas, waiting for Santa.

If there was a bug, as he'd said, she'd caught it then. And it had never gone away. She could feel the fever pitch in her father's voice and as he talked, that same vibe rose in her chest.

"A mobile casting van," Dad said. "Isn't that clever as all hell? Seems these people got the idea off an old episode of *The Apprentice* and figured it would be a hit. Damned good idea. My buddy Rich from the psychology department is running it. He knows people, that's for sure. He's going to be a great casting director, soon as he gets to Steve Bochco. He sold him that dog that woofs at the end of all the shows he's produced, do you know that? 'Course, the dog is dead, but Rich is sure Steve will remember him and show a little movie networking gratitude."

Olivia remembered that episode of Donald Trump's show. But it had taken place in the movie mecca of New York City. Maryland wasn't exactly *the* destination for actors and producers.

"They're going to hit their stride. Just gotta get the right marketing going." He gave her a one-armed hug. "But that's okay. I know you're going to repay that loan and I can put it back in the bank before your mother even notices it's gone."

That, Olivia suspected, had already happened. "But Dad, what if I don't? You had a lot of retirement money; I only borrowed twenty-five thousand. What happened to the rest?"

"Well, you know, spend a little here on Rich's business and a little there on some other things, and before you know it, it's all gone."

A lump of lead sunk to the pit of Olivia's stomach. She never thought he'd go that far. When he'd loaned her additional money she needed for her start-up, he'd assured her it was just savings. If Olivia had known her father would touch his retirement, she would have turned the money down. "It's *all* gone?"

Her father shrugged. "Hey, what's life if you don't take some risks?"

She looked at her father, sixty-two and in the last years of his job. Except for the safe nine-to-five job, Harold Regan had always lived on the brink. He didn't just buy one lottery ticket, he bought a hundred. He didn't bet on one losing pony at the horse track, he bet on every race and only left the track when his pockets were empty.

Now, his pockets really *were* empty. And a good portion of the blame for that went to Olivia herself. Because she'd let him down. Because she hadn't made the profits she'd expected.

And worse, she might never do it.

She glanced at the flyer on her countertop, advertising the Frosting on the Cake competition. Five words flashed back at her, big and red.

Top prize: Fifty Thousand Dollars.

If she won, she could pay her dad back and give Pastries with Panache a much-needed financial shot in the arm.

Yeah, *if*. Her chances of winning were slim. She had better odds betting on a three-legged horse at Suffolk Downs.

Still, there had to be a way.

"You're right, Dad," Olivia said, pouring her soup into a bowl and taking a seat beside the man who'd inspired her and now was counting on her to pay back some of that inspiration. "If you don't take risks, you can't reap the rewards."

Olivia picked up the flyer. If she was going to win this thing, she'd need to pull one well cooked rabbit out of her chef's toque.

Olivia's You-Don't-Always-Get-What-You-Want Blueberry Muffins

1/2 cup margarine
2 cups flour
1 1/4 cups sugar
2 eggs
1/2 cup milk
2 teaspoons baking powder
1/2 teaspoon salt
2 1/2 cups blueberries
2 tablespoons sugar, divided

You may think you have it all planned out, but someone's about to throw a monkey wrench into your life. Keep busy making batter and everything will eventually work out eventually...won't it?

Preheat the oven to 375 degrees. Line 12 muffin cups with paper or non-stick spray. Don't want your muffins to get as stuck as you are right now. Cream the sugar and the margarine then add the eggs, one at a time. Mix in the milk.

If you want a really great texture, sift the dry ingredients before adding them to the wet. If you don't have time and don't mind a few lumps, just mix 'em on in (hey, your whole plan is full of lumps now anyway; seems apropos).

Toss the blueberries with one teaspoon of sugar, then fold them into the mix. Fill the muffin cups 2/3's of the way, then sprinkle the muffins with remaining sugar. Might as well make this as sweet as possible—a little sugar helps take the edge off the worst day. Bake for 25-30 minutes, just enough time to formulate another strategy to get your world turned right-side up again.

CHAPTER TWENTY-FOUR

The next morning, Josie pushed through the door of the shop and found Olivia at one of the tables, an empty pecan pie plate in one hand and a tissue in the other.

"I had another dream, Liv," Josie began. "And you know my dreams are always…well, lots of times… right. In this one, there was this duck—" She slipped off her coat and hung it on the rack, then noticed her sister. "What's wrong?"

Olivia shook her head. "Nothing. Really."

"Uh-huh. I can read the sorrow in your aura, so don't lie to me." Josie came up beside Olivia, draping an arm over her shoulders. "Come on, sis, what gives? Don't make me get the tarot cards out."

Olivia opened her mouth to tell Josie, to let the whole story pour out, but she couldn't. She couldn't add that burden onto her sweet, innocent sister's shoulders. The shop was Josie's dream, too, and telling her the whole thing was going down the drain would pop the bubbles of Josie's optimism.

"Just worried about the business, that's all," Olivia said finally.

"Nothing to worry about," Josie said, waving a hand at her. "Your horoscope today said "a big decision will work out fine." Good times are on their way."

"You know I don't believe in those things."

"Well, you gotta believe in *something*. That's how it works."

"How what works?"

"Life. It's all about believing." She nodded, as if that was the answer to everything.

Olivia shook her head. "Sometimes you have to have money for those beliefs."

Josie dismissed that with a palm. "Money, shmoney. Faith doesn't cost a dime, you know."

Olivia bit back another argument because she knew it was pointless. Josie wasn't the kind to be discussing finances with anyway. She'd charge a new TV, confident the money would be there before the bill came in because the moon was in the right position in the sky. Or the sediment at the bottom of her coffee cup had told her so.

Olivia worked on facts, not coffee grounds.

Josie leaned past her sister and picked up the flyer on the counter. "Hey! This was exactly what was in my dream, except there was this duck, too, carrying brownies in his beak."

"Uh, I don't think they allow ducks in the Worth Hotel."

Josie giggled. "Sure they do, long as they're on a plate." She waved the paper. "You giving this serious thought?"

"No. Yes." Olivia shook her head. "No. I can't do it. It would be a disaster." She let out a little laugh. "You know how I get when I have to cook in front of other people."

"That was at culinary school. It was different."

Olivia shook her head. "They're still talking about me over there. Me and that exploding soufflé."

"Hey, what's a little too much baking powder between friends?"

Olivia chuckled. "Seriously, Jo, I can't compete in that thing."

"Well who says it has to be you beneath the toque?" Josie picked up the tall white chef's hat on the table and slipped it on her head, then took Olivia by the shoulder and turned her to see their reflections in the mirror by the door. "We look a lot alike when my hair is covered up. No one would know."

"*I'd* know. And if Mom and Dad find out you're competing instead of me—"

"They won't. Besides, I'm the quirky one. I'm used to being a disappointment." She grinned. "Come on, Liv. I know what I am—as flaky as our pie crusts. I'm never going to be like you, all statistics and plans."

"Oh, Jo, that's not true. I couldn't have done any of this without you. You're the magic behind everything."

Josie laid the toque on the counter then crossed to the hot water pot and poured herself a cup of tea. "I envy you, Liv. You jumped off the bridge with both feet. Me, I'm just sticking a toe in. I'm a bit more of a scaredy-cat. Might be why I've never stuck with anything as long as I have this."

"Being scared can be good." Olivia sighed. "It can keep you from making a huge mistake."

"Or a great decision." Josie sipped at her cup, the scent of the raspberry lemon brew drifting through the space. "But, I'll let you in on a secret."

"What?"

"I'm not working here because I need the money to pay for beauty school. Or because I wanted to help you out. Or because I felt bad for you when I saw that first cheesecake you tried to make." Josie shook her head at the memory. "That thing had more cracks in it than your average city street."

"Not to mention the nice little valley of raw cream cheese in the center."

"I was hoping you wouldn't bring that up." Josie grimaced. "I just ate breakfast."

Olivia laughed. "Sorry."

"You know why I work here?" Josie didn't wait for a response. Her face was more serious than Olivia had ever seen it, giving her youthful looks a more adult cast. "Because I *love* it. I love to bake. I love the smell of cinnamon rolls and chocolate cake. I love that I can create something with my hands and a couple hours later, watch someone eat it with that dreamy look on their face that says it tastes like heaven."

"But I thought you loved beauty school, too." Olivia looked at her sister, sure this was all a phase.

As much as Josie loved this, Olivia knew that some-day, her sister would drop it for a new passion. It was just the way Josie was.

From the first day, Josie had been here, working alongside Olivia, never complaining, always believ-ing in a rosy future. And all Olivia had done was dis-appoint her sister by running the business into the ground.

Which was exactly why Olivia was going to keep her financial secrets to herself and protect Jo as long as she could. If the Pastries with Panache ship went down, Olivia would throw the life preservers to her father and her sister.

"Listen," Olivia said, "why don't you go home early today, work on your color homework. I can handle the business."

"With one hand tied behind your back as always, right?"

"What's that supposed to mean?"

Josie sighed. "It means you never let me in, Liv. You never let anyone in. I know the business is doing badly; I'm not that stupid."

"I never said—"

"You didn't have to." Josie swallowed, her green gaze on her sister's. "You did it just by keeping silly Josie out of the details."

"Jo, I don't think you're silly. You're just...not the business type."

"How do you know if you don't let me try?"

The question hung in the air between them, heavy and loaded.

Olivia rose, grabbed Josie's coat off the rack then pressed it into her sister's arms and gave her a gentle nudge toward the door. "You've got another life out there, Jo. Another career. Waiting for you to take it."

But her sister didn't budge. "You're not listening. I'm here because I love *this*, Liv. Not beauty school," Josie said, putting up a hand and stopping Olivia's protests before they could be vocalized. "I was the one begging you to take me into the business, remember?"

"I know. But Mom and Dad think you're getting that beauty certificate and going to work for that salon in Newton when you're done…"

"Living up to my potential, finally settling down, yada-yada. Well, news flash, sis, I don't want to be a hairdresser when I grow up. Not anymore."

A panic bell sounded in Olivia's head. That had always been Josie's safety net. Josie, the butterfly, who flitted from one career to another. Josie, the one who needed stability more than anyone Olivia knew. Josie, the one Olivia worried about more than her own self. "What do you mean, not anymore?"

Josie grinned. "I quit beauty school today."

"You did what? But…but…but you were almost done."

Josie plopped into a chair and waved a hand in dismissal. "That was all a mistake."

"A mistake? But…" Olivia's voice trailed off. What could she say that would change Josie's mind? How could she make her flighty sister see the importance of job planning, 401ks and health insurance?

Hadn't this lesson in entrepreneurship taught Josie anything? Olivia had taken all the risks, handled all the crises because she knew the dangers, while Josie lived in rainbow-hued bliss. She couldn't understand the risk she was taking by doing this; she needed the security of another career to fall back. "Why would you do that? What was wrong with being a beautician?"

"Soon as I mixed my first bowl of highlight cream, I knew I didn't want to spend the rest of my life perfecting Jennifer Aniston's haircuts on women who look more like Little Orphan Annie. And I knew something else." She gestured toward the shop. "*This* is my dream. To make Pastries with Panache the best damned pastry shop in the city."

Josie had always been the one to believe in the shop, no matter what obstacles they'd faced, or how few customers came in. Mom called Josie a "Pollyanna"—meaning she put a positive spin on everything, including the existence of aliens.

Still, during the last few difficult months, Josie's emotional—and baking—support had meant a lot, and had kept Olivia going on the days when it seemed pointless to roll out of bed and make more tarts no one was going to eat.

Olivia wrapped her sister in a one-arm hug. "It already is a success and you deserve a lot of the credit, sis."

"All I did was show up and toss around some flour."

Olivia laughed. "You did a lot more than that. Thanks to you, this *is* the best damned pastry shop in the city. Our only problem is the entire population of Boston doesn't know that."

"Well, they will." Josie reached for the toque and settled it back on her head. "On Saturday, Pastries with Panache is going to take home the Frosting on the Cake prize and turn Boston's baking world on its bundt pan."

Olivia opened her mouth to give Josie ten more reasons why it would never work. Then she spied trouble outside her shop. The protestors were back—but with a different tactic this time.

Free samples.

"Do you see that?" Josie asked, pointing out the window at the spandex-clad carb-killers stalking the lunchtime walkers. "Eww. What *are* those?"

"I think they're…" Olivia made a face. "Pork rinds."

"And people are *eating* them? Haven't they heard about those alien pigs in Hawaii? Some people think they came from another planet. I mean, how'd they get on an *island?* I swear, no one thinks about these things." Josie cupped her hand over her eyes to see better through the sunny window. "Hey, there's Lauren and Murph."

Two of their regular customers were indeed dipping a curled, fried pig skin into a tub of sour cream dip. After the taste test, the pair from CitiBank smiled and headed into Sweets without Sin.

"Traitors," Josie muttered. "Maybe *they're* the pod twins. The Lauren and Murph I knew were totally addicted to pie. I swear, it's *Invasion of the Body Snatchers* all over again." She wagged a finger at Olivia. "Watch out for suspicious plants."

Olivia might be out of ideas, suffering from stopped-up cash flow, and trying like heck not to think about a certain bachelor who had turned her life upside-down, but damned if she was going to go down without a fight.

Nor was she going to lose her business to a fried pork skin.

"Two can play at that game," Olivia said. "I'm getting some muffins." She crossed the room and grabbed the platter of fresh-baked muffins in the case.

"I have a good right arm," Josie said, flexing for evidence. "Want me to help take out the fake Lauren and Murph?"

Olivia paused, her voice softening. "Aw, Jo, you've helped too much. I wish you'd reconsider beauty school."

"It's done and I'm happy as hell." Josie's face turned serious again. "This is where I'm supposed to be. With you. Look at my aura." She waved her hands around her head. "It's happy." Then she slid her arms into her coat and turned to face her sister, taking the platter out of Olivia's hands. "Besides, where else am I going to find a job where I can throw muffins at aliens?"

Daniel's What is . . . Regrets?
Easy Chocolate Mousse

8 ounces semisweet chocolate

3 eggs

2 tablespoons espresso

1 teaspoon rum

1 cup whipped cream

The woulda-coulda-shouda syndrome is alive and well inside you right now. You ran away from your responsibilities, now it's time to step up to the plate instead of playing your own game.

Melt the chocolate in a double boiler, then cool it. Meanwhile, beat the eggs in a separate bowl until foamy, then add them to the chocolate. Mix in the espresso and rum, beating until the mousse is as thick as the clog in your throat. Fold in the whipped cream, turning over and over until you've smoothed out the mousse and your life.

CHAPTER TWENTY-FIVE

Daniel halted inside the doorway. Ten feet away lay a pale, thin man who didn't look a thing like his grandfather. Shadows smudged beneath his closed eyes. An oxygen line sat askew beneath his nose. IV tubes ran down into his arm while a machine kept a steady watch on his heartbeat.

The man in the bed seemed twenty pounds thinner and a hundred years frailer. Daniel lifted a chair and brought it over to his grandfather's side, afraid to touch the man who looked as vulnerable as a kitten.

In the next bed, a man in his fifties was watching *Jeopardy* with the volume so high the speakers crackled. He, too, was hooked up to a heart monitor. "This ocean is the largest in the world," Alex Trebek read to the teenage contestants.

"What is Lake Huron?" the guy in the bed shouted. "No, wait. Lake Erie!" When "Pacific" was revealed as the answer, Grandfather's roommate let out a dramatic gust. The machine beside him beeped a warning at all the excitement.

Grandfather's eyes fluttered open. "Daniel." The word came out in a slow rasp.

"Yeah, it's me." Daniel laid one hand on top of the old man's. "How you doing?"

The elder Worth shifted, raising himself up a little on his elbows. "Bored as hell and ready to go home."

Daniel smiled. Apparently, a heart attack wasn't strong enough to tamp down Grandfather's spirit. "The doctor said you were lucky. They caught it early and as long as you take it easy, you should be back to normal soon."

Grandfather waved a hand in dismissal but the movement was slower, more exaggerated than his usual quick snap. "Quacks. What do they know? I feel like I got hit by a truck."

"In Latin, this means 'do not follow,'" Alex read.

The guy in the other bed jerked to a sitting position, his finger punching the remote like he was really competing. "*Ibid!*"

"What is *Non sequitur?*" answered a kid who looked about ten.

Grandfather rolled his eyes at his companion. "I'm getting a private room this afternoon. Too many damned sick people around here."

Daniel chuckled. "That's the point of a hospital."

Grandfather scowled. After a moment of silence, punctuated only by questions about George Washington, Grandfather cleared his throat, reaching for Daniel's arm. "I need you to do something for me."

"What? Anything."

Grandfather's emerald gaze zeroed in on Daniel's. "Take my place at Worth Hotels."

"This eight-letter word means lineage." Alex Trebek paused, waiting.

"What are bindings?" the roommate answered.

Ancestry, Daniel thought, with half of his brain, the half that wasn't running away from the question his grandfather had just poised. A question he didn't want to answer, but knew he had to. "Grandfather, I...I can't take over the business. I don't have the experience—"

Grandfather waved again, pushing the objections away with a shaky palm. "You're the only one I trust."

Grandfather might trust him, but that didn't mean he'd ever have the passion for the company that his namesake had had. "What about John Abbott? He's been your right hand man for years."

Grandfather shook his head, dislodging the oxygen line. "Those Marriott people have been wooing him like a hooker talking to a dimwit in a Ferrari. I can't trust him."

"This part of the brain is used for making decisions."

"Ooh! I know this one!" Grandfather's roommate slammed his thumb on his remote. "What is the coronary artery?" The TV flickered, then switched to a rerun of "Full House." "Damn. Now I'll never if I was right," the guy muttered, flicking furiously to rejoin Alex.

Daniel looked at his grandfather, who was still waiting for an answer that wasn't in the form of a question. If Daniel went to work in the family business now, it would mean giving up everything he'd worked for in the last few days. His dream of making his own way, under his own rules, would get sucked up into the great Hoover vacuum of Worth corporate life. He'd end up stuck on the same hamster wheel he'd been doing his damnedest to avoid. He tried one more time to dissuade Grandfather's plans. "Grandfather, I've never worked at the hotel. I wouldn't know how to do your job."

"What's there to do? You show up, look intimidating and fire someone once in a while. Can one of the idiots in the mailroom and people start taking you seriously." His grandfather paused, readjusted his oxygen line, then sank into the pillows. "I always pictured us working together," his grandfather said, so quietly Daniel almost didn't hear him. "Your father died before…" Grandfather shook his head. "Remember how you used to come to work with me on the weekends? You'd sit beside my desk, doodle on my notepads and tell me that someday, you'd be the big boss."

Daniel chuckled. "Yeah, and one of my first acts would be making room service ice cream free."

Grandfather smiled, a facial gesture that surprised Daniel. It had to be the morphine talking. "I never told you, but I did that."

"You did?"

"Anyone who wants to can get a dish of chocolate. Anytime. No charge."

Daniel's chest constricted. "My favorite flavor."

Grandfather nodded. Then he drew in a weighty breath. "Please, Daniel. Do this for me."

Daniel let his objections go. Across from him was a man who did, indeed, look like he'd become well acquainted with the underside of a truck.

For the first time that Daniel could remember, Grandfather Worth wasn't ordering him to do anything. He was *asking*.

Knowing Grandfather Worth and his stubborn streak, there was no way he would have ever asked nicely, much less said please. The pre-heart attack Grandfather would have preferred his grandson crawl into Brigham & Women's, pledging undying corporate fidelity and begging to be reaccepted into the family fold.

In the last few minutes, Daniel had seen an entirely new side of his grandfather. One that needed him, as much as Daniel had needed comfort on the worst night of his young life. Ironic, wasn't it, that the bridge between himself and Grandfather would have to be built on the very thing Daniel didn't want?

Alex Trebek flashed on the screen again. "This whiskered fish will eat almost anything, including smaller fish in the same species."

Grandfather's roommate waved his remote like a five-year-old who needed a potty break in kindergarten. "What's an orca whale?"

Weariness flooded Grandfather's face. "Daniel?"

Daniel couldn't turn Grandfather down. Whatever his own wants might be, they took a sideline to family. To a family that truly needed him, for the first time in a long, long time. Maybe ever.

Daniel reached for his grandfather's hand and gave it a small squeeze. "You can count on me."

"Sorry, wrong answer," Alex Trebek said.

And with that, Daniel's plan for a new career separate from the Worth name went down to the bottom of Dream Lake, along with the bottom-feeding carnivorous catfish.

Pauline's Impress-the-Date Crackers and Cheese

1 8-ounce block cheddar cheese, sliced
1 package Ritz crackers

Arrange all in an attractive circle; wouldn't want your daughter's date to think you're uncouth. Serve on paper plates, all the while keeping your husband under control and your daughter from dashing off. You need time to see if this handsome bachelor is going to be a good fit with the family.

Of course, if he isn't, then don't waste a single slice of cheese on him. Any guy who doesn't treat your daughter right definitely isn't worth the good crackers.

CHAPTER TWENTY-SIX

On Friday night, Olivia stood in the center of her apartment's living room and tried really hard not to feel fifteen years old again. Her parents sat on the sofa, expectant smiles on their faces, their ongoing argument tucked in the closet with the suitcases.

A truce had been called—because Olivia had a man coming over.

When Daniel had called an hour ago, she'd been so surprised to hear his voice that she hadn't thought about her parents being here. All she'd been able to concentrate on was the deep, husky tones and the simmering heat they ignited. She'd thought about him—a lot—over the last days and had missed him more than she wanted to admit.

It was a different kind of missing than when she'd dated Sam. With Sam, it had been more like a curiosity about where he was and whether he was thinking about her. Back then, hours would go by and then with a start, she'd realize she hadn't thought of Sam once.

With Daniel, well, that hadn't been the case. Thoughts of him came as regularly as the ticking of a second hand.

She truly missed Daniel's company, his conversations, his touch. His teasing grin and those blue eyes that seemed to see right through her, reading the secrets she'd managed to keep from everyone else.

"I can't wait to meet your gentleman," Mom said. "Maybe he'll be The One."

The One? Lord, it made him sound like Neo in "The Matrix". Here to save the world and Olivia's lacking love life. She might have missed him, thought about him constantly, had this constant heat of need in her gut, but she wasn't going to marry him.

She wasn't going to marry anyone right now. She had bigger fish on her plate than a ring and a veil.

She should have met Daniel in a dark alley. Or a street corner. Anywhere but here. But when he'd called that afternoon, with an invitation to dinner, her mind had flown the coop.

Clearly, he wasn't the only one with a craving. Her thoughts hadn't just been on his conversational abilities, that was for sure.

"Olivia, don't you think those heels are a little high? You're going to break your neck." Her mother gestured toward the three-inch Enzo pumps. "Harold, don't you agree?"

Dad shrugged and reached for a Ritz topped with a slice of cheddar off the tray on the coffee table. Mom slapped his hand and he dropped them back into place.

Leave it to her mother to get out *appetizers* for Olivia's date. She hadn't just stopped at cheese and crackers, either. A sticky stack of Rice Krispie squares sat on a small floral plate beside a crudité of olives and tiny pickles.

Olivia groaned inwardly. It was eighth grade all over again.

"Stop pacing, dear," Mom said. "You'll get all sweaty."

Olivia reached for her coat on the hook by the front door. "I'll just meet him downstairs." As far away from the parental inquisition as possible.

"Why? Are you ashamed of us?" Her mother's face turned down into a frown of disappointment.

"I'm a little old for pre-date approval, Mom."

"What if he's a serial killer? If we don't meet him first, how will we ever give the police a good description?"

Olivia didn't bother to argue the logic of meeting the next Ted Bundy and then wishing her daughter well on her date. "Mom, he's not a serial killer."

"How do you know? I see them on *Dateline* all the time. They look perfectly normal and bam! Next thing you know, you're in a ditch somewhere and he's in your car, driving to Mexico."

Olivia sighed. It was pretty clear where Josie got her tendency to believe in all things unexplained.

Where was Daniel? According to her watch, he was ten seconds late. The minute he rang the bell to get in the building, Olivia was going to bolt. She'd deal with her mother's predictions of a grisly murder later.

"You're our little girl," her father said, sneaking a piece of cheese and popping it in his mouth before Mom's wrath descended on his wrist again. "We care about the company you keep."

"For Pete's sake, it's just dinner."

Her mother raised a brow. "With men, it's never *just dinner*. Isn't that right, Harold?"

Dad raised his hands, refusing to acknowledge the baser intentions of his sex.

The doorbell rang. Finally. Olivia buzzed Daniel into the building, anticipation boiling within her.

"I remember when I met your father," Mom continued. "We went out for dinner and didn't come home till one in the morning." She waggled her eyebrows. "He definitely wanted more than three courses."

"Eww, Mom. Please don't tell me that."

"Well, it's true. Harold was quite the player in our younger days."

"Knew you like a fiddle," he said, reaching for another cracker.

Olivia stepped to the peephole and looked out, vowing to go to church more often. This conversation had to be a preview of hell.

And then, she saw him, striding down the hall like a man with a purpose. He held a bouquet of yellow and white roses in one hand and a bottle of white wine in the other.

He looked damned good in a white button-down shirt, red tie and dark blue pants. Heat stirred in her gut, rushing through her veins. Damn. She had missed him.

He'd been in every cake she'd tried to decorate, every chocolate chip she melted, every muffin she stirred. Thoughts of him simmered in her dreams, in her thoughts. He wasn't just dessert before dinner. He was the whole enchilada and the Belgian waffles for breakfast the morning after.

"He's coming, Harold," her mother said. "Behave yourself. And for God's sake, put down that pickle."

Olivia opened the door and for a few seconds, forgot everything except Daniel. His deep blue gaze, the smile that had become as familiar as her own face. "Hi."

"Hi yourself," he said. "These are for you." He handed her the roses and wine, placing a quick, chaste kiss on her cheek.

"Why don't you ever do that for me?" Mom gave Dad an audible punch.

Oh yeah. Her parents. Olivia flashed an apologetic smile at Daniel. "My parents are staying with me for a while," she explained. "Let me introduce you." She turned, praying her parents would contain themselves and not embarrass her like they had in front of her prom date, insisting they pose for pictures that re-enacted the entire dance. "Mom and Dad, this is Daniel. Daniel, these are my parents, Pauline and Harold Regan."

"Olivia, really," her mother scolded. "Doesn't the man have a last name?"

"Worth," Olivia coughed.

Her mother's eyes widened. "As in the hotel?"

"Uh...spelled just the same," Olivia said, side-stepping the truth. If she told her parents he was *the* heir, her mother would be hauling her off to the first justice of the peace she could find. To Mom, a man with a dependable income source was better than a lifetime subscription to *TV Guide.*

"Damned fine beds they have there," her father said. "Me and your mother broke one in on that vacation to Chicago in eighty-two. We—"

"Dad! Don't. Please." If there was anything that could send Olivia off the deep end of mortification, it was her parents talking about their sex life. She preferred to think she'd been conceived in a vacuum, in a test tube, in outer space...anywhere but in their bed. Or worse, a Worth Hotel king-sized.

"It's a pleasure to meet you both," Daniel said. "Your daughter is quite a woman."

"That's my girl," her mother said.

"It's because she's got her father's blood in her," Olivia's father said. "Makes her a risk-taker, I say."

"I'd rather she inherited your nose," Mom muttered.

Olivia grabbed Daniel's hand. "Well, we better get going if we want to make our reservation." She had no idea if he'd made a reservation or not and frankly didn't care. She'd call one in to Burger King just to get out before her mother started in on her life choices.

"Are you saying I'm a bad influence on my children?" Dad pivoted to face his wife.

"Daniel," Mom said, putting on a bright face. "Won't you at least stay for some hors d'oeuvres?" She gestured toward the appetizers, as glaringly middle class as a minivan in the driveway.

To her surprise, Daniel tugged Olivia's hand and led her to the sofa. "It would be my pleasure, Mrs. Regan," he said. And so they sat down, with Olivia squished between her mother and Daniel.

Her mother beamed, handing him a Dixie plate loaded with a Ritz and cheese, two olives and a Rice Krispie square.

"Thank you, Mrs. Regan. This looks delicious."

"Oh, why thank you," Mom said, blushing. "I just threw it together."

Daniel had just done something no other man she'd dated had been able to do—made mega brownie points with her parents. To Sam, meeting her parents at Thanksgiving last year had been an irritation he needed to get through before he and Olivia returned to their hotel room for the night. He'd sulked all the way through the mashed potatoes, making less conversation than the deep-fried turkey.

But Daniel—Daniel seemed genuinely interested in getting to know her parents. Their worlds were as far apart as Venus and Pluto, but he closed that gap by biting into a Rice Krispie square and proclaiming it "delicious."

"I told Olivia she should have made you something," Mom said, clearly sizing him up as a potential filler for Olivia's lonely future. "She owns that shop and yet wouldn't bake a *thing* for her guest. And you should see her kitchen. Not a single decent ingredient."

"Overload the guy on sugar and the next thing you know, he's falling asleep on the table," Dad put in. "Plus, he looks like a meat and potatoes fellow to me."

"I enjoy Olivia's—" Daniel began.

"A girl needs to sweeten up a date," her mother went on, as if Olivia and Daniel weren't there. "How do you expect her to ever keep a man interested?"

"I'm interested—" Daniel tried again.

"We love you, Olivia," Mom said, giving her daughter's knee a pat, clearly not hearing Daniel at all, "but we both know you can be as gentle as a cactus sometimes."

"You're not exactly a daisy yourself," Dad muttered to his wife.

Mom put a hand on her hip and gave him the evil eye she'd perfected with three children, daring him to repeat that. "Are you telling me *I'm* unpleasant?"

He shrugged, grabbing the Rice Krispies for himself. "If the thorn in your side fits…"

"*Thorn in your side?*" Her mother rose and yanked the tray of marshmallow molded cereal out of her husband's grasp. "How unpleasant do you think it would be to starve?"

"Now, Pauline, calm down. All I'm saying is that sometimes, you're a bit...prickly." He grinned and reached for her hand. "And sometimes, prickly can be fun."

"*Harold Regan...*" her mother began.

That was it. Definitely time to bug out before her parents started marriage World War Three, or, in their case, war number three hundred. "We're running late," Olivia cut in, jerking Daniel to his feet. "Thanks for the treats, Mom."

"Oh, don't go," Mom said, her voice now polite and high-pitched with sweetness. "Ignore your father's innuendos and we'll have a fine time."

"I'm used to the ignoring," Dad muttered. "Just put a bowl of food before me and stick me in a corner."

"Don't exaggerate, dear," Mom said. "I always offer you a seat at the table before I ignore you."

"Uh, we'll be late," Olivia said again, making her way toward the door.

"There's one of those cookie dough tubs in the fridge. I could make—"

"No thanks, Mom." Olivia shouted a firm good-bye and managed to get Daniel out of there before her mother could prepare a tray of slice-and-bake cookies—and show Daniel the uglier side of a long-term relationship.

"I'm sorry about that," she told him once they were safely on the sidewalk outside her building.

Daniel chuckled. "They're not so bad. It reminds me a bit of being at Lewiston's house. His mother was a nice lady, but if you crossed her…watch out. You got it with both barrels *and* the reserve TNT. But at the heart of it all, she loved her kids." He shrugged, as if that wasn't a big deal, but Olivia got the distinct feeling it had been.

"And you," Olivia said softly, realizing the rich boy had found something special in his butler's home, "became an unofficial member of the family?"

Daniel shrugged. "I guess so. I was an only kid, so it didn't take much to make me feel included." He let out a little laugh, as if it hadn't meant a lot.

But Olivia could tell it had. As annoyed as her parents made her, Josie and Ben, the three of them knew Mom and Dad loved them. Her childhood had been, for the most part, a fun one, overflowing with her father's adventurous spirit and her mother's caution-filled love. No matter what had befallen the family economically, the three Regan kids had never wanted for anything.

Especially love.

Olivia looked at one of the richest men in Boston and realized he'd lacked the one thing in the world that was always given away for free. "Hey, if you ever want to be part of a slightly dysfunctional family, you're welcome to mine."

He chuckled. "I'll keep that in mind. For the future."

She left those words there, turning them over in her mind. A future. With Daniel. Other than her financial projections for the shop, she hadn't thought that far ahead with anything. Especially a man.

A future she'd have later. Much later.

The winter air bristled around them, zipping a chill up her skirt and through her sweater. Olivia drew her long wool coat closed. Before she could button it, Daniel had his arm around her, taking her into the protective, warm circle of his own cashmere coat. "Thanks," she said.

She could have turned him down, could have enforced her independence as she always did. Or she could be smart and for just one second, let this gorgeous, interested guy take care of her.

And revel in the feeling. For a single, simple moment.

"Wouldn't want you to be uncomfortable. Ever." His smile seemed to shut out the world around them.

Was he doing what he had done with the women in her shop and pretending she was the only woman in the world? Or did he really mean it?

She looked into his cobalt eyes and saw something she hadn't seen when he looked at the other women. A depth, a layer that said this was for real.

He was for real.

Fear raced through her, chased by desire. Should she take this chance? Trust this feeling?

Trust him?

Olivia drew in a breath and took a huge leap off the bridge again—this time with her heart.

Tonight, she would trust him. Allow herself to need him. And let him inside the part of her that she had guarded as closely as her PIN number. Maybe it was because she'd been weakened by missing him.

Maybe it was because he'd been sweet with her parents. Maybe it was simply because he'd shoveled her walk, carving a path straight to her door.

And maybe it was something more—something she refused to acknowledge right now.

He opened the door of a white Cadillac Escalade and gestured for her to get in. "You got your car back?" she asked when he had climbed in on his side.

"I got the whole life back," Daniel replied, dangling the keys in his hands and staring at them as if they were strangers. "I'm now working at Worth Hotels full-time, running the company."

She blinked at him, stunned. "But...I thought that's what you didn't want."

"I still don't. But my grandfather is ill and he needs me. Saying no isn't an option."

Olivia heard the tendrils of sadness in his voice, the regrets of things undone. Yet at the same time, she felt a newfound respect for him, for giving up his independence, his dreams, because his family needed him. The moonlight cast him in a soft glow, glinting off his hair. She reached out, laying a hand on his. "You're a good man."

He shook his head. "No. I'm just an average guy trying to do the right thing. For once."

"I disagree." In her grasp, his palm felt warm, comfortable, as if she'd held his hand a hundred times before and could hold it a hundred times more. "I'm impressed. Very much so."

He hesitated, his hand on the gearshift. "You're impressed that I went to work for my grandfather?"

She turned in her seat to face him. In the dark, everything between them multiplied, intensified. Suddenly, Olivia didn't want to talk anymore, didn't want to think whether getting more involved with Daniel Worth was a good idea or not. She simply *wanted* Daniel.

Wanted a little piece—okay, a big piece—of this man who'd turned her expectations, her life and her heart upside down.

Olivia had never met anyone like him, someone who could throw away a fortune and then step up to the plate to fill in for a pair of shoes that didn't fit. She wanted to wrap herself in him, in his world. For tonight—before the real world intruded and forced her to push her own needs aside again.

"I'm not only impressed," she said, grinning. "I'm….well, more attracted to you than ever. I'm one of those twisted women who finds a responsible man sexy as hell."

The familiar tease lit the blue in his eyes and his mouth lifted up one corner. Damn, how she liked that smile. A quiver of need shot through her, hard and fast. It nearly took her breath away in a powerful rush.

This time, Olivia wouldn't shush those demands.

"What if I told you I cleaned my room today?" Daniel said. "And helped take out the trash?"

She laughed. "I'd tell you that's the most sensual thing anyone has said to me all week."

He turned, moving closer, his lips brushing against hers. "You're one easy to please woman, Miss Regan."

"Now you're wrong," she whispered against his mouth. "I have expectations. *Big* expectations."

"Then maybe I should fulfill them." He kissed her, his lips capturing hers as easily as they would a breath of air. Too soon, he pulled away, leaving her wanting. Frustrated. "What about dinner?"

"We'll order in." Right now, she didn't care if she ever ate again. All she craved, all she needed, was him. Touching her, kissing her, quieting that hungry need pulsing within her for him. Only him.

"But—"

"No more buts, Worth." She swung her body over the gearshift and into his lap. She tugged up her skirt, watching his eyes widen as she did, then straddled him, one leg tucked on each side of the bucket seat. "I know what you said about waiting, but I don't *want* to wait. I want you. Now."

Desire exploded in Daniel's brain, sending fire to his groin. What was that he'd said about waiting? He'd had a damned good reason before, but he couldn't remember it now. Hell, he was lucky he could remember his own name right now.

On his lap, pressing against his groin, was a beautiful, desirable and intriguing woman. All he had to do was put his car in gear, drive like hell over to his house, then carry her up the stairs and into his bed. Nirvana waited just on the other side of Boston.

He lowered his mouth to hers again, tasting the sweet spice of Olivia. She moaned and cupped his head, asking for more with her touch, her kiss, her tongue. *Damn.*

She was incredible, this spunky woman who made him want more out of himself for the first time in his life. In that moment, Daniel realized the most dangerous thing he'd done hadn't been walking out on the Worth fortune.

It had been falling in love with Olivia Regan.

Olivia's Surpassed-Your-Expectations Génoise

1 cup all-purpose flour
pinch of salt
4 eggs
2/3 cup sugar
1/2 teaspoon vanilla extract
4 tablespoons butter, clarified and cooled
Chocolate Icing from Lewiston's Boston
Cream Pie

Oh. My. God. Words can't even describe how you're feeling right now, so just lay back and revel in it. The man is a master at what he does—no wonder women quack at him.

To top off this awesome, amazing time, you need chocolate. Preheat the oven to 350 degrees and lightly butter a deep cake pan, then line it with parchment. Dust the parchment with flour.

Sift the flour and salt and set aside. Put the eggs in a heatproof bowl over a pan of simmering water. Beat the eggs and then gradually add the sugar (pretty much the way he teased you with sweetness, a little at a time), stirring and cooking for 8-10 minutes. When the mixture is thick and ribbon-like, remove it from the heat, and stir in the vanilla. Beat until cool.

Fold in the flour, reserving one-third of the dry ingredients. Stir in the butter, then add the remaining flour. It should look fluffy and airy, pretty much the way you're feeling…after.

Bake for 25-30 minutes. After it's cool, top with the chocolate icing. Indulge repeatedly—the cake and the man.

CHAPTER TWENTY-SEVEN

When she was a junior in high school, Olivia had read her first romance novel. Fifteen years later, she couldn't remember the names of the hero or heroine, or even much of the plot, but she did remember one thing. The hero had made the heroine feel cherished.

When she'd finished their story, Olivia had closed the book and lay under the pink striped comforter in her twin bed, wondering if she would ever meet a man who would do that for her.

Until today, she hadn't. Until Daniel.

He had carried her up the stairs of his townhouse, his lips on hers the entire time, teasing, caressing, promising. She wrapped her arms around his neck and gave him back as good as he gave, feeling a surge of electricity with each step that brought them closer to his bedroom. Moments later, he crossed the threshold into a massive room—bigger than her entire apartment—and decorated in rich hues of burgundy and forest green. Without breaking his stride, Daniel carried her to the bed and laid her gently on the down comforter. Olivia sighed. It was like sinking into a cloud.

"It's a king, isn't it?" Olivia said.

"Of course."

A smile curved across her face. "Perfect."

He lowered his mouth to hers again, kneeling beside her on the bed. Slowly, he kissed along her lips, down her jaw and then down her neck, pausing at the V of her sweater. Olivia moaned and arched up against him, wishing she could snap her fingers and her clothes would magically disappear.

She reached between them, tugging his shirt out of his waistband and sliding her fingers against his bare skin, along the waistband of his pants, dipping her touch beneath the edge, to run a teasing path along his hips.

Daniel groaned and rolled to one side, pulling her on top of him. She straddled his waist, tossing her hair back and out of her face. His hands went to her shirt, fingers deftly slipping the tiny pearl buttons out of the holes of her cardigan. She slid it off her arms, then raised them so he could slip off the matching tank. In seconds, she was wearing only a lacy pink bra. Close enough to naked. For now. Cool air rushed against her chest and her nipples peaked beneath the fabric.

Daniel reached behind her, unhooking her skirt and tugging the zipper down as far as he could. Without a word, Olivia moved to one side, allowing him to pull her skirt down and off, tossing it aside.

"Oh, God, Olivia, you're…incredible." He ran a palm across the flatness of her belly then slid his warm fingers along her hips, teasing at the edge of her matching panties.

"You're not so bad yourself," she managed, retaking her position across his waist. She smoothed her palms along the hard planes of his torso. Well-defined muscles met her touch, solid and firm. The kind a woman could lean on. The kind that embodied strength, security, masculinity.

Everything that had been missing from her life until now.

Sam had been softened by his desk job, his muscles about as firm as a cheap mattress. But Daniel… Daniel was a hundred-percent male. Everywhere.

Between them, his erection pressed against her, hot and hard. She shuddered, then squeezed her thighs against him, wanting, needing what was still too far away.

"I want to see you," Daniel said, his voice low and hot. "All of you."

"Is that an order?" She grinned.

"Absolutely."

Still smiling, she reached behind her back, undid the clasp on her bra and slid the pink lace off one shoulder, then the other, cupping her breasts with her palms, holding the scrap of fabric in place a while longer. The slow tease lit a spark in his eyes. "Patience is a virtue," she said, repeating his words from the last time they'd been in bed.

"It's damned hard to be virtuous when you're sitting on my lap in nothing but your underwear," he said, the words nearly a growl.

"You're right. I really shouldn't be sitting here in my underwear." She tossed the bra to the side then slid off him just long enough to peel her panties off and drop them to the floor. In an instant, she was back on him. "There. Is that better?"

"Much." He reached up and cupped the soft flesh of her breasts, drawing his thumbs across the sensitive tips. A shiver raced down her spine and a little mew of need sounded in her throat.

"It's a lot more fun when both of us are naked, you know," she said.

"I was always taught that it's polite to let ladies go first." Daniel grinned. "And to take care of the lady's needs before your own."

She caught the heated glimmer in his eyes as he grabbed her waist and rolled her to her back. Oh. My. God. This was going to be good. So good. "Daniel…" her voice trailed off as he began to show her how wonderful going first could be, with his mouth, his fingers. Then, finally, when she thought she could stand no more, he tugged off his briefs with one hand.

He paused only long to sheath himself with a condom from the bedside table, then slid into her, filling her want with his length. She raced her hands up and down his back, thrusting her hips upward to meet his deep, long strokes.

They moved in concert, fitting each other as perfectly as two pieces of the same puzzle. He buried his face in her hair, kissing the tender places along her nape, then nibbling lightly on her ear. The sensations scorched her nerve endings, setting everything within her on fire.

Olivia closed her eyes, and images of everything she'd ever dreamed of filled her mind, tinged with the fire of passion. Making love with Daniel Worth was a fantasy come to life—

The kind that had fueled all those Cinderella dreams, yet with a decided adult flare. For the first time since she'd met Daniel, Olivia stopped worrying about her business.

And worried instead about her heart.

Then he reached a hand between them to cup her breast, his thumb circling the nipple. He increased the pace of his strokes, sending her mind and pulse into a frenzy. Olivia thrust against him, matching him stroke for stroke, feeling the impending crescendo rushing through her, blinding her sight and stopping her breath. And then, in an explosion all of her needs were answered, as her orgasm swept over her like a tidal wave. A second later Daniel called out her name in a sweet, soft whisper, then reached his own climax.

This time, Daniel fulfilled someone's expectations. In spades.

An hour later, Olivia lay in Daniel's arms, every muscle in her body feeling about like a limp tissue after a few very good rounds of sex. Daniel had kissed and caressed, and used parts of her body she didn't even know were erogenous to coax her to one dizzying orgasm after another, before she said to hell with ladylike behavior and climbed on top of him to give the gentleman back as good as he'd given to her.

He'd cried out her name when he climaxed, his fingers tangled in her hair, his lips against her neck. Something beyond desire rushed through her then, adding a crescendo to the last climax that made something in her heart take flight.

Toward thoughts of a future. Of more than tonight. Crazy thoughts, she reasoned, brought on by too many pheromones in the air and pooling lactic acid from her especially spirited ride atop him.

"You were amazing," he whispered, his fingers toying with her upper arm.

"You weren't so bad yourself."

"I hear practice makes perfect." He raised a brow.

"In that case," she said, grinning, "I think you need a *lot* of practice."

He chuckled heartily. "You're going to kill me, Olivia. Don't you think three times is enough?"

"For now. I'll let you take a breather." She rubbed a hand across his chest, enjoying the solid feel of him beneath her palm.

"Okay, so how about a tamer subject? One that doesn't have anything to do with sex?"

She chuckled. "Wouldn't want to get me going again, is that it?"

He smiled. "At least not until we've eaten." He curled her against his side. "So how's the business going?" he asked. "I'm sure people have forgotten all about that stupid newspaper article."

Her libido dropped to near zero. "Let's not ruin a perfectly good evening with talk about business."

"That bad, huh?"

"Let's just say I better add a whole new menu of meat and cheese items if I want to survive." She wriggled closer against him, enjoying the warmth and comfort. For one moment more, she told herself, she'd lie here and shut out everything else.

"I've been thinking," Daniel said. "And I'd like to make you a deal."

"A deal?"

"Worth hotels uses a lot of pastries. The downtown Boston location alone goes through tens of thousands of dollars worth of desserts every year. I'd like to hire Pastries with Panache to handle that."

A huge contract like that…it would be the answer to what she needed. An easy answer, dropped in her lap, like a gift from heaven. "But don't you have a chef on site?"

"Yes, and he can still do his job. He'll simply have less work to do since you'll be picking up all the slack. That'll leave him free to concentrate on our catering end." He tapped her nose with his finger. "Leaving all the rest of the business for you."

Olivia raised up on an elbow. What Daniel was offering her was incredible—too incredible. "No. I can't accept that."

"Olivia, don't be proud about this. You told me yourself that business is slow. That you're having financial problems. Right now, I'm the head of Worth hotels and I have the power to do something about that for you."

"And when your grandfather comes back to work, what will happen then?"

Daniel grinned. "With a bite of your cheesecake, I'm sure I can persuade him to keep Pastries with Panache on board."

She jerked to a sitting position. "I can't believe this."

"I know. It's a great opportunity."

She climbed out of the bed, standing in his room stark naked and not even caring. "Would you have made this same offer if you had met me on the street?"

"I don't know," he said. "Maybe. If you bribed me with one of those muffins." He grinned.

"I'm serious, Daniel. The only reason you're doing this is because you feel sorry for me. I'm not a Baby Bell that the big Ma Bell has to take under her wing. I'm perfectly capable of earning my own business. On my merits, not on the favors I do."

"Is that what you think this was?" He gestured toward the bed. "A down payment on the contract?"

She put her hands on her hips. "Wasn't it?"

"No, Olivia. It wasn't anything like that." Daniel rose, moving to stand before her. "I made love to you because I care about you."

She shook her head, pulling on her underwear and bra. "Yeah, as a charity case you need to give a handout to."

"That's not what this is," Daniel said.

Maybe not. But if Olivia took this offer, what would it prove? That she needed to be bailed out by her rich boyfriend? That she couldn't do this on her own? If she accepted Daniel's deal, she'd never know if she could have succeeded on her own.

And for Olivia, that was the entire point.

Olivia tugged on her sweater, haphazardly fastening a couple of the buttons, then reached for her skirt. "Oh no? Because that's what it feels like to me."

"Why are you so stubborn? I'm trying to help you, not take over your company."

"I would think that you, of all people, would understand why I want to do this on my own. I want my shop to make it because I was a smart business-woman. Not because I slept with the richest bachelor in Boston."

He shook his head. "You're impossible."

"No. you're just back to being your old self."

"What are you talking about?"

"Oh no? What was the first thing you did when I met you? Pulled out your checkbook. Then you were doing it to get rid of me." She choked back the hot sting of hurt in her throat, then grabbed her shoes and purse off the floor. "Now you're doing it as a tip."

He followed after her, charging down the stairs behind her hurried pace. "Olivia, you're wrong."

She wheeled around on the bottom landing. "Am I? Or are you just falling back into your old habits?"

Before he could think of the right words to stop her, Olivia was gone.

Olivia's Make-It-Quick
Baked Bananas in Orange Sauce

2 bananas
1 tablespoon orange rind, grated
1 tablespoon honey
1 tablespoon orange juice
1 teaspoon vanilla

Keep it simple—you don't have the time or energy to be messing with anything more complicated than a couple of fruits. Preheat the oven to 450 degrees, then slice the bananas horizontally and lay them on four individual pieces of foil.

Mix all of the sauce ingredients together, spoon the sauce on top of the bananas, then seal the little foil packets and put them on a cookie sheet. Bake for 5 to 10 minutes—just enough time to realize you're about to make a huge mistake.

CHAPTER TWENTY-EIGHT

Olivia was in the middle of a perfectly good dream about a naked and penniless Daniel Worth who was offering her his body for recipe research when the lights came on and somebody started shaking her awake.

"Liv, wake up." Her father's voice. He gave her another nudge. "It's Josie."

Olivia bolted upright. Her sleepiness disappeared in an instant. "Josie? What's happened?"

"Seems her appendix has had enough. It burst early this morning and they rushed her into Mass General, to get it removed."

Olivia ran a hand through her hair, processing the words. Josie. Sick. Panic rushed into Olivia's chest, sucking the air out of her lungs. "Is she okay?"

He nodded. "In fact, she was asking me to sneak in some of those cinnamon rolls you sell." Dad chuckled and patted Olivia's hand. "She's going to be fine."

Olivia swung her feet over the bed and reached for her robe on the wingback chair in the corner. She stood, pulled it over her nightshirt and belted the terrycloth across her waist. "I'm going with you. I want to see her."

"But...isn't today Valentine's Day?" Dad asked.

Olivia was already in her closet, looking for a pair of jeans. Anything clean and decent that she could throw on. Clearly, she'd been spending too much time working lately because the clean clothes pickings were slim. "Yeah, but what does that have to do with anything?"

"Aren't you supposed to be somewhere this morning?"

It took a second for her brain to make the connection. And when it did, it came with a rush of panic. "The Frosting on the Cake competition. Oh God. I forgot."

Well, she hadn't forgotten *exactly*. She wasn't the one who was supposed to be there this morning. But her parents didn't know that. No one knew except Olivia and Josie.

"You can make it over there if you hurry," her father said. "Go win that fifty grand. I know you can do it, sweetie. I've tasted your petit fours."

"But, Dad, I wasn't going to—" Olivia cut herself off. She couldn't tell him Josie was the one who was supposed to be going. That Josie was the one with the cooking skill. That Josie was the one everybody should be looking at to win this thing, not Olivia.

Because Olivia Regan was a fraud.

She was a culinary school dropout because no matter how hard she'd tried, she'd never mastered a single pastry dish. She'd come home every night, trying over and over again to get her rolls to rise and her cakes to be moist, but it hadn't worked. She'd been about to quit, to admit she couldn't make all those statistics and business demographics work with a single cupcake, when Josie had stepped in.

In five seconds, Josie had mastered meringue.

That was when they'd made the plan. Josie would do the baking in the mornings before she went to school and Olivia would run the business. It seemed like a perfect plan—one that kept Josie employed and would give Olivia more time to learn how to cook. Olivia had figured that by the time Josie finished beauty school and had her future secure, Olivia would be able to take over the cooking.

It hadn't exactly worked out that way.

"Come on, you better get moving," her father said. "That fifty grand isn't going to walk over to you, you know."

"I—" But Olivia didn't finish the sentence. How could she? Her father was counting on her, counting on her business to be the one that paid him back and launched his daughter into the first Regan entrepreneurship success story.

Pastries with Panache needed to win the Frosting on the Cake. They needed the prize money desperately. If she didn't pull off a miracle, her father's retirement years would be spent packing groceries at the Stop 'N Shop just so her parents could afford canned tuna.

Olivia knew Josie had written out a plan for the competition, along with all her recipes and some kind of astrological chart for preparation order, designed for maximum luck. Back at the shop, the box of ingredients and utensils was ready to go.

Olivia could follow directions, more or less. How hard would it be to just implement that?

Besides, hadn't Josie said that with the chef hat on, no one could tell them apart?

Olivia could only pray that was true...and pray that she grew a flour-colored thumb in the next couple of hours.

Olivia's Nothing's-Going-Well Rocky Road Wedges

1 cup butter, softened
1 cup brown sugar
2 eggs
1 3/4 cups flour
1/4 cup unsweetened cocoa
1 teaspoon baking soda
1/2 teaspoon salt
3 cups semisweet chocolate chips
1 cup nuts (your choice), chopped
1 cup mini marshmallows

The heat is on for you to make something amazing, but you're not so sure you're up to the challenge. Heck, any challenge right now. Try making these bars because hopefully any judge can be swayed by a little chocolate and marshmallow.

Preheat your oven to 350 degrees. Take a breath, get some perspective. Think positive. Cream the butter and sugar then add the eggs one at a time. In a separate bowl, mix the flour, cocoa, baking soda and salt, then add that to the wet ingredients and mix until well blended. Deep breath. You can do this.

Make two 8-inch circles of dough on a cookie sheet, then bake them for 15 minutes. Sprinkle with marsh-mallows, chips and nuts, then bake another 3 minutes. Allow to cool for a few minutes, then stack your circles and serve. And pray like heck that everything is going to work out.

And you won't end up completely humiliating yourself.

CHAPTER TWENTY-NINE

When Olivia had been nine, she'd been riding a Ferris wheel that got stuck at the top for fifteen minutes. Dangling fifty feet above the ground, the wind swinging the hard metal seat back and forth, had set off a wave of panic as strong as a hurricane. Olivia held on and prayed, until the ride was finally fixed and returned her to the safety of the ground.

Olivia now stood in the center of her temporary kitchen, set up in the Worth Hotel ballroom while hundreds of people filed into spectator seats to watch the Frosting on the Cake competition. She felt a lot like she had on that Ferris wheel.

Only a hundred times worse. And without a safety belt to prevent her inevitable fall.

Olivia's heart raced, sweat beaded her brow and her feet seemed cemented to the carpeted floor. She sent up a prayer, swallowed hard and hoped like hell she could move when it came time.

The clock on the wall turned from 8:59 to 9:00. A skinny man in a tux stepped up to the microphone at the front of the room. "And our competition will begin in three…two…one!" A buzzer sounded and the announcer waved a toque like a checkered flag. "Chefs, start your ovens!"

Olivia glanced down at Josie's handwritten notes. In her nervous hands, the paper shook and blurred. Oh God. What was she supposed to do again? For a full minute, Olivia couldn't remember if she was here to bake a pizza or a puff pastry.

Take a deep breath. You can do this.

She inhaled. Exhaled. Inhaled again. Then she crossed to the stainless steel counter of her cubicle, laid Josie's notes on the flat surface and then breathed in and out until her heart stopped beating like a jackhammer.

This was a challenge like any other. She reminded herself that she liked challenges. Liked standing on the edge, not knowing what was coming next.

Except that this was like standing on a cliff, overlooking shark-infested waters with a hungry grizzly nibbling at her heels.

Olivia glanced down at Josie's list. She squinted, trying to make out her sister's scribbled notes. Number one: cheesecake. She could do this. It was *just* cheesecake, after all.

Except she'd failed cheesecake making. Three times.

Fourth times a charm, Liv. She unwrapped the foil on a package of cream cheese and dropped it into the bowl of her Kitchen Aid mixer. There, that wasn't so bad. She turned it on and watched it slowly turn the lumps into a soft whipped mixture. One after another, she added the necessary ingredients, keeping the mixer moving.

A cinch. Right?

She checked the clock. Plenty of time. Just dump it in the pan, put it in the oven, let the heat do the rest and Voila! In an hour, her cheesecake would be ready.

She hoped. The memory of her culinary school cheesecake attempts still churned in her stomach. And probably in her instructor's, too.

Beside her, the other eight chefs were bustling around their kitchens, mixing and pouring, whipping and blending. Not a one looked like he needed an oxygen tank, unlike Olivia who was ready to hyperventilate at the thought of starting another dish.

The cheesecake mixed, Olivia poured it into a springform pan that she'd added graham crackers to earlier. Too late, she realized she'd forgotten to preheat the oven. Cursing under her breath, Olivia scanned Josie's notes for the baking temperature. Was that 325? 350? Or 375? And did it say bake for sixty minutes? Or ninety?

Olivia decided to err on the side of heat—the memory of her runny cheesecake still pretty vivid—and turned the oven knob to 375. While she waited for the stove to preheat, she returned to the list. Number two: raspberry soufflé. Oh God, not one of those. The last one she'd made had caved in on itself like the Grand Canyon. Only without the pretty vistas. And tasting a lot like rock face.

Olivia closed her eyes. The image of Josie and her parents came to mind. She couldn't let them down. Couldn't let her business down.

If she won, everyone would be secure. But if she lost—or worse, hyperventilated and passed out face first in a bowl of chocolate frosting—the ignominious loss would end up splashed across the newspapers, destroying any shred of sales she had left.

If that happened, Olivia might as well capitulate to the low-carb craze.

Soy flour, here I come.

Daniel stood in the back of the room, watching the nine pastry chefs bustle around their kitchens like chickens worried about making their egg quota. To his right, three booths down, was Olivia. The only one not bustling.

She stood there, reading over a piece of paper, a measuring cup in one hand, and a puzzled look in her face. She glanced up at the clock, then back down at the paper. And still didn't make a move.

Clearly, she was in trouble.

Daniel skirted the velvet rope blocking off the audience area and started walking toward Olivia's booth.

A pudgy security guard stepped into his path. "Sir, you can't be in here. This area is reserved for the chefs."

"I'm Daniel Worth," he said. "I just wanted to, ah, see if the chefs were satisfied with their accommodations."

The security guard backed up, his face red with embarrassment at not recognizing his boss. "My apologies, Mr. Worth," he said, gesturing toward the open ballroom. "Please, go ahead."

"Don't apologize for being diligent. That's an important quality in our security staff."

The other man beamed, then afforded Daniel an even wider berth. "Thank you, sir."

Daniel wanted to make a beeline for Olivia, but he took the time to appear nonpartisan. He paused at the first two booths, chatting with the chefs in conversation snippets as the others hurried to concoct their next dish. Then he ambled over to Olivia's booth, trying not to look like he was spying on her. She had taken something out of the oven and was tasting a piece that had broken off.

When he reached her, she grimaced. "Yuck," Olivia whispered under her breath.

"Don't hold back on your feelings," Daniel said.

She jerked around, startled. Then her face fell and she let out a gust of frustration. "I don't know what to do with this thing," she said, gesturing to what he now saw was a cheesecake. At least, he *thought* it was a cheesecake. The fractured custard had a hard, burnt circle running around the outside edge and a puddle of yellow in the center. "Hell, with any of it." She gestured around the small confines of her makeshift kitchen. "I can't do this. I thought I could, but I just…can't."

"What do you mean?" He stared at the array of bakery equipment around her, all very similar to what she worked with in her shop. Was the new environment intimidating her?

"I don't know how to make this," she whispered, pointing to a recipe for something called a Japonaise torte.

"Don't you sell those in your shop?"

"Yeah, but *I* don't make them. Josie does."

"Oh, I'm sure you can do it," Daniel said. "You're a smart woman. I know you can improvise. Remember, I've seen you drive." He gave her a grin, then noticed one of the judges watching their conversation. If he lingered any more, he was afraid they might suspect the owner of the hotel was trying to influence their decision and disqualify Olivia. "I have to make my rounds. But let me wish you good luck, even though you don't need it. I know who the best baker in Boston is."

As he walked away, he noticed Olivia's face, still looking as panicked as a chipmunk caught in a landslide.

Josie's Winning-Isn't-Everything Chocolate Ganache

1/2 cup heavy cream
4 ounces semisweet chocolate

Have a little chamomile tea before you start, so you can relax and center yourself. Deep breath in, deep breath out. There, that's better. You need to have your mind in the right place if you're going to compete against the big boys.

Bring the heavy cream to a boil, but don't burn it. Pour the hot cream over the chocolate in a separate bowl and whisk until smooth. That's all there is to it! As easy as finding a ghost on Halloween.

As you spread the ganache over your cake, believe in the impossible. Miracles can happen—especially when you top them with a little chocolate.

CHAPTER THIRTY

Seeing Daniel had surprised Olivia, which was pretty dumb considering she was once again in the ballroom of a Worth Hotel. The same Worth Hotel, in fact, where she had bid on him two weeks ago.

What a difference fourteen days could make. Back then, she'd never anticipated anything beyond using him for the ad campaign, then moving on. Her business would rebound and Daniel Worth would be nothing more than a pleasant memory.

But that wasn't how things worked out. Her business was worse off than ever, the ad campaign with the Worth heir had set off a negative backlash of publicity, and low-carb people were set to inherit the Boston dessert market.

And worse, she'd started to care about Daniel. She'd been fooling herself if she thought she didn't because everything within her betrayed her best intentions when he'd come over, and being so sweet—damn him—and checking on her.

Right now, she had no time to think about Daniel Worth. She had to concentrate on winning.

This was her last ditch effort to pull Pastries with Panache back from the brink of bankruptcy.

Olivia took a deep breath. She could do this. She *had* to do this.

She could concoct a recipe. Sort of. That frittata with apples and oranges hadn't gone over well with her culinary school instructor. It had come back *up* quite well, unfortunately.

She glanced again at Josie's recipe, only half of which she could decipher, and figured she could wing it. Based on Josie's chicken scratches— complete with what looked like hieroglyphics of moons, suns and stars peppering the words— winging it was pretty much the only option.

"Olivia, you can do it! Win, baby!"

Olivia jerked around, knocking a filled measuring cup of flour onto the floor. When the plume of white dust cleared, she saw them. Standing in the ballroom entrance, beaming with pride and expectations.

Her parents.

Mom offered an encouraging smile and a little wave. Dad pumped a fist in the air and shouting "Whoo-hoo, Olivia!" at decibels that the lead singer of Green Day would envy.

She'd *told* them not to come. *Begged* them to stay home. And yet here they were anyway, her own personal Pastry Cheerleaders.

Fantastic.

She turned back toward her kitchen and saw that the flour dusted the carpet and nearly every square inch around her, even her shoes and her black dress pants. Who knew such a small amount could make such a mess? Across the way, she caught one of the other chefs snickering at her white-dusted space.

Even more fantastic.

Olivia scanned the recipe for the torte again. She could make out almonds and egg yolks. But the rest of the ingredients in Josie's scrawl were pretty much a blur. As were the instructions.

Oh, damn. She knew Japonaise torte was a complex layering of meringues, butter cream frosting and chocolate. Meringue wasn't exactly Olivia's forte, either. Come to think of it, she pretty much sucked at anything involving eggs.

No jobs on a chicken farm for you.

She looked down at the recipe a second time. Raced through her memory for everything she knew about making meringue.

Uh, not much.

Thought of everything she knew about making frosting.

She knew *how* to frost, could make some pretty damned life-like flowers and a lattice work that would rivaled a Longerberger basket, but as for *making* the frosting—

Well, Olivia's talents ended at licking the beaters.

She skimmed the rest of the directions. Chocolate curls. Phew. Now *those* she could make. In fact, she was the best damned chocolate curl maker in the city of Boston. Give her a vegetable peeler and a hunk of chocolate and she could make a hell of a curlicue of cocoa.

Decorative work, she had that mastered. As for the meringue and the frosting, well, she'd just have to wing that. And hope no one ended up with food poisoning at the end.

"You can do this," she told herself. "Your parents said so."

Olivia glanced at Daniel, standing along the sidelines, watching her. *He* believed in her. *Josie* believed in her. And for the first time ever, both her parents believed in her.

If only faith were enough to create a minor miracle.

An hour later, however, when her raspberry soufflé came out of the oven inverted and tasting a lot like an expired carton of milk, Olivia knew she was fooling herself.

She couldn't do this. Not if Emeril Lagasse himself stepped in and put his healing hands on her recipes.

"Come on, Liv! Kick some bagels!" Dad was watching her, pride in his features. Beside him, Mom sat with her fingers laced tightly together, that go-get-em smile still tight on her face.

None of them knew that her cheesecake looked more like scrambled eggs than dessert. Or that her soufflé had left the oven looking like a crater on the moon.

Then an idea came to her. Chocolate ganache. Everything tasted better with a little chocolate on it. If she poured enough on the cheesecake, maybe everyone would think she was a real baker.

Yeah, and those people at the Big Foot Gift Shop made a pretty convincing case for their plaster footprints, too.

Olivia wasn't ready to give up yet. Not while there was still a chance to pull this thing out of the fire. She turned to the refrigerator, withdrew the heavy cream, then measured it into a Pyrex cup. She dumped it into a pan and flicked on the gas, moving fast to make up for lost time.

Olivia turned to the cheesecake. Maybe if she trimmed the sides a little, she could remove the worst of the burnt parts. With swift, careful movements, Olivia shaved along the perimeter of the dessert, taking it from a nine-inch to an eight-inch. Okay, there was hope. Albeit, not much, but at least some.

Then she started chopping up a chocolate bar, grabbing a whisk on her way to dump the pieces in with the cream. She paused. Sniffed.

Was something burning?

Oh, shit. The cream.

One of the first rules of dessert making—keep an eye on your cream when it's boiling. Or at the very least, don't leave your common sense at home.

No matter what kind of magic she tried to create with the chocolate chunks, the ganache would taste more like ashes than decadent glaze. Two out of her four dishes were ruined. There weren't enough ingredients, or enough time, to recreate them—assuming she could even get it right the second time around.

The other chefs were bustling about their kitchens with smooth, practiced, confident moves. One chef had a three-tier white chocolate cake sitting on his counter, another had a set of cupcakes, elaborately decorated with edible flowers. A third was putting the finishing touches on a quartet of puff pastries, drizzling caramel sauce over them.

Then here she was. The biggest fraud in the room. She couldn't even heat cream, for God's sake. What business did she have in this competition?

Losing was a foregone conclusion. For the first time since Olivia had drawn up the plans for the pastry shop, she had to admit defeat.

She had no idea what the hell she was doing. No instincts to fall back on. No—

No passion.

That's what she saw in the faces around her, the smiles beneath the toques. A passion for their jobs, their work, their creations.

How stupid could she have been? In all the statistics and demographics, in all the business plan software and talks with the banks, never once had that word been mentioned.

And clearly it was the most essential ingredient for success.

Olivia stood in her kitchen, covered in flour, holding a pan of burned cream and finally admitted the truth.

This wasn't going to work.

"Come on baby, I believe in you!"

She cringed at the sound of her father's voice. What had she been thinking when she'd taken Josie's place? Or more to the point, when she'd opened a business in something she hadn't mastered?

Josie was the one with the brains in the family. It sure as hell wasn't Olivia, who had been stupid enough to believe she could make a go at working for herself.

That she was up to the challenge.

Daniel returned, his blue eyes filled with concern. "You okay?" He hesitated. "Do I smell something burning?"

"Yes." Olivia sighed, took off the apron and tossed it onto the counter. It lay there in a heap, a white flag of defeat.

"Olivia, what are you doing? The contest—"

"Is over for me. I don't know why I thought I could pull this off."

"You're doing great. It's probably just the pressure talking."

"It's not pressure." Olivia's voice had risen with her panic level. She wanted out of here, out of this nightmare that wouldn't end, out of the burnt, flour-covered mess she'd made. "It's a disaster." She gestured toward the smoking cream, the ruined cheesecake, the flop of a soufflé. "I can't do this, Daniel."

He smiled, not getting the point at all. "You're a wonderful pastry chef who's simply got a case of the jitters."

She shook her head. "*No.* I'm *not* a wonderful pastry chef. I never was."

"I beg to differ," Daniel said. "I've tasted your cheesecake and snuck your muffins."

Her cheesecake. *Her* muffins. If Daniel only knew. Never had Olivia expected the lies to get to this point, to go this far. She had kept thinking that some of Josie's skill would wear off, and Olivia would eventually be the one behind the mixer.

Olivia ran a hand through her hair. The lies weighed on her shoulders, as heavy as a ton of flour.

"Go, Liv, go! Go, Liv, go! Go, Liv, go!" Her dad had stood and was leading a one-man wave in the front row.

What had she done? The monster Olivia had created had now grown to epic proportions, as destructive as Godzilla. Suddenly, keeping up the pretense became too much.

Why bother when she sucked at it anyway?

The carnage from her lies was as widespread as a roach infestation. And neither was going to do her business any good.

"You can do this, Olivia," Daniel said. "You're a great—"

"No," she said, cutting him off with a wave of her hand. "I'm not. I'm not what you think either."

"Go, Liv, go! You can do it!"

"Honey, what is it?" Daniel stepped forward, his voice so soft and full of concern, she wanted to cry. "Tell me."

"Go, Liv—"

"*I can't cook!*" she shouted the words, wanting only to shut out that understanding look in Daniel's eyes, to stop the family support rally echoing in the ballroom. "I can't bake! I can't puree! I can't blend! I can't do *any* of it!"

Silence descended over the room, heavy and thick. The chefs stopped what they were doing and turned to stare, mouths agape. Daniel's jaw dropped, his eyes widening with surprise.

And hurt.

She'd lied to him. To everyone. She wasn't sure what was worse—the silence, or the disappointed look she saw in the familiar eyes looking back at her.

"Olivia?" Dad's quiet voice cut through the silence. Begging her in one plaintive word to tell everyone it wasn't true, that he hadn't poured his retirement into another flushable Regan loser.

"I can't do this." Olivia exited her kitchen, leaving the entire mess behind. "I'm sorry."

Then she bolted from the room like a lifer who'd just scaled the walls at Alcatraz.

Daniel's The-Right-Words-Aren't-There Chocolate Macaroons

8 ounces almond paste
2/3 cup granulated sugar
1/4 cup confectioners' sugar
1/4 cup cocoa powder
2 egg whites
sugar

If you don't know what to say, you're probably a hell of a lot better off keeping your mouth shut than saying the wrong thing. All she needs right now is a man who sticks his foot in his mouth. Actually, both feet. And those aren't small feet, either.

Stuff your mouth instead with these. Preheat the oven to 375 degrees and line two cookies sheets with parchment paper. Beat the almond paste and sugars together for about five minutes, then add in the cocoa. Mix in the egg whites gradually.

Wish finding the right words were as easy as this. Pipe the macaroon mixture onto the prepared pans in one-inch circles. Just before baking, sprinkle them liberally with sugar. Then bake for 15 to 20 minutes. While you're waiting on the macaroons, work on convincing her that you're not all bad and that most days, your intentions are good.

You're a guy. Tact isn't part of your DNA.

CHAPTER THIRTY-ONE

Daniel wanted nothing more than to run after Olivia and take away that defeated look in her eyes. But the demands of Worth Hotels—of his other life—took precedence. While he stood in his grandfather's stead, he needed to put the business first.

It took him a few minutes to perform damage control and convince the rest of the chefs they could still go on, with an extra five minutes of cooking time to make up for the interruption. There were a few grumbles, but overall, the other eight were happy to have one less cheesecake standing in line between them and the fifty thousand.

Next, he headed over to Olivia's parents, still sitting in the audience, stunned and immobile.

"I don't understand," Harold Regan said when Daniel reached them. "Did she say she *can't cook?*"

"I'm as surprised as you are, sir."

"But...but...but she told me..." Harold's voice trailed off. "I gave her the money, she started that business—"

"You gave her the money?" Pauline said, wheeling on her husband. "Why on earth would you do that?"

"It was her dream. She thought she could afford it on her own, but all the stuff with the city and the equipment took more than she expected. So I kicked in a little."

Pauline's gaze narrowed. "What money did you give her, Harold? Exactly?"

A storm was whipping up between the Regans, one that was attracting an audience. Daniel lowered his voice and leaned in toward them. "Uh, can we take this discussion out to the hall? It'll be more private there."

But the Regans didn't hear him.

"You gave her the money…" Pauline began, "or did you push her into this business thing? Did you encourage your daughter in another of your get-rich-quick schemes?"

"It was nothing like that. Olivia wanted to work for herself."

"Because of the example *you* set. Did you ever think of telling her not to do it?"

"No, Pauline, I never did." He drew himself up and faced his wife. "I support my children."

"I do too, Harold, but not in things that risk their futures."

"You mean things that are safe. Predictable as rain in April."

She nodded. "If they don't take risks, they can't lose."

Harold reached out a hand to his wife. "Not every risk is a losing one, sweetheart. And they're not always someone's fault. Sometimes things fail. Just because."

Pauline bit her lip and averted her face, tugging her hand out of her husband's.

Daniel got the feeling the Regans were talking about something other than Olivia's business. Something between the two of them, something that clearly was part of the San Andreas Fault in their marriage. "Mr. and Mrs. Regan," he said, trying again, "why don't we go find Olivia? I'm sure she has an explanation."

Pauline drew in a breath, then got to her feet, clutching her purse to her chest like armor. "I'm not listening to anyone's explanations. Especially not yours," she said to her husband. "I knew *you* were crazy, but I can't believe you encouraged your daughter to jump off the same bridge."

Then she stalked out of the room, leaving a befuddled Harold behind.

He draped his arms over his knees and faced Daniel. "I just wanted my daughter to have her dream," he said. "Who knew it didn't have any yeast?"

It took an hour before Daniel finally found Olivia, sitting on the roof of the hotel. Twenty stories below them, the city of Boston went about its late afternoon business, the cars and people looking like miniatures on a Hot Wheels track.

She looked so forlorn, sitting there on the corner of a stainless steel ventilation unit. Her shoulders hunched about her, and her hair whipped against her face in the brisk winter wind.

"Don't jump!" Daniel said, only half kidding. Though Olivia didn't seem to be suicidal right now, he didn't want to take the chance.

Olivia pivoted and gave him a weak smile. "Don't worry. My life insurance policy isn't big enough to repay my parents for the disappointment bill."

Daniel took a seat beside Olivia and draped an arm over her shoulders. She tipped her head, leaning into his embrace. "It's okay, Olivia. Everything will work out."

"No, it won't." She let out a breath and looked to the sky, as if the gathering storm clouds held an answer. "Don't you see? I tried. And I failed."

"It happens," he said, pushing a lock of hair off her forehead. Her emerald eyes connected with his, waiting, he was sure, for him to supply the right words. No one had ever relied on him for something like that before. Just another one of the areas in Daniel Worth's life where he hadn't had to perform like the rest of the human race.

He drew in a breath, choosing his words carefully. He wanted to get this right. Because Olivia mattered to him, more than she knew. And, because he was a guy and his chances of saying the right thing at the right time were as good as Larry Bird's returning to pro ball. "You have what it takes to bounce back," Daniel said. "This was one competition. In the grand scheme of things, it's a small thing. I know your business will succeed despite what happened today."

"How do you know?" Olivia said, drawing away from him. "You don't understand. You haven't taken a risk like I have."

"I walked out on my family fortune, Olivia. That was a risk. A hell of a risk."

She shook her head. "It's not the same. Your fortune was always there to fall back on, and you didn't let someone who loved you invest in a horse that couldn't run." She let out a bitter laugh. "Hell, one that couldn't even get out of the starting gate."

Clearly his words hadn't worked. So he offered the only other thing he had. "Olivia, let me help you. I can pay—"

Olivia rose, drawing her coat about her like a shield against the snow that had started falling. And maybe, against him. "I don't want your money, Daniel, don't you understand that? I didn't go into business because I wanted to make a ton of money."

"What other reason is there?"

She stared at him for a long time. "You really don't know, do you?"

"Everything in my family is about making a profit." He shook his head and cast his gaze toward the darkening sky. "When I was little, my grandfather gave me a quarter for every goodnight kiss I gave him. Then it became dollars for good grades, for doing chores. Said it would all make me smart about using my talents."

Her face softened and she reached to brush a hand against his cheek. "I'm sorry."

"Don't be," he said. "Money is part of my world. Always has been."

"A world you left."

He snorted. "*Tried* to leave." He shook off the thoughts about the Worth family expectations. "But this isn't about me. It's about you."

She sighed. "I don't know anything about me right now."

He'd been wrong. He had one other thing to offer Olivia. He stood and drew her into his embrace, buffeting her against the biting wind and smattering of snowflakes hitting them. "It's going to be okay," he said softly. "*You're* going to be okay."

"I didn't do any of this for the money," she repeated, her voice muffled against his chest. "I did it for love."

"Love?"

She nodded, focused on him. "It's why I opened a pastry shop when I couldn't cook. It's part of why I've stayed with it, even as the business went down the tubes. For Josie." Olivia leaned her head against his shoulder. "I asked her one day to help me with my culinary school homework. She took to it like a fish to the ocean. You have to understand Josie. She never sticks with anything for longer than a couple weeks. But this…this she loved. As the months wore on and it became pretty damned clear I wasn't going to learn how to bake—at least not without divine intervention—we made a plan."

"You'd take care of the business end and she'd do the cooking."

She nodded. "Josie needed stability; I needed a chef."

"Businesses are started on those kinds of partnerships every day. Surely you can make it work from here on out."

Olivia drew back, shaking her head. "No. I can't let Josie be sucked down into my failure. I have to protect her."

Daniel tipped her chin to meet her gaze. "She's a big girl. She can handle the truth. And maybe more of the business than you think."

"No. You don't know Josie. I've protected her all my life. She could never get out of bed on time for school. Or worse, she'd get distracted by some book she was reading on UFOs and forget completely to go to school. I usually brought two lunches with me because I knew, somewhere along the way, Josie would lose hers. She loves this business, but she doesn't know what business is really like. I can't let her become a Regan family failure."

Daniel studied the amazing woman before him. She'd awakened something new in him, something powerful. Something that had changed his view of his world, and made him want more from a life he'd once thought had everything. Until she came along, he'd lived in a world where everything was bought and sold, where affection was a luxury and individuality could cost you everything. But then

Olivia Regan had plunked down her last nickel for him and taken a huge gamble. All while knowing failure was a distinct possibility. "You did all this... for someone else?"

"I wanted to work for myself and Josie needed something she could stick with. I figured I'd learn to cook and in the meantime, take care of her. When I dropped out of culinary school, I intended to do anything but bake for a business. But then, Josie..." Olivia shrugged. "Well, when you love people, you make sacrifices. You make choices that help them find their dreams."

Daniel moved behind her, his arms stealing across her waist. He wanted to shield her, to protect her, but knew Olivia would resist. If there was anything Olivia Regan was good at, it was not needing anyone. "At the expense of your own?"

She shrugged. "It was close enough." Then she stepped out of his embrace and turned to face him. "Besides, haven't you done the same thing? Giving up what mattered most to you, to help the people you love?"

"Olivia, I'm no saint, no matter what color you use to paint my life. I might have done something right today, but it's not the same as what you did." He smiled. "You're the bravest woman I know."

"I'm not brave at all." She turned away, facing the edge of the building, snowflakes dusting her hair like confetti. "I'm just trying to take care of my family."

Daniel came around to stand in front of her, refusing to let her look away and avoid the real subject. "What about you?"

"What about me?" She raised her jaw defiantly, but it trembled, belying her strength. "I'm fine, no matter what."

He traced along the curve of her chin with his thumb. "You don't look fine."

Tears welled in her eyes, but Olivia stubbornly kept them from shedding. "I just need to figure out what to do." She sighed. "I have no idea where to go from here. Or how to fix what I have done to my family. Did you see the looks on my parents' faces? They were so hurt that I'd lied to them, that I was a failure."

"Your parents understand more than you think," he said quietly. "They'll be okay with whatever you decide."

"But how do I know what to do now? They don't cover this," at that, she waved a hand toward the lower floors of the Worth hotel, where everything in her life had gone up in a plume of flour dust, "in the business books."

And then, he knew the right words, the ones he needed to hear right now, too. Maybe if someone had said them to him sooner, he'd have trusted himself instead of following the Worth family plan, like a sheep being led to slaughter. Maybe he'd have trusted his own instincts, instead of agreeing to something that could never work.

He pressed a hand to her abdomen. "The answers are there, Olivia, in your gut."

She shook her head and stepped away. "That's the one part of myself I never trust."

"You know what my gut is telling me now?" He didn't wait for her reply, needing to tell her, to let loose the feelings that had been building in him for days. "That I have fallen in love with you."

She backed up, warding off his words. "Don't, Daniel. I can't take another risk like that. You may listen to your gut, but I don't. When I opted to go into pastries, I researched the hell out of it so I knew I was thinking with my head, not my emotions. I can't afford to do that with business and especially not with men. All it does is get me into trouble."

Then she turned and walked away, leaving Daniel on the roof of a hotel that bore his name but had no similarity to the life he wanted to lead. Everything he wanted, he realized, had just left the building.

Pauline's The-Truth-Is-A-Jumble Easy Apple Cobbler

4 ounces butter, melted
1 cup milk
1 cup sugar
1 cup self-rising flour
8 cups apples, peeled and sliced
1/2 cup sugar
1 teaspoon cinnamon
1 teaspoon nutmeg
1/4 cup brown sugar

Oh, dear, it's all a mess now, isn't it? That's what happens when you hide things from the people who love you. Honesty really does pay (and so does finding a steady job).

Preheat your oven to 350 degrees. Mix the first four ingredients together, then spread the dough in an 8 by 13 pan. Mix the apples, sugar, cinnamon and nutmeg, then spread those over the dough. Crumble the brown sugar over the top and then bake for one hour.

The cobbler might be as easy as pie, but telling the truth…that's a little harder pill to swallow.

CHAPTER THIRTY-TWO

Daniel Worth had been right, damn him.

Three days after their conversation on the rooftop—and after a long, serious talk with herself—Olivia stood beside her sister's hospital bed, her gut churning like a rock tumbler. There was no other way, not anymore. The fallout from the Frosting on the Cake competition, and the ensuing publicity about the pastry chef who wasn't, had killed all business at the shop. Well, except for the curious, who stopped in to ask her what the hell she'd been thinking.

She stood there, working up the courage to tell Josie it was over. She couldn't let her sister go on thinking there was a shop to return to when she was discharged today. Olivia had popped in for quick visits over the last three days, avoiding any conversation more involved than "the weather stinks" and especially avoiding her parents. She'd put in overtime at the shop, returning to her apartment only after Mom and Dad were asleep, then leaving again before they awakened.

Still, despite all those hours, and multiple, fruitless attempts at creating some of the shop's specialty items, business had slowed to almost nil. Ben had been her best customer all week.

And she didn't even charge him.

Now, she needed to finally come clean, to stop avoiding Josie's questions. "Hey, Jo," she said quietly.

Josie's eyes fluttered open. "Hi, Liv! How are you?" She wiped the sleep from her eyes, then pushed the button on her bed, raising her head a few inches.

"Fine. It's...ah, snowing again." Her courage deserted her, as it had every time before, when she saw her sister in that bed, looking pale and thin.

"Nope, no small talk this time. You're not leaving without telling me what happened. I know you took my place at the Frosting on the Cake competition, Dad told me. But no one will tell me how it turned out."

Olivia sighed. "It was a disaster. My baking incompetence was exposed to the world. And Mom and Dad."

"Ah, they'll get over it." Josie waved a hand in dismissal. "I kind of figured that might happen since your sun is in a triune position this month."

"My what is where?"

"Anyway, since I'm just lying here all day, I've been working on lots of new ideas for the shop," Josie went on, clearly not upset about the loss, "We could do something like Starbucks. Add some wireless Internet access, invite writers and groups like that…"

Olivia lowered herself to the edge of the bed and drew in a deep breath. "Josie, I have something to tell you."

"What? That the doctors were aliens who gave me a big booty implant while I was under?" Josie lifted the sheet and peeked at her butt. "Nope. And no breasts, either. Geez, you'd think if the aliens were going to abduct me, they'd at least do a little lipo as a consolation." She laughed, the tease clear in her eyes.

"No. It's not that." Olivia paused, unable to get the words out.

The laughter dropped from Josie's features. "What, Liv? You can tell me."

"I have to close Pastries with Panache."

The words hung in the silent hospital room, heavier and more oppressive than the too-warm temperature and the cloying scent of antiseptic.

"Close the shop?" Josie repeated. "Are you sure?"

"You know we've been struggling. Winning the Frosting on the Cake competition, or at least placing in it, would have given us a great boost. But with that low-carb place across the street, our business took a huge nosedive and it hasn't recovered." Olivia sighed. "And then I went and blew all that money on the sexy bachelor ad campaign—"

Josie reached out and grasped her sister's hand. "With my blessing. If I remember right, we both supported that idea."

"Yeah, but *I* was the one running the business side. And I let you down, Jo."

Josie shook her head, a warm, forgiving smile on her face. "No, you didn't. You did your best."

Olivia snorted. "It wasn't my best, not by a long shot."

"We'll rebound. We always do."

"No, Jo, not this time. I'm going to sell. Everything. If I cut my losses now, the sale of all the equipment and fixtures should be enough to pay back Dad. As for the bank loans…well, I'll work on those."

"How?"

Olivia grinned. "I'll get a real job."

"You have a real job, Liv, running Pastries with Panache."

Olivia let out a sigh of defeat. "I can't do it anymore. And I can't expect you to stay with a company that's going under. If you get out now, there's still time for you to finish beauty school and take that job in Newton." Olivia gave her sister's hand a squeeze. "We tried. But it didn't work out."

Josie sighed. "I don't understand. We had all the right ingredients. Great food, great location, great-looking women behind the counter…"

But Olivia didn't return her sister's smile. "I was missing one thing."

"What?"

Olivia knew now what that feeling in her gut had been. She'd taken it as excitement for the challenges of business, telling herself she loved what she was doing and it would all work out. But when she'd gotten quiet with herself, and really listened, she realized it hadn't been excitement at all. It had been panic that she'd made a colossal mistake. Another Regan disaster. "I never had that hunger for the job, for the industry, for going to work every day. At least not for pastries. *You* had it in spades. You loved what you did at the shop. But—"

"But you didn't," Josie finished.

Olivia shook her head. "I thought I would. I mean, all the signs pointed to a great career."

Josie laughed. "Signs? Now you're starting to sound like me."

Olivia thought of Daniel's words, and realized how true they were now. How had she missed it? How had that been the one thing she hadn't accounted for in her business plan? "Do you know what I feel in my gut when I get up to go to work every day?" She didn't wait for an answer. "Worry. Anxiety. Frustration. Not the excitement I see in your eyes when you come to work."

Josie laughed, a blush extending into her cheeks at the unexpected praise. "I think that's the caffeine rush. It takes a lot to get me out of bed in the morning."

"Do you remember how Dad used to get when we were kids and he had a new idea? Or a new invention he wanted to back? He was like Ben at Christmas—pinging off the walls, talking non-stop."

Josie nodded. "He'd get up at the crack of dawn, making plans, doing research, talking to his friends about the latest thing. His whole world centered around whatever he was investing in."

Olivia smoothed the blanket with her palm. "When I went into business for myself, I did it because I wanted a taste of that. I wanted to feel what Dad felt because it seemed so...fun. So magical." She drew in a breath and admitted the truth to herself and her sister. "But I thought I could be smarter. That if I researched and planned enough, it would work out. But it didn't. I was wrong."

"Maybe you picked the wrong business, Liv."

She shook her head. "And maybe I'm the wrong person to be in business. Period."

Josie thought a second. Beside them, a rerun of "Oprah" played on her roommate's TV. "You know those cows that got sucked up by aliens to the Mother Ship for experiments?"

Olivia blinked at the conversational detour. "Uh...no."

Josie wagged a finger at her. "You need to watch more Discovery Channel, sis. Anyway, there were these cows and they just disappeared, then returned a day later with their inner workings all missing. No kidney, no liver, no heart. It was all clean cuts, too, without a drop of blood. No evidence at all except their little empty spotted carcasses."

"Josie, you don't know that it was aliens."

"But how do you know the alien theory *isn't* true?" Josie asked. "All I'm saying is that sometimes you gotta have a little faith."

"I don't believe in faith or miracles or portents from witches. I believe in cold, hard facts. Faith doesn't put money in the cash drawer."

Josie sat up and leaned forward, her eyes bright. "But how do you *know?* You never had faith, Liv. Not in yourself, not really. If you had, you would have chosen a business *you* loved, not one I did."

"I—" Olivia began, then cut herself off. Josie, the one who based her theories on the position of the moon and the sight of a strange flower in a garden, had nailed the truth right on the head. Daniel was right again. Her sister was more perceptive than she'd ever thought. "You're right. I didn't have faith in me. But you always did."

"Hey, I believe in the Loch Ness monster, too," Josie said, chuckling. "My philosophy is you gotta believe if you want to receive."

Olivia wanted to trust what Josie was saying, but the worry in her gut only began churning faster. "That's what Mom used to say about Santa, Josie, until we found the presents in the back of her closet."

"You never know what could happen if you trust in the impossible," Josie said. "Stranger things have happened. Look at the cows."

Olivia wasn't sure she was going to put her faith in Josie's theory that there was a life lesson in alien tampering of farm animals.

"Maybe the right business is out there, waiting for you to find it," Josie said.

"Oh no, I'm not going down this road again. Once is enough."

Josie's eyes filled with a wisdom Olivia had never seen before. "You're good at business, Olivia. You just need to work in the right one."

She shook her head. "If I'm so good, why am I shutting the doors?"

"Because you didn't have any faith in the impossible." Josie sobered. "You never had faith in me, either."

"Oh, Jo, that's not true."

Josie raised a brow. "You've been looking out for me since the day I was born, Olivia. But you seem to forget I'm a grown-up now. I can handle more than you think."

"Josie, I…" But Olivia realized she had done exactly that. Kept her sister in the dark, on purpose, because she didn't think Josie could handle the truth. "You're right."

"Trust me, Liv, and you might be surprised. I may believe in alien abductions, but that doesn't mean I can't be a good businesswoman. And hey, you never know. We might get a few customers on Mars." She smiled.

Olivia laughed. "Long as they like our danishes, we're all set."

"Speaking of things you refuse to trust," Josie went on, "what about Daniel?"

Daniel. She'd avoided him, too, over the last few days. Avoided the questions left unanswered between them. Avoided dealing with her feelings, which were as topsy-turvy as her stomach lately.

"What about Daniel?" Olivia repeated. "There's nothing going on there."

"Liv, I may be a bit ditzy, but I'm not stupid. You're half in love with the guy."

Heat stole across her cheeks. "I am not."

"Uh-huh. Believe and you shall receive." Josie grinned. "And I get the feeling that with a guy like Daniel, you'll receive and receive…"

Olivia shook her head. "I don't want him for his money."

"I was talking about his bod, silly. He's a hunk, he's interested in you and you're interested in him. So what's holding you back?"

The heater in the room kicked on, blowing a shudder of hot air into Josie's space. In the hall outside, a patient rang for a nurse and another screamed for her dinner. Olivia drew in a breath, then faced her sister. "I guess I'm afraid."

"Of what?"

"Of being wrong. Again."

Josie wagged a finger at her. "But you forget that you already have the key ingredient with Daniel."

"What's that?"

"Hunger for him. I've seen you look at him. You're like John Edwards discovering a new spirit on the other side." Josie squeezed her sister's hand. "Go for it. Fall in love."

Olivia shook her head. "Sorry, but I'm not in the risk-taking business anymore. Too many people can get hurt. Especially me."

As if on cue, her parents peeked their faces around the curtain separating Josie from her roommate. Her mother was clutching a *TV Guide,* her face worried yet hopeful. Dad looked tired, but still wore a smile.

Guilt rocketed through Olivia's chest, sharp as a spear. Avoiding them wasn't going to make the problem go away. Or produce some money miracle. She'd faced the truth with Josie—now she needed to do the same with them.

"Before you say anything," her mother began, "your father and I want to apologize to you, Olivia. We ah, eavesdropped on your conversation."

Oh God. They'd been listening? "You heard? Everything?"

Her father nodded. "I had no idea, honey, that things were so bad. Or that Josie was the one doing all the baking."

"I didn't mean to lie," Olivia said. "I just wanted Josie to have a job she was good at, and could stick with. And I wanted to be the first successful Regan entrepreneur. I really thought it would work. That I'd pay the money back in a few months and everything would be perfect." She drew in a breath and swallowed the facts. "But since that didn't happen, I'm going to sell everything and get your money back."

"Olivia—"

"No, Dad, I *have* to do this. I won't let my mistakes burn up your retirement. I let you down and the least I can do is repay you."

"Oh, don't worry about that," Mom said. "We'll be fine."

Her mother telling her not to worry about money? And actually being chipper about it? For a second, Olivia wondered if Josie's alien abduction theories were true.

Then she took a closer look at her parents. For the first time, she noticed her mother's pageboy was tousled and the first four buttons of her shirt were done up in the wrong order. When she glanced at her father, she saw his tie was askew, with the long skinny end caught in his belt buckle.

"Their moons are all lined up again," Josie whispered, following her sister's line of sight.

"Their what?"

"What your sister is trying to say," Mom said, clearing her throat, "is that your Dad and I worked out our problems." Her mother held up the *TV Guide.*

"You settled your differences with a channel guide?" Olivia shook her head, definitely feeling like she was in an alternate universe. "But I thought that was the least of the issues."

"Oh, but this isn't any ordinary *TV Guide.* It's the one with George Clooney on the cover." Her mother flipped it around, displaying the sexy smile of the former *ER* doc. "Your dad won it on eBay for me."

Dad shrugged. "It was nothing. Besides, your mother did most of the bidding."

"Oh, it was so exciting, Olivia," Mom said, coming closer to take a seat beside her daughters. "You have to try it sometime. I'd bid and then someone else would bid over me, so I'd bid higher and then they'd up their bid. The price went over twenty dollars and I thought for sure I was going to lose out.

Until finally—" She glanced at husband. "Go on, honey, you tell it."

Her father drew himself up, straightening his tie and clearing his throat, as he always did before he told a story. "I said, 'Pauline, lace up your boots because we're going for broke.'"

"And he raised them fifteen dollars. Before you could say boo, we'd won!" She waved the *TV Guide* again like a victory flag. "We had it FedExed right out."

"But I thought you hated risk," Olivia said.

"That was before I knew it could be fun." She gave her husband a whack on the arm. "Harold, you never told me this was fun."

"Pauline, a little risk is fun. There. I told you now."

Her mother rolled her eyes, then returned her gaze to her daughters. "Afterwards, we even called up Uncle Morty."

"You did?" Josie asked. "Why?"

"Your mother was still floating on eBay fever," Dad said. "And she told Uncle Morty she wanted to buy a bidet for the house—"

"And I'm going to tell all my friends at bridge and at church that they need one."

Dad beamed. "Your mother has a brilliant marketing campaign for them."

"Yep," Pauline said, raising a brow. "I'm thinking *hot flashes.*"

Olivia gaped. "Hot flashes? What do they have to do with bidets?"

"Well, a smart woman starts at the source, if you know what I mean. I even have an advertising slogan: Cooling relief, without the hormones."

Olivia blinked. Who *were* these people?

Dad drew his wife into a one-armed hug. "'She's brilliant, I tell you. An idea a minute now."

"Anyway," Mom said, "we also wanted to tell you that we won't be back at the apartment tonight. We're, ah, going back to the hotel. To, ah, celebrate."

"*Back* to the hotel? When were you *in* the hotel?" The heat in the room must have affected Olivia's brain because it seemed like a million things had changed in the past few minutes.

"They went out for oysters for lunch today," Josie explained. "Ever since, there's been no dealing with them."

Mom wagged a finger at her eldest daughter. "The next time that Daniel comes over, I'm serving him oysters, too. Before you know it, I'll have one of my kids married off."

Olivia cringed at the image of her mother using raw oysters with a side of Rice Krispies as bait to lure in potential mates for her daughters.

"There's something else we wanted to say," Dad said, approaching the bed and laying a hand on Olivia's shoulder. He turned to look at his wife, raising a brow.

"I was wrong," Mom said quietly. "For not supporting you."

Olivia let out a laugh. "No, you were right. I was crazy to risk that much. I've learned my lesson. I won't be doing that again."

Her mother reached out and took her daughter's palm in her own. "Don't. I did that and spent my whole life in fear."

Olivia gaped. "You...you were in business for yourself?"

Her mother waved a palm. "For a little while. When I was young. It was before I met your father."

"She was quite the little entrepreneur," Dad said, beaming. "She was simply ahead of her time."

"I really thought pet costumes would go over well." Mom sighed. "But people just laughed at my Great Dane vampire cape and my poodle booties."

"Now it would be hot," Dad said. "You should try again." He leaned toward his wife, his eyes bright with the excitement of a new business venture. "We could get another dog and use him as a model."

"Another dog?" Mom considered that. "Hmm... It would be easier than trying to wrangle Ben's cat into a leotard."

Dad nodded. "Exactly. And we could be rich."

Mom sighed, apparently not believing the way to wealth lay in doggie undies. "Dear, don't worry about that business," her mother said to Olivia. "It'll work out. You'll see. Your dad and I have faith in you. Even if you can't cook. You'll find a way around that." Her mother leaned in closer, a shadow of the perpetual worry back in her eyes, telling Olivia not everything had changed, thank goodness. "Won't you?"

"Thanks for the support. But..." Olivia got to her feet, gave her sister a quick hug then turned to go. "My mind is made up. Josie's right. I shouldn't work in a field I'm not passionate about."

"I think you're just selling the wrong thing," Dad said, rising and spreading his hands wide to punctuate his excitement. "Oysters, my dear, are the wave of the future!"

Grandfather's The-Lies-Are-Thick Chocolate Chip Scones

3 cups flour
1 tablespoon baking powder
1/4 cup brown sugar
1/2 teaspoon salt
1/4 teaspoon baking soda
5 tablespoons butter, diced
4 ounces semisweet chocolate chips
2 eggs
3/4 cup buttermilk
milk, for glazing

In *Gone With the Wind*, Scarlett O'Hara is willing to resort to *anything* to protect the family. "If I have to lie, steal, cheat or kill" she says. I can see Scarlett's point. I'm of the opinion that if the family name is at stake, you should do whatever it takes to protect it. Even if it costs you the very thing other people need from you.

Since these are served with tea in Britain, they're as proper as you can get. And right now, you need something that reminds you of the world you have fought so hard to control.

Preheat the oven to 450 degrees. Mix the dry ingredients. Hurry now—time is money. Cut the butter into the dry ingredients until your dough is as crumby as the foundation you've built everything on. Stir in the chips. Mix the eggs with the buttermilk and then add them to the mix. Cut the dough into 12 wedges, then brush with the milk.

Place on a parchment covered cookie sheet, then bake for 10 to 15 minutes. Enough time to formulate a new plan to restore the family name to its former glory. Because if you don't, it could cost you more than you ever imagined.

Chapter Thirty-Three

"Don't jump," Daniel's inner voice told him as he walked into his grandfather's hospital room two weeks later, a magazine tucked under his arm. But it was too late—he'd already made up his mind and he knew if he backed out now, two weeks would turn into three, and then quickly spiral upward until he was accepting a gold watch and collecting retirement from Worth Hotels.

He hadn't heard from Olivia in all that time, despite calling her, stopping by the shop, and in general, trying to get her to talk to him again. She'd been as mum as the Sphinx, refusing his flowers, his chocolates, and most of all, his overtures toward resurrecting what they'd had before.

He had tried to get back to his old life. Hung out with the guys at the country club, dated a bit with the usual crowd from doubles tennis. But it had lost its appeal—if there'd been any appeal left to lose.

He found everything in his life as lacking in substance as cotton candy. Too sweet, too fluffy and really bad for his heart.

What he wanted, he realized, couldn't be bought. Couldn't be hired. And damned sure couldn't be persuaded to have anything to do with him.

He couldn't fix things with Olivia, but he could damned well try to fix the rest of his life.

He found his grandfather sitting up in bed, scowling at the television and clicking the remote over and over. "It's about time someone came to visit me," Grandfather said when he saw Daniel. "I was ready to buy my own TV station just so I could watch something decent."

"Nothing on?"

"Let's see," his grandfather flicked through the channels, "soap opera, Drew Carey and Bob Barker and that twenty-year boon for corporate marketing, or reruns of some show called *Sex in the City* where the women keep talking about some guy named Manolo Blahnik." Grandfather shook his head, then turned the nineteen-inch screen off. "No Turner Classic Movies on this thing, nothing to watch where manly men are blowing things up and waving around guns. Just a bunch of girly shows where everyone wears pink."

Daniel laughed and pulled up a chair to his grandfather's bedside. "At least you have your private room now."

"Just when I was beating my roommate at *Jeopardy!*, too." Grandfather tossed the remote to the side and shifted position. "I get out of this prison in a day or two, but have to stay home for a few weeks.

And rest. What the hell kind of quack advice is that? I can't rest."

That, Daniel knew, was true. Grandfather would be back at work, back on the golf course, and back on the stage within a day of leaving the hospital. Sitting still had never been one of Grandfather's strengths.

Daniel handed the magazine to his grandfather. "I wanted to show you something. Turn to page seventy-two."

Grandfather gave Daniel a suspicious eye, but did as he was told. He skimmed the page, then looked up at his grandson, nodding in appreciation. "Great piece on Top of the Hub. A little different from the average restaurant review, too. I like this social life addition." He tapped at the page. "Never seen anything like it before. But what does it have to do with anything?"

Daniel drew in a breath. "I wrote it."

"No you didn't." Grandfather squinted at the byline. "It says some guy named Joe Smith did."

"It's a pen name."

"Well, no shit. I could tell that just by the Smith." Grandfather went to toss the magazine onto his end table, then paused. "Wait a minute. Are you telling me that *you're* Joe Smith?"

"Yes." The admission soared through Daniel. For the first time in his life, he was admitting to his writing in public. Well, to one person besides Lewiston. He'd work up to the rest of the world.

Grandfather scowled. "What the hell is wrong with your own name?"

"I wanted to do this on my own. Without hundreds of years of bloodline behind me."

"That heritage is something to be proud of, boy. Your great-great-great grandparents came over here with the Mayflower. There've been Worths in this country as long as there've been people. We're *Worths,* goddamn it, not Smiths. The Worth name opens doors. Why would you throw that away like it was a dead raccoon on the side of the road?"

"Because I want something else." Daniel leaned forward, connecting with his grandfather's steely gaze. He drew in a breath and did something he should have done a hell of a long time ago. "I don't want to work in the hotel industry. I never have. I don't even want to be a part of the business world. It's not who I am."

Grandfather shook his head, dismissing his grandson's words like a craving for pistachio ice cream. In other words, Grandfather was sure it would pass. "You can't spend the rest of your life drinking and screwing women. I won't allow it."

Daniel bristled and forced his temper to stay put. He knew Grandfather was lashing out because he was disappointed. "That's not how I spend my days."

"You call this," at that, he smacked the magazine, "a career? What kind of security does this give you? None. It's as fickle as a tom cat. And less productive." Grandfather chuckled at his innuendo.

But Daniel held his ground, his words low and even. "Is that why you never went into acting?"

Silence extended between them, filling the room with tension as thick as peanut butter.

"I act." Grandfather dropped his gaze to the magazine, flipping the pages as if the cover story on the Catholic diocese in Boston was the most interesting thing he'd seen all week.

"Part-time in community theater. Didn't you ever dream of something more? Of a career on the stage?"

"There's no room for fluffy ideas like that at Worth," Grandfather said, his temper rising to match his voice. "When you grow up, you settle down. Become a company man, my father always said. That bullshit is just that—bullshit you can't afford."

"What if you had the chance to do it all over again?" Daniel asked quietly. "Would you have become a company man? Or would you have taken a different path? The road less traveled, as Frost would say."

Grandfather tossed the magazine onto the small table beside him, then cleared his throat and adjusted his blanket, his gaze not meeting Daniel's. "I don't dabble in what-ifs, Daniel. All they do is lead to expensive mistakes."

Daniel was through dabbling in what-ifs. He'd had a taste of the "if" and he wanted it to become the reality. He couldn't stomach the other alternative— the stuffy world of a suit and corporate bottom lines that meant as much to him as a slice of Wonder bread.

"I love literature, Grandfather," Daniel said. "I love to read. To write. I don't love business."

"You tell me this now? After I paid for your goddamn MBA?"

Actually, he'd told his grandfather a hundred times, but never before had Grandfather taken him seriously. Or listened to anything other than what Grandfather wanted to hear. Nor, Daniel knew, had he been all that forceful in presenting his thoughts. It was a case of one not listening, and the other not talking loud enough. "I thought I could do what you wanted, but after the last two weeks, I…" Daniel shook his head. "I can't."

Grandfather dismissed him with a palm. "You're spoiled. That's the whole problem. Too used to getting your own damned way."

"Maybe I am," Daniel admitted, cocking his head toward his namesake. "It seems to be a family trait."

The ghost of a smile crossed his grandfather's face, then he wiped it away as quickly as it came. "Are you saying what I think? You won't work for me? At all? Ever?"

"You don't *need* me, Grandfather. I don't know what the hell I'm doing anyway."

"Stick with me. I'll teach you." Grandfather reached out and laid his age-softened palm over Daniel's hand, clutching it tight, secure.

Was that desperation he heard in his grandfather's voice? Need?

Impossible. Grandfather would never show vulnerability.

Yet… Daniel hoped, maybe, this was one time when his Grandfather could understand. Listen. And sympathize.

"If there's one thing you've taught me, Grandfather, it's to fight for what I believe in, even if it isn't what everyone else wants. I believe in me. For the first time, I believe in what I can do. Without the Worth name behind me."

Grandfather yanked his hand away. "I didn't teach you to abandon your family in a time of need."

"I'm not. I'll stay at Worth until you're back to your old, chipper self."

Again, a tiny smile crossed Grandfather's face.

"I'll stay, because you asked me to," Daniel went on. "But you've already got a good, loyal and smart man at Worth. I'm not doing anything but taking up desk space."

"You're not talking about that fool John Abbott, are you? He was talking with the Marriott people—"

"To find out how they ran their business and to see if he could steal their director of marketing. Not to get a job."

Grandfather paused. Swallowed. Drew in a breath. "He didn't tell me that."

"Because he knows you. You wouldn't believe anything but cold, hard facts. And now that he's wooed their director over to Worth, he has evidence of his loyalty for you. John's a good man," Daniel repeated. "And he told me he's always considered you to be a father figure. You brought him up in the business, taught him everything he knows."

Grandfather's gaze went to the window. Something weighty seemed to settle on his shoulders, sliding him under the white covers. "He's not my son. Or my grandson."

The words lanced Daniel. He was the grandson who was clearly a disappointment. Who wasn't living up to his Grandfather's dreams. Who had turned out to be the black sheep in a family dedicated to maintaining the herd.

Why had Daniel thought his grandfather would understand? That things could change? That, somehow, on the basis of shared frustrations for things that had been bypassed because of the Worth family demands, they could find a common ground? He knew Grandfather was hurt by what he saw as a defection, but he'd hoped...

As always, his hopes were empty. Unless Grandfather gave up at least a centimeter, there was no hope of finding a middle ground.

Daniel rose. "I love you, Grandfather. But I can't work for you."

Grandfather jerked back to face Daniel, his eyes turning to ice. "If you won't take what I'm handing you on a goddamn silver platter, then you're not my grandson anymore."

Daniel laid a hand on his grandfather's arm. "I know you think I'm betraying you, but I'm not. No matter what happens, you'll always be my grandfather because I'm still a Worth, even if I don't work in the hotel business."

Grandfather's Adam's apple worked up and down. His face was set in a stone mask, yet something glimmered in his eyes. Disappointment? Anger? Frustration? He wouldn't say, nor would he yield at all. Instead, he yanked his arm out of his grandson's grasp.

And then, Daniel knew what that something was. Betrayal.

"You were never a true Worth." The words came out of his Grandfather's mouth in an angry, bitter whisper.

The words seemed to reverberate in the room, bouncing off the cream walls, careening across the small, quiet space. Daniel backed up a step. "What do you mean?"

His grandfather turned away, mute.

"Grandfather, what are you talking about?" Daniel moved closer, the words demanding, nearly begging. Never a true Worth? Because he'd abandoned the business?

Or because of something else?

For a long time, his grandfather didn't say anything. Then he let out a heavy sigh that seemed to deflate his entire body, sinking him further into the covers, making him become a small, frail man. "You're...adopted, Daniel."

Daniel stumbled back, falling into the chair again. "I'm...what?"

But Grandfather merely shook his head, giving no more information. "Go and do what you want," he said, the anger gone from his voice, replaced by something weary and heavy. "Be a writer. But be a damned good one so you don't embarrass the family."

"Grandfather, please. Tell me. Who are my parents if they're not Worths?"

"Don't ask me," Grandfather said, his voice hoarse. "Ask the man who knows you better than I do."

His grandfather refused to tell him anymore. When Daniel left the room, he swore he saw the shimmer of a tear sliding down Grandfather's face. But before he could turn back and try to mend a broken fence, Grandfather had flipped the TV back on and was feigning huge interest in Samantha's latest method of achieving orgasm.

Lewiston's Making-Up-For-Lost-Time Apple Pie in a Bag

7 apples, sliced
1 teaspoon cinnamon
1/4 teaspoon nutmeg
1/4 cup sugar
1/4 cup brown sugar
2 tablespoons flour
2 ready-made pie crusts
1/2 cup butter

You've already spent enough time dusting, polishing and cleaning up other people's messes. Time to make something fast, easy and just for you.

Preheat the oven to 375 degrees. Mix the apples, cinnamon, nutmeg, sugars and flour together in a re-closable bag. Turn it several times to help the ingredients meld well, a heck of a lot better than the people in your life have. Put one crust into a pie plate, then pour in the apple mixture. Dot with butter, then put the other crust on top, being sure to cut a vent in the top. The last thing you need is the pie exploding—like everything else is about to—and creating an even bigger mess for you in the oven.

Bake for 40 minutes. Enough time to avoid the subject by dusting everything in sight.

CHAPTER THIRTY-FOUR

After he left the hospital, Daniel went home, still puzzling over what his grandfather had said. Adopted. How could that be? How could that secret have been kept from him all his life?

And who did Grandfather mean when he said, "ask the man who knows you better than I?"

Daniel headed up his front stairs. Before he could grasp the brass handle, the heavy oak door was opened for him. "Lewiston. Thanks."

"Good evening, sir." Lewiston took Daniel's briefcase from his hands, then took his coat. He laid the leather attaché on the hall table, then hung up the coat, all in quick, precise movements that didn't waste a step or a breath.

Daniel sank into the carved leg armchair beside the hall mirror. He kicked his dress shoes off, leaving them beside him on the marble floor, then loosened his tie. "What a day."

"Between the new job and worry about your grandfather's health, I'm sure these last two weeks have been rough," Lewiston said.

"It's not that," Daniel said. "The office isn't so bad. Though how Grandfather stands being indoors all day, I'll never know."

"I like a little outdoors from time to time myself." Lewiston picked up a rag off the small table and went back to dusting photo frames. Grandfather Worth, in his stern business shot, Grandmother Worth standing outside the Botanical Conservatory she had donated to the city of Boston, Daniel's parents on the back of a yacht.

Tucked behind the official family photographs was one of Daniel's favorites, a tiny picture in a silver frame that Grandfather hated because it didn't "match the décor." Daniel rose, crossed to the table and picked it up. "Do you remember this day, Lewiston?"

Lewiston paused, the rag still. "Yes. Very well."

He said the words so softly, Daniel almost didn't hear him.

Daniel rubbed his thumb over the glass, tracing the image of the two people below. "That fish was huge. Twenty pounds, I think."

Lewiston chuckled. "Almost bigger than you."

"That's why you had to help me reel it in." Daniel chuckled at the memory, and the photo of himself and Lewiston, wearing droopy fishing hats decorated with lures. "I about fell in trying to get that damned fish on the boat."

"I kept a good grip on your waist," Lewiston replied. "Didn't let you go."

Daniel replaced the frame on the table. "That's what you're good at, Lewiston. Holding on to me so I don't make really stupid decisions."

The butler picked up the photo of Grandfather and circled the glass several times with the dust cloth. "That's my job, sir."

"No, it's not. Your job is to answer the door, take my calls and keep me on track with my schedule."

Lewiston stopped working and blinked in surprise. "I'm sorry, sir, if I have overstepped my bounds."

"Hell, Lewiston you overstepped them on my first day of kindergarten. Don't you remember, staying with me in the classroom?"

"You were upset, sir. Didn't want to stay."

"No, Lewiston, I didn't want *you* to go." Daniel reached out a hand to the other man's arm. Wondering. Putting the pieces of his past together, trying to finish the puzzle. "I was afraid you wouldn't come back to get me."

Lewiston's normally stiff demeanor washed away. His face softened and there was a sheen in his blue eyes. "I'll always come back for you."

"Why?"

"Well, that's my—"

"No, Lewiston. I just told you what your job is. You're the butler." Daniel paused, his gaze seeking that of the man he'd known all his life. The pieces had been clicking into place all the time, but Daniel suddenly knew. Knew for sure. "But you're not the butler, are you?"

"Sir, I have no idea what you're talking about." Lewiston retreated to polish the hall mirror.

Daniel wasn't going to let this drop. He crossed to Lewiston, their twin reflections peering back at them in the mirror. One man, a couple of inches taller than the other, impeccably dressed head to toe in black and white. Then the younger man, in a navy suit and white shirt that had been starched enough to withstand a hurricane. In all the years Lewiston had been with him, Daniel had never seen their images quite like this before. Now, he felt like slapping himself because it seemed so obvious. "Why? Why did you do it?"

"I really do have to get to the cleaning, sir." He waved the rag, avoiding Daniel's gaze. "I need—"

"Why, Lewiston?"

"The hall is atrocious and if your grandfather comes by—"

Daniel shook his head, refusing to let Lewiston back away, refusing to let him use the housework or the telephone or anything else as a barrier between them. Daniel was done with walls built on lies, with a life built on thinking he was someone he wasn't. "Why have you been more of a relative to me than my own family?" He stared at Lewiston in the mirror. "Is it because you *are* family?"

Lewiston swallowed, his blue gaze meeting Daniel's in the mirror. "You know?"

"I think I always did." Daniel put a hand to his chest. "In here."

"That's impossible. I never—"

"You didn't have to." Daniel swallowed, the truth sinking in with finality. "Why didn't you ever tell me?"

"It wasn't appropriate."

"Wasn't appropriate?" Daniel spun away from the mirror and crossed to the photos again, picking up the one of him and Lewiston, proudly hoisting a catfish between them. "Do you know what a difference it would have made to me? To know *you* were my father?"

Lewiston took the photo from Daniel's hands and replaced it on the table. "It would have made a big difference. You would have been poor, living in a two-bedroom apartment with a father who had no talents but waiting on people."

"I wouldn't have cared about the money."

"I wanted more for you than that. I wanted you to have a good education. A good upbringing."

"A good upbringing?" Daniel snorted. He picked up the picture of his parents and thrust it into Lewiston's grip. "Those people hardly knew I was alive. I spent every holiday with you. *You* planned my birthday parties. *You* took the pictures of me at graduation. You did it all."

"They loved you. In their own way."

"No, they didn't. I was an accessory, Lewiston. Something my mother could trot out at garden parties and show off. My father didn't even know my favorite color. But you knew. You knew *everything*."

"It was my job."

Frustration boiled in Daniel's gut. "Don't give me that job crap! I don't want to hear it. I want to hear—" Daniel cut himself off and turned away, reaching for his briefcase. Ready to leave again.

Then, Lewiston's hand was there, once again taking the leather case out of Daniel's grasp and laying it on the hall table. "I wanted more for you than I could give, Daniel. All I wanted was to do what was best for you."

Daniel's gaze went to the floor, as if the oak parquet held the answers he needed. "What would have been best for me would have been living with someone who loved me."

"Daniel…" Lewiston said softly.

And then, he did look up, studying eyes that were a twin of his own.

A half-smile crossed Lewiston's face. "You did grow up with someone who loved you."

Something hot stung at the back of Daniel's throat. He cleared it, but the sensation remained. He was a grown man, for God's sake, he shouldn't need anyone. Shouldn't need to hear those words.

"Why would you do that?" Daniel asked finally, the words as quiet as the ornate hallway. "Work in this family? Work for my grandfather?"

"Because I love you," Lewiston said softly. "I couldn't bear to be away from you."

"So you became the butler?"

Lewiston shrugged. "I didn't see another solution. Your mother had already given you up for adoption before I found out that I had a son." He loosened the tie at his neck, as if opening up allowed him to also relax his meticulous dress code. "Did I ever tell you I was in the army?"

Daniel shook his head. He could see, though, how the military would fit someone who liked order as much as Lewiston.

"That's why I didn't know about you until after your birth mother signed away the rights. She told the adoption agency she didn't know who the father was. They believed her. Or they didn't press her. They had a wealthy couple who wanted a little brown-haired boy to carry on the family name."

"My adoptive mother..." Daniel let the question trail off, not even sure what he was asking.

"Couldn't have children. And your grandfather wanted an heir."

Daniel snorted. "Was that what I was? An answer to another one of Grandfather's ultimatums?"

Lewiston shook his head. "Maybe it started out that way, but when you came into this house, your grandfather changed. The world began and ended with you. He bought you everything you ever asked for." Lewiston smiled. "Saying no wasn't something your Grandfather did easily with you."

Daniel shook his head. "But I didn't want things. I wanted a family, a real one."

"You know your grandfather," Lewiston said gently. "He's never been good at expressing his feelings. So instead of saying what you wanted to hear, or handing out hugs, he bought you everything he could."

Daniel looked at the man who had been with him for as long as he could remember. "You."

Lewiston nodded. "He figured out who I was pretty early on. When your parents went to adopt you, your grandfather hired his investigators to check everything out."

"And eventually the trail led to you." Daniel lowered himself onto the loveseat, the story sinking into his mind, all of it making sense. Snippets of his childhood came back to him— his Grandfather's unexpected animosity toward Lewiston that Daniel now understood as jealousy for the way his grandson had taken so easily to an outsider. He thought of his mother, who had dismissed her "son" from her life like he was a skirt that went out of style. And the whispers...the whispers he'd heard from time to time over the years, always quickly squelched by Grandfather. "Didn't he fire you?"

"He wanted to. I begged him to let me stay. So I promised him I would never tell you the truth. I couldn't bear to let you grow up without me."

Daniel shook his head in disgust. "My grandfather blackmailed you."

"No, Daniel, it wasn't that." Lewiston laid a hand on Daniel's arm, the touch as familiar as his own. "It was your grandfather's way of protecting you."

"From what? From being your son?"

"From a life without choices." Lewiston waved at the fancy furnishings, elaborate paintings, crystal chandelier. "Money, Daniel, gives you choices."

"What choices? I've been destined to go into the family business since the day I learned how to read. I didn't have any choices."

Lewiston's was silent for several seconds. The moment rocketed Daniel back to when he'd been ten and Lewiston had given him a long lecture about Little League baseball and the importance of playing the game with integrity, not winning. The words had stuck with him all his life.

"Do you know why your grandfather really wants you to work at Worth?" Lewiston asked, not waiting for an answer. "To keep you close to him. I'm not the only one who loves you."

"To…" The information sank into Daniel's brain. When they did, they socked him in the gut. "He did it to spend *time* with me?"

"Think of it this way," Lewiston said. "You and I have always been close. We've spoken the same language. Fishing trips, camping, playing catch in the yard. But your grandfather doesn't speak that language. The world he's comfortable in, and the one he wanted to share with you, is the business world."

All of a sudden, the myriad elements of Daniel's life clicked into place. What had once been a confusing jumble of expectations and rules now made perfect sense. He realized Grandfather's stiff upper lip, his emotional distance—all of it—had been entwined with what he had learned today.

Grandfather hadn't hated him.

Quite the opposite. He'd loved him enough to let another man live in his house and play father, when he knew damned well doing so would cost him his grandson's affections.

What had Olivia said? *You make sacrifices for the people you love.* Daniel swallowed, feeling the full import of that weighing heavily on his heart.

"I never knew," he said quietly. "But now that I do, it changes everything."

"What are you going to do now?" Lewiston asked.

"Like you said, money gives me choices. And I'm going to make some choices of my own. Starting right now." He gave Lewiston a long, tight hug, trying to put years of their relationship into one embrace. "Thank you. For everything." He pulled back, his gaze connecting with a mirroring one that was filled with unshed tears. "Dad."

When Daniel left his house, Lewiston was bent over the glass credenza, swiping away with the polishing rag in tight, fast circles. But this time he wasn't wiping away dust.

Olivia's Giving-Up-Is-Easier Strawberry Shortcake

1 pint strawberries
1/2 cup sugar
1 package prepared shortcake shells
whipped cream

The easiest way out is to let go. Since you're not in the mood for serious baking, let the grocery store do all the work for you. Mix the berries with the sugar and let sit for ten minutes. Ladle the sweetened strawberries onto the shortcake, then top with whipped cream.

There. Calories, sweetness and sustenance, all in a few minutes. And with no oven involved, your chances of screwing up again are greatly reduced. The fire department will thank you for that.

CHAPTER THIRTY-FIVE

The sign might as well have been a dunce cap. Olivia stood outside Pastries with Panache and heaved a sigh. "For Sale: All Contents and Fixtures."

Across the street, she heard the crowd lined up outside Sweets without Sin let out a rousing cheer.

"Don't worry about the neighbors. All they need is a good sugar rush and they'll come to their senses."

Olivia pivoted and found her neighbor from Gift Baskets to Die For standing beside her. Maria Pagliano had always been a great customer at Pastries with Panache, being a woman partial to a sweet. She and the other owners of the small shop next door had also been some of Olivia and Josie's greatest supporters, sending business their way and offering advice in the first stressful days of the start-up. Olivia would miss all four of them a great deal.

Olivia smiled, a weak smile, but one nonetheless. "I think they're celebrating that they managed to shut me down."

"You're really closing?"

Olivia shrugged. "I didn't make it. It happens to businesses all the time." She heaved a sigh and stared at the "For Sale" sign. "I don't see another choice."

Maria studied her for a long second. "You seem almost...relieved to be closing. Sort of like you just dropped off a blind date with bad breath."

Olivia laughed, then sobered quickly. It took a minute, but she realized Maria was right. "I am relieved, in a way." Saying the words, though, made her feel guilty, more of a failure. She closed her eyes, trying not to see the imprint of the sign on her brain. "Anyway, I need to give this back." She pressed the key to the shop into Maria's hands, giving back the place she had rented all these months from the next-door proprietors.

"We'll wait a bit before putting it back on the market," Maria said. "In case you change your mind, there'll be a storefront here for you."

Olivia shook her head. "I won't be changing my mind. But thank you."

"Ah, that's what I said," Maria replied, flashing her diamond engagement ring. "Food has a funny way of changing the most stubborn mind."

"Food? Or men?"

Maria laughed. "In my case, it's both."

Olivia shook her head. "I'm done with the food industry and I'm done with men."

Maria arched a brow at her. "Uh-huh."

"No, really. I'm going to work at Wal-Mart or something and forget all about this entrepreneurial thing." She nodded firmly. "And definitely forget about men."

Maria propped a fist on her hip. "And why would you give up men? Just saying it is heresy, girlfriend."

Olivia laughed. "Because they're a lot more trouble than they're worth."

"Or…" Maria began, her eyes softening with the wisdom of having been there and done that, "is one particular man pushing buttons you thought you'd done a damned good job of hiding?"

Olivia shrugged, non-committal. Not wanting to admit the truth. That Daniel was damned good at seeing past all her layers of bravado and getting to the heart of who she really was. That he represented challenges that scared her—more than bankruptcy did.

"Come on, I saw that millionaire sex god." Maria said. "Don't look at me like that. Every woman on the street watched his comings and goings."

Olivia chuckled. "I thought you only had eyes for Dante."

Maria grinned. "My heart's committed, but my eyes still appreciate a piece of cheesecake when I see one." She wagged a finger at Olivia. "I saw you walking down the sidewalk with that hunk of burning love. You are hooked, girlfriend."

Olivia waved a hand, dismissing the thought with a gesture, but knowing it didn't dismiss so easily from the rest of her. "Nah."

"Listen, I know you didn't ask for my advice, but I'm the kind of person who's going to give it to you anyway. When it comes to work and love, don't always listen to your head. Your heart is usually a lot smarter than the whole rest of you put together. Listen to it. It'll tell you what you need."

"I'm not—" Olivia cut herself off. She glanced at the shop window, at the business she'd opened because she'd been thinking with her head and not trusting her heart. She thought of Daniel, of the way she'd pulled back from him whenever her heart got too close.

She had silenced the voice of her heart. Afraid that listening to it would cause her to make another mistake. Instead, she'd compounded all of her mistakes with too much rational thinking. Clearly, the wrong part of her anatomy was in charge.

Time for a change of leadership.

She turned to Maria and gave her a quick hug. "Thank you."

"For what?"

"For giving me an instant college education in what's good for me." Then she turned and walked away from one thing that wasn't right for her, bound to find the other. Behind her, she heard a chorus of "Ding, Dong, the Sugar's Dead" from across the street.

"You look like a guy who invented the next wheel." Madison came up beside Daniel in the garden and took a seat on the curved concrete bench beside him. "I won't ask if you struck it rich, since that's a redundant question in this family. But something is definitely different about you, cousin."

He turned to her, not bothering to hide his smile. "I did strike it rich. In a different way."

She tipped her head, eyeing him with a question on her face. "There's another way besides making Grandfather happy?"

"Actually, I quit working for Grandfather."

"Again?" She let out a gust. "Some people never learn. How many trips are you planning on taking down Poverty Lane?"

"He's not going to disown me. We've found some common ground. And I think he's realized that I'm never going to be like him."

Madison snorted. "Grandfather change? That'll be the day. He's always wanted you to be his carbon copy."

"I can't. I'm not a Worth."

"What do you mean, not a Worth?"

Daniel drew in a breath. "I'm a Lewiston."

Madison's jaw dropped open. "No way."

He nodded. "It's a long story, one I'll tell you later. But suffice it to say I realized today that there's more to being wealthy than money." He grinned, feeling the weight of the Worth life lift from his shoulders. Leaving him free to do other things…like pursue the woman he loved. "There's more."

"More? Do I need to get out an inhaler to hear this part?"

Daniel drew in an icy breath, and with it the sweet clean smell of freshly fallen snow. "I'm in love."

Madison pressed the back of her hand to Daniel's forehead. "Did you catch malaria on that Caribbean cruise you took at Christmas?"

He laughed. "No."

"Who is it? Laura Templeton? Susan Jensen?"

"No one in our circle. She's an ordinary girl." Daniel chuckled. "Actually, she's as far from ordinary as you can get."

Madison studied him, a smile curving across her crimson lips. "Oh, you got it bad, cousin. Really bad."

He grinned. "I know."

"So what are you doing here? Why aren't you with her right now?"

"I'm coming up with a strategy."

Madison drew her coat closer around her neck and shivered in the cold. "A strategy? What are you going to do? Divide and conquer?"

He chuckled. "If necessary. Olivia is a bit…hard to handle."

It was Madison's turn to laugh. "She sounds perfect for you. You need someone to keep you on your toes."

"I want to do it right," Daniel went on, not entertaining Madison's analysis of his needs with an answer. "So I'm thinking. Planning. I need a good plan if I'm going to convince her to marry me."

"Whoa, now I know you're sick. Worth men only get married when there's an inheritance at stake."

He arched a brow. "What about Worth women?"

She waved her hands. "Me and marriage aren't a good mix. In fact, anything that involves a commitment lasting longer than the spring collection is a bad idea."

Daniel rose and clapped Madison on the shoulder. "Someday, some man is going to come along and change your mind."

She snorted. "That'll happen when poodle skirts come back into fashion."

Daniel was done thinking. It was time to take action. He was done waiting for Olivia to come around. He was going to find her and not let her go until she listened to him. "I'm off. Wish me luck."

"Luck? I think I should commit you to an insane asylum," Madison grumbled. "But yes, I'll wish you luck, you grinning fool."

He gave Madison a quick kiss on the cheek, then headed off to start executing the first part of his plan—to convince Olivia that some risks were worth taking.

Especially the ones that came with a ring.

Daniel's Winning-Her-Heart Buckeyes

1 1/2 cups peanut butter
1 pound confectioners' sugar
4 ounces butter, softened
1 teaspoon vanilla
16 ounces semisweet chocolate chips

You've screwed up royally, so the only thing left to do is bring her some chocolates as a peace offering. Mix the first four ingredients together and shape them into one-inch balls. Chill on wax paper for two hours, enough time to formulate a good plan for convincing her you aren't a total jerk.

In a double boiler, melt the chocolate. Dip each ball into the chocolate mix, leaving a circle in front to create the "buckeye," then cool on waxed paper. These one-bite delights are sure to win her heart.

And if that doesn't work, up your ante.

CHAPTER THIRTY-SIX

The next morning, Olivia's phone was ringing before she even got out of bed. She stumbled to the receiver and mumbled a greeting.

"Miss Regan? I saw your sign and I'm interested in buying the contents of your shop. Can you meet me over there right away?"

Damn. She hadn't thought it would happen this quickly. She should be glad there was a buyer so fast, because it meant she could repay her father and move on with her life. But still, a sense of loss rippled through her.

Olivia agreed on a time to meet with the buyer, then headed over to the shop, stopping first at Gift Baskets to retrieve the key. When she pulled up, she saw a tall, older man in a crisp navy suit, a slight paunch evidence of his desk job. "John Abbott," he said, extending a hand.

"Olivia Regan." They shook, then Olivia withdrew the key, unlocked the gate and the door and led the man inside. All the while, she wanted to hit rewind, to give herself a little more time before saying goodbye. She'd handpainted the decorations on the wall, chosen the dishes and the décor herself. But, she'd also made a promise to her father, to repay him. And she couldn't do that by admiring her decorations in an empty shop. "As you know, all the fixtures and equipment are for sale. I rent the space from the people next door, but if you wanted to maintain the location, I'm sure they—"

"I'll take it," he said, withdrawing a check and a pen from his inside pocket. "How much?"

"But…but—" Olivia felt like screaming that she wasn't ready. She couldn't do this yet.

"Miss Regan?" John asked. "Are you selling?"

"I…I—" She should. If she were smart, she would cut her losses, sell the business, and get the hell out of town so she'd never have to drive by this street again and think of what could have been. But her heart broke at the mere thought, and she found herself more attached than she'd expected.

Because Pastries with Panache had wriggled its way into her heart.

"I can't," she said finally.

"Good." John Abbott smiled and put his check away.

"Good?" She stared at him. "What was this? A test?"

"No, not at all. I assure you, I'm interested in your product. But I'd prefer *you* were baking it instead of me."

She shook her head. "I can't bake. It was all my sister. She's the one with the talent. Maybe you should be talking to her."

He nodded, taking that information in. "But you were the one running the business, right?"

She snorted. "Badly."

He shrugged. "Businesses that shouldn't fail do sometimes. What if you had more time? More money? Would you do it differently?"

"Absolutely." Olivia pressed a palm to the glass display case, now standing empty and sad. "But it's too late for that."

"Not if you have a standing order for your cheesecakes. Say…twenty to start?"

"Twenty? Every month?"

He smiled. "Every day."

"Every…day?" The word squeaked out of Olivia. "But that's—"

"A successful business." He eyed her. "If you're up to the challenge."

And then, she knew. Knew where John Abbott had come from and who had sent him. "Daniel Worth put you up to this, didn't he?"

"I do work for the Worth hotel chain, but the younger Mr. Worth has nothing to do with this. Someone sent Mr. Worth Senior one of your cheesecakes as a get-well wish, with a little note about how it was the perfect dessert for his star sign or something like that. Whoever sent it was right. It was the best damned cheesecake Mr. Worth ever tasted." John blushed. "I tried it too. Not sure if my star sign was right, but the cheesecake was. Mr. Worth insisted I buy them for the downtown hotel."

Josie had done that. Well, damn. Apparently Olivia wasn't the only one who liked to use inventive marketing techniques. Her sister was clearly smarter than Olivia had imagined and far more smart about reading people than she'd thought. She put out her hand. "You have a deal, Mr. Abbott. Twenty cheesecakes a month."

Which would mean hiring people. People who would work for peanuts. And who would believe in the business, as it started to get back on its feet. She knew exactly who to call. Time to unfold the sofabed again.

"And when you send over the first order, include a sampling of your other treats." John spun on his heel, appraising the shop. "If it tastes anywhere near as good as the cheesecake, I think we might have the beginnings of a beautiful friendship." He grinned. "Sorry. That's one of Mr. Worth's favorite sayings. He's a bit of a movie buff."

"Daniel?"

"No, his grandfather. That's who I work for. The younger Mr. Worth is off pursuing his own interests."

Which likely meant other women, Olivia thought. Not that she could blame him. She'd rejected him as firmly as Donald Trump would reject a man trying out for the Miss America contest. Besides, it was all for the best, especially now that she had so much to think about with her newly reopened shop.

"So, do we have a deal?" John asked.

Olivia grinned. "Definitely." She sealed the deal with another handshake, and when she did, the charge of excitement she thought had been gone forever rose again in her chest.

Apparently, her sun was no longer in a triune.

After John Abbott left, Olivia stood in the center of Pastries with Panache and spun in a circle. The shop's cozy atmosphere seeped into her pores, as if it were a part of her. She'd missed this, more than she thought possible.

For a half an hour, Olivia polished and dusted, imaging the future of her little shop. She could be an entrepreneur—a successful one—by concentrating on what she was good at instead of continually stressing over the things she couldn't master. And by trusting in her sister, who had as much heart invested in this business as Olivia did.

When she paused for a coffee break, the door opened, releasing the familiar jingle of the bell. She turned. Joy bubbled up in her chest. Maybe she hadn't lost him. Not yet. "Daniel."

"Hi, Olivia." He took several steps forward, bringing him within inches of her. "Before you say anything, I have something to ask you."

"And I have something to tell you."

"No, let me speak first." He cleared his throat, then took one of her hands in his own. "I love you, Olivia Regan."

The words took flight inside her. He loved her, despite everything. And he hadn't given up on her. "I—"

He pressed a finger to her lips. "No, don't say it. I don't want to hear your reasons why we aren't right for each right now. I've worked out this whole speech. Call it a persuasive marketing strategy." He grinned. "I did learn something at Harvard, after all."

"Daniel, I—"

"I know, we hardly know each other. And I'm not a man famous for my commitments. But with you...everything changed." His blue eyes softened, the light casting them in ocean shades. "Everything. You've made me want more, Olivia Regan. A lot more."

"But—"

He ticktocked the finger in front of her. "No buts, not yet. I'm not done selling myself to you."

She grinned and zipped her lips, deciding not to tell him he didn't need to sell her anything. She'd already bought the package.

"I love that you're a woman who dives into life head-on, without a life preserver or a rescue boat nearby. You're a fighter, but you do it with grace. And principles. And you would do anything for the people you love. Even sacrifice yourself."

She shook her head. "You're wrong. Diving in headfirst is stupid. You can end up with a broken neck."

"A beautiful woman once told me that I had no idea what it was like to sacrifice." He took both her hands in his, rubbing his thumbs over the backs, sending a warm tingle up her arms. "You're right. I didn't. Until I saw what it cost another person to sacrifice for me."

"What are you talking about?"

"It turns out, I'm adopted." A look of wonderment filled his face, as if the surprise was still sinking in. "And the man I've always known as my butler is my real father. Lewiston, uh, I mean my father, took that job so he could be close to me."

"He…he's your father?" Though the revelation came as a surprise, it all made sense. She had noticed the love Lewiston had for Daniel, and the way he seemed to protect and care for him. Much more than an ordinary employee would.

"After I discovered the truth about who I am," Daniel said, "I decided I didn't want to ever waste another second of my life. On anything. I've seen what it cost someone to keep how their feelings to themselves, and decided I wasn't going to do that anymore."

She held her breath, afraid of speaking, of breaking the magical connection swirling around them. He took a step closer, wrapping her in the depths of his gaze. Olivia's pulse skittered. She considered running from the emotion purring between them, but knew if she did, she would regret it forever.

If there was one thing today had taught her, it was that losing something because she hadn't fought hard enough to keep it was far more painful than giving up on it. So she stood her ground, her heart soaring with every passing second. "And so you came here today, to tell me how you felt?"

"Without you, the past two weeks have been empty," he said, a smile curving across his face. "You challenge me, Olivia Regan, and I think that's a very good thing."

"I challenge you?" A little laugh escaped her. "How do I do that?"

"You make me want to be better than I ever thought I could be. You made me brave enough to walk away from a family fortune—twice—and to take a chance on believing in myself. You have guts, Olivia."

"I don't know about that." She glanced away, taking in the empty display case, the silent shop. "Guts don't always equate glory, you know."

"But you weren't afraid of failure, and that inspired me to do the same." He reached out and cupped her face, his touch tender and light. "I'm in love with you, Olivia, and I don't want to spend another day without you."

"In love?" She repeated the words, not fully believing them yet. They pounded inside her, resonating in every beat of her heart.

He nodded, his blue eyes locked with hers. "I love the way your face scrunches up when you're trying to concentrate. The way you protect the people you love as fiercely as a mother lion. The sound of your laugh, the spark in your eyes when you're excited." He chuckled. "Or mad."

She cocked a hip forward and rested her fist on her waist. "What about the way I drive?"

"Well...everyone has a few faults." He grinned. "What do you say? Is your heart available?"

She considered Daniel, a smile playing across her lips. Inside, she was processing the words *I'm in love with you,* cautiously trying them out on her emotions, wondering if she dared to return the feelings. "Hmm...I don't know," she said, teasing, delaying. "I'm pretty expensive."

He grinned. "That's right. I believe you said the only way I could have you is if I bid on you at an auction."

She raised her chin, eyeing him, offering a challenge. In that, Olivia felt comfortable, on her own two feet. "And if you did, what would your opening bid be?"

He spread his arms wide, indicating himself. "One bachelor, slightly used."

She laughed. "I think even the janitor could trump that. There are some cute and less used men in maintenance, you know."

"Okay, then. A bachelor who has seen the error of his ways."

"Hmm...that's not much." She crossed her arms over her chest. "I still think the janitor has you beat."

He trailed a finger along her jaw line, tracing the outline of her chin, her lips, the subtle dimple in her cheek. Desire raced through her, urging her mind to give up the fight to her heart. "And I know how to make you moan."

"Really?" she said, feigning nonchalance. "I've forgotten. It's been such a long time, I can barely recall moaning with you."

"Time for a refresher, then." Daniel covered her mouth with his own, kissing her with the same reverence and passion as he had before. His lips consumed hers, igniting a fire that had been dormant for the past two weeks, waiting for him. For this.

It was as if he'd thrown a gallon of gasoline on a pile of embers. Everything within her sprung awake. She wrapped her arms around his back, pulling him closer, pressing her pelvis to his, returning his kiss touch for touch.

She took his bottom lip between her teeth, gently pulling on it and teasing the edge with her tongue. He groaned and then, with clear reluctance, pulled back. "You are distracting me," he said, a little breathless.

She grinned, her pulse still racing. "That's the point."

"I've offered you a bachelor and raised you a kiss," he said, peppering smaller kisses along the perimeter of her lips, making her ache again with want. "Is that enough to win your heart?"

"It's a damned good offer," she said. "But I don't know. Those janitors can be pretty persuasive. They do housework, you know."

"Oh, is that it? You want a man around the house?" He grinned at her, and just when she thought he was going to come back with a silly offer like a broom and dustpan, he dropped to one knee and pried open the lid of a small blue jewelry box.

She gasped. She stopped breathing, thinking, feeling anything, and just stared.

A single diamond glittered up at her, perfect and round, not too big or too ostentatious. Exactly the kind of ring she would have picked herself. Daniel Worth had the money to buy the biggest, fanciest engagement ring in the city of Boston, something she would have hated for its blaring bling. But this... this was absolutely wonderful. He'd known her, understood who Olivia was.

Maybe she should put her heart in his hands.

"I'm upping my ante," Daniel said. "And throwing in a marriage proposal."

A lump lodged in her throat. Marry him? This was going way beyond what she'd expected. She'd thought they'd go back to dating, have a few laughs. Olivia hadn't thought past that. And her mind certainly hadn't journeyed down the wedding aisle. "Daniel—"

"Jump off the bridge, Olivia. Trust your gut." He pressed his hand to her abdomen, just as he had two weeks ago. Heat extended through her stomach, as if sending a message.

Trust me. Trust Daniel. Trust in love.

Jump off the bridge. Take a risk.

Her heart beat double-time. She backed up, waving him off. "I can't. I—"

He followed her steps, not letting her escape. "Why is it that you take risks with a two-thousand square foot business and a two-ton car, but you won't take a risk with a two-hundred pound man?"

She shook her head, staring at the ring, afraid to touch it, and yet also afraid to let it go, to let him walk out of her life again. "I like being behind the wheel."

"Sometimes it's good to let someone else drive." He took her hand in his, the velvet-soft box between their palms, then closed his other hand over theirs. "You never know where the journey may take you."

"But what if I'm wrong?" she said, her voice small and unsure. "What if we end up hurting each other? What if..."

"And what if the low-carb people took over the world tomorrow and eradicated sugar? Anything can happen, Olivia."

She looked around the shop, and thought of how Josie had surprised her, proving that sometimes, Olivia Regan, with all her facts and figures, could be wrong.

There was no probability chart for love, no warranty that it would all work out and she wouldn't be left emotionally bankrupt in the end. All she could do was trust in him, and herself, and let the future handle itself.

Olivia's gaze met Daniel's. In the depths of blue, she saw only love. No hidden agenda, no lies. Nothing but pure, honest emotion.

Anything can happen.

Even a happy ending.

"Yes," she whispered, closing her eyes for a brief second before making the final leap. "I'll marry you, Daniel Worth. Because I love you, too."

He whooped, then slid the ring out of the box and onto her left hand. As she'd expected, it fit perfectly, as if it had been custom-made for her finger. The light above glinted off the diamond, shooting an array of sparkles around her hand.

"I guess that means I'm off the quacker tour?" he said, grinning at her.

"I'll still give you two quacks up." She pressed her lips to his neck, trailing kisses down the side. Inhaling the warm, steady scent of his skin, and realizing how very much she had missed this. Why had she ever considered letting him go? Being right here, in his arms, was everything she'd ever wanted. "In the bedroom, though."

"Mmm…my favorite place to use my quacker."

She laughed and wrapped her arms around him, their chests meeting, heartbeat against heartbeat. "Now, about who's going to be the driver in the family…"

He took her left hand in his and held it tight. "We'll get a chauffer."

And when he kissed her, she knew being married to Daniel Worth was going to be one hell of a ride.

Jake's Recipe for Happily Ever After

1 wealthy playboy
1 daredevil pastry chef

Mix the two often, throwing in a dessert whenever things get too tense. Turn down the lights, turn up the Sinatra, and let the wine breathe while the two cozy up on in front of the fire. For a man who never thought you'd get married, the thought is suddenly as appealing as a new Porsche.

Oh, and it helps if you have a former bachelor friend who's made it work himself. Gives the rest of us shmucks hope that we can become productive members of society. Or something like that.

EPILOGUE

"You know," Jake said, pouring himself another scotch and soda, "I think you and your wife are crazy."

Daniel looked at him. A crowd of people milled around them, plates and wine glasses in their hands as they waited for the auction to start. "Why do you say that?"

"How many people do you know who bungee jump off the side of a bridge after they get married? As you went over the edge I swear I heard the priest giving you two last rites."

Daniel laughed. "Being married to Olivia is pure adventure. The bungee jumping seemed appropriate."

"And then her parents following with their own parachutes? I had no idea she came from such a daredevil family." Jake shook his head. "Plus, she's got everyone in society buzzing about her elaborate cakes. She's a hell of a decorator."

After that little fire in the kitchen of the townhouse, Olivia had decided her talents lay in decorating, not baking. Her sophisticated designs had netted her several awards, which were framed on the walls of Pastries with Panache alongside Josie's Frosting on the Cake win from this year. Things had changed in the little shop, enough that there were now three shifts of bakers, working around the clock to keep Worth hotels and a large portion of the city of Boston supplied with desserts.

Within a month of introducing the shop's confections to the hotel menu, reservations were up ten percent. Wedding bookings and special events were up thirty percent. Those numbers had Grandfather singing in the shower.

And, he'd cut back on his hours at Worth Hotels to act more often in community theater. He was now starring in a revival of "Annie" and seemed made for the role of Daddy Warbucks.

Across the room, Daniel spotted his wife, who was making her way through the crowded ballroom with a series of zig-zags and near collisions. Apparently Olivia didn't need her Volvo to drive dangerously. Daniel chuckled, and waved her over to him.

"It's all going very well," Olivia said, pressing a kiss to her husband's mouth. As always, it sent a thrill through him and he wished they were alone so he could take that kiss further. A lot further. "I think we'll raise a lot of money for Juvenile Diabetes tonight."

"Those sugar-free cheesecakes are a huge hit," Daniel said. "I've even seen some of the Sweets without Sin people here."

She smiled. "I knew I'd eventually win them over with a little Splenda." She turned to Jake. "Has he told you about his book?"

Jake shook his head. "Joe Smith has a novel?"

"Nope. This one is coming out under Daniel Worth." Olivia leaned against him, sending a proud, adoring look his way. "And it's great. You have to buy a thousand copies and give them out to everyone you know."

"A thousand?" Jake looked at Daniel, grinning. "I'm not sure I can blow that much of my allowance on him."

"If my one-person PR campaign has her way," Daniel said, giving Olivia a squeeze, "I'll be on the *New York Times* list."

"You should be," she said. "Now that you've taken your writing out of the drawer, it's time to show the world how incredible you are." She tiptoed her fingers down the front of his tuxedo shirt, her green eyes sparkling. "And I think I need a reminder, too. Our place, tonight?"

He captured her hand in his and gave her palm a soft kiss. "Your wish is my command, Mrs. Worth."

"I do like the sound of that." Olivia gave him another kiss, then headed off to help the harried chef keep the dessert line moving.

Beside him, Jake cleared his throat. "Daniel, I, ah, wanted to apologize."

"For what?"

"For not being there when you needed me. When I want to, I can make a damned good selfish bastard."

Daniel shrugged. "Water under the bridge. Besides, you taught me something I never learned at Harvard."

"What's that?"

"Self-reliance."

"Maybe I'll try that sometime." Jake took another sip of scotch. "Maybe."

There was a tap on Daniel's shoulder and he turned to find Josie behind him, beaming with pride. "I knew this was the right day to do this," Josie said. "All the stars said so."

Jake pivoted and when he saw Josie, his eyes widened with interest. "Why, hello. I don't believe we've met."

She smiled and looked him over, her gaze clearly appreciating what she saw. "Nice aura." She put out her hand. "Josie Regan, Sagittarius."

"Uh, Jake Lincoln." He took her hand in his and didn't immediately let go. "And I have no idea what I am, except interested in you."

As Daniel walked away to join his wife, he was sure there was more than one couple in the room whose moons were destined to cross.

EXCERPT FROM
THE BOSS COURTED TROUBLE

Book Five in the *Sweet and Savory Novel Series*

M adison Worth knew she was in trouble the
minute the manure hit her Prada heels.

Actually, the trouble had started months ago in
New York, during the Fall Collection Show. One little incident with a chocolate cake and Kate Moss,
and all of a sudden, Madison had been labeled as
difficult. Temperamental.

And the unkindest cut of all—a diva.

That one hurt the worst. It wasn't like she went
around insisting all the orange M&Ms be removed
from the candy dish. Or pitched a fit because someone handed her a Dasani instead of Evian. Why, she
rarely ever complained about having to smile and
cavort in the ocean for a swimsuit shoot in February.

She was *not* a diva. Not even close. The cake
throwing had been completely justified. Maybe not
smart, but explainable.

It had merely been a bizarre twist of fate that
Kate Moss's face had to come between Madison and
winning an argument.

So now, because of that, Madison stood in the
circular dirt driveway of the Pleeseman Dairy Farm,

located in one of those no-name, blink-and-you'll-miss-it towns in the Berkshires of Massachusetts, trying to ignore the brown lump on her seven hundred dollar strappy sandals. The late July heat only intensified the odor, the experience. Madison forced herself not to turn her nose up in distaste, not to retch right there on the driveway. That wouldn't do, not when she desperately needed this job. If she'd had a choice, she'd have been out of here on the first private jet.

But those days were far behind Madison Worth. So she was forced to put up with the crud. Literally. She put a hand on her hip, the other shielding her eyes from the sunshine.

Ahead of her, the poop perpetrator—a massive green and black truck thing—a dump truck?—chugged along the curve, leaving a cow patty trail in its wake, several of which bounced off the dry, caked dirt and spattered in her direction. Ewww. She shuddered, resisted running as fast as she could back toward the sanity of New York, and instead raised her hand, waving, trying to catch the attention of the driver. Surely someone should be outside, ready to meet her, to show her to her dressing room and then escort her to her hotel suite.

To civilization and crisp, white sheets.

But the tractor, truck, whatever, kept right on chugging toward a barn and trio of silos on her left. A one-horned goat trotted along behind the machine, baaing and nipping at stray blades of grass along the path. The breeze picked up, whisking with it the heavy, distinct smell of manure, tinged with sour milk. Madison grimaced, swallowing the bile in her throat.

If she hadn't already looked at her calendar and seen Sunday on the little block for today, she'd have sworn it was a Monday, given the particularly crappy start to her day.

She'd put up with worse, hadn't she? That photo shoot in Greece, with the grabby photographer who had a habit of "making sure" her top was properly adjusted for the lens? The video she'd shot on the yacht, which had turned into a disaster when a storm whipped up, sending most of the crew and the models scrambling for the nearest bucket. Her agent had gotten an earful about that particular job, and as consolation had sent Madison a case of Dramamine and a hot-off-the-runway pair of Jimmy Choos.

This, too, was a job, like any other. And one she had to do without complaint, if she ever wanted to restore her career to its former beauty.

Now *there* was irony—modeling for a cheese company, steeped high in the scent of manure, as a way to get back into the pages of *Women's Wear Daily*.

Madison picked her way further up the drive and past the cow landmines, still waving futilely, and in between, waving her hand at her chest, trying to head off the perspiration before it started to show. Why had she worn a suit? Who was she trying to impress out here on Green Acres?

Anyone who wanted to hire her, that's who. She didn't care that Eileen Ford had dropped her from her model roster faster than Britney Spears could say "I do." That all the other top agencies in town had turned her down, refusing to see her, lest she darken the doorsteps of their Naomi Campbell built offices.

That she had had to go groveling back to Harry Blenkins, her agent from the early days, and listen to him chortle with glee, in between Marlboro hacks.

One—okay, maybe two or three—crying jags in front of the camera did *not* constitute a breakdown. She still had her looks, her body and most of all, her ability to model the pants off Cindy Crawford. And she was damned well going to prove it to the industry—

As the spokesmodel for the Cheese Pleese Company.

Behind her, her Benz made an odd clicking noise as it cooled, definitely a sign of owner neglect. It had sputtered to a stop halfway up the drive, leaving her to navigate on her own.

Surely, she had landed in hell, she thought, avoiding yet another dung disaster.

Around her, the scent of manure seemed to multiply, to take up residence in her nose. A bird swooped down, nearly decapitating her in its journey toward a nearby birdfeeder. And leaving her a nice surprise on the opposite Prada heel.

That was *it.*

Forget the whole damned thing. She couldn't do this. She wasn't *that* desperate.

Madison tugged her cell phone out of her purse, flipping open the cover. She had not driven all those hours along the crowded turnpike to be crapped on—literally. "I'm out of here," she muttered, holding one in-need-of-a-manicure finger over the first listed contact. In an instant, she could erase the manure, the cheese factory, that itty bitty nervous breakdown during Fashion Week.

All she had to do was push a single button. Well, that and maybe grovel a little. Okay, a *lot*.

One phone call would put her back into her Manhattan apartment, give her Benz some much-needed TLC, and send her on a shoe shopping spree that would make Imelda Marcos salivate.

She hesitated. One button. One call. And it would all go away.

And leave her right back where she'd started, except without any cake ammunition. Madison clicked the phone's flip top closed.

Aw, hell.

Somewhere along the way, Madison Worth had gotten the insane idea that she needed to grow up.

"Hey," Madison called to Mr. Green Jeans on the truck, making her wave bigger, using her phone to catch a glint of sunshine. "Hey!"

Farmer-guy put his foot on the brake, turned, cupped a hand over his ear and stared at her. If he was surprised to see a five-foot-eleven blonde in designer duds standing in the drive, he didn't show it. He just gave her a blank look, then one short nod. "Ma'am," was all he said.

"Do you know where I can find Jack Pleeseman?"

The engine of the tractor continued its low rumble. The guy lifted a shoulder, then dropped it, and shook his head. "Can't say that I do. He's a pesky one to keep track of. Always off on one idea or another."

Idiot, Madison thought to herself. She hated dealing with anyone lower on the totem pole than the top. He was probably one of the worker bees, which meant he had no idea of the boss's whereabouts and wouldn't be a bit of help anyway. Madison waved a never-mind hand at him, squared her shoulders and marched the rest of the way to the front door.

She'd do it herself. It wasn't like she was completely incapable of self-care. Most days, anyway.

The tractor backfired, releasing an explosive boom and a plume of black smoke that surrounded Madison, surely turning her pink Chanel suit gray.

Okay, so, this wasn't the high profile runway work she was used to. It wasn't the cover of *Marie Claire* or hell, even an inside quarter-page ad. It was small town, hokie work, the kind the other models laughed at behind their thousand-watt mirrors.

But it was going to be Madison's saving grace, by God. If not, she'd have to find a real job and Lord knew she wasn't fit for anything more involved than returning a purse to Bloomingdale's.

She reached the porch and made her way up the steps. The wood was worn in places, the white paint peeling back to reveal a gray of years gone by. Each step let out an ominous squeak. And then, just when she reached the top, the spiky heel of her right shoe poked right through the landing.

And stayed there.

Madison yanked, but the porch still held her hostage. She had two choices—stay there and wait for rescue or bend over, undo the pain-in-the-ass buckle and take off the shoe.

Since her only chance for rescue seemed to be Hector the Tractor Guy, who had already chug-chugged away, backfiring like Patriots fans belched, she opted for the second choice. Madison bent over and tried to get her acrylic nails under the teeny buckle to slip it out of its brass tether. She nearly had it off and then—

The red tip on her index finger popped off, flying across the porch. It skittered across the wood, then slipped through a crack.

"Better watch out for our bull," a voice said behind her. "Big George sees that view and before you know it, you're having a calf."

She whirled around, her skirt whooshing against her bare legs, and faced the man behind her. It wasn't the tractor guy—it was someone far younger. He was taller than her, probably six foot two, and tan in a rugged sort of way that said he spent time outdoors, not at the Mist-N-Go booth. He had broad shoulders, easily defined by his pale blue cotton T-shirt and jeans that hugged along his thighs, tapering down to cowboy boots that were dusted with dirt. His hair was dark, with a slight wave, offset by even darker eyes, the same color as a good chocolate.

He may have been good-enough-for-the-runway gorgeous, but Madison hated him on sight. Because he was *grinning* at her. Like he found her predicament amusing.

"I'm stuck," Madison said. "In case you didn't notice. Could you find the boss or better yet, help me? Like the gentleman I presume you are?"

"That porch," the man said, ignoring her and rubbing his chin with one hand, that grin remaining on his face, "why, it's nabbed many a woman. My cousin Paul married the last one who got her foot caught."

"You're joking."

Still that smirk. "Only if you're already spoken for."

Madison let out a gust, gave her shoe a solid yank, pulling it from its wooden prison—

And sending her off balance, scrambling for purchase against the peeling wooden columns. Before she could fall to her humiliation on the cow patty drive, a pair of strong arms had scooped her up and carried her onto the middle of the porch.

"Put me down," Madison said. "Before I—"

"Sue me for saving you from falling on your ass?" The man tipped forward, dumped her onto the porch, then stepped back, crossing his arms over his chest. Madison teetered. Then, as only a woman who had spent her formative years in three-inch heels could, regained her balance.

"You're pretty damned ungrateful," he said.

"And you're pretty damned touchy-feeling. You could have helped me without using your hands."

He quirked a brow at that. "Hmm…now there's a talent I haven't yet cultivated. Picking up a woman without using my hands." He thought a minute. "Can't say I want to learn to do that, either."

Madison bit back her first retort. And her second. She was here to work on her self control, with the bonus of earning a living. Lashing out at the hired help might make her feel better, but it wasn't working toward her goal. "I'm looking for Jack Pleeseman," she said, naming the man who had hired her, and who held the fate of her career in his hands. "Do you work for him?"

"Nope."

"Do you know him?"

The guy considered this. "Better than most."

"Can you point me in the direction of where I might find him?"

"Don't need to."

Madison took a step forward, pointing her naked nail at his chest. "Listen, buster. I have been spattered with cow crap, used as a Port-a-Potty by a low-flying bird, and suffocated by tractor exhaust. I am in no mood for your games."

"Too bad. Because you sure seem like you'd be fun to beat at checkers."

A shriek of frustration resonated in her mind. Whoever this guy was, she was going to make sure Jack Pleeseman fired him for treating her so rudely. "If you won't tell me where your boss is, then I'll find him myself, wherever he is on this godforsaken hell-hole farm." She pivoted on her heel and reached for the brass doorknocker.

"'Fraid you won't find him in there," the man said.

"And why is that?" Madison lowered the knocker hard against the door anyway.

"Because he's standing right here."

The manure had been nothing. This time, the shit really hit Madison. Square in the face.

About the Author

*N*ew York Times* and *USA Today* bestselling author Shirley Jump spends her days writing romance and women's fiction to feed her shoe addiction and avoid cleaning the toilets. She cleverly finds writing time by feeding her kids junk food, allowing them to dress in the clothes they find on the floor and encouraging the dogs to double as vacuum cleaners. Visit her website at *www.ShirleyJump.com*, follow her on Facebook at www.facebook.com/shirleyjump. author or follow her Twitter at www.twitter.com/ shirleyjump.

www.ingramcontent.com/pod-product-compliance
Lightning Source LLC
Chambersburg PA
CBHW070349260626
47161CB00001B/74

* 9 7 8 1 9 3 7 7 7 6 8 5 5 *